WINE
OF
SATAN

WINE OF SATAN

— A Tale of Bohemond, Prince of Antioch —

By

LAVERNE GAY

CHARLES SCRIBNER'S SONS, NEW YORK
1949

TO
MY MOTHER

Contents

My lords, before this tale begins, know this. Much fancy clings about the mighty; for heroes trail through time, as comets do, their starry dust. But when, in your new Italian wanderings, you find the scars and markings of events told here; when you view some saucy scribings on a certain countess's tomb; when you toast with Southern shepherd-folk in Norman apple-jack instead of wine; and when, at last, you gaze on bronze and silver serpent-headed doors that sailed by pirate-ship to Antioch and back again, don't say, my lords, you were not warned herein, it would be thus!

The Prologue

[1]

IT WAS HOT enough on the roof on the Cinq-côte Tower to scorch your breechclout, and Marc, wriggling in his mother's arms, let the world know about it in a steady wail. But the whole castle lacked a better vantage place—the whole town, for that matter—so Albarada continued to lean as far out of the bull's-eye as she dared without toppling into the steaming moat below.

"Hush, *hush*, Marc!" she told the babe. "How can I hear the gate bells if you bawl so?" She thought of clapping a hand over the tiny, wide-open maw with the pink tongue vibrating lustily within, but judged better of it and drew him back in the shade of the ashlar wall and swayed him a little. His nursing was done, but she dreaded to leave her post a second. Above his red face she kept strong, sixteen-year-old eyes strained on the steaming hill-town below. A stinging sirocco, hot from Sicily, had blown up with the sun at zenith. Noon, and still no sign of Robert! Could those devils have set an ambuscade? O God! Bring that cloud of dust, that progressive scattering in the circular streets, to tell her he was pounding home at last!

She thought of the town with its flat-roofed two-storied houses and shops and its rich palazzos as a great, ring-backed snake. She thought of it as a dragon coiled in a nest of vipers. Yet she could envy the masses below: the hawk-eyed Moslems; the Saracens with their white flea-filled head rags; Pisan sea-pirates; Amalfitan merchants; heavy-pursed Jews; the sullen Lombards and the oily Greeks—all the riffraff that filled Melfi town and spilled over its walls to wild Italian moors beyond. At least they went about their living, breathing business, despicable as it might be, while she, married to the greatest of the Twelve

Norman Counts and the most exciting man in all Italy, was locked in this tower, alone.

Albarada, praying her baron home, was full of wrath and resolution. To be given at nine to a stranger was a bad enough beginning. To wake from virginity, in due time, in the arms of the fabulous Count Robert de Hauteville called Guiscard the Wary, was getting better. But what early good was it, if he *still* went marauding from Salerno to the Middle Sea, alone? She could count on her fingers the times they'd lain together. Well, no more of *that!* There was a son now. Moreover, there was a new mode of life filtering down from France. Guiscard wanted New Normandy here in the South, did he? Then let him be a true French knight and keep his dame in honor at his side. (What a heavenly prospect!) But sweet Sant' Nicholas, was it too late?

The big trap door behind her interrupted these thoughts with a *scrawtching* sound. She turned, to see the blond, cropped head, ruddy face and husky mailed frame of Richard the Seneschal heave themselves onto the battlement. He shot a frantic look out over the town, and as though he had spent his last penny of hope thereby, he jerked around to her angrily, squinting in the hard light.

"Where the devil *is* he? The mules of the Pope and those other heaven-hounds cross the Venusian Bridge already . . . Mother of God! The herald came hours ago! Where *is* he?" He waggled a finger roofward at his feet. "As for the counts, the whole pack of 'em—Fitz, Peter, Gautier and the rest—are standing around below this very second, grinning like jackals. I tell you, he's been *stopped* somewhere! Now. After all our plans. God knows it won't be a de Hauteville called Duke, if *they* get to the churchmen first!"

"Pig!" she exclaimed, and turned on him hotly. "It's like you, Richard de Hauteville, to mind the vesting now, when Robert may well be dead of their dirty schemes! You've far less heart than the *rest* of the cut-throats waiting in this donjon . . . Robert is ambushed, waylaid, murdered like a sheep—I *know* it, Richard! He's *dead!*" She burst into tears.

This appalled Richard. Bad enough to be wild in love with his young chatelaine, without making her cry, to boot. Save for the mite dozing at her breast, he had a mind to fold her in his arms. His liege's wife, but damn! Adorable and so much alone . . .

"May Heaven provide for him!" she sniffled out, and with both arms full of little Marc, elbowed her sash meaningly at the seneschal. He fished the kerchief from the dizzying precincts of that supple waist, and offered it.

"Heaven always has, so far—in everything," he said. He watched her dab at her dimpled face, so full of woe. There was no sound besides his sigh, and the warm wind soughing at the walls, whipping the veils about her tear-stained cheeks.

Then they both jumped at once. The sudden clangor had them fighting for shoulder-room at the bull's-eye. Below, three riders pounded through the gates, rattled over the bridge and into the bailey.

"Guiscard! Guiscard!" shouted Richard. It was greeting and battle-cry. Then he and the young countess raced to the open *trappe*. Richard restrained himself with difficulty to let her be the first, pushing and plucking at her shoulder as he started mother and child down the narrow winding steps that led to the keep below.

The air in the hall was close and heavy with the scent of men in their best clothes. Their agitated chattering sounded strangely hollow in the high vaultings of the roof as Albarada, descended from the battlements, found herself stopped at the arch of the inner balcony by the press of those who waited. She craned her neck, stood tip-toe, and was just in time to see the porter pull the door ajar and the three soldiers swing into the gloomy keep, as though on a gust of the sirocco. Big Hugh Falloc and Geoffrey Ridelle were with him, all three helmed and hauberked and their white grins standing out like Saracens' in their dusty faces. Guiscard came foremost, and a woman, young and anxious-looking, accosted him. He lifted her up and swung her around, setting her headdress quite awry with the violence, while his big voice boomed above the noisy murmuring.

"Your lord is well again, Madame! I left him hearty in Calabria, and here is his kiss." He delivered it resoundingly, with a noisy smack.

Albarada pushed forward through the crowd above. She felt her heart beating and her face flushed. She prayed not to swoon. Behind her Richard called, "Welcome home, Messire Robert! What a sight to our eyes! What *kept* you, man?"

Guiscard looked up to the *entresol* and grinned. He was a big man, even for a Norman, and a young one for forty-five. He took the shallow steps three at a time. Albarada barred him at the top.

"Ho, my dear!" he cried, and folded her, babe and all, in a great bear hug, which set the lad to squealing against the links of steel.

"Look out, Robert! You'll crush him!"

"The babe!" he exclaimed, moving the swaddles with a grimy gauntlet. "The great red rose!"

"He's *your* rose, Robert . . ." Albarada bit her lip (no time for tears!) and lifted her face for its proper kissing. But he only stood and bathed her in his bearded smile, his eyes with the soil-caked corners laughing mischievously. "My sweet one, you have gifted Guiscard magnificently," he said, but there seemed to be some other thought intruding even as he spoke. "Now, where's my tub, my little one? That pack of monkish rascals'll be here, and I not decent!"

At this, Albarada, happy with connubial duties to attend, went off. He strode to the bend of the buttressed arch that cut the balcony in half and stood beneath it, facing the balusters. He doffed his helmet, threw it to Richard, and leaned out over the crowd, grinning. Never handsome, he passed for it and better, with his breezy bluster and his lusty looks. But now his face was a strange and savage-looking mask, with the dank, red, ear-length hair dishevelled over it, the ragged beard upon it, and the white streak left on his nose and forehead by the nasal of the helm. The impudence of a much younger man was in his glance as he took a rapid survey of the counts and their retainers in the hall below. Fitz, Peter, du Chaine, and the rest of the Norman masters of South Italy stood awkwardly about, staring up at him. Their smiles, those who tried one, even, were less than hearty. This day, with the papal mission here to invest a de Hauteville with the dukedom they had *all* aspired to, was no time for French masquerie and courtly protocol. The de Hautevilles, frankly ambitious, were frankly hated. Fitz Bebena, the pug-faced lord of Monopoli, seemed about to cast an insult into Robert's very face from where he stood below him, scowling sourly, resplendent in a Byzantine pallium of watered silk. Guiscard, while they waited, jerked off his leather gauntlets and shook them jauntily. His voice, for him, was quiet.

"You sent an escort for me, did you, bonny Fitz?"

The slight whispering fell off like last wine trickled from a barrel.

"They're still in the pass, I think, Bebena." He shrugged and hooked a thumb at Hugh Falloc, the large, dirty-blond-headed count who stood beside him, leaning dourly on his heavy sword. To Hugh, who once had killed an over-impudent Greek herald's horse with his fist's blow, Guiscard owed nine lives, several of them at the hands of such as these. Hugh, with a nature much less subtle than his liege's, let his blue, slightly protruding eyes be frankly full of knowledge of them all, let them gleam with hatred in the shadow of his conical steel cap.

"Great Michael, Robert!" he growled. "How can you joke with them on it? Even a grave dug there in the road!"

"For Saracens, Hugh. They hunted Saracens!" Guiscard spread his hands, knit his brows in a deprecating frown. "Too bad Falloc is so hot-headed . . . Took the lads for an ambush and cracked their skulls like a pair of eggs before I could tell him his error." He clucked his teeth. "My impulsive Hugh!" He stopped in the stone-dead silence and gave the fallen ones the courtesy of a sigh before he said, with a sudden change of mood, "But look you now!" favoring all with a grin. "We're all here together, all Twelve, like the chosen ones of old on Maundy Thursday!" He shot a glance full of mischief at a robed and tonsured figure by the wall. "My lord the abbot frowns. Do I blaspheme, father? If so, you'll shrive me of it presently, for I am, as usual, greatly in your need. But I only meant, Your Piety, that with the holy crowd from Rome approaching to bless us all today, we'll carry the Norman gonfanon among the infidel like them appointed in holier times than these. May God be kind!"

His Gallic fervor caught at the crowd. They responded with a great, eager shout. *"Dex ais!* God aid us!" It was none the weaker for the lords who did not join in.

He turned then, and pushed through to his chamber, with happy Albarada in his wake.

But when the others followed, Richard and Hugh and Geoffrey Ridelle, she looked at him quizzically, and tried to close the door on them, for her lord's ablutions. But Hugh pushed past her, lowered his towering frame to a fur-covered chair and took off his helmet. Geoffrey, when she sought him, was already seated on the rushes, making a mess of his sweaty dust-grimed face with his rubbing of his hand across it all, as men will do to refresh themselves.

"Well, Richard," Guiscard asked the seneschal, "you must be full of news? There's much to know of you presently." He was doffing his dusty clothes. The link byrnie slid to the floor with a clinking and his tunic quickly followed. Below the white breechclout, his legs were sun-blackened and his neck, since he scorned a gorget, glowed like dull fire. But wherever the armor came away his flesh was white and firm and muscular beneath the fine, red-gold hair, and overlaying all a thin coat of grime clung to him from the ride.

Richard began to chatter. The others drew round like spikes to a lode-stone, shutting the Countess out. Having seen to the tub-filling, she hesitated. Pride pricked her to leave but stubbornness kept her there. And longing. Eleven months, after all, and now perhaps a few niggardly hours of him . . .

But there was only his quick voice from that wall of masculinity. "What of the men from Rome? *Ow!*" She heard him hit the rushes. *"Deu de Deu!* Would you boil me, little one?"

Heavens, the *cold* water, of course. She went to jump, then anger struck with a rush. She glared at the Count's General, Ridelle, still massaging his face and scratching his inky curls in cross-legged luxury on the floor. He was humming a snatch of war-tune in the mellow voice his friends had of him in idle moments.

"Geoffrey," she interrupted him, "there's the cannikin; fix it yourselves!" And rage, like a physical hand, propelled her toward the door. Lord, what did they think she was? One of their plump, dark Calabrian serving-bawds? The door, as she slammed it after her, exploded like thunder.

The conference at the tub turned as one man, wincing, but blame, as it happened, fell on a lad bearing wine, cheese and steaming birds on a tray which Richard the Seneschal had ordered for their freshening. "Look what you're doing, Etienne, and mind you watch the Acarenza saved for the Count's arrival!"

The lackey crossed to the chest that Richard indicated. But swish! Off went a capon, two quail and the cheese, so that nothing was left but the wine-casque standing lonesomely on his tray. Falloc and Ridelle, with their poached spoils, retired to a pair of couches to ravish the dripping fowl, while the seneschal broached the wine for Robert.

Guiscard reached for the cup and quaffed it at once and with a sound of bliss. The red drops danced from his hand as he rubbed his bearded mouth.

"And now," he said, taking brush in hand for his scrubbing. "What about Rome, Richard? You must have sung like a swan to bring them to Melfi, 'the robber's-nest', the 'hold of the Calabrian Cattle-thief'. *Cattle-thief!* Lord, I must dress carefully! What legates are coming?"

"Legates my eye," said Richard, and smiled.

"Don't tell me they bring a *pope!*"

"*The* pope, Guiscard! A protégé of Hildebrand's, a pious fellow named Nicholas. All that business is over, of anti-popes and such."

"*Well!*" said Robert, and fell to scrubbing vigorously, lost in happy speculation. "So Hildebrand sends a pope. . . . Who else?"

Gerard said, nonchalantly as he could, "Oh, some bishops, a hundred or so."

The brush stopped abruptly on the sudsy chest.

"A hun—— Damn me, what *is* this—a church council?"

"Exactly, Robert! They don't come all the way from Rome just to make you Duke of Apulia . . ."

"*And* Calabria," Robert prompted, waggling a soapy fist.

"*And* Calabria. No. They held a council to reform our country abbés."

"Reform! That brings one name *only* to mind . . ."

Richard, practically bursting with delight, just nodded his blond head.

"Hildebrand *himself!*" cried Robert. This time the brush was flung against the farther wall. Down went one of Albarada's tapestries. "Geoffrey! Hugh! Listen, you gluttons! This is magnificent!" He heaved himself from the tub.

Gerard handed him a robe in which he wrapped his great body, hardly dry, then hugged his young retainer. "Good boy, Richard! This is indeed a victory for the de Hauteville gonfanon! Ah, what an appetite I have now! Did Etienne fetch more wingers from the scullery?"

Assured of his meal by the varlet's removal of the serviette, he sat himself down and fell to with a relish. He was all smiles.

"I'm proper too, for my eating—not like those dirty pigs on the beds!" He waved a drumstick at Geoffrey and Hugh. "Look at them, wolfing their rations, as if they snatched between skirmishes in the field!" He glowered at them mockingly.

"You must learn to live like gentlemen now, my lusties. We grow rich and powerful, we stealers-of-cattle! We can well afford to grow respectable!"

For a while they all ate silently, each with long thoughts to dwell on, thoughts of their blue-blooded roots in Normandy which they'd long since fled, under a legal cloud or for the crime of being born later than brothers who inherited their feudal patrimonies. These were the dispossessed.

Half through a pigeon pie, Guiscard asked Richard, "Do you know where we rode to, these last few days, before heading up for Melfi? To Salerno, to see Prince Gisolf. For see, the friendship of Rome itself it wooed and won; why not Salerno's? Have we not leagued with Lombards against Greeks since first we came here? But Gisolf, the fool, won't even listen to offers of friendship. And the man goes deeper into his vices every day. Richard, that heathen tortures his prisoners after breakfast like you and I'd play chess. He's crazy, you know, mad as a roebuck in the autumn rut. I can't abide him—and we quarreled again as ever. He had me actually thrown out of his hall, tossed out by my breech-seat, like a blasted beggar. And all the while that sister of his—that handsome virgin they call Sigelgaita—she laughed. Damn my sockets, but she laughed. At *me!*" He tapped his chest with his napkin, not braggardly, but in a muse, staring before him into some inner dream.

"Let her laugh. Next time I clap eyes on that handsome hide of hers . . . God of God, what a woman!"

He looked up suddenly, at the seneschal. "Richard, I'm in love! And I think—Why—Blood! I know she looked on me with favor, though she laughed . . ." He took a shuddering breath, full of excitement, and laid his hand on Richard's wrist. "When this Nicholas comes today, this new pope, he must cut my marriage ties."

The young man gasped and pulled back as though stung, but the Count continued calmly enough.

"I've been *thinking* lately, how the child Albarada is in my blood-kin, and it bothers my conscience."

They all stared. Young Richard had his mouth wide open.

"Now—listen." Robert shrugged a shade impatiently. "No need for fussing on this thing." He appealed to the two others. "Think back, friends. Don't you recall how it was that I wedded her at the first? That cold keep in Argentano and all our wine gone? Not a byzant standing between us and a bony death? Her uncle spoke of her dowry and her family willing . . . But would you expect that I'd *love* her, whom I first knew as a babe? Besides," (turning to the seneschal with a wink) "look *Richard* here with that handsome blush! It's come to my ears, don't fret, how I keep the seneschal from his love. 'Steeth, it's *natural!* I grow older every day—a dotard soon—and she hardly yet a woman!"

He gave one of his broad, warm smiles. "Why should *I* stand in your way, you two?"

Over the hot, embarrassed protests of the seneschal, Guiscard's voice boomed out.

"Come now, Richard! Leave it! I've got to hurry!"

For indeed as he spoke, the faint peal of the city gate bells could be heard, distorted and vague in the roaring swirl of the sirocco.

[2]

It was a mild, warm afternoon some few days later when Hildebrand, the papal archdeacon, the terrible monk from Cluny, rode out of Melfi with Guiscard, his brother Count Roger, and the Pope. He was seemingly unaware of the oaths and imprecations churning none too privately in the long procession of abbés strung out on mules behind them, but indeed he knew the brethren, as long as they lived, would talk of the Council of Melfi in 1059 as the low point in their lives, and he cared not a fig. There were notable exceptions, of course. Desiderius the Lombard, brilliant young Abbot of Monte Cassino, was one, and there were others. As for the rest—God send them thorns and bristles, trials and tribulations to harden their hides and the fibers of their mewling souls!

To overtax the Pope, however, was another matter. Guiscard had courteously given Hildebrand the pace to set and he set it slow, with many haltings, while he watched unceasingly the pale, rather frail-looking face of Nicholas II who rode at his side.

The sun was slanting steadily westward, cocking a fiery eye behind the great Vulture, that huge blue volcano that guards Apulia like a sentinel, and they were threading the outer reaches of Venosa where the Pope was to consecrate the new de Hauteville abbey. They were soon to reach it, doubtless; the windy Guiscard for once was silent, and Hildebrand felt the need to think. This man de Hauteville, whom to hold in converse was like breasting a tide, what did he want? Hildebrand marshalled the facts to two. De Hauteville supremacy among the counts, and the dukedom of all this South Italian entity for himself. In return he would go the whole gamut of the feudal pledge. A boon indeed. It would be good to have the powerful Robert bound, both on pain of sin and by knightly obligation, to come to the aid of Rome. So far so good. But one request of Robert's jarred. His divorce. His excuse—the secretaries had found it valid—was consanguinity. The marriage was within the blood-tie, therefore wrong. It was wrong in the law. But what of the spirit? And the motives?

Hildebrand woke from his troubled reverie to find the procession splayed before him in the abbey yard, waiting for him and the Pope to enter. Quickly he dismounted and went to Nicholas's aid. Robert was there before him, holding the papal stirrup, reverently, with a pious expression on his ruddy face.

But as the three of them entered the abbey porch and passed beneath the square Norman belfry to the narthex, Hildebrand had a glimpse of the child-wife, Albarada, sitting sad-faced on her palfrey, and by her side, a nurse holding Robert's babe. He frowned.

The long-robed prelates took their places on the semicircular stone benches about the sanctuary, with Hildebrand on the Pope's right and the young Abbot Desiderius on the left, and the ceremonies for the abbey's consecration began. There was an added feature to the day's performance in the shape of de Hauteville's corpses to bless. The bodies of three elder brothers—Drogo, Humphry and William Iron-Arm, the first who had ventured south to seek new lands—had been exhumed and brought to Venosa to be more suitably interred. Awaiting their bones were three exquisitely sculptured sarcophagi, which Guiscard, as his custom was, had raped from a Greek town. These sat incongruously dainty beside the grim Norman stone pillars. But for the present, three plain black boxes stood centered in the nave. While Nicholas spoke out suitable eulogies of the gentlemen within, Count Robert and his brother Roger stood over the coffins, their heads bowed piously. Nicholas had a cold, and as his weak voice rasped on, Hildebrand observed the scene with a jaundiced eye . . .

Roger de Hauteville was handsomer than his brother—slimmer, blond rather than tawny-red. He looked to be the ideal of Norman nobility. But under that refinement, Hildebrand had heard, lay unsuspected ruthlessness, and behind the gentle brow a cunning to match any, save perhaps Guiscard, who indeed kept his wary eye on the youngster. Roger, who had already made good in Calabria, now conceived daringly of the conquest of Moslem Sicily, the Isle of Fire. Like an eager boy, Roger, with Guiscard by to second him, had advised Hildebrand of the plan—to rid Sicily of the heathen under the actual banner of the Church. The idea was at once fine and terrible. The Moslem menace was all too real, the concept of a holy war was a great one—but Hildebrand could wish it were the lawful feudal nobility who had conceived of it. If these southern brigands, the disinherited of Europe, began it, would the thing catch on with a fine zeal, or would it start a wildfire the outcome of which no man dared guess? He had instructed Nicholas already about this Sicily thing, so there was no use to fret further on it. Oh, but he prayed the decision was right. The cause was good—but the means? These splendid de Hautevilles, were they the chosen instruments of good? How could you tell? Their piety was brash. It had a brassy note to it like their war-horns. Was that merely the fault of their manners—or was it the hint of a terrible flaw beneath? Yet, one thing was certain. Tancred de Hauteville, courtier and hunting companion to William of Normandy's father, had spewed a brood of king-makers from his loins. And these two were the prime of the lot.

But Hildebrand, with mere men as his tools, wished he could mold them in the fiery furnace of his own zeal. Couldn't they see what was foul dross of *this* world and what was pure gold to save up for *the next?* The two of them, standing flushed and handsome under the apex, receiving the sounding accolades—both of them bent on power and love—while the worms went writhing in the casques before them! *There* was the proof of it, there in those mouldering casques, could they but gaze on them with the eyes God gave. But lands were far more beckoning than Heaven now, and a lover's kiss more potent than the stink of the grave. What a powerful brew the devil mixed to get his wordlings drunk on!

And as if to honor the Deacon's suspicious thoughts, Guiscard now started to fidget and crane, and cast his eyes unpiously across to the outer nave where the women stood in the far side of the abbey. What was up with him? wondered Hildebrand, and couldn't resist following the Norman's gaze. His curiosity was rewarded by the sight of a white profile against the wide curve of a pilgrim's hat. Princess Sigelgaita of Salerno! Gisolf and his sister had visited Rome too often for him to mistake the outline of that strong, white-skinned, wilful face. What was she *doing* here, and in this guise? The rumor, then, was true. So *this* was the cause of Robert's churning so madly for divorce! This woman, long a disdainful virgin, whom Gisolf couldn't even by threat of his own rack marry off, was smitten at last, and for Robert Guiscard. What a pair!

Even as he watched, the white profile slipped from view behind the bowed heads of the other women, and the next sight was her somber back moving out through the throng. A white hand at the brow as though with the humors. *Sly pilgrim!* thought Hildebrand, as Guiscard took the bait. For Robert had handed his prayer-scroll to Roger and now pushed his way from the church. The final glimpse of him was the fiery de Hauteville hair taking flame in the sunlit doorway of the abbey porch.

And now he returned, the churchman to his book, to find Nicholas

staring at him. The Pope had finished the obsequies some moments
back, it seemed, and now waited on Hildebrand for last orisons of
death. . . .

[3]

Guiscard jumped to his destrier with a mighty leap, startling it
from its somnolent cropping in the abbey yard. It reared up snorting,
and wheeling to the bit, leaping to the rowel, scrambled over
the chantry steps, took the cactus fence in a white-eyed leap and went
charging down the dusty road whence it had come so short a time ago
so leisurely. This felt more like his master. This was haste, urgent,
yet joyful. There was hurry in the whip, panic in the spur. Neither
flight nor battle, it had the joy of summer in it, the rush of a swollen
spring.

"Wait!" cried Guiscard and gave a great halloo. But the swift white
dust ball ahead of him on the road swept on. Her start was a short
one—he pounded the stallion with his heels for joy and exultation.
The abbey, the Pope, the power about to be given him, everything
gave way to the tumult in his heart. Springtime in the breath of summer. Fierce joy that he had never known. He would give up lands,
kingdoms, Heaven itself for this surge of delight that filled his limbs
and spread his lips to a grin. He couldn't help it. Sigelgaita, that beautiful brazen one, could have chosen no more captivating thing to do
than to seek him, here and now. The first glimpse of that bold profile,
prim and sober in the pilgrim's weeds, had set his innards whirling.
And now? Now the passionate virgin would find what it *meant* to
tease the heart of Guiscard in love!

God, that was a fine beast she rode! He spurred his own impatiently and began to gain. At a rise in the road, she turned to look
back and he had a momentary picture of her fleeing upwards, framed
against the hulking mass of the great blue Vulture, before she plunged
down from sight. But his own progress was so winged that before
long he could see her white under-kirtle foaming at her knees, for
she rode not side-saddle, but hugging the mare's flanks like any man.
A heavy braid of yellow hair had loosened from that ridiculous hat
and was sweeping back. Soon he'd be able to catch it in his hand.
But suddenly, where the road crossed, she swerved and sped several
rods up the Herculean Way before he could turn his destrier. "Blood!"
He thought he heard her laugh on the wind. He wheeled at last and,
leaping the fosse beside the road, scrambled across the goat pasture,
riding at her from an angle. At this, she whirled and fled into the dark
woods of scrub-pine that stretched south to Forenza. It was fatal. In a

trice he plunged after, caught up, snatched her bridle and had her stopped. As he dismounted, she leapt from her horse, and was backed against a tree, her riding whip in one hand and a sharp-pointed deadly-looking baselard in the other. Her hat lay in the dust where it had fallen. The sunlight slanted through on her bright gold hair, and her tawny eyes glinted dark beneath bold thick brows that almost met above them.

"Great Saints, Sigelgaita!" cried Robert. "What am I, a Saracen, that you fence me so?"

Her words came jerkily from her heaving breast and her voice was husky with a sort of passionate terror. "Don't touch me, Guiscard. Don't touch me. This has a good Lombard blade that I don't mind using on Frenchmen any more than Moors!"

At this, so savagely put forth, Guiscard backed up a little, and stood by her sweating palfrey, grinning. The autumnal air and the mingled scents of the animals and the dead grass at their feet were strong in his nostrils. Old memories stirred, of his robber-days when he'd captured prizes on the road: a fat merchant's belt, a bishop's gold, a wench or two for a few sunny hours on the Calabrian meadow. Just looking at Sigelgaita, his youth seemed renewed. This beautiful Lombard was to be his life's crown, and her coming today like this was like some splendid act of love. He could be patient with her teasing then. He flung an arm across the neck of her black horse and stood watching the play of sunlight on her features, the stain of wrath and outrage—he could scarcely call it fear!—drawing rapid shadows across the golden-colored eyes. Sigelgaita and her wide-cheeked face, too generous mouth, and rather muscular stance, was too bold and powerful for a proper maid, they said. Sant' George, she was too much woman for a common man! There was the truth on it. But not for him. God, how perfect she was, for him! He stood watching her, grey eyes hard on her amber ones, while his fingers played with her horse's mane.

"What makes you *dream* I'd harm fair pilgrims on the highroad, magnificent maiden?"

"I believe you've been known before to follow such pursuits."

"Yet, with a lead on me, you erred so badly as to take to the trees. You had quite a start, you know."

Her eyes smouldered at him for a second; then, "If you are such a boon to women on holy pilgrimage, let me proceed on mine."

His brows went up. "You are indeed on a shrine-road? Where? Compostela? Rome? Jerusalem? Even our own St. Nicholas at Monte Gargane? This is the wrong direction for them all. Don't dally, Sigelgaita. I know why you came! Let's thank the saints, together, then, can't we?"

"For what?"

"Why, that our hearts caught flame together at your brother's court!"

He moved toward her then, but she uttered a sound only to be described as a soft snarl, like a young lioness he had met once in the Calabrian hills. "Come closer, Robert de Hauteville, and I'll stab you dead as a vineyard fox!"

Robert was a little dashed, and began to wonder if she meant it.

And as if she saw his vanity wilting at her threats, so obviously in earnest, she let her eyes soften a little, and when she spoke again there was a pout to her full, wide mouth.

"Would you hinder me on my penitential road? The Bishop of Salerno set me the task for the sin I told him lately."

"And that?"

"That I love a wedded man."

His face cleared. "But listen, sweet palmer, it may be that your penance is vain, that you may be innocent!"

"What do you mean?"

"The Pope finds my claim of cousinship is true. He will free me tomorrow."

"And what of your son?"

He laughed, huskily, with a sort of checked passion. "You yourself, my beauty, will yield Guiscard many a lusty heir."

He drew nearer. He was done with words. And seeing this, she shook her head, swept her hat from the ground and walked through his reaching arms to her horse. He felt for the moment the beating of her heart where his hand brushed across her bodice, and saw the hot flame glowing in her cheeks. But she said, "Don't defile my pledge, Count Robert. I must complete it, now that my word's given."

He hastened to hold her spur as she mounted, side-saddle this time, and sat gazing down at him. Her pose was prim enough. But the tumble of her hair all dishevelled and the lambent sweep of her eyes on his face had Guiscard clinging to her cloak, imploring her. "Come back to Venosa, Sigelgaita. Just till this thing is settled. Now, more than ever, I must have you or I'll perish of it. Listen, sweetheart, we could make our shrine-journey together, for in truth this hour of seeing you has torn such a rent in my soul it would take a pilgrimage to the Tomb itself to mend it . . ."

He would have gone on in his fevered pleading, and indeed he meant it, but she laid a cool hand on his lips.

"Go back, then, Robert. I will follow, but not full to the abbey. *Go back*, Guiscard, and hurry. They will be waiting."

[4]

Albarada stood in the abbey, flanked by Richard the Seneschal and Beratine, the nurse. She had never known such cause to weep, so many reasons. She had missed no more than Hildebrand the spectacle of Robert slipping through the crowd, and had watched him re-enter and take his place again with Roger. What embarrassment he had caused, making the Pope prolong the ceremonies, murmuring prayers till his return! It had Hildebrand red as a beet. His small, fierce, freckle-spotted face seemed ready to burst with anger and his eyes snapped dangerously.

What excuse had Robert to leave at such a time and in that woman's wake? Who was she, this Sigelgaita they had told her of? Everyone was so anxious to make her understand. She, Albarada, was her husband's cousin—terrible sin. She must let them free him of his sinning, they said, and Guiscard himself seemed bent on mixing her up with his queer logic. The night before, in their chamber, when she had known the worst, and had wept, screamed, pleaded, and at last had fallen to kicking her heels against the wall in a fit of humors at this terrible decision, Robert had stood there saying how lovely she was, how good, young, beautiful she was, and therefore he was letting her marry Richard! Good lord, what wild, strange reasoning!

Well, Robert was fooled if he thought she'd let him go. In the flesh, yes—for she'd scarcely had him. But always she would wait, whatever happened. She looked about at other tombs in the abbey, which were meant to hold the de Hauteville clan, and suddenly made a vow that she too would rest there, in the one next to Robert's. Wouldn't it be *something*, if at last she could lie in peace with him forever? Such love as hers, she thought determinedly, was not to be murdered lightly, even by his dallying. Her love was a live thing, grown like a weed while she waited months on end in Melfi Tower. What did the Lombard woman know of that? She wanted his power and his name.

Even now the first step in his wild ambitions was being confirmed. The Pope's weak, wheezing voice was calling out the new-made title . . . "Robert, Duke of Apulia and Calabria . . ." there was a pause. Then Nicholas added, "And by God's grace, of all Sicily!"

A great shout seemed ready to shatter the sanctity of the chapel. *This* was a call to arms for the Seigneur Christ! But the singers in the chantry-stalls broke like a torrent into song and the mob went spewing from the church to gossip of it.

As Albarada walked with her husband from the abbey, the babe behind, in the nurse's arms, began to cry for sustenance. She turned to take him, there was a place in the belfry tower where she had gone before to give him peace. But Robert caught at her arm as she did so, and the look in his eyes told her this was his last goodbye.

"Believe me, Albarada, I am sorry for this, to give you cause to grieve so."

She shook her head. Didn't he see she suffered far too much to speak? Why didn't he go?

"And the babe," he was saying, "he *is* a rose, my Albarada—fair and stout."

She was shy. "Beratine says he looks so *much* like you, messire . . ." as if indeed she spoke to a stranger. Her strength shattered, her ears splitting with Marc's squalling, she thought wildly, "Why *doesn't* he go?"

"Of *course* he looks like me! For I am the seal and he, the little one, is the signet of it!" Then, as though caught by this whim, he pulled the great seal-ring from his middle finger and turned it on the infant's arm. Then he offered it.

"Here. When the boy hits the mark of my shoulder on the pillar in the hall by the dais at Melfi, give him this, and send him to me. Do you promise?"

As a sleep-walker might, she took it and turned away. . . .

Up in the belfry room, she let the babe take comfort at her breast, wishing she were dead, emptied of all feeling, so that this living death would go. There were no tears now. Dry-eyed she stared out the little window-square at the towering cone of the Vulture in the west. A movement below caught her glance. The pilgrim's weeds, the strong white face. So then, that was it. The creature waited for him even now. She saw Guiscard come up, and taking the woman's hand he seemed to push up the sleeve and bite with a kiss the bare white arm. The woman drew back with a laugh and her ebony horse reared, neighing, as she galloped off. Guiscard mounted to follow and, as he spurred to the road, a sob escaped from Albarada, and as though resenting it, the babe bit suddenly into her flesh, and she blessed him for the sharp, numbing pain.

BOOK 1

THE WAR-CAR

CHAPTER I

The Black Duchess

SOME THIRTEEN YEARS LATER, on a still, warm evening, a solitary horseman appeared near the sea-town of Bari in the south, where the de Hauteville brothers had been lying for two years, pressing a siege.

The Normans lay resting, after victory on the six-hundredth day, their camp-ground murmurous with soldiers at mess or dice, and smoky with supper-fires just started at the tents. The city, red-gold in a brilliant sunset, rose sheer on the cliff above them. Behind them, a shale bank jutted up, with only a cleft where merchant caravans, in more peaceful times, came through to Bari.

A pair of sentries, loitering at the tag-end of a watch, had for some time seen the horseman riding from the hinterland. One of them rose from his haunches, put up his spear against the fellow as he came, and raked with a practiced eye the husky destrier the lad was riding.

"Where do you ride from?"

"Melfi."

"*Alone* all that way?"

"Yes."

"What road, then, from Apulia?"

"The Appian Way, of course, then through the mountains."

"What's your age?"

"Thirteen."

"Well. That bay you ride would credit a belted knight, much less a wet-ears like yourself. Did you steal it?"

"No, it's mine, from my mother's stables at the—"

"What's your business here?" The sentry was enjoying himself. The lad's face was growing redder than his hair, which was bright enough, in the hard light.

"I've come to see the Duke," was the boy's announcement.

"The Duke! My! And what to do, if I may make so bold?"

"I—— Just that I've come. He'd expect me now."

The burly one shook his head. "I *know* those he expected. You're not one." He started to chain the postern.

"No, listen! I was *told* to come."

"Wherefore?"

"I'm as high now as the nick in the pillar at the hall at Melfi. I—"

"Great Michael!" snorted the other guard squatted against the shale. "Send him packing, Jules! He's either lying or touched, and my stomach sticks to my back already." He sniffed the air, and glanced at the fires below, where the spitted meats grew steamy on the coals.

Above them the boy nearly jumped from his saddle. "No! I must see the Duke!"

The first guard grimaced at the other. "What *lads* they send on high affairs now! What do they call you, weighty one?"

"Marc de Hauteville."

The sentry smiled, but his manner grew a shade less bantering. "Come now. Some proof of the name you carry."

"I have it here." A gull flew up from the heath. The horse shied. Marc checked the bay, pulling it up in a high smart rear, and spattering them not too accidentally with shale and recent mud. Then he leaned over and showed them the seal-ring thonged to his neck. Jules's eyebrows rose, and the other sentry roused himself for a look. While they conferred on the talisman, Marc stared at the scene below, his belly churning.

He had the feeling he had come on a great stage between acts. The town, far up on the crag, stained red and purple now in the changing light, had stout vines slung from its walls to foil the probing of the battering-rams. The battlements themselves were strangely bare. Below, poised here and there on the rocks, stood the rams and cats, their sockets empty, their slings limp. There were strange noises from somewhere in the city, but far-off sounding, as if they emanated from the banks of evening clouds behind it. And down in front was the quiet camp, with arms stacked neatly at the tents and the garrison lying at ease.

The sentries grunted together, shrugged. "The Duke's seal, all right. No doubt of it here." They raised the chains.

Marc's heart pounded at his ribs. He pulled at his belt, at his gauntlets. Except for his new steel corselet, what a sorry mess! He tried to smooth the bandage on his leg where the devil-born roadman had lodged a dart-point meant for his back. But ouch! That made it bleed again! Be damned to his draggled plumage! He picked up the reins and allowed the young bay to find his way between the boulders into the compound.

There had been a heavy afternoon shower. The flat surface of the encampment gave to the destrier's hooves in deep scrogging holes as he worried it along. Several horses had been tied at the cleft, and he saw, now, he had made a mistake not to leave his own with the rest. Some soldiers glanced up from their throwing of the dice and he heard their remarks followed by bursts of derisive laughter. Perhaps he was crippled. A young tout like that should be able to rein in, even if the nag *was* too much for him! He went the gauntlet that he had begun, reached a large olive tree and swung off, grimacing a little as the bandage pulled at the edges of his wound. As he tethered Ouragon he felt his face burning hotter than his sore leg and cursed that he hadn't a fald-cloth, a shield, some piece of heraldry with the de Hauteville lion painted on it. If the confounded siege-hounds knew they were yapping at the heels of the son of the Duke himself—what a shutting of big smart mouths!

He went, walking carefully among the bowls of arrows and the bristling stacks of bows. He hoped he would be spared the necessity of asking questions of the garrison. Sure enough, his eye caught at a great scarlet pavilion emblazoned with the crude device he sought, and he headed for it, boots slogging.

"Ho, there!" came a roar. "Come back, young whoreson with the head of a blind mole! What's the plan, boy? And where do you think you're bound?"

The burst of questions had no sooner assaulted him like a load of slag from a catapult when huge fingers dug into his shoulder and stopped him in his tracks. "Come over here!" roared so close to his ear and with such an accompanying cloud of wine-drenched breath that he twisted in the rock-like grip as much from physical revulsion as anger. He pulled around smartly to face his hinderer; but when he saw the big hulk of an officer framed in the tent-flaps with his huge fist raised, and strong teeth bared for his benefit, he saw he might well do the fellow's bidding.

The great paw on his collar-bone pushed him into the tent. A low fire burned in an iron bowl in the center of the shelter, and the far corner was taken up by another rough, a darkly handsome fellow with salt-and-peppery brief curls and sharp blue eyes, who sat cross-legged, with the lute in his arms. A huge eared cider-jug, uncorked, sat mulling by the brazier. Marc was pushed into a camp chair; and when he tried to adjust to a sitting position therein, was pushed back. From this appointed place he opened his lips to state his business, but the giant above him barked out across his tentative beginning.

"Now Geoffrey, let's have it. Sing loud!"

Geoffrey made a try.

> *"The snarling trumpets call beside my wall;*
> *Love hears them chide,*
> *Love leaves my side,"*

and sourly broke off.

"What the devil, Hugh; that's three times now. That's enough. Besides, that's a *woman's* song. Why should *I*—"

"No— Now Geoffrey, go on," the big one coaxed with a peevishness which, with his grizzled face and his stature, seemed comic. "Try the other, then. You know which I mean!" He had unhooked an old-time mace that was slung from the tent-beam, and swung it in a clumsy fashion, as he started himself, in a voice like a rasp, on a livelier tune.

> *"Broach the cider and pipe the reeds.*
> *Pound the tambour and brush the viol;*
> *Our bones too soon will blend with weeds*
> *So make us merry our little while!"*

Marc moved at this point and got a slap from the mace in his new corselet. He knew, from the jar and the dull clang of it, that his corselet was no longer new. He sat back sighing. The farther rough, it seemed, was addressing him.

"Look!" he said. "Can you slice it? *He* is the one who is sick-of-the-moon, but *I* am the one who must sing! Always of late, must I sing to him, like a cat on a castle gate, while he snivels and sighs and— Vaugh! It's disgusting at his age! Homesick; lovesick as a squeaking boy for his wife; his old Viking beldame who waits in his castle on the coast. He's missed getting to Bull Joy now three months, so every night I must sing like a bird, though I croak in the bargain!"

His eye sought the jug. It was picked up, tilted and appreciatively smacked-over, then he turned to Hugh.

"Ask the Duke for leave, Hugh! Each night I sing; by day I can't *talk!* Ask the Duke for a fortnight! Since when has Guiscard refused Hugh Falloc a simple boon? Elsewise I swear by Easter I won't have pipes enough for 'Attack' or 'Ease,' and Guiscard will have me water-carrier for cat-wailing all night to *you.* Bah!" He laid the lute, not too carelessly, beside the cider-jug and folded his arms.

"You're a *windy* old scart," growled Hugh, and turned to their guest. "What's your errand, boy?"

Marc was short-taken at the sudden attention; but he felt more at

ease now. What a mercy to meet, right off, the famous Hugh and
Geoffrey!

"I am the Duke's son," he said.

"His *what?*" Hugh cocked his head and squinted down at him.
"Wild yellow hair and a hot grey eye. H'm, might *be*, especially in
Calabria. That complexion, I s'pose, you have of your mother, whoever the bonny trollop was. But don't blush for it, son, that's *good
blood*, however you came by it! Now what is't you want of him? A
bounty? A horse? New bow and shafts? He'll not see you lack
these things, with his mark so strong upon you!"

He stood up, red to the ears; he showed them the seal-ring; he said,
"I am Marc de Hauteville, son of Albarada of Melfi."

"Whump!" the other officer got up and leaned over the fire to look
first at the token, then at Marc. Geoffrey Ridelle's judgment of manpower had been relied on by Guiscard for twenty years, and his
slightly bibulous condition could not befuddle dead-eye appraisal
of a soldierly build, a thoroughbred stance. Now he missed no detail
of the cap of red hair, inclined to hold to curl at the edges, the high
rounded brow and the large, prominently planed face. The nose
was good, quite broad at the nostrils but lacking the usual hump.
He had an extremely well-formed mouth and there was a glimpse of
superb teeth. But that and the rounded chin, the blue shadow under
his nether lip—let the maids discover them. Geoffrey passed quickly
from the face. He took in the fine shoulders—a little sloped and a
little bent, as in an athlete—the narrow waist and hips, the sinewy
legs in the dirty, bloodied hose. He was certainly unkempt looking,
as though in recent road-trouble. But, judged Geoffrey, the lad's bearing would never be a matter of oiled mail and shined spurs.

"Robert did better," he said from the side of his mustache, "on
Gerard's niece than on Sigelgaita. This is better off-throw than young
Clutchy-purse, by far . . ."

Marc caught the well-bandied name of young Roger Borsa, son of
the Lombard woman. He clamped his teeth tight and looked at the
iron bowl of fire.

Hugh Falloc had suddenly sobered. "Shut up, loud-mouth! How
can you sing so nice one minute and talk like a serf the next? Your
father," he told Marc, "is on the other side of the town tonight, on
the sea wall. Doubtless we'll take you there. But Madame commands
this camp. We'll report first."

"*Who* commands?"

"Lady Sigelgaita. You had better show yourself now, or there'll be
some to answer for!"

Marc frowned, then gave a shrug so much like Guiscard's that
both men grinned. Geoffrey Ridelle came, not without some difficulty,

from the other side of the fire-bowl and laid a hearty hand on Marc's shoulder.

"Glad you have come to us, lad. I fear we've been barbarous with you, hey?"

Marc smiled and said nothing; but he had an immediate liking for these two to add to his hero-worship.

"And mind you hang on to your talisman!" Geoffrey called as they left him.

Walking along beside Hugh the Horse-killer was like trying to keep pace with the free stride of some mountain animal. Yet from the aura of leather and wine and horse-flesh emanating from the gigantic warrior, Marc derived a protective friendliness. It felt comfortable to be going to face the redoubtable Black Duchess under such a sponsor.

Sigelgaita was seated at the end of a long camp table as they were ushered in. Late shadows obscured the interior spaces of the pavilion, but Marc was aware of silken curtains, several wide couches and besides the page, a great glistening black man standing near her chair. The two guttering cressets by the Duchess's head threw shadows on her face, so that he realized her features only gradually. She was eating a bowl of something; her arms as she raised the spoon to her lips glimmered with innumerable shining tight gold bands from wrist to elbow. She was wearing a long garment of heavy silk, black, that clung in deep ripples to her body. Hung on a tent-pole above the board, catching the cresset's glow on shield and shoulder-buckle, was a suit of steel *maille*. The tips of the round, pointed breastplates on the cuirass caught sheen from the light and flashed. She had not looked up.

"Your ladyship," said Hugh, "this is Marc de Hauteville, son of Albarada of Melfi, come for his page-service with us, and to join his father."

She slid further into the Greek chair she used, tilted it backwards and flung an arm across. Marc was conscious of power in that superb, relaxed body. She wore a girdle of round gold medallions. He saw them shimmer with the rise of her quickened breath. She scarcely glanced at him, however.

"Don't come to me with wild statements like that, Hugh Falloc. This boy is fifteen at least."

"Well, Madame, I didn't ask him that. What age have you?"

Marc heard himself say, "Thirteen," but absently, with his mind not on it. So *this* was the one whose name went unsaid in his mother's presence, whom Albarada spoke of in the most degrading terms, on certain terrible occasions. He had half expected Sigelgaita to be horned, at least.

Hugh was saying, "Well, he's large all right, but it's him. Look at the shanks of him, and the hair."

"Every man in the army has good shanks, and half have yellow hair!"

She glanced up from under thick dark brows, the light falling strongly on the gold braids, the handsome white face, the wide red mouth. Her eyes, as she turned them on Marc, swam with brown specks and were lambent as a cat's. Somehow, the very fact of her head's turning shot a thrill of awe—he'd sooner die than call it fear—up his spine. The turning of her head and the look of her face made him feel as if the sun had swung at mid-day and blazed in his eyes. Without looking away from him, she said, "Falloc, you're drunk. And on Palm Sunday Eve. You see *me* here, with my bowl of frumenty and light *Acarenza* to wash it, and you—potting yourself like a swine on the Abbot's applejack!" She turned to him then. "Go back to your tent, Hugh. I'll manage this."

Marc looked at Hugh and saw his large eyes bulge a little. But the purr-like voice went deeper, strangely quizzical,—"Go *on*, Hugh! And mind you, clear your head. We'll go to the sea-wall soon and hear about Roger's naval fracas . . . *Well!*"

This last seemed to settle things. It was with some misgivings that Marc watched Hugh Falloc's big mailed frame fade back from the pool of cresset light.

She pushed back the board with a hard grate that sent the smell of broken rushes to the nostrils, and rose out of the circule with a lithe, powerful movement. At thirteen he was as tall as she, but he stepped back.

"And now, my bold fellow, don't you know what happens to ones like you who seek to build nests for themselves with false feathers? Or can't you imagine?"

A woman shouldn't smile that way, thought Marc—she looks terrible. But she was reaching for her cloak. Great gods, she really thought he lied!

For the third time he was glad of the seal-ring slung from his neck.

Her movement was smooth but swift as she caught at it; *he* was the one who perked forward a little and had, at that proximity, a whiff of the powerful perfume of her black silks.

The device, a shield charged on field sable with red flanches bearing de Hauteville lions rampant, the center foss enfiled by a row of fox-ears for Guiscard's chief ordinary, seemed to demand as much scrutiny of the Duchess as if she had not had sight of it on every piece of gear that Guiscard had claim to. He wondered a little what she was thinking, but any reaction of hers took second place to what was giving him joy.

For this was who he was. The seal and the signet; himself, *himself* and Duke Robert Guiscard. Each time he looked at it he could see his life before him, exciting, colorful and full of meaning as the device itself.

Since Beratine, the nurse, had told him the old secret, his life had changed. Only two years now he had known, but for that time he had lived an existence apart. The sons of the Counts, rolling about the castle-yards in their fathers' absence, the sons of Albarada and Richard—he had felt superior to these in a special, secret way. For the fact, at first dim, became more vivid and inescapable. He was the first-born son of the most powerful prince in Italy. He endured his mother's ministrations, his step-father's love, with patience only, and thought ever of the day when the natural burgeoning of his strength would give him the right to the seal—the passport to his shining inheritance. He thought of this not as gold, lands, or power. He thought of it as being with Guiscard, learning what he must in order, some day, to ride, fight, and live beside him. This alone—what ample patrimony!

And so, as the Duchess stared, he felt not relief only. He saw here the very beginning of his life. The white hand tossing the cloak to the page was the sign that his talisman had guided him home; that was the fact, despite all the sentinels and Sigelgaitas in the world.

"Why didn't you present this *first?* You showed it to Hugh Falloc, I suppose . . ."

He felt utterly calm now, and he looked at the broad, vivid face almost insolently without caring what thought was in his eyes, and nodded.

"You are a great, healthy lad," said the Duchess. "Go on to Count Hugh, then, and tell him to give you a place in one of the pavilions as page."

Marc frowned.

"I should like, of course, to see my father."

"Oh? Well, you *will*, sometime soon."

"Tonight?"

"I'm afraid not."

"Why?" asked his new-found boldness.

"He is very busy and in great travail."

"Why? Is he ill?"

"No." She took an audible breath; her eyes seemed to smoulder at him a moment as she played with the array of bracelets on one forearm. "There has been a great victory here, clinched by Count Roger's triumph over the Byzantines today in a sea-fight off Bari. With no food from the Greek Emperor, the Barinese have, of course, surrendered. The Duke is anxious to secure things here, for the march to Sicily."

That explained, then, the air of interlude in this encampment.

"Then I can *go* to my father on the sea-wall," he said, emboldened by her conversational tone.

It was softly said, but it sounded final: "No."

"Are you forbidding me?"

"Orders, my lad." And she really smiled. "Now return to Falloc's tent."

The Suffering Lord knew he was only too happy to leave, but as he turned to go, she said, "Wait!" and pointing to his feet asked, "What's that?"

He looked down. His wound had bled on the floor.

"Your pardon," he muttered. "I hadn't realized . . ."

"Let us see it."

"It's mending, Madame."

"Let's *see* it!" Again he was aware of the glisten in the yellow eyes. He pulled the bandage down.

"That must be tended," she said.

"Yes, I'll arrange."

"Come here." Her voice was soft, but the effect on Marc was like a shout. "Unwrap it."

As Marc unwound the dirty clout he watched her move to a brazier and pull it to the board. At a jerk of the white hand the shiny black varlet alertly came forward.

"My medical chest."

As the black brought the instruments and put them on the board, Marc mightily cursed his luck. He knew of the skill of the woman of Salerno—that she, like her brother, had drunk deep of the well of medical knowledge there. It was fairly certain that though Gisolf pursued certain macabre experiments in his castle of Maia Torre, the Duchess, to anyone's knowledge, used her secrets but to heal. Nevertheless, as Marc watched her place pincers, a knife, a salve-box and a probe, beautifully polished, at her immediate use, the silk tent of the red lion seemed indeed to close on him like the keep of Maia Torre . . .

He watched her work with swift, cat-like energy. She was, he felt, taking a real interest in him for the first time. But the thought simply summoned cool twinges to the region of his ribs. That feeling was soon transferred to the fire in his leg as she probed the wound none too gently with something the devil must use to tickle the sinners in hell. He bit his lips as she swiftly cleaned, cauterized, anointed and wrapped it . . .

As he took his leg off the trestle, it still hurt like fire, but the swollen, sick feeling was magically gone.

"Now mind you rest in Falloc's tent tonight." She looked at him as if she expected some obeisance besides his murmured thanks, but those strong, smooth hands, as she presented her finger-tips, had his blood upon them. He bowed and left the pavilion.

He was half-way across the compound heading for Count Hugh's

quarters, when he came to himself and realized he did not mean to
return there. He was burning with frustration. He *must* see Guiscard.
Besides, how could he abide waiting till morning for a look at Bari?
His fatigue was gone. It was as though he had come to the village
for the first time, like a peasant freed from the glebe for a holiday, and
the town must be his oyster even these first hours. The sun had dipped
behind the crags now, casting the encampment in shadow. But above,
the tips of the turrets of Bari's palaces were gilded still. Day was not
gone, and he would catch it at the tag-end.

He climbed up one of the steep paths, scrambled up on a ledge
and made his way along a rock wall. He blessed his youth, for he
might be any page-boy bent on an errand for Guiscard's officers, and
he met many such on the way.

The further he climbed on the ledged crag that swung around
the city, the more distinct became noises he had heard as only mur-
murings before, and as he gained at last the seaward side and
flattened himself against the rock, for it was narrowest here, his eyes
were blinded by the harsh, sudden light, for out on the Adriatic the
sun sat like a great red bowl, and under its fire the sands glowed like
wine at his feet.

He slid along the last few rods and onto the sea-wall and walked
along easily, taking everything in—the harbor, blood-crimson in the
final rays, strewn with débris of battle; the high, empty walls of
the city and the pavilions of the Norman officers spread beneath them.
Behind him the sun sank and night fell with the abruptness of a sea-
side evening, and as the light vanished, he saw torches catch in
pavilions, a soft glow gradually growing. Voices, muffled with tent-
silk, sounded warm and companionable, and rendered the sea-wall
silence more desolate and still. Marc shivered. He had seen the red
tent among them, a larger pavilion than Sigelgaita's, but with the same
leonine device, and the half-formed plan to accost his father now
abruptly crystallized.

"Who is it that goes without a lance?" came a voice. And, as Marc
turned, the voice, sharply caught, gruffened, and barked a brisk, *"Dex
ais!"*

Marc had wheeled in the dimness, to face a large, kite-shaped
buckler, luminous in the twilight, over which a youngish, fuzz-faced,
helmeted head appeared.

"Dex ais," the head repeated.

Marc gave back for lack of a better answer the usual "God aid us."
He saw by the guard's look that this was not enough.

"So I thought. The Duke will be less than pleased that they still
get through, for all our watching. *Come on, you!"* He glanced about,
apparently in a hurry to take his prize before anyone horned in, like a
dog with a bone.

"Hey!" said Marc. "You've got your bow strung backwards! I lack your word here, maybe, but am of the Duke's retinue. I'm his son and was about to speak to him in his quarters."

The guard laughed. "Do I look like a babe? His son, which you're not, would scarce be sneaking about. Do you come, or have my steel in your backside?"

They were engaged in a duel of glares, when a voice beside them had them both standing stiff as lances.

"So; you chose to ignore my orders."

Sigelgaita's words received full emphasis from her appearance. She was, except for a helmet, in full military dress. Even in the darkness she was handsomely terrifying. Big Hugh Falloc, even, looked less huge where he stood beside her, bearing a small hand-faggot.

"Haven't you seen the Duke?" Hugh boomed.

"He was not to leave your tent, Hugh," her ladyship announced in a voice like curds. Hugh subsided then and looked at Marc as if he smelled something.

Voices now sounded near the Duke's pavilion; laughter and a scuffling of feet. A crowd of soldiers were milling about it—noisy, boastful, on top of the world. Marc, in all this, was feeling dashed. He was not being escorted, accompanied or presented to the Duke. "Led in custody" was the phrase—he had heard it so often at his step-sire's military court in Melfi. Led by the ear, so to speak. Behind him, the worried-looking guard tagged after in a travesty of his duty, and while Hugh forced a blustering way through the crowd, it was the silent Sigelgaita who had Marc firmly by the sleeve of his wilted jerkin.

So *this* was the moment he had dreamed of so much up in Melfi. Over his lessons—French, Greek, Latin and Arabic—which his mother had insisted on, he had mooned on this first meeting with his father. And the athletic exercises which good Richard the Seneschal had ordered for him, he had done them faithfully, the sooner to reach the height of the pillar-nick. And he had achieved it at thirteen, two years sooner, they told him, than rightly suited a page's service.

Between then and now had been the terrible quarrel with Lady Albarada. Uncognizant that Beratine had tattled about Guiscard's request and the pillar-nick, she had raged when he wished to go. That bitter, bitter farewell; from his mother's lips, at the last, the ancient curse—*mal vignai e mal andre, ill to you coming and going*— and the long, hard journey into wild Calabria. He wondered now if it had been worth the pains.

As they approached the pavilion, Marc had a sudden sick picture of how he would look to Robert—not unlike a renegade being dragged up in disgrace. It occurred to him now for the first time to regret his defiance of the Duchess Sigelgaita.

"Boil me!" roared a voice. "Hugh the Horse-killer!"

A big ruffian with a huge torch had shouldered into them. He changed the faggot and stuck out a grimy gauntlet. He reeked of sweat and leather.

"Grie Duval," responded Hugh. "Not since—but where? Argentano? Bull Joy? Reggio? A long time! Whose company do you command? Your own lances only, perhaps?"

"And some of the Count's. Going to Sicily too?"

"Aye."

And then, since the Duchess behind them cleared her throat, the two gossips broke up with a mutual *"Dex ais";* and Hugh pushed through to the red marquee and raised the silk.

The Duke's tent as they entered was filled to overflowing with men gathered in knots of talk. The actual victory had been postponed for the morrow, when they would enter in triumph to the town of Bari. Tonight, apparently, they were absorbed in future war plans. The names hanging in the atmosphere—Trapania, Palermo, Catania— all bespoke Sicily. Hugh tapped a broad-backed knight on the shoulder, who drew up frowning from his stoop across the trestled desk, and seeing the Black Duchess, made room. The Duke himself, busy with a stylus, looked up from the rolled-out sheet of vellum before him. He broke to a great grin.

"Ho, wife! What do you think of your Frenchmen *now,* my beauty? What do you want, sweetheart? A palace? A basilica with monks in it, to pray for your soul's forgiveness? Anything in Bari"— he flung out his arm—"yours!"

Marc, enthralled, thought how singularly handsome this ruddy-faced man was, with the fine grey eyes, short beard and reddish hair. The hair was faded lighter than Marc's own, and grey showed in it. But for the rest, Marc forgot his troubles, and as Hugh Falloc with a grin pushed him forward and announced him, he stood tall as he could and looked straight into the grey eyes across the table.

"Not *this* great lad!" cried Robert. He rose, came around the board and clapped both hands on Marc's shoulders. The boy, under their hearty dig, felt like melting at his mailed feet. "You could only *be* what? Thirteen? Well!" He stood, taken aback with undisguised pleasure. He had never read a battle-plan more closely than he scanned his son's face. "I had not thought to have an equerry so young—but you're big enough for it! God knows you're stout enough—Well!"

Sigelgaita's voice broke on Marc's ear then like a tocsin.

"Robert, there is something regrettable. The boy's in custody to this guard."

"In custody? *What* guard?" Guiscard said. He was still looking at Marc.

"Raoul, here. He was on the sea-wall against orders. He was already assigned to duty at the landward camp. Now Count Hugh tells me he not only failed to report back there to his pavilion, but he deserted entirely and came to the wall."

Guiscard frowned at them all, puzzlement in his face. A pool of silence had grown around them. The rest in the tent were all turned from their work-boards, listening. Count Hugh, staring at Sigelgaita, looking dismayed, found nothing to say except a lame, "He was excited, Robert—his first night . . ."

The Duke turned to Marc. "Speak up, boy! What *is* this? Surely they make a jest about your defection?"

Marc was about to push some words from his constricted throat but Sigelgaita filled in the only chance he had with, "Raoul wants to withdraw his arrest. He thinks, I suppose, since the lad's your kinsman . . ."

Robert frowned. Sigelgaita had neatly cut ground from under any thought of leniency with *that*. He asked Marc the direct question.

"You *deserted* the camp you were ordered to?"

"Yes," nodded Marc, too utterly panicked to speak further. He then had the agony of seeing the subtle change in his father's face. It reddened a little too. Marc became aware of the others there, listening. God's Eyes, he thought, by his very sonship he had degraded the Duke a little in his men's eyes. He gripped the edge of the table, fortifying himself with a sidelong vicious glance at Sigelgaita and stood waiting. His father had broken off staring. He was pacing in the small space left by the press of those about. The sword in his baldric, rattling, was harsh in the silence. Big Hugh spoke again.

"He was carried away, Guiscard! And after he goes in the field awhile and knows our war-ways—"

The Duke halted and wheeled on the hulking officer.

"None in our ranks," he said, "can be 'carried away'. No soldier," he turned to Marc, "or son of a soldier, can know this 'carrying away'. Give him thirty strokes."

"Oh, but no, Robert!" spoke up the Duchess. "Not *that*, for *him!* For such cool boldness in mischief, such hot, quick punishment would be less than fitting. We must prove ourselves appropriate in this!"

Marc turned to look at her, his hackles rising. She was white as ash. She wore two stout braids of hair secured by a jeweled fillet. She put a hand to these and patted them.

"Don't *frown* so, Robert. Am I ever without device?" Almost archly she turned to the dishevelled and bloody apparition in war-mail who stood lounging near. Of all, and in spite of the great battle-tiredness visible in his face and form, Guiscard's brother, Count Roger, was smiling a little. The others were too tensed to smile. To a man, they expected a tremendous quarrel to snap and break like lightning under the silk. But where others had no stomach for even the fringes of the storm, Roger looked ready to enjoy himself.

"What is't you wish, sister-in-law?" His eyes, in the grime of his face, had a hard, brilliant, nearly opaque look, like obsidian.

Sigelgaita, heavily whimsical, returned his grin. "You go, I believe, through Calabria, by horse, while we take sail to Reggio when we're done here. Could you arrange as you go, to put some military manners in this lad's head?"

Roger looked at the Duke, as though measuring the anger growing in his brother; then, shrugging easily, replied, "I daresay, Lady 'Gaita, but of course. One more fuzz-face will scarce incommode our numerous company. Has he a mount?"

Marc found his voice.

"I'll take the lash!" he said, his tone low and tight. Damn! His eyes were burning. The lash, the lowest lackey's post—anything—save to leave the Duke's command. But he mortally feared to say more, for the tears that were imminent. He looked at his father, his young mouth carefully set. Only those near him could see its tremble.

In the tent were others besides trusted captains, old friends and Robert's family. There were young subalterns, soldiers nearly strange to Guiscard, from Roger's army, men in whose presence the Duke would not quarrel. Robert was as flushed now as the Duchess was pale; his breathing was quite audible.

Suddenly his voice filled the tent.

"Great battling Sant' George! Is this a war-council we hold here, or a training-school for boys?" He turned to the erstwhile silent young sentinel, who had spent his time being as inconspicuous as he could.

"Take him, Raoul, and as we go in tomorrow, leave him in custody in the tent here, and await my further orders!"

Marc had another glance from his father, fleeting and unreadable. Then the Duke abruptly returned to his maps. The pack of officers closed in on him, the pavilion returned to military bedlam.

Marc turned and looked at Sigelgaita. Her face was expressionless, bland. He wanted to lash it to a pulp. His look caught at the jewel on her fillet. Black onyx set with Guiscard's crest. The beasts, the fox-ears and something more. The iron crown of Lombardy, in exquisite miniature, was inescutcheoned there above the enfilment. Immediately he rued his scrutiny of the thing. His aim, to outstare the Duchess, turned back upon himself. For now, as fatigue and the pain from his leg closed the darkness in upon his vision, he seemed to be looking down a dim corridor at a female monster with an extra eye set horrifically above her own. The spell held him. He could not look away. Even as the guard spoke and pushed him from the pavilion into the outer dark, his tired eyes saw that face yet floating in the sea-mist, in an after-image.

CHAPTER II

Eclipse of the Talisman

MARC HAD NOT SEEN the Duke again. But surely he would; any hour, any moment now. Long, still eternities of waiting, these days and nights. He would never forget them. He paced and paced in the silk tent, alone with the rats and shadows, and pondered his abandonment. He could hear the sound of the city. The humblest squire, the youngest page was having his fill of Bari. Why couldn't *he?* Was his foolishness so gross that he could not ride in the rear, with varlets and fools, through the gates of that shining city? Was he less than *they?* Who was he? The seal-ring no longer showed the answer.

It lay unlooked at, ignored, between his shirt and his naked breast. For a week he had not touched it.

An old sailor who brought him food, he questioned closely. How did the triumph go? Was there a massacre? Were they punishing Bari for the long hold-out? (He had seen the counts of Melfi and their hard way with a stubborn citadel.) But no, the ancient assured his young questioner. The Duke was foreign to such a policy. There was a great triumph, to be sure—with processions, prisoners on display and all the rest of it. But no Barensi felt a Norman sword. Guiscard's yoke was always, if not sweet, at least fair, and therefore not too badly taken. The Norman renegade, indeed, would fetch hard fare, with Roger all for hanging. The Duke might well consent to this. Lack of loyalty, breach of discipline from his own—these were the things he would not tolerate.

Marc, wincing at the ancient's remarks on this delicate theme, came to examine his military sin. At first only resentment, and no sorrow for it whatsoever. Only one fear rankled. Was his father lost to him now? And the thought of the Black Duchess sat across his soul, a bar to penance. Only eventually did he feel regret for having offended; fresh resolve spurred him to mend; until finally he waited more eagerly than ever to see Guiscard again.

Once he had those bold grey eyes looking full in his, by God, he'd confess, man to man, and be exorcised at last of the devil in him!

But his purge was not to be completed. The fact was, Guiscard was gone already, that final day, when Geoffrey Ridelle brought him blinking like a young owl into the light of morning. This he failed to believe at first.

"You mean, my father has already left the city?"

"Yes, boy," Ridelle informed him. "His *battles* go by sea to Reggio where we will rendezvous with him for Sicily later . . . But say there, fellow!" cried the knight. "Your helmet—it blinds me, so polished! You'll make the rest of us look like scullerymen with your spit!"

"You can get a lot of shining done in a week," said Marc, between set teeth. He was having a hard time with the knottiness in his throat. So— His father had left without even—

"Ah, indeed yes," Ridelle chattered on. "A deal of shining and a deal of thinking and a deal of tears, eh? Oh, but *yes!*" he said to Marc's stabbing glare. "Tears at thirteen, boy—and it's best that way. But your punishment, had Guiscard the thing to give, would've been the lash. The lash for boys; like a spoon of summer physic! A dose of the leather gurgling merrily in thy guts. The knot of that balkiness of yours breaking with the gripe of the nine-tails on that stubborn hide. The hide of a horse on the hide of a hot de Hauteville. A healthy combination, lad, and you'd be better for it! Cleaned out; done with it; ready to be made a soldier of! But did Robert have the say? No!"

He poked Marc sharply in the ribs. Then setting hands to hips, he executed a jingling dance with his mailed shoulders. Instantly one caught the whip-like intensity of Guiscard, the curious spell of the Duchess, heavy but something magical. He was at once artful and naïve, vicious and comic. He had pulled some damp locks from his helmet so that they nestled coyly against one cheek.

"What says the Black Duchess?" he chanted. "What wishes La Sigelgaita? What is the final word of my little wife? Bah!" he grimaced. "I tell you things are changed about this army since we got the woman's touch to it! Love and war—a bastard combination, young de Hauteville. Remember that. Let us rest here."

It was hard enough going for Geoffrey, all spurred as he was in the clumsy toe-curled mailed boots. They had come, half trotting, half sliding down the self-same path from the sea that Marc had scaled with such ill omen the week before. But Geoffrey seemed in a hurry. Now Marc saw why. From this ledge the landward side was clearly visible. Confusion, dust, a hubbub. They were striking camp. He watched three tents crumple, mushroom an instant with the caught breeze in their sides, then fall. War horses leapt and neighed, resisting the grooms and the long-unfelt caparisons. Pack mules, lashed with gear, strung themselves from the declivity hard up to the shale bank, already in motion. One by one, like an ant-line, they were disappearing through the cleft.

Marc's head throbbed; a fierce hurt stung in his chest. He wished to lose himself watching the busy scene below. He hoped Ridelle had permanently left off badgering. He wanted his silence only. But, as they rallied to continue the descent he found his mood once more intruded on.

"Now take Falloc. He's itching as if from the lousebug for the march. To fight the infidel? No! To get to Bull Joy! Hugh has two loves too, you see—the army and his family. He has a son too, you know. Mihera would be near your age, I guess. Perhaps we will take them on to Sicily as we go; Lady Godhilde, Mihera and my young girl, Zoë . . ."

He desired Marc's interest. He solicited it with a short, sharp jab in the ribs.

"Your 'young girl'?" said Marc, making shift to be civil.

"Aye; my Zoë. Hugh's lady at Bull Joy keeps her for me all these years." He shrugged. "What else to do? Just a soldier, a follower of the Duke. No lands or title to my name, like Falloc . . . I have been too free-of-heart, perhaps, to keep some donjons for myself! So, what could I do with a babe, and always on the go? Her mother I brought from Normandy. But this savage land, this wild Calabria—*hélas,* my sweet Ursule, she died. She—she was like our Normandy appleblossoms, mind you, soft and smooth and fair like that. I think she pined for the dews and the rains on our soft green heaths at home."

Marc, listening now, felt himself oddly moved at this recital. All the music of Geoffrey's voice was in it, and a sort of breaking.

"Had she lived, all might be changed. I might maybe be a lord with many lands. Bah, I'd have owned the world, if *she* asked it! Do you know how a cloud of incense throws up shadows on the wall of the basilica when the sun comes in, and makes it tremble? Then you know how my heart loved her and loves her now . . ."

They threaded along together. For a time the only sound was Ridelle's mailed feet crushing the shale-rock under them. Then Marc saw him laugh, black mustache curled up, his bright eyes snapping in the leathery face.

"That Zoë—a little rascal, *une coquine!* She won't even *look* the way I want her! Each day at Mass I pray she will bring me back, but just a little, my Normandy blossom. Just a wee, small bit to be like her lady mother . . . soft, *blonde,* delicate, like that . . . But *sangre Dex!* Each year of her life (she has only few), she grows all the time to look like *me!* That won't be bad for *her,* of course. I look in my shield. I am not an ugly fellow, ay? But still, still, it is a pity."

He began to sing, half to himself.

> *"The trumpets call beside my wall,*
> *Love hears them chide,*
> *Love—"*

Marc had sighed audibly in annoyance. The song had snatched him, from the brief diversion of Ridelle's history, back to his own dark thoughts. And now from the depths of his funk he fetched a glare to Geoffrey.

"Ho, no songs today? It's awful, how gloomy you are! But I'm not one to resent it. But here, now! Don't let your present fortune vex you overmuch! I take you to meet your aunt, Count Roger's Lady Judith— an angel from Heaven itself!" He kissed his fingers in a Gallic gesture of approval. "Now there's a sweet woman! She's asked especially for you, my lucky!"

To the deep silence greeting this, he sighed. "Hey now, rouse yourself, Marc de Hauteville! She'll not *like* that scowl on your handsome face! Just think how much better off you are than that beautiful jackanapes there!"

Another sharp, staccato poke.

"See, up on the mantle of the battlement, high up, directly below that wheel of buzzards there? *See* how my fine Norman traitor, Duke of Corinth, rides his war horse so lightly!

> 'Vainly he spurs,
> Vainly he seeks grassy earth when the saddle galls . . .'

Say! I must get my lute!" He kissed his fingers up to the battlement. "Jocelin, you inspire me as you *never* did in life! I'll make a song on you, my pretty, to plague Falloc with of nights on bivouac! Ah, but here she comes now, the Lady Judith. I must find your uncle and sound the call to march . . ."

Marc squinted up at Bari. The numberless lion-crested flags blew gay from every spire, and below them, thrust out from the wall itself, was the renegade, swinging gently in the morning wind. He wore his Byzantine armor of fine gold mesh; it caught the climb of the sun and made him sparkle and seem to dance. But the dark crew of winged visitors swooped and got busy with him, even as Marc gazed.

He was often to think of this in after years; how, turning from that sight, his eyes went from ugliness to beauty; from disgust to heavenly delight; from a nightmare to a perfect vision. For there sat a lady on a golden-colored palfrey—the loveliest lady he had ever seen—and she was smiling at him. Great golden braids bound her head and these were crowned by a little chain cap. The wealth of hair cast a soft shadow over the most delicately aligned face. Her form, in a blue, gold-girdled gown and grey silk mantle, seemed like a slim taper cup porting that beautiful head. Marc stood rooted. He would have been little surprised to see her vanish into air. Visions indeed!

"Bother that Geoffrey!" the vision laughed. "He runs to war like a stallion when he hears the horns. But I take it, from your resemblance to your sire, that *you* are Marc. Your father bade me watch for you, and it gives me pleasure!"

How was he? Did he need more clothing? A heavier jacket? The journey would be a hard one . . .

Balm, incense, medicine for a sore young heart. *His father had asked.*

And as he still stood and gaped at her, unable to speak, she laughed. Brave, game laughter, its gaiety troubled with a note of deep fatigue. There were blue shadows under the pretty eyes. "Come, Marc," she said briskly. "They're wanting us now. We'll ride in the van with your Uncle Roger."

This prospect mollified him some. He sought Ouragon, mounted him and spurred smartly up past the main ranks, thinking that it was good, at least, to be a de Hauteville.

CHAPTER III

Mileto Keep

"WHAT KEEPS THAT whoreson herald, d'you think?" Count Roger shouted, more to himself than to the horsemen going abreast of him.

He had dispatched the varlet hours since, to warn his staff at Mileto to have things ready when he came, to have the camions started with all the gear to go to Sicily. All measures must be taken to prevent delay. They had already lost, in the hard march to the coast, too many precious days—at Cosenza, at Belmonte for the pack-mules to be relieved and realigned, and then maddeningly at the village of Oliva, where Lady Judith, under grave warning from the army leech, must needs take rest. There remained just time, if no other thing occurred, to meet Guiscard and ride the right wind out of Reggio.

They had come, skirting the Tyrrhenian all the way, from the bleak passes of the old sheeplands, gradually and relievingly to mild-climated villages, stretches of sunny hills. A strange, harsh radiance lingered everywhere, caught half from the hard blue-greenness of the sea and half from the sun's reflections on the sharp-ridged headlands running like giant cats' paws to the shore. Here, too, boomed the surf, a cadence more leisured yet more powerful than the beat of the cavalcade. Far out, sails showed, but faintly. Trade-craft stayed seaward here, avoiding the half-hid river mouths and the pirate-haunted bays. Meanwhile settlements thickened on the shore. On the road the dark grey slabs of the old Popilian grew wide till at last they had afforded four great destriers galloping on abreast.

Hugh, Geoffrey, Marc and the Count rode forward. Lady Judith and her grooms came next. For the rest, the line stretched back like ragged seaweed to the last reaches of the mountain trails.

Going along in such a company, Marc de Hauteville rode in a dream. His father was absent, to be sure. But this was his crowd, they were on their way to meet him, and the future would take care of itself. Only one doubt nagged: from camp talk these nights past, he knew that the Duke and Count Roger would part ways, after Sicily— Roger to stay south while Guiscard ranged as usual in the highlands. Yet Roger kept treating *him*, Marc, as his personal equerry, with long instructions on the tending of his gear. It would be a misery to think—

but that was *too much!* He recalled his father's face, his smile, and burned with affection and trust. But when his mind insisted on a portrait of the Black Duchess too, his knuckles grew white about the Spanish plate-and-cuirass he was carrying for Count Roger on his saddle.

The breeze, as it happened, was blowing the tassel-tailed banners in their own faces as they achieved the last hill that crowned the windswept promontory overlooking the Count's main castle, called Mileto Keep.

The Count had spurred forward for the last short stretch. All in the van watched as the arresting figure, slim and armorless, went flying up the crest. But there, instead of plunging on downward from their sight, the Count pulled his mount up short and wheeled it, rising meanwhile in the stirrups. His charger looked to be dancing on the ridge. A murmuring rose and rumbled. What was amiss?

For ahead the Count had waved a gauntlet. "Come!" and the arc of his arm was lengthened by his great, long Norman sword.

Ridelle and Falloc, stalling on the crest as the Count had done, nearly had young de Hauteville, lad, horse and armor, on them in a heap. But Marc wheeled dextrously, skirting the precipice, and went plummeting down the road, his eyes wide as saucers at the scene before him.

Below, the castle of Mileto, five-dongeoned and flying de Hauteville flags, was visible, but smokily, for it was ringed at some distance in a circle of fire. Marc had seen the Counts of Melfi burn crops thus. The way was an old one, for quick sieging. A ring of trees or vines was fired systematically each day, till the occupants, seeing their fodder of years' standing shrivel to ash, came gingerly to terms. But Marc had no memory of such fantastic war-makers as started to spew from the fiery precincts as the Count's vast Calabrian army hove ever more numerously into sight. No finely mounted knights were these, come to besiege a fellow-baron. This was a ragged ribbon of raiders, without discipline and apparently without command which streaked from the neighborhood and hastily hit the road toward Bull Joy; a crazily assorted mob on a motley string of horses that ranged from heavy chargers, doubtless stolen for the occasion, to scrubby bang-tails. Marc failed to fathom the nature of this company with its sashes about its heads, with trousers that bagged and were bootless, till someone shouted, "Pirates!"

Roger and the rest rode at them, felling them easily as they fled in weaponless panic. Marc, hampered as he was, managed to swipe with his short, slim estoc at one pantalooned ruffler who swung out too near him. The random stab hit home. It was Marc's first war-killing, and he watched, fascinated, as the man seemed to toss his firebrand aimlessly aside, then slump after it in the dust.

They were all doomed, these unfortunate incendiaries. Half of Roger's army strung out after them. It would be a few minutes of massacre there on the road, no more.

"Come on!" Roger ordered his companions. "Let them manage it. We'll go through to the Keep. Fetch my lady."

He waited while they rallied there in the confusion and smoke, and while the men beat a gap in the fired apple-trees. Then, as the others came, Roger scudded his mount quickly over the hot earth, motioning back through the smoke for them to follow. Marc, full of curiosity and with the Count's accoutrements as excuse, plunged next, and watched as Hugh Falloc, his heavy face scowling in the heat, drove his neighing destrier through the glowing débris. The Countess, long since ill and exhausted with this march, looked large-eyed and pale as death in this last extremity. A far different cut of woman than Guiscard's man-like Sigelgaita—Judith endured these hardships for Roger's sake alone. She was yet no faint-heart; and now as always, she set her beautiful face gamely to the test and went through, guided by Geoffrey Ridelle.

The Count had meantime drawn his silver rouser. But before his blast could sound there was a clanging and screeching and the chains began to scream through the lanyards and the great portcullis went staggering like a giant and came toward them. Their mounts reared as it slammed down, spewing dust, before they pounded to the *pont-levis* planking and up through the bailey gate.

The face of the tall figure waiting high up under the barbican of the Keep was transformed by the tongues of firelight to a mask of flame and shadow. Deep blots of darkness under eye and brow and lip obscured identity, but the clothes, dark and plain, were the unmistakable skimpy gabardine and frugally wound turban of an Amalfitan Jew.

"Maurus of Amalfi!" Roger exclaimed, and even for Marc the picture began to suggest itself.

For Maurus, lately baptized Piereleone after two churchmen who had sponsored his notorious conversion, was for many reasons a well-known and widely respected man. With his palace in Amalfi as base, he managed counting-houses from Rome to Antioch, even owned markets, it was said, on the road to Cathay. His ships plowed all seas. He was a man of brain and courage and holder of as much power of a sort as any here. Piereleone, Maurus of Amalfi, was rumored to be the richest man west of Constantinople.

Roger did not bother with civilities. "Well, Maurus," he demanded, "what's the meaning? You here, my hall sieged, and my crops ruined?"

But the slender Jew was not looking at him. He gazed past the Count's destrier at Hugh and Geoffrey riding up behind, and his eyes had the look of a man appalled by his present knowledge. In quiet, economically clipped phrases in which there was a hint of the schools

of Alexandria, he answered the Count, while his intelligent, dark glance
flicked strangely between Ridelle and Falloc.

"It is true that I brought destruction on your crops, Count Roger.
But know you, alas, that orchards were the least lost on this terrible
day."

He raised his voice against the noises of the troopers beating out
fires.

"I landed, from my Egyptian galley, at Bull Joy this afternoon. I
was returning from the bronze kilns at Alexandria."

"Bull Joy!" repeated Hugh, spurring up, his brusque voice gruff
with alarm. The coastal town, site of his own castle, was only a short
shift farther down the road.

"Hear me out, Hugh, Geoffrey." Maurus spread long Oriental
hands, frail before the stompings of their huge mounts. "You will
know soon enough. With me on the galley were the great bronze-and-
silver doors I had ordered cast for the new basilica at Amalfi. They
are of fabulous price, and save for the duplicates Duke Robert Guiscard
has in the works there now for his gift to Monte Cassino, they are
unique. On the ship too was a brace of elephants, for the doors must
be borne over hill-roads to the town. There was no other way, since I
knew Prince Gisolf had his sea-rats hid about the bay. Of late he does
all to ruin us, since Amalfi far out-trades Salerno now in the East. He
seeks, of course, to strike through me, and for long now I have lived
in fear, with my own son under constant vigilance in the palace, since
the Lombard stops at nothing. At any rate, today I dispersed my escort,
made port at Bull Joy, let the beasts off the craft and meant to take the
hill-road to Amalfi straightway."

Here he paused, scraping his hand through his short, neat beard. It
closed as he did this to a dark, knuckled fist.

"If only I had done it thus! But, Javeh forgive me, I thought it to
be safe, and I stopped, Hugh, at your Keep in Bull Joy to see your
family as I have done so much beforetime. I am very fond of the boy
Mihera . . ."

He drew a shuddering breath, as Hugh's face broke suddenly to
sweat.

"She—Lady Godhilde was playing the viol," Maurus said, and
turned to Ridelle. "Your young daughter was singing to it when they
came. I saw their craft later from the road. Four swift gats, Saracen-
manned, from Africa. They came on us there in the peristyle while
we listened to little Zoë singing. I had known the foul Teligar was in
Salerno's pay, but until I saw him there in the door, I had discounted
the possibility of being dogged clean from the Middle Sea. Your wife,
Sir Hugh, sprang up and they stabbed her. It was all very quick, very
violent, and I know not yet how it happened that I was allowed, with
all of them crowding in, to make my escape, except that it was only

through Mihera's struggles that I did so. I saw him deliberately make shift to draw them so that I might break. I shall never forget his action while I live. I fled here for help. What else—against so many?"

Hugh lunged down from his saddle and with a roar grasped Maurus by the front of the striped scarf knotted at the neck of his gabardine.

"Maurus, you misgotten! You son of a Hebrew unnamable! *You're* safe, I see— But my wife, my son . . ." He had lifted his huge fist and would have brought it down on the merchant's skull had not Geoffrey dismounted and restrained him.

"Wait, Hugh! This is nothing, your killing him. It would get us nothing. The children, Maurus!" Geoffrey cried. "Killed? Taken? Taken, my God, to the Monster Prince?"

"Taken. But not to Gisolf. Listen," said Maurus, his French coming strangely stilted, more used as he was to Greek and the strange tongues of the East. "When they had the doors, the Saracens changed their plans. It was *I* they were hired for, not the doors. The doors were a piece of luck. So they left me pocketed here, and fled with the doors and the children, doubtless across the old Pass of the Merchants to Gerace and the Beach there, where no one, neither the Prince, nor you, nor any save their own godless kind can follow them. They will lose no time. Ships leave there nightly for far places. Gisolf will never see them now. They will sell the doors, and the children too they will sell, to Egyptian brothels, where Teligar plies a steady trade."

"My God!" said Geoffrey, pale under his tan. "When was it—this afternoon, you said? Two, three hours?"

Maurus nodded. "Time enough, with luck. Their sort sails under hood of nightfall."

Hugh Falloc's mount snorted as he rattled the reins. "Then, by God, what do we wait for?"

"A plan," said Maurus. "A plan. How can you reach them? How find them, or even get in? Forget you no Norman enters those gates? Gerace pays tribute for the fact that you do not enter. Don't you recall?"

"Good Lord," said Geoffrey, "he's right. Guiscard was captured there in the old days and that was the price of his rescue."

"To hell with tribute!" shouted Hugh. "We'll enter it now quick enough, because, thank God, we've an army to do it with!"

"Ah, but you *haven't*, Hugh!"

They all turned at the voice of Count Roger, who had dismounted and was leaning against the portcullis chain with his arms folded.

"I have gathered these troops expressly for the *coup* on Sicily. It's all planned. The time's set for the rendezvous with Robert, and do not deceive yourselves about men."

It was Maurus who broke the strained silence after this.

"Hugh," he said, "to ransom them is better. It's *time* that counts."

"Ransom them?" Geoffrey said. "With what?" glancing at Roger.

The Great Count merely shook his ringlets and gave Geoffrey his straight, cool glance.

"The monies and treasure we have gathered for the campaign are in close trust from the towns of Calabria"—touching his great golden-shod baldric—"and it's all pledged as sacredly as my blade here to the Faith for Sicily. It will serve that end and none other!"

This time even the Jew stared at the handsome face, before he said to the two knights, "Listen. I have thought of nothing else these hours as we waited. I myself have monies. I can get to the Beach, and I have means to find what ships they trade on, these tools of Teligar."

Hugh Falloc growled. "To damnation with your dirty coin!"

"What choice *have* we, Hugh?" said Geoffrey, his blue eyes snapping.

There was a rustle of silks as Lady Judith, looking taller than her frail self in her silver saddle, unclasped her riding cape and flung it to the stones. She was brightly flushed. She drew off her jewels one by one, unclasping them from her throat, her arms, her fingers, and finally, from her slender waist, unfastening the great jeweled chatelaine with the ruby coat-of-arms, and tossed them all to the garment.

"I pray these will help; I'm ashamed there isn't more, seigneurs. But this can I further pledge for my heart's honor, that, if you succeed, I shall take the children in my own care to Sicily, and you shall have no further fear for their welfare there." As she spoke, her clear glance sought the faces of the two knights, but avoided the sight of her husband. She sat in the saddle, tall, beautiful and very angry.

While Judith had been thus engaged, Maurus had unwound the purple sash from the waist of his gabardine, and now threw sack after jingling sack to the cape. "These also, Lady," he said. Then he tied up his sash again and it was amazing to see how thin he really was. At another time Marc would have laughed.

"I think we have enough and more there to secure the children."

Big Hugh, distraught and maddened with grief, was not impressed. "You can well be generous with your gold for this debt of honor, Maurus. But maybe there's new villainy. Maybe you think to get the doors."

The Jew sighed. "Listen, Hugh. I *know* my debt of honor, which I can never forget, and I confess I regret the doors. Who would *not,* for there is something I have not said of them, but I shall now, as a token of my will. You know how pilgrims fare lately in the East, and how the cry rises to take the Holy Land from the Moors. For this they will need money, and already there have been killings and strippings of Jews for their gold. I planned to forestall this bankruptcy for myself in good time, by taking the half of what I had in gold coins and filling those doors with them, thinking that in the house of God where I have been freshly converted, they would be safe. No one would know of the gold within them. The opening of them is very simple but it is a secret that only I know."

There was an exclamation from Roger. "Is this true, Piereleone?"

"Aye." Maurus spread his hands. The Count shook his head and started pacing as Maurus continued.

"The pirates do not know this of the doors. But even so, to buy them back would take seven times as much as I have given you. Think no more about it. Listen, I can gain to the town in secret, but to be seen on the Beach," he shrugged, "for me—pure death, and my death would serve you nothing. Someone else must be the purchaser. It is a simple thing, once you are there on the Beach and bear the parchment of a high-placed person whom I know there. But it must be an inconspicuous one. No one patently of the Norman conquerors, or one strongly armed, or a known knight. I have thought, as we spoke, of this well-favored lad among us. Who is he?"

Marc felt his pulse rise as the slim Hebrew finger pointed at himself. It was the Count who answered, very quickly.

"The boy is my equerry, and completely sound. You have my full consent to his employment."

The Jew nodded. "It is settled then. We should take a force for protection on the Pass. Once in Gerace there's comparative safety, but beforetime . . . Fifty knights, Count Roger. It would delay the sailing no longer than a day."

"Delay the sailing! Are you mad?" cried Roger. "Guiscard will rage!"

"Guiscard would not refuse this thing," said Maurus with cool dignity. "Have you *seen* the brothels of Egypt, Seigneur? Very interesting. All sorts of pleasures such as Alexander himself never dreamed of, for the men of the sea as they enter port. Young girls learn well in the school of exotic love. All manner of devices, some very painful, whose uses they perform for the rest of their rather short lives. The boys will be castrated, of course, have their eyelids dyed purple and their nipples made sensitive with the Cut of the Demon, and be sent to the wealthy emirs of the East for more unusual pleasures. Have you ever . . ."

It was Geoffrey who turned to face Roger and said in a voice as cold as steel.

"Leave it, Maurus. We take the men. There is no question in it. Come." His eyes sought Roger's and the mouth beneath the black mustache was a thin line.

But Roger hardly heard. He seemed preoccupied. He plucked at Marc's stirrup.

"Come," he said. "You need strength for the task. We will seek something in the scullery while they fetch fresh mounts."

As Marc trailed Count Roger into the hall, he felt dizzy as with a sickness or from too much wine, the result not alone of hunger, which was but one of his woes at the moment. In answering Maurus's question about himself, Count Roger had said not, *This is Marc de Hauteville*, but *This is my equerry*, and Marc could only think that his worst fear had grounds, and that Roger meant to keep him in his retinue. Like a puff of smoke the hope evaporated of joining Guiscard's party when they met at Reggio.

They had passed through the great-hall, huge, cold, and wearing the neglected air of a great house long abandoned to the occupancy of servants, and climbed stone steps to a high dim corridor, where Marc, preoccupied with his gloomy thoughts, nearly sprawled on a heap of arms left carelessly in the middle of it, which Roger had gingerly stepped around. Indeed there were discarded pieces everywhere— old weapons, dented shields shining dimly in the glow of the occasional torcheres, and Marc saw that they were on a sort of balcony giving on a huge beamed upper room, apparently the armory of the old castle. An aged retainer sat at the one brazier in that cave-like area, half warming himself by it and half using its dull light to repair a link hauberk which he held on his knees.

"Turn your back on your hall," grunted Roger, "and the varlets consign it cheerfully to ruin! There'll be leather exercised on loutish ribs before I presently leave." But the Count seemed to smile a little, in spite of his words, as though his mind played with other thoughts than that of his dingy castle. Marc meantime caught scents of meat turning and was silently blessing their apparent advance on the scullery when the Count abruptly hesitated.

There was nothing here. Bareness, dimness, ill-smelling rushes underfoot; a few rusty arms bracketed on the walls as elsewhere. But Roger dealt with a chain on his baldric, pulled out a key and forced aside an old cuirass hung on the wall. He displaced at the same time the piece of tapestry under it, a faded bead-piece depicting Stephen stoned. They both coughed with dust as Roger disturbed the antiquity.

"I've fretted on this cache," said Roger, peering beyond the iron door he unlocked and into the cavity behind it. He looked relieved as he retrieved a large leather coin-pouch which he shook.

"A fine tune it plays, aye? Better than Sir Geoffrey's lute, I think! But *la*, it's a cumbersome piece . . . so I told the fat soul who was burdened with it that day we so happily met him! I tell you, nephew, were his abbotship to chaffer at fair like a jay at a crow-nest, he'd not make a finer thing of it than we will now! Here—bind that still-unbelted young girth of yours. It will warm thee in more than *one* fashion!"

Marc applied the *bourse* obediently beneath his baldric while Roger gazed down at him, slim, golden and smiling in the dusky gloom.

"You know of course, how to use it! It is much, *mon* Marc. It is five thousand michael-pieces, *more* than seven times the sum the Jew named. You could purchase the Amalfi doors . . ."

Marc started a little. "But they said—"

"Aye, they *said*—But *you*, Marc, shall buy the doors." The steely look flashed in the gloom. "They'll send you in alone. It'll be *your* word that the slave ship had gone and the treasure-gat had not. See?"

Marc's fingers fumbled on the last fess of the belt. It was very quiet in the armory vault. He could hear, from the gallery, the faint chink of rings on the hauberk that the ancient mended.

The Count had sucked in his smooth jaws with amusement and when Marc looked up at him, he laughed, a startling sound in the echoing vastness. *"La*, it's *fine* to be a de Hauteville, aye? Luck, cunning and good sense are the heritage. *Use them*, and they'll not grow rusty. And look you—see how it is, if you meet the Duke of Reggio with a lively task well done? I'll tell him a fair tale on it, and name you for his retinue, against both custom and the Black Duchess . . . There'll also be stints of those monies for *you*, Marc, aye? Come . . ." clamping strong, hearty fingers into Marc's arm. "Secure the doors, forestall the Jew, and bring both Jew and doors to me at Reggio. I will deal with it then."

They descended from the armory and as they passed through the main keep, between the din and the tumult of his gut, which was still empty, Marc could not deal with his strange crowding doubts about the present turn. As in a dream, he joined the mêlée of horses, men and clanking gear in the courtyard.

But before they started, in the last flurry of oaths and the shouting of a company bent on a quest, Marc looked up to observe Lady Judith. She was standing at the *porte cochère*, jewelless, girdleless, beautiful in her austerity, and she seemed to be gazing intently out at him, though her eyes were shadowed by darkness and by the coping that hung over her like an overhang on a shrine. He found himself brushing his hand across his sash where the coin-band bulged. There was no connection between her questioning gaze and the affairs of men, yet Marc, as he waved in her direction, felt his face go hot with something other than courtly worship of a great and beautiful lady, and his emotions puzzled him.

"Good lad!" said someone beside him, and he turned in the saddle to see Roger smiling up at him, with one hand laid admiringly on his mount's sleek neck.

"Be hearty, nephew! Press Ouragon and ride with luck!"

CHAPTER IV

Pirate Beach

HALF AN HOUR LATER the old Roman block-road that led to the Pass of the Merchants struck fire from hooves of fifty Norman destriers. Whether by chance or because of their capable number, no ambush or attempt at ambush was met. The spring moonlight made dappled streaks on their ranks as they passed through the wooded region of Piano de Dioja and then spurred upward to the lofty Pass itself. Here they rode fast and it seemed to Marc, in the light-headedness born of excitement and his hunger, that they rode among stars in these naked mountains. Toward the end they saw water far out, gleaming, white-flecked under the moon, and Marc's heart beat fast; it was his first glimpse of the fabulous Middle Sea. Then they dropped into dark pockets. They went riding in hot, muggy, sweet-scented air through olive-groves and lemons until, finally, above them loomed white-walled, lofty Gerace. As they presently pulled up, curses, mutterings and vicious slaps could be heard, for these lowlands swarmed with mosquitoes.

"Now," said Maurus the Merchant, who had ridden silent after Marc, "from here on, we go it alone."

One of the men cried out. "Make short work of it, will you! By morning these winged beasts would have us in shreds!"

Hugh and Geoffrey loomed pale and grim in the dimness, Hugh accosting the Jew with a last-minute threat and a steely gripping of his gabardined arms.

"Don't come back," Marc heard him growl, "without Mihera."

Meanwhile Marc found considerable trouble in facing Geoffrey's eyes, anxious and pleading in the shadow of his steel cap.

"My little Zoë, you recall, is dark, as I told you, and she favors me. She has hair that is short, of many curls, like a cap, Marc. You cannot mistake her. Go now, and may God be good!"

Maurus, grasping Ouragon's reins, led off into darkness. The young destrier flinched and twisted.

"Check him, lad," said the Jew. "He must follow docilely; it is narrow here." Marc caught his heels to the colt's sides and tightened the bit. He could see nothing. They were in shadow from a great overhang of rock, and far below he could hear a roar and a surging, and he knew that they made a precarious journey on one of those gorgy bitten-in places above the sucking sea.

They presently hesitated and Marc knew by the dim whiteness above them that they were against walls. Maurus dealt with a length of heavy chain that was caught to an iron pin in the bastion. A square of light opened and a gruff voice confirmed in Greek the merchant's surname, "Piereleone! Aye, enter."

Maurus and Marc pushed through.

Once in Gerace they traveled freely, achieving the steep streets between high, white houses, dodging carts, drunken sailors, and a pedlar or two. Certain of the groundlings they passed looked back at the strange duet, the lad on a fine horse, clad well in good French links, and the hooded Jew. At a corner of the high street where one of those turreted white palazzos jutted out, Maurus dismounted and told Marc to await him there.

"I go, now, for your leave to the Beach," he said, "but meantime take care and use the shadows. This town looks ill on red-headed lads with bold hawk faces." He gave the boy a kind, reassuring glance and glided into darkness.

This place, thought Marc, must be the very summit of the town. The whole thing seemed to rise to this peak from a thousand steep streets and crooked alleys in one continuous structure, for all the world like a rambling castle—not an extraordinary effect to one raised in the wilds of south Italy where all such towns were an accumulation of Greek villas, Lombard keeps and Norman donjons—yet Marc tonight felt the threat of such a place, the ease with which one could be swallowed in it and not heard of again. What was to keep these rufflers from taking him even for his horse? And if it were known by chance that here sat the Duke's son, the magnificent ransom . . .

Such speculations, turning as they did on his own importance, seemed agreeably chilling at first blush, but he found himself fairly relieved when Maurus once more materialized from the depths.

"Come. Now, we can go to the Yards, and you can enter. Remember, you're but the page of a rich lord, one of the trusted patrons of this illegal market place, seeking slaves for his hall."

This time they traveled downward, traversing the tortuous cobbles of Gerace, and Marc felt sea air assault his face like perfume after ordures of the streets, and presently they came out on a sandy roadway directly bordering a narrow moonlit beach. These were the famous Pirate Yards, the taking-off place for all manner of unlawful traffic—pirates, slavers, and hawkers of stolen goods. From here corsairs transported all manner of exotic loot to Alexandria, Byzantium, and even to Antioch and beyond, where the Turks ruled. Here on the Beach swarmed a concourse of nations, the dregs of each and the fugitives of many, and all ties and all histories were by mutual consent forgotten. There was one international bond that joined them—gain. And their language went according to the minting of the coin—the ducat, the soldus, the rubel, the michael, the byzant, the pence. Tonight as always, scores of night fires bloomed on the sands and these, with the light from torches carried, and the dull glow from the yawning mouths of the pirate ships drawn up for their loads, made the creatures laboring in the ruddy gloom seem indeed like Hell's stevedores. They used small and speedy craft—gats, yawls, and slender long-ships with their single sails wound up on the masts, and clustered near each mooring was a pot-pourri of tents, lean-tos and shacks from which voices floated up to the two men watching above—singing, cursing, laughing . . . A dancer swayed by one of the fires; at another two men wrestled, and Marc's blood chilled a little as he heard at intervals some high, thin screams from a long queue of people being hustled forth, far to the end of the concourse. The merchant drew Marc from his wide-eyed surveyal of the colorful scene.

"You see," said Maurus, "there is no time to lose. Look you, take this ribband; keep it prominently showing on your saddle. It is Igor's sign itself." The Jew spurred, wheeled and pulled back into darkness as Marc directed Ouragon on down.

With his badge of license for trafficking with thieves, Marc threaded the busy ribald mob, stopping only occasionally to worm Ouragon through a procession of loaders strung from loot-piles to their caravel. Once he waited while crested hogsheads were briskly borne galleywards, and he stared down, wondering what high lord had been relieved of his finest wine.

He was half-way up the strand when he saw them, elephant shapes looming out from the darkness, harnessed with stout chains, a great shining double-piled object hung swinging between. God of God—the doors. He had in truth as good as forgot them. He pulled up and watched. Great St. Michael, but they were handsome and huge! And to think of their secret! A mere few words of bargaining and his byzants could command them, a fortune for the de Hautevilles and a fine pleader of his dubious favor with the Duke. It seemed dull to hesitate. But he could feel Maurus's eyes up there on the breeze-swept road. Was his heart to be crasser than a man of trade's? And Hugh and Geoffrey . . . Where, in a deed like this, would be the quality of knighthood taught at Melfi, and present in the queenly question he had so vividly felt in that last glance of Lady Judith?

But as the cumbrous pachyderms set their broad feet on the lip of the high-pooped caravel, Marc's fingers itched for the purse. It was a natural enough thing to have come upon the doors—the corsairs and beasts could have bested the Normans by but minutes of time, yet to Marc the happening assumed the hues of magic. *La,* was it not his saint's favor? His saint in a prudent, worldly mood, to be sure, yet working wonders for him, all the same . . .

It did not occur to Marc, at the moment, to recall whose realm this concourse likely was!

He temporized. He approached the tall, parchment-faced Egyptian who stood barking unintelligible orders and prevailing on his stevedores with a monstrous whip. But on being questioned, the fellow wrinkled his thin yellow face and made signs that he did not understand, so that Marc must patiently try Arabic, Italian hill-jargon, and even a few Hebrew words he knew. It was Greek that finally penetrated.

"When does the vessel leave?"

The man shrugged. "Now . . . Very soon, now."

"Can the cargo still be bargained for? Those doors?"

"The captain would hear you, I guess, if you'd catch him aboard. Come you from Igor?"

"Even so." He showed the ribband.

"Aye. Well, you can inquire. They're a great nuisance, the doors, but they're worth much money. Have you such monies that would speak for the Egyptian doors?" His eyes were lighted now, and he moistened his grey lips so that they shone thinly in the weird light. The moon sat low on the troubled strait beyond, and the star-hung veil of the deep Sicilian night was closing in on them. Marc was feeling uncomfortable, instinctively recoiling from the evil aura of the atmosphere around him, though he wished to seem like a man much used to matters of the half-world.

"I *have* monies," he said levelly, "and I may be back."

The burly one stared as if doubting his wit.

"May I inquire, young nobleman, why you shop about? You'll not find *another* two pretties, look you, like those doors! What think you this *is?* A fair?"

He threw back his long head and speculated; he was eyeing Marc and his rich clothes and his fresh young strength like a cat surveying a mouse.

"Where is she headed?" was Marc's next inquiry, jerking his head toward the vessel.

The Egyptian started, seemed to hesitate and again flicked his yellow, heavy lidded eyes to the badge.

"To Antioch, as it falls out. But what's it to you?"

"Nothing. I was merely curious." The tumult from the slave-ship farther down the strand had been crowding upon Marc's ears like a tocsin, and with some half-formed plan of making a gesture thence and returning for the doors, he wheeled Ouragon and passed more quickly up the avenue of galleasses, his mount's hooves heaving sand to the fires.

Presently he laid a hand on Ouragon. "There, boy. This is it. Let's see about it." He did not bother to dismount at first, but sat and surveyed the fire, the slave-masters and the long, lamenting human queue, hoping in spite of himself that those he sought would not be found there.

The slaves were being put aboard like so many hogsheads, and like so many hogsheads were being suitably marked. Most of the wretches were apparently being transported from one bondage to a next. They stood brutish, unresisting, leaden, so that the pair Marc sought stood out unmistakably by even the single distinction that they went unwillingly. Hugh's son, a husky light-haired lad, was being peaceable enough, but only because extra-devised twists of rope on hand and ankle had secured him, and the hatred that stared from his intelligent wide-set eyes was spirited and sharp. He looked capable of spitting venom, especially each time the hulking slaver gave another jerk to the girl who went similarly manacled ahead. She struggled like a wildcat with resistance and terror. They had consigned a husky varlet with his full attention to manage her alone.

The tangled mop of dark curls was flung across her face. She kept tossing them back so that long, slanted blue eyes that could have been Geoffrey Ridelle's might stare with loathing and terror at what befell the unfortunate woman who knelt ahead at the fire. This last was a dusky wench, the apparent veteran of many a flesh-mart. She submitted to the fresh brand pressed quickly to the nape of her black neck with a thin, high, and not unmusical scream, a sort of obligato to her immemorial fate.

Marc looked on horrified. It had been easy to plan the other thing, seeing his father pleased thereby, and himself a hero. But that was before he actually must deal with the sight of these youngsters like himself, and the visions about them that crowded on his mind. The slaver was having a scurvy time with Zoë. She was by no means a delicate commodity, but strong-limbed and lithely muscular, with the last overlay of childhood just fading from firm contours visible through her torn dress. Just now one bare shiny knee had emerged from a tear in her tunic as she sought to use it on her burly captor. Queer to think of that beautiful young body ten years hence, raddled and ravished from disgraceful traffic, that high spirit beaten away by every newly despised panderer for whom she must become a willing pasture.

Thoughts are swift things, and Marc had long since leapt down from Ouragon and accosted the bare-armed captain by the fire. The boy Mihera, indeed, had seen the strange lad staring at Zoë, and his glance had flared with a half-formed hope. He watched Marc intently.

The trouble came in pulling the huge troll from his tasks, in engaging his attention at all, and Zoë had now been dragged quite up to the flames. Marc became frantic, ran to the brander and sought to deal with him, and was immediately set upon from behind.

"What're ye about, youngster?" the captain growled. Marc saw Mihera lunge also, only to be checked back, all hobbled as he was, and knocked sprawling. As for Zoë, the giant bent her easily forward on his knee, ripped the tunic from her neck, and grasped the rich, tumbled hair to make place for his instrument . . .

Marc went wild, threw off the first and second slavers, snatched out his belt purse and jingled a fistful of michaels at their staring eyes.

But by that time Zoë was on the far side of the fire.

The blond lad and the girl were soon consigned to the young purchaser, and the captain shouted up to them as all three mounted on the bay, "The great lord for whom you bought this tasty piece is not likely to misplace his tender beauty, by God! There's a well-seared tab there, fresh on her pretty carcass!"

The low heavy laughter of the brute echoed after them as they galloped off.

Back on the Pass where the company waited there was heartfelt, happy welcome. Geoffrey Ridelle crouched on his spurred heels in the road, and kept running one hand tenderly through Zoë's curls, while he busied the other with Marc's gauntlet, pumping it and grinning up at him. Zoë, however, was weeping bitterly, and Marc saw how really she was little more than a child. She kept burrowing into Geoffrey's shoulder, repeating the same words over and over.

"They *did* it, papa, they *did* it! They put that terrible mark *on* me!"

Mihera sat on a new mount that Hugh had brought down for him, and both sat silent with the others there in the midnight moon. Marc did not know what to make of Mihera. Did he hold it was *Marc's* fault about the girl? One would *think* that, from his silence, indeed from his hostility, as with Maurus they had ridden from Gerace. What rankled in Marc, was that though Mihera did not know of the vacillation, the indecision, the time lost at the pirate-sloop about the doors, he seemed instinctively to sense something, which he unerringly laid to de Hauteville. But Marc, recalling that Saxon blood flowed in the veins of Hugh Palloc's son, returned him stare for stare.

It was insupportable that a de Hauteville be glared down by an English hay-head.

And anyhow, later on, as they retook the road to Reggio, it came to Marc that the sharpness of Mihera's expression was something natural to him, or at least not directed to himself only, and he left off sparring with those intelligent light-lashed eyes and the cool judgment he encountered there.

It was a little startling, after the forced march to Reggio, to see a good half of the great, painted Norman fleet already pushing out to the whirlpools of the strait. Apparently as soon as the first of the trickle of late horsemen had been seen descending from the white road-ledge to the beach, several of the galleys and low, fat dromons had flapped their sails out taut and were under way almost without benefit of the doubled-ranked oars in each of their sides. There was an uproar of departure, with the excitable Greek troops clashing tambors above decks, while down in the hold-stalls the stallions neighed.

"Holy Stephen!" roared Hugh. "The whoresons would push off without us, damn me if they wouldn't. Equerry!" and as Marc hastily spurred up: "Post down there and tell those de Hautevilles to keep their breeches on! By God! I've half a mind to stay behind in these parts and beat out lands for myself, like Fitz and the rest!"

And Hugh trailed a string of invectives through the air all the way down to the water's edge where, assigning his mount with the rest of the horses being herded onto the planks of Guiscard's galley, he roared on up to the Duke's deck and up to the high poop where Robert was.

Young de Hauteville, trailing along behind, had some vague hope, with all the confusion, of staying on the flag-ship; but with the Count's michaels still in his belt, he was a little concerned for the plan, and thus preoccupied, was about to cross the gangway behind Hugh to gain to the poop when he went cannoning into a lad with a wooden bowl of fruit, and sent the whole mess across the main deck, with the lad sprawling after it.

Seeing the flash of velvet and satin in which the youngster was dressed, Marc instinctively hastened to pick him up. But the boy, who looked to be some two twelve-months younger than himself, wheeled about and made at him with a small dirk which he had swiftly pulled from his sash. Marc took him by the shoulder with one hand and with the other easily disarmed him, at which the lad let loose a string of guard-room oaths such as Marc had scarcely yet had ear to. And from above, over the noises of the ship, the sea, and this child's cursing could be heard the roar of Guiscard's laughter. Hugh, too, had forgotten his sorrow and his spleen to grin at the violent little scene. Marc looked up; he saw Sigelgaita standing between them, handsome and flushed, holding her glittering mailed skirt up a little as if it were a brocade gown, a swatch of links clenched in each hand, so that some of the red under-kirtle she wore appeared beneath it. The expression of her face—grave, alarmed, flushed with ill-controlled anger—told Marc that this must be her son, Roger de Hauteville, whom the army called *Borsa*, Clutchy-purse, from the way he saved the pennies they threw at him on the march.

"Oho!" roared Guiscard. "Do y'mind, Hugh, the giant in the Viking-gest who goes about charging into everything, with his huge clumsiness? He knocked the wine from Wotan's hand, I think it goes, and otherwise filled Asgard with laughter wherever he went. *Boamundus Gigas* was his name . . . Hey, son Bohemond' Gigas! And hold there, young Roger! No knives, mind you, between brothers!"

The two looked at each other. Marc saw a black-haired light-eyed lad, slight-built and on the slender side, like his name-sake uncle. The face was pure Lombard—square forehead, heavy mouth and sullen, lambent eyes. And presently on the poop the two boys stood at opposite deck-rails, grandly ignoring yet secretly staring at one another, while Guiscard dominated the noisy scene, calling for the flag-ship's final push-off. Their own galley was indeed nearly under way when someone came aboard calling, "Marc de Hauteville! Count Roger requires his equerry!" And Marc had the pale satisfaction of sincere regret in the Duke's eyes as he sent him off with a last reminder.

"Mind your tasks, son. A good lad with a serviette and a boot-clout is a good man with a sword, we find, and later on, with the crest of a general."

The words were accompanied by a warm grip on the shoulder, but they sent him poorly consoled from the deck of the flag-ship *Normandy*.

The whirlpools that menace the jutting bays of Reggio and Messina are something to cross of a morning when the wind is right and there is only a ship or so to worry on. But with a sailing delayed and the best breeze all but missed and the whole sheeted stretch filled with craft starting, all hands are likely to be on deck, bent upon missing no moment of the perilous noisy passage of a war-bent company. But on the bright blue, lateen-rigged long-ship of Count Roger de Hauteville, three young people lingered dejectedly under the stern-shrouds, uninterested in all that was going forth. Lady Judith, emerging from her cabin for a view, encountered them there, and thought them the gloomiest trio she had ever seen. Zoë Ridelle, her little neck swathed in ointments and bandages for the fester of her burn, lay belly-down on a sunny place on the canvas, resting her chin gingerly on the backs of her hands, her piquant little face a study of woe. Hugh's son, glowering and cold-faced as a young Viking, was holding the nether

tip of Count Roger's upright kite-shaped shield while Marc de Hauteville squatted down to it with polish.

Mihera looked around briefly as the Countess approached, and at
the same time Marc plied a strong shove with his oil-clout so that the
shield slipped from the tow-head's hands and clanged to the deck. A
ridge of the aft capstan scraped across it as it fell. Both boys stood
looking at the considerable scratch it had made on the buckler's
gleaming surface.

"Hay-head!" hissed Marc. "You'd be better set to the stable than
to tasks like these!" He recovered the buckler. "Here. I'll try to fix it;
lose it once more and I'll give you a taste of this clout, I swear!"

An expression of extreme resentment crossed Mihera's face, and
Marc observed it. But his own spleen still smarted from an uncomfortable interview with Roger on the thing at Gerace, and he had chosen
since to behave as if Mihera and the girl were the direct spoilers of
his fate.

"Look you," he said to Mihera coldly, "you're lucky not to be
chained on a pirate-ship this day, instead of part of a knight's company!"

"*Va*," said Mihera with a wry face. "I'd count myself luckier yet
to be back in Bull Joy, where there are neither slavers nor arrogant
fat-heads to contend with!"

Marc started. "Mind your tongue!" The girl Zoë was watching
them with a frightened expression on her face, and the two lads had
almost forgotten the presence of Lady Judith in this preliminary bout
for fisticuffs.

She checked them lightly. "Come lads, no quarrels this fine day.
Deal later with the buckler . . . Mind you the hubbub! Is it not all to
the liking of warlike princelings?"

Judith seated herself on the capstan, and let the cool air beat about
her braids, raising her wimple out after like a sail. Roger was somewhere forward, but she did not seek him, thinking that from now on,
in Sicily, her loved one would always be near. For such had been the
promises: Guiscard's, that after conquest he would leave the Isle to
Roger, and Roger's own that he would be content to rule his southern
kingdoms there from Palermo or *Balerm* as the Moslems called it. To
Jordan, Roger's natural son, would later fall the stewardship of affairs
on the mainland. Judith and Roger would at last be home, together. In
the peace and security there, she looked forward to mothering these
three young offshoots of the stormy South Normandy nobility.

"Have you heard the new ballad the minstrels are versing on the
decks?" she asked. "I am told that young Zoë, here, sings nicely, so I
beg you to bear with my own small gifts . . ."

The Countess leaned forward, her fair brow wrinkling a little with

the effort of the words which were new to her, though easy to the
tongue. Lusty words, some of which indeed fell strange from her
ladyship's gentle lips:

> *"Bohemond', Bohemond', Bohemond' Gigas,*
> *Sir Clumsy will serve us well;*
> *Hear how this huge and mighty lad*
> *Will slay the infidel!*
>
> *"No lance he bears, no mighty sword,*
> *Yet hark to his battle-charge!*
> *Though his wits are thick, his arms are strong*
> *And because his feet are large!*
>
> *"Bohemond', Bohemond', Bohemond' Gigas*
> *There's joy in the company,*
> *For woe to the Moor, swift death to the foe*
> *When Bohemond' takes to sea!"*

Mihera and the girl Zoë were laughing as Lady Judith left off, but
Marc looked in a fair way to the sulks.

"*Now* what pricks thee, lad?" asked Lady Judith.

He shrugged. "Surely you didn't think I should be *pleased* with
that bell-cap's gest!"

"No one thinks to *make* thee a bell-cap, Marc. None but thyself
can make thee a fool. You mustn't seek, in a song, *honor* or the lack
of it! Hast thou yet *earned* honor, Marc?" She laughed as Marc
flushed with realization of his own ill nature.

"But look, Marc, I can tell you this, that when every minstrel in
the company has wind of it, you will no longer own the name you
were born with. It's just as if Duke Robert had bent you over the
lustral-font and bade you christened!"

The polish-clout fell aside. The buckler, abandoned on the stern-
bench, caught flashes of warm flame from the Sicilian sun as Marc
stood there, his expression unreadable, looking out across the sea.

BOOK 2

THE CAROUSEL

CHAPTER V

St. James of the Lepers

HIS NINETEENTH BIRTHDAY. Marc, Bohemond de Hauteville had lighted, as the Countess had made him promise, five candles for the five years he had spent here in Palermo. From these small, blue flames he moved to the great arched nave of St. James of the Lepers, where the huge death-tapers bloomed like flowers on the stone bier of his countess, Judith of Sicily. It was the first anniversary of her death; and with the same sense of desolation he had known when first she was gone, he stood among the smoky bowls and looked down upon her effigy.

Around him, the other tombs, enclosed in their black rails, were dark and cold. But here the flames brought warmth to the sculpturing of the patient monks, till Judith seemed herself lying life-like on that stony couch. For minutes Bohemond lingered, and as he looked he seemed bemused, as though some fancy held him.

"Should I leave," thought Zoë Ridelle, cowering in a prie-dieu near the bishop's poppy-headed stall, "or should I stay and pray? Lord, will he think I've spied on him when he goes?"

A pure coincidence, her decision to stop for a brace of paternosters before proceeding to her lute-instruction. Ordinarily, and for an ordinary girl, there would be nothing strange in the fact that Bohemond de Hauteville had happened into the new church for an orison on

Lady Judith's death-day. Hadn't the Countess been mother to the two of them, and Mihera Falloc, too, since the Sicilian Crossing? But Zoë besides being Zoë, was in no ordinary state of mind where Bo was concerned. And so this chance encounter took on the weight of history, the poignancy of fate.

As Goeffrey Ridelle's daughter knelt among the tombs, anyone could see no sculpt coldnesses there could match the fairness of her own profile, which her Maker had chiseled as though, in all His sculpturings He had become bemused with this *one*, and took more time to the thing. Yet Zoë in these devout visits consistently prayed for beauty, to be showered, endowed, covered with it; and the corollary of her plea was simply, "O Lord, make Bohemond love me!"

But today the petition begun so devoutly had floated away on the candle-smoke, and likewise her attention, which dwelt, more than brooding saint ever dwelt on crucifix, on that figure at Judith's tomb, her young spine melting in idolatry. To be sure, the object of such devotion was not to be sneezed at. It wasn't only that the early promise of his looks had been generously kept, from the set of the red head on the big shoulders to the heavy sinewy legs which showed the new-fangled hose to such perfection. It was rather that some alchemy of de Hauteville blood had set a lofty look about him; about his mouth and in the depths of his eyes. Noble was the word you thought of. And then there was an ingredient which his life thus far and the nature of Bo himself had added—a sensitive, sort of shunted look, which you saw in him, in the way he moved, if you were aware, as most maidens found themselves to be. It was caught, sometimes, in moments of luck, in the intense gray eyes.

Now, as he stood by the tomb, Zoë had full observance of that look she adored in Bohemond. She was finding it, to her pangs, more exciting than a rush of music, more soul-piercing than a midnight star. It fetched her up with a beating heart against her final orison . . . "O God, make Bohemond, when he loves, love *me!*"

But even as he turned, made the sign of the cross and came walking up the aisle, his Venetian boots shuffling a little on the stones, she saw his usual expression fall dark across his face. It came like a slap, like the bar of shadow that struck his cheek and scraped across it as he passed a stained-glass oriel in the transept wall. To be sure this look of his, oblique and a little hard for one so young, went better with the flamboyant cap of red hair. This was the usual Bo that everybody knew, with the sharp raw humors and severe, blind heart.

As he passed her prie dieu, Zoë took her lute from the stones and gave him a poke with it in the side.

"*Sant' George!*"

His startled expletive fled between the pillars and echoed up to the great altar where, as he passed from the church, Zoë set her eyes to ask forgiveness. But since youth can go from stars to earth in the instant you can say "Friar Jacques," the somber air of St. James was disturbed by a girlish giggle . . .

Having made shift to let a decent time pass before deserting the basilica, Zoë did not emerge till some time later. But she saw no one waiting for her, no one with new Venetian boots. At this warmest time in Palermo, when the sun seems to cast its most killing look on Sicily, all took their sleep like proper Saracens. Even the Normans rested, while their women kept to quiet tasks in the palace grounds. None sought the streets save beggars who sat cross-legged and snoozed where they were, heads thrown back and bristly mouths respiring like so many bellows. Zoë had a glimpse of several through the lintel of the church, and she dreaded, now, to step to the street. As she reached forth to wet her fingers with the lustral water, her hand was seized by an arm from the shadowed door. The Palermo heat died before this chill alarm, until Bohemond stepped to the light.

"Oh, Bo!" she gasped, "how you scared me!"

"Good. That's what I meant," propelling her by one small elbow down the shallow steps. "God knows you deserve it . . . What are you *doing* this time of day, minx? Alone and on foot?"

Zoë pulled off, since his hard hand hurt so. "I was bound for the Nuns of the Villa for my lute lesson. What would you have me *do*, the white mare throwing a shoe and it not fixed yet?"

"Then where's that old scold Berthe, that she doesn't tend you?"

"Busy, of course, with the girls in the Bower. *Everyone's* readying for the joust tomorrow. Such fussing with ribbons and curls as you never saw!" She gave him a sidelong glance. "I s'pose I *know* where *you're* going . . . Is my guess right?"

He grinned. "If it's to the tilt-yard—yes."

"Of course. That's all you think of—training, fighting, going at somebody in the dust! You never have fun. Remember how we used to hunt and ride?—Mihera and you and I? And now even *him* you keep tilting from morning till night! Well—so! You're the best. The acknowledged champion. You'll doubtless prove it, in the knighting-joust tomorrow. You're Jacques-on-the-spot at the *lists*, all right," she pouted "—but never, *never* at the Hall, Bo! Never at the dances!"

"What's the matter? Not partners enough?"

"Oh!" she deprecated. "It isn't that! But they're *goats*, beside your dancing! You danced better than those goats *now*, as we stepped down those basilica steps, then they do in the whole long evening of country sarabands."

She was quite breathless and flushed, but Bohemond was not taken

by her flattery. He was too used to these outbursts, from a childhood
spent in company with her strange, mercurial temperament. What
suddenly struck him was that Zoë was no longer a child. She had the
curling dark hair of a child and the curving face that still flushed
like a child's, and the utter lack of guile. But a deepened intensity in
her, the bright, sweet, passionate glow of her, made his breath seem
to catch. This new thought, this dangerous thought, since so he must
learn to view it, flicked through him only lightly, only swift as a rush
of wings, and had not altered his manner which remained quizzical,
nor his glance which coolly met hers.

"Now, listen once to me," he said as they came to the yard. "Why,
pray, aren't *you* fussing with the others, for tomorrow's doings?"

"I? Oh. I hadn't thought of it much yet. I—"

"You never think is *right!* Look, sweetheart, you're growing to
quite a ladyship yourself, you know, and better be busy with it!
Meanwhile, it's *one* reason (besides my good nature), that I'll *take*
you to the Villa of the Dames. Why, these fine lepers here might try
to snatch such a lovely!"

Another of the snoozers had waked and now approached them,
shaking his clack-dish. But Zoë observed neither him nor his loath-
someness. She was so taken with Bohemond's compliment, even thus
questionably put, that her side was quivery and things in her back
stung like a thousand needles. But she said calmly, "What would you
suggest, Bohemond?"

Ouragon champed restlessly at the cathedral wall as his master
approached. But Bohemond left him tethered, sat Zoë down on the low
stone churchyard parapet, and fell into their old mood of easy com-
radeship. Cocking his fair head in speculation, he put up a hand to
the dark, wayward curls that flowed about her shoulders among the
veils.

"This would be better *up*, of course. A good nose, quite wonderful
eyes and all, but—let's see—you *smile* wrong."

"*Smile* wrong?"

"Yes."

"How *should* I smile?"

"Well, *prettily* and not too much. Parting your lips just so and no
more. Let's see you do it."

Zoë smiled.

"No. Don't *grin* when you smile. A few of those teeth of yours
are a treat, but not all marshalled into view like a troop of men-at-
arms!"

"Like *this?*" said Zoë, heartily diverted.

"Yes, that's it. *See,* now! Your lips are more delicate, like archer's
bows, like—like wings, like—"

"*Are they, Bohemond?*"

"Yes, damn it—I *said* they were!"

She pouted at this sudden unnecessary gruffness.

By this time several beggars had come and gathered about. Although their eyes which had been closed were open now, their fearsome mouths were in the same agape state. For never had they seen such a queer making-of-love as this young Christian seemed engaged in, with his pointing at the lady's face, and his scowling and his scratching of his head.

"Come on," he said shortly. "I'll ride you to the nunnery." He lifted her to the saddle and mounted in front.

Ouragon pranced off as though proud of the capacity of his back which was now ample enough, since he was in his seven-year prime. But, as they passed out of the gates, the pigeons (who, like beggars, seem to prefer church-yards whence by the nature of things folks emerge more charitable-minded) flew from Ouragon's hooves till he thought he was swimming in the feathery things. Therefore he reared twice, and Zoë slipped to the ground. Several of the stricken ones stepped forth as if fain to set right this tumbled heap of beauties; but the young squire dismounted, stooped, and had her back up in a trice.

"Clumsy," he ill-naturedly said.

"You should *sell* this nag, Bo—he shies at nothing!"

He scowled. He flung an arm at the birds. "Those aren't '*nothing*'! They're pigeons! He shies at *pigeons*, not *nothing!*"

She sent him a small smile, her lip-corners denting minutely, which he ignored as he climbed to the saddle.

"*This* time you had better hold on."

This Zoë did, and finding his back too broad for her arms' span, must have her cheek against his shoulder-blade. And thus they rode out of the church-yard.

It was only a short way to the Villa of Holy Dames, but, as they trotted along through the hot, sleeping streets, she made leagues of cubits, hours of minutes by her savoring of each jounce and second. The balminess of the air, the rhythm of the ride, had a spell-like music, and she fell into fits of happiness, not knowing *what* palpitations, quiverings and harrowings went on in her person, till she scarce could bear it. Bohemond looked around once and frowned, from which she realized she'd been leaning against him like a page of a book against another, as if she would leave her imprint on his soldierly back.

She held to him more lightly then, and, as they drew up before the old Greek villa that housed the nunnery, he slipped from the saddle and lifted her from Ouragon's ribs. She was aware of his face near touching hers, of the curve of his firm, full mouth. Below his lower lip there was a shadow, blue-tinted . . .

Then her feet struck ground.

Bo's gray eyes still scanned her face as if he still took inventory there, or so she hoped, but his tone had the coolness of a merchantman as, mounting Ouragon, he remarked, "You know, Zoë, something else. *You* shouldn't be interested in hunting and riding and the rest, save as pretty accomplishments, like your lute songs. You should think now constantly of your future, as chatelaine of some lordly manor, baroness of wide lands, like those other doves in Berthe's Bower, like a true *jeune fille*. Listen," hooking a forefinger in his dagger-belt and squinting down, "you know what you need?"

She pulled her eyes from his face which she had been conning like a monk his manuscript.

"What, Bohemond?"

"Choose a chevalier at Roger's court . . . Pay him attention . . . Coy, flirtatious, gay—you know how they do—and fall in love."

The lips that were like bows, like a pair of wings, fell open.

"I need to fall in love!" they repeated rather blankly.

But Bohemond had shaken rein, and without further ceremony spurred on toward the tilt-yards. The echo of hooves returning to Zoë from the dark red pavement was like laughter, like cackling of fiends.

She walked to the Villa door. There was an old Greek open-mouthed comic mask whose tongue was a wooden bell. This she set in motion by a tug on the silver baldric; she harked to its clacking while she waited for the gate-nun to give her entrance.

CHAPTER VI *The Tilt*

"LIFE'S A RARE THING in Sicily!" people were used to say. They meant the wild ways given rein to here, beneath the mask of knighthood. High mass, prayers, votive lights kindled piously—these started the day. High jinks dogged it to its close. Chivalry, high revelry, were synonymous in wild Palermo. Norman blood, not far enough removed from Vikings who sired it, and southern suns between them made mock of restraint. Youth here was short—as short as its civilizations, and hotly brilliant.

In view of all this, the knighting-rite itself was appropriately lusty. Elsewhere the *accolade* was topped by the kiss of peace from lord to lad. But here, indeed, the final salute was a swift, mark-making, tooth-endangering blow from Count Roger's gauntlet . . .

There were but four new squires to be knighted this year. But all were distinguished, being sons of prominent lords, none meaner than a Count-apparent. A motley crew, the four, fit spawn to the Barons of the South. Guiscard's son, Borsa de Hauteville, had spent his pre-belting weeks under the Count's tutelage, joining Roger's only male heir, his illegitimate favorite, Prince Jordan. These, with Bohemond de Hauteville and Mihera Falloc, would make a fine lot for the winter *accolade*. The previous day would be marked by jousting in the lists, in a special tournament known as the Squire's Carousel. It was always a gala time, with shops decorated, masses said in high ceremony, and northern lords down for a winter holiday. Here troths of state were often plighted and a squire's talisman might identify for the first time his chosen lady.

The Winter Lists at Palermo were held in Castletown, western-most of the two brown-walled cities that made up this filthy but beautiful Arab paradise. All roads leading from the purple mountains to the plains of the Golden Shell came into Castletown, for it was the elder. To its old Roman fort and the castle of the infidel, the Normans had added a square donjon of their own, fronting the ruins of a round theatre set in the hillside like a dish, whose remains they had put to use as a jousting arena. From this old Saracen Castle clean to Bar-el-Bahr, the harbor gate, ran a red-marble-paved street known as the Row, as Simat to the Arabs.

Thus it was that along about the third watch, after late matins, the whole gay company of Normans set out from the Select, where the Emir and his *divans* had once ruled, and crossed into Castletown.

"Slow down!" Bohemond called to Mihera Falloc. "Make way; we could ride together!"

Mihera looked back. The padded lance-rest bulked up large on an already husky shoulder tip, and the broad face over it was an echo of the mighty Hugh. Mihera was blond, white-blond, and the thick thatch sheared in a line from ear to brow and around to ear again, too much in the Saxon way, fairly shouted his maternal heritage. His habitual expression could stem from both. He always looked bored and a little irritated.

"Fall back, *Englishman!*" Bohemond called again, his laugh flicking at the nick-name. It little moved Mihera. He raised a slight shrug against the badgering and went on apace.

The day of the tilt had a new note in its sultriness. A wind rose that was more than the breeze of yesterday. Warm gusts of it whipped dust into dusty eyes where the natives swarmed, ranked on the cobbles. Remarks in Arabic flew thick and fast as the panoply surged by.

The squires and their mounts might be dully caparisoned, compared to the splendor there. But what they lacked in show, they fully made up in youth and lustiness. The worst looked well-endowed today, as a bride does at her wedding. Borsa de Hauteville rode first, as his high birth had it. His swart, bat-like face glowed darkly with much scrubbing and his link shirt sat well on his slight form. Soft green boots with thin cross gaiterings of leopard pelt played down the ill-developed stringiness of his legs. Bonny Prince Jordan, all smiles, rode next. His vivid, half-Saracen features looked more spirited than ever between Borsa and the wry-faced young Falloc who rode, slightly self-conscious, close after him. Bohemond rode last.

The Row, usually dung-strewn from the Harbor to the Gate, had been scraped free of its filthy crust and spread with pungent-sweet fronds of cypress bushes. And, brushing the knights' helms as they passed beneath them, long flags hung, stretched sill to sill from the white-washed, precariously sagged dwellings.

Bohemond felt good. He was bursting with news he had kept since sun-up, and wished to share it with his friend Mihera. He smiled at the stiff back—it seemed fairly bristling at him—and called once more.

"By God, it's good to be riding to our Carousel, aye, Mihera?"

This time Mihera answered. His steel shaft, jutting up from the *épulier*, was a hot gleam athwart his features.

"Yes—at least it's done with!"

Bohemond thought he hadn't heard right. He kicked Ouragon and pushed ahead. The crowd flared, chattering with anger at the sudden closeness, till of necessity young Falloc made room.

"It's this wind," said Bohemond cheerily. "It makes the heathen spleeny. But what's up with *you*, Mihera?"

"Nothing. Except that I don't like it . . ."

"Like what? The tilt?"

"The tilt. Not the tilt, nor this fine useless parading nor this nausea of show, nor anything about it."

"Good Lord!—The first taste of what it *means*, the knighthood!" Bohemond was puzzled. "What *would* m'lord like, then?" he asked, half-joking.

"The sea."

"The sea?" Bohemond echoed, at a loss. "What of the sea? An infinity of water . . . Lord, I like it too, to *look* at . . . What talk's this?"

But Mihera, with unwonted alacrity, replied to the first query.

"What of the sea, you say? I like it *all*, friend. At Bull Joy many shippers, merchants, even Viking Lords came, friends of my mother's people. (Do you forget she was born while her own mother looked for a long-beak to show off Dover Head?) Well, these took me for sails, days, weeks at a time, and once, with the sea-lord Piereleone, for one whole summer. And now, I too would spend a life-time on that 'infinity'."

"By the Rood, Mihera! Why no word of this before?"

"To you?" Mihera smiled—a broad parting of wide lips without humor, but his deep-set lashless eyes now showed an almost boyish happiness. The crowd cheered, thinking he greeted them. But he was unconscious of their stares. They were forgotten.

"Where do you think I *spend* my time, when not with you and your eternal knight-talk and your worlds to conquer? Down at the sea-wharves, Bohemond, on the rim of Castletown, where you'd scorn to go. But sea-folk are there, and I could listen and talk and hark to all things concerning it, till I felt a little less like bursting. Only thus could I stand this jousting and this thing of the Frenchiness with you till the time was out."

De Hauteville's nostrils flared.

"Why bother at all?"

"Sir Hugh, of course—I promised my father to take the knightly rank. But now it's done." He smiled his broad, dry grin. "I had news today. It came on the great black bireme that sailed in last night from Salerno."

"So did *I*!" cried Bohemond. "That's what I meant to tell you! My *own* father sent the ship special, from the sieging there . . ." He stopped. "But, what were you saying?" He checked himself politely, laying a light hand on his destrier, who seemed as restive as himself.

"Well," Mihera began, "you know how it was with my old friend Piereleone, Maurus of Amalfi . . ."

Bohemond nodded. For indeed, Palermo had talked of little else for months. A grim tale, too hideous to be told at table with the women by. It began when Amalfi, worn out by the savage raids of the Prince, had asked Guiscard to make the town his in exchange for defense, according to feudal custom. Since Maurus was expediter of the desperate plan, the vengeance of Gisolf came hard and swiftly. Kidnapping Maurus's fine and well-loved son, he had held him for fifty thousand ducats, which, when they might be paid, he doubled to an impossibility. While Pope, Duke and every person of influence in the environs of the tragedy pleaded with Gisolf for a meed of decency, the Prince spent long days in Maia Torre, slow-torturing the young Piereleone, and sending old Maurus the grim mementoes of it. The thing, the details of which revolted even a violent Italy, had an end at last, but with death only, when the Prince threw the youth, half-living, from a high cliff to Salerno Gulf.

"Old Maurus is naturally half-ill from that long-drawn-out horror," Mihera now told Bohemond, "and from word of doctors and in line with his oft-spoken wish since the affair of the pirates that time in Bull Joy, he has asked to adopt me as foster son. It is a thing in use, I understand, with emirs of the East. He will train me to sea-ways if I want it."

"To *trade*, you mean?" asked Bohemond, not bothering to hide his shock.

"To trade," said Mihera with cool emphasis.

"Well," said Bohemond, after a time, "there's no need for a necromancer to see your future and the fortune in it." Then, with contempt spilling suddenly over the rim of his try at understanding, "But by God, Mihera! What of your father's lands? Great fiefs to take charge of, and fight for, and your honor as a knight? Do these things mean nothing? To rough it against the infidel, to subdue monsters like our fathers do, even now at Salerno avenging Maurus? To all this you prefer the *sea*?"

Mihera said nothing. He had his stubborn look.

If there was snobbishness in Bohemond's attitude to young Falloc's dreams, he would not have admitted it. He sincerely felt nothing but a great wonder.

"Isn't that the way of it!" he mused. "All my life I have wanted those things you leave so lightly. Land of my own, my father's good will, a place of knightly rank and you . . ." He suddenly swore. "For these things you scorn, by Heaven, I must plan, scheme, pray and sacrifice and come to my rights in some way obscure and devious as my dubious heritage! Today, for instance! God granting, I *must* win this tourney in order to gain, after perils I dare not think of, my own rightful place with Robert!"

"*Perils*," Mihera singled out the word, "what mean you, *perils*?"

"Did you know what the task will be this year for the champion's endeavor?"

"Naturally not, since it's not told, here, before the tourney."

"*I* was told. The news of it came with that ship we speak of, and I had it secretly, from one close to Roger."

"What, then?"

"It is this. Prince Gisolf, with the city half-starved and murmuring about him for weeks now, thinks of surrender. But he wants a hostage. Some son of the Twelve Normans at the Palace first as a surety of his life."

"Good Lord! You mean, to go in *alone*? What reward, surviving it?"

"The Golden Spurs, of course, but more—a high post immediately in my father's command."

Mihera whistled. "For once I've got luck. You and Jordan are the better ones. Borsa I'd out-thrust with hands tied, but thank God my indifferent skill will take me no farther! I can't fathom Roger, though, to consent to it, with his beloved bastard at the tilt. A wager on *your* skill, of course . . . The Count must be banking on it!"

Bohemond grinned. "I hope he's right. I've wanted nothing else in my life so badly."

Mihera shrugged. "If *that's* your idea of luck—well, luck *to* you! For the rest—new times, new ways, Bo! But I regret it won't be together! We've had fine times here, you and I and our pretty Zoë . . ."

The subject of women, or of Zoë in particular—Mihera found himself wondering which caused the swift flush on de Hauteville's face.

" 'Sblood!" Bohemond swore. "What a pert piece *that* is. Looks, sighs, playing the very devil! The Count should wed her off before—no discretion!"

Mihera stared, frowned, then broke to his rare, gusty laughter.

"By God, Bo . . . you're rare!" he said. "Looks, sighs, and pretty words—let us have more of this!" He paused, catching his breath. "Listen! With the rest of us, your sweet friend is a very monument of discretion!"

"So?"

"So! The girl loves you."

Bohemond frowned. "Leave it, Mihera. I've no time for love. Such love's not for me."

"Good God, why? And what's more, how *not*?" His tone was oddly careful. "No appeal for you there?"

" 'Steeth, you're a nosy bugger! I'm no monk. I've thought of her, of course! I thought more last night about her than I did of the tourney! But it cannot be . . . Unless, of course, she were an inn-wench, which she's not, or merely like some of these fine, titled peahens we know of hereabouts!"

Mihera's jaw tightened. He shot a strange glance at young de Hauteville.

"I see. And a troth is unthinkable, since she's no high-born demoi-selle with a *dot* . . ." He shrugged. "Well, it's none of my business then, if you are all Norman with the notions of a *grand seigneur* and a stream of ice for blood, but touching the other—don't thank your-self for being *noble*, Bo! I'd kill you!"

"Well!" surmised Bohemond, "*you* love her! Welladay! . . . You *love* her!" he said to Mihera's silence.

"Were any to ask—yes. It's Zoë I think of when I think of love . . ."

Bohemond laughed. "How grim you are about it, Falloc! Such a pretty thing of love!"

"It's not my *way* to say it otherwise," he growled, reddening a little. "*You* could of course . . . on *anything*, you could! If you went to the privy-room to relieve yourself, you could announce it high-flown like a trumpet-call!" He looked away, his eyes suddenly naked. "Besides, why hold to the thought, when it's *you* she dotes on?"

It was Bohemond's turn to anger. "I tell you, leave it, Mihera—it's no good. I'm no contender in it—now or ever. Remember that . . . Have you told her how you feel?"

"Great Michael no!"

"Well, now! And how would she *know*, otherwise? Speak up now! In the tourney! In fact, if you don't, I'll do it *for* you!"

Mihera's protests were drowned in the sudden flare of trumpets far ahead.

"Well, then," cried Bohemond, aroused to the fray. "To the Carou-sel! For you, love, and for me, the victory! Let's go!"

They spurred to the others. They all pranced four abreast through the gates of the Saracen Castle.

The Beauty Throne stood white, beautiful and eloquently poignant in its emptiness there mid the color and noise that rioted in the list-pavilion. It had a mantle of late roses cast over it like a chaplet, a salute to the dead Countess. All contestants dipped their lances there as they passed.

The squires were moving out when Bohemond felt a pluck at his lance-tip.

"*Bohemond! No talisman for your joust!*"

For an instant he was at pains to recognize the small picture of ravishment that sent her glance directly out at him. Zoë had her hair all coiffured up, and, save for one long, sooty curl snaking out on a bare shoulder, it was bound securely by some sea-blue silk, the very hue of her eyes. Against this and the softness of pale green gown she wore, she was radiant. On the bench-back she had flung one of the new short capes from France. Scarcely knowing it, he was staring a little, till she repeated.

"I *said*, Bo, your talisman! See—Borsa sports the silk of the maid of Flanders; Prince Jordan has I-don't-know *whose* glove on his saddle-poll, while *you* . . ."

"What of Mihera?" he said quickly. "See, he goes ribbonless too, though wearing, I swear, the very skin of his heart on his gauntlet for your favor, Zoë!" He was very earnest.

"Zut!" said Zoë. "It would be that I'd given it to a brother, then. So don't meddle in that!" She wore a small grin of mischief. Presently, her eyes sparkling, "Bo—you wear it! Please!" She tugged the silken hair piece from her coiffure . . .

"Oh no, Zoë, *don't!* Your— The hair—it's fine, wonderful . . . it looks . . ." He trailed off vaguely. "Zoë," he began again, his tone suddenly low and very intense in the noise about them. "Don't squander yourself on such as me . . . The unfavored son on the tag-end of my father's escutcheon." He was at pains to control the growing huskiness in his voice. "You and I—we must go our separate ways, for our mutual benefit. My God, sweetheart, don't you see?"

But to Zoë, who still thought the thing had something to do with two who kindled one another, the argument was vain. She let his stiff words hang where they were in the surcharged atmosphere. So Bohemond, feeling inept and aware he had made a sorry try at things, added with scant judgment what he felt was a jocular touch to the proceedings.

"Besides, Zoë, it's always for the squire to seek and the lady to grant, this talisman thing, and if I have seemed to ask it, I'm sorry . . ."

He saw her skin flame, her eyes blaze. Wine-glow on lapis lazuli he thought wildly. . . .

"Don't sc 'd me, Bohemond! As you implied now, we are not like to the rest, we two. So you can be as reluctant as you wish (as no knight ever was) and I can be bold, as no lady . . ."

He grinned. For an instant he let himself look deeply in those sea-blue eyes. He learned there how a woman's glance might be, if she wished it, the very seat of mirth, mischief and man's destruction.

The harsh blare of new horns pulled him from this dangerous reverie. With the other three, he reared, wheeled and spurred in practiced unison toward outer tents that blew beyond the pale. But presently, in his own running shadow, he observed something foreign. He glanced about at his lance-tip. There, floating from it tied in haste, was the little blue hair-piece. He thrust a scowl backwards; he saw her sitting primly by; he saw that she smiled—not *too* much—just a few small pearls set charmingly in view.

The wind rose steadily in the next hour, while visiting champions matched their long-accustomed blows. By the Interval, little whirl-winds danced in the dust and snapped in the blue silks of the bright pavilions. The Count's pavilion grew restless, waiting, and Roger requested a lute-song from Zoë.

As the notes sounded, sweet and delicate beneath the silk, the company relaxed, stopped their nervous chatter and subsided to small groups visiting at their ease. Roger talked highly to the guest on his right hand, one Count Stephen, ranking heir to the French lands of Blois. The nobleman was idly watching the pretty musician as her slim, sun-tinted hands brushed across the lute, her single dark curl trembling a little on her white neck with the rhythms that she struck. He was giving to Roger only half-attention, until presently the Count mentioned Golden Spurs.

Zoë had been lost in some reverie of her own, but her notes now quieted some and her head slightly lifted, one bare, alert ear toward the great golden Chair of the Emir in which Roger sat.

"But why won't Guiscard simply *take* the city?" the young lord of Blois was asking.

Roger shrugged. "Because Gisolf sets torches as soon as not, and would leave to Guiscard only ashes for his pains."

Stephen gasped. "Even beautiful Salerno he would burn?"

"It is what he has threatened."

"Monster of a man," Stephen shivered. "And to think a knight would go as hostage there . . . God! *That* I would not, for a place in the Host of Heaven!" A somewhat delicate young man, he blanched at the mere thought.

Roger laughed, in a sort of crooked humor. "That, young sire, is almost exactly the prize the fellow will *win*, except for uncommon luck!"

Zoë had turned and was openly staring at the Count, her eyes narrowed somewhat, and her fingers plucking only ragged bits of tune. Stephen of Blois was also casting him a puzzled look.

"But your own *son* competes!" he said, and added, not thinking, "it's well that Bohemond's *so good!*" Seeing his host stiffen, he hastened on. "Oh, Jordan is *good*, better than our best at the lists for the younger knights at Paris that I attended last spring! But all say Bohemond is unsurpassed." He broke off, embarrassed at his conversational quandary.

But the Count seemed unperturbed. He crossed his knees, drew the rich folds of his weightless mantle about them, and presented to Stephen his handsome profile. "Such is the course projected; no use to ponder on it now."

On a sudden, a strange, harsh twang resounded from the lute. Roger looked up, slight annoyance in his handsome face. Zoë's mouth was a little "O," her hands thrown up, the broken string swaying in the breeze.

"Regrettable!" she said. "I must fetch my own! It is still in the litter." She was flushed now, and her eyes were glistening.

"Ye gods, no!" disparaged Roger. "Don't vex yourself. The squires tilt presently . . ." and seeing she was already risen, "*Here,* Zoë! I shall send a page, of course . . ."

"No, sire! Do not bother. He— I'll go . . ." There was a thin note in her voice. "I'll go."

Her soft garments billowed in the wind, and as she stepped lightly by, the eyes of Stephen of Blois followed her appreciatively.

"By the Head," he commented to the Count when she had gone. "That Demoiselle Ridelle is a maid of some spirit, eh? and quite a fascinating piece, to top it!"

He twirled his new French pointed lip-tufts and wondered idly when the fair *trobador* would return.

The grooms and litter-slaves were gossiping at the gates when Zoë came flying into the tethering-space. She looked like a night-vision in the day, wild-eyed and scared, but grimly purposeful. She waved them away and ran her eyes quickly over the stallions snorting at the posts. Skittish murder, most of these; mounting most would mean a bite on the backside and a swift rolling in the dust. Which, then? She stopped, nonplussed. Then, hard by the gate she spied Count Roger's tall, gentle chestnut, with the great jewelled pillow on his saddle-cloth and the languid look in his eyes. In a trice she was on his broad back, out the gate and, at a pounding gallop, went clattering up the Row.

The grooms, when presently she returned, made a great fuss over the chestnut's lather. There would be beatings for the horse-sweat on the Count's caparisons. Zoë searched, eyes narrowed, among the younger grooms and found one suitable for her projected task. She motioned him after her as she struggled with the great clumsy pigeon-basket, staggering back in the direction of the listing-grounds. It was just by a hairsbreadth that she remembered the lute. With quick words and a threat or two she relieved herself of the cage and launched the lackey toward the lists. And after a short shift at the litter, she was mounting into the Count's pavilion once more, her stray curls tucked to rights, her capelet straight on her shoulders. None marked her even, for her entrance was happily lost in the trumpeted calling of the victory joust. She slipped to the bench beside the Count of Blois. He smiled warmly and she asked, "How went the earlier tilt?"

"As you'd think," shrugged the young veteran of the tourney-stands.

"Jordan upset Borsa and Mihera lost out to Jordan. So you see, it is just as all surmised it. Bohemond engages Prince Jordan for the last."

At that moment Borsa de Hauteville, his yellow eyes lighted with chagrin at his recent mouthful of dust, joined the others in the royal company, lowering his elegant mail-clad body on the bench. The Frenchman leaned down with a hand on his shoulder.

"Congratulation, Prince Borsa. Luck rode with your broken lance!"

Borsa was puzzled. "What do you mean?" Then, glancing about at everyone. "What goes on here? Why does everybody hang so on this next event? Except of course that it tickles the fancy to see the Bastard and the Half-Bastard going it together . . ." He played with his sash, smiling lazily, alert to see Zoë bridle at his secret sobriquet for Bohemond.

Indeed her eyes raked him, and breathless from anger and her recent exertions she snapped, "There's more to this than the honor-place at 'Squire's Board' this night. . . . Ask your *noble* uncle!"

When Borsa came again to her side, his face reflected a strange alertness, as did all eyes there as the final fanfare flung itself to the sirocco. The thing this day had an edge of death to it.

Bonny Prince Jordan spurred to the sand, dipped his lance happily in the Count's direction and with a flourish galloped to the list's far end. As he held there, bent a little across his mount's neck, Zoë was aware of his good looks, his clean-cut face and his laughing eyes. Guiltily aware. And she saw, besides the device sinister on his shield's left quarter, the motto, "The Hand of the Lord Raised Me," which was Roger's own device, taken after a Saracen skirmish when St. George was seen to lead the Norman charge. Somehow she turned the sight to a consolation. St. George was a powerful adversary to the devil, so maybe the joust was in other hands than one's own . . .

Then, from the far side, the cloud of hoof dust that went straight to her heart and turned it over. Bohemond shot out in his turn, bowed briefly to the Count and went to his appointed place.

Zoë held her breath. Now. Was that urchin under the boards where it was his business to be? Woe betide him if not. She lifted the Persian rug and placed her sandal at the platform edge, anchoring it. She watched the page hand Bohemond his helm. He fussed a moment with the lance-haft, getting some favorite hold, and her heart seemed to leap with him as he started the long charge. She stamped on the boards. It was horrible to brace the soul for the next thing—and see nothing occur. Nothing but the flash of Sicilian sunshine on his shield, as he pounded by. They met dead-center like a pair of thunderstorms. The clang of their lances on one another's buckler brought a roar from the crowd. It was a tribute to them both, this dead-tie attack in which neither was unhorsed, for the blow of weapon on iron had been a lightning-clap, a thing of thunder. But their lances were still whole, so back they went, their mounts pawing with excitement, the riders grinning back at one another over their *épuliers*.

Zoë was aware of a slightly perfumed breath as Count Stephen spoke again at her shoulder.

"This is a *sportman's* match. The true blood . . ."

Zoë nodded, gritting her teeth. Bohemond wheeled, set himself, and started the running charge once more. This time Zoë jumped up and down with both feet and under cover of all the shouting, let out a string of Norman and Arabic oaths that would credit her father.

"Zut! You little whoreson down there!" she said in part. "Now! *Now!*"

She screamed as the pigeons came. Whrrr . . . The whole, gay company of them, streaming out like a wide white ribband, flinging themselves out from the pavilion. Fluttering, they rose on panicked wing, right in front of Ouragon. The timing was perfect. Ouragon's eyes reddened. He neighed and reared while Jordan came bearing on. Bohemond flung out with his lance wildly. It struck Jordan in the shoulder and pierced through ring and fess, but not before his own lance shattered against Ouragon's chest like a kindling-stick. Bohemond unbalanced, fell from the horse and lay in the dust, prone. The whole list-stand was on its feet, silent for a time, for the thing had been completely unorthodox, all swift confusion. Then the cry came.

"Jordan! Prince Jordan wins!"

Zoë, paralyzed, was watching the center of the list. Ouragon mortally wounded, had toppled on Bohemond and lay heavily on his leg. But she saw Jordan yank the beast up with a pull of his good arm. Bohemond rose from the ground as though dazed.

"Saint Michael be thanked," she breathed.

She saw Count Roger leaning out, heard the awful curses spewing from his handsome mouth and the one word, "Jordan," as though he were already looking his last on his beloved son.

Zoë sat very still, and the list-ground drew her eyes again like a magnet. Jordan's face smiling in his luck, his courteous regrets to Bohemond, Bohemond bending near his dying steed . . . She looked at her lap and hid her hands there. None must see the wide white band and learn that the pigeon vendor had the ring that the Countess had given her. She stared at the empty Beauty Throne, almost seeking some consoling sign, as if maybe the Countess's shade still lingered. But no; there were only winter roses, blowing jauntily in the wind.

CHAPTER VII   *The Bower*

THE HALL OF THE EMIR in the Select was ablaze that night with long, slender onyx-hasped cressets touched with cinnamon and balsam-of-Alexandria. They rested daintily, poised in silver sconces. Other flames concealed themselves in small wall-coves hidden from the tables so that the light falling on the feasters there had a suffused and moony glow.

The light-fingered architecture of the East, the delicate, unanatomized decor, was light and lifting and infinitely restful. The sirocco might well be aboard this night in Sicily, might well lift a cloak of sand and fling it at the moon. But here in the ancient Saracen chamber life was pleasant, with no sound but soft music made by lutists hidden in the screens. Only distantly could the storm be heard.

Count Roger sat like some splendid deity with the beltless lads at his board. He still wore a somber under-cote of mourning, but of exquisite silk, from the Syrian looms of Castletown, and his long, ringleted shoulder-length hair gleamed bright above it. There was a glinting edge of gold that ran like fire about his sleeves and the edge of his pallium. The Count's life spread long and golden before him, and he had liked its prospect. His spirit did not writhe and fuss at fate as did his brother Robert's. The eagle of unending ambition that clawed at Guiscard had happily passed him by. Since that long-ago night when Roger had first set his destrier's hooves on the narrow strip of land about the Golden Shell, pale-washed in the wan, Sicilian moon, he had loved this Isle of Fire. Sicily was the soil he loved, and it was all-satisfying.

But Jordan was the very core of this land-love, sired as he was on a dusky maid in its soft hills long ago.

Thus it was that on this night of rejoicing, Roger was unwontedly quiet, and that every toast he drank with the rest sat bitter in his mouth. The cries of *"Moult preux!"* and *"Moult valoureux!"* lingered in the light air like weights to his spirit, spoiled as they were by the vivid fact of Prince Jordan and *Maia Torre.*

They had all toasted, and now Borsa stood to toast again, and Roger roused vaguely from his worried torpor.

"To Prince Jordan," Borsa was saying, "for his skill in the Carousel and"—turning a little tipsily—"to Bohemond, for a long life and continued safe-keeping by the ladies!"

It was a supreme enough insult—to toast a list-loser. Cups, half-lifted, stopped in mid-air. Silence fell, except for the insipid whine of the Persian pipists in the screens.

But Borsa plunged on.

"The Bastard goes on his *own* honor, as is right, but"—belching grossly—"the Half-Bastard hides behind skirts . . ."

"Wait a minute, Borsa!" Bohemond was on his feet. "What are you talking about?"

And while they listened, mouths agape, he told the tale. The finding of Zoë's urchin and a small meed of elbow-twisting had armed him well, and he spewed it all out on the foul breath of the wine-dregs.

The upshot could be nothing less than it was: Bohemond, distressed and shouting, demanding the peril at Salerno for himself, with the Count only too glad to give it; Prince Jordan, his injury swathed in linens attesting to his impotency in the matter, despite his indignant protests. It was a sorry feast. And out of the mess that Borsa had vomited forth, Bohemond distilled as he might a few scraps of his tarnished honor, and consent to go to the task at Maia Torre. He made his regrets early, and with several more quaffs from the already too-often lifted wine-horn, and with his whole world wryly changed, he scraped back his feasting-chair and hurried from the Hall.

He flung from the castle to the windy night and walked the length of the gusty colonnade. The wind was an enemy and he dodged to the small shelter of a portico to await its lessening. He thought of his key, but as he sought it in his sash, his hand felt some other thing and he pulled it before him. The blue hair-piece curled about his fingers, glinting and blowing in the ruddy light. He went on, squinting, his eyes stinging from sand in the wind, and knocked softly on the door of Berthe, the old one, the dame seneschal.

No answer came, but the heavy door yielded to his sturdy push. There were three marble steps and a low, ornamental gate of Moorish iron, and then all was quietness.

Berthe, the key-keeper, was an old friend. Was she still awake? He tapped on the inner door. No answer. Then he heard footsteps on the colonnade, and no longer avoiding the moon, he stepped from the pillar and went out to meet her . . .

He was fumbling at the lock. He had been fumbling with it for some time. The wind was howling high about the parapet and in the space between the walls of the castle close; it seemed to be trying to pull him bodily from the tower and he was cursing softly. He paused;

he looked at the great, iron-studded door with the florated grill-work as though it were an enemy. The fine sand-sting was raw on his face and in his eyes, maddening him. He thought of giving up. He tried once more, fitting the key in the cavity that was shaped like a pome-granate-blossom. The thing scraped over at last, and at a lunge from his shoulder the hinges gave to.

There was a vigil-shrine with an amethyst-colored lamp glow-ing by her bed. The high, faintly boat-shaped couch had the covers wrinkled over. He smelled the perfume-like summer blossoms and he thought it emanated from the vigil-shrine by the bed. There was a high amber-glass casement along the far wall, leaded with pictures in it, like a bestiary.

She was standing against the amber casement, cool against the night. She was looking at him and there was a smile on her lips; he could see the lamp's reflection in her eyes.

"I have watched you come," she said, and inclined her head a little to the yard below. She seemed far away, and he stood, holding the silk.

Warm shadows moved across her face and on the thin silk of her gown as she came forward. The silk was cool in his hand and he was calm now, cast, as it were, in her own small dream. She put out her hand as though to take the ribband from him, but folded his fingers in hers instead and came up against him, firm and cool. It was as simple as that, and he felt his arms go round her with a thrill of tenderness and strange surprise.

He looked at her then, holding her face up, and he heard her breath catch in the half-opened lips as she drew off and went toward the window. Turning, she seemed to draw the light. He saw the small, bright globe of her breast gleam out beneath the silk and, like a man waking from one dream to the next, more compelling, he moved, his new links dappled by shadows, and took her in his arms.

"Zoë, oh Zoë," he said.

They stood there and he felt her heart beating hard against him and she was cool yet warm against him, and through his sudden joy came the small thought: how different it is, this thing of meaning . . . This tenderness. He held her gently.

"Why did you come?" she said.

"To bring—" He abandoned one pretense and changed the truth a little and said, "Because of you, of you . . . You are trembling."

"Yes."

"Are you afraid?"

"I was, but now—"

"What were you frightened of?"

"To know why you came."

"Why did you *think?*"

"Never mind now." He did not look, he had his eyes closed, but he knew there was her smile of mischief. He smiled too.

"About the Carousel? And your doings there? That?"

She trembled again, and he thought she might cry.

"Don't speak of it any more, Zoë."

Truly he had forgotten it, but the thought of it now again brought a heat of anger. This and the hurting awareness of her, closed-pressed, the length of her lithely up against him in the yellow night, one bare foot on his boot, had him standing hard against her. And he drew her face about and his mouth was against her hair and he sought her lips. They trembled and her whole body trembling set him suddenly afire and the fierce feeling came to his arms and his mouth burned closer onto her, forcing her head back. The touch of her, soft, and the cool smoothness of her fired his wanting and he crushed her roughly and he felt her stiffen to resist. He felt terror growing in her, and she twisted, crying, "Bohemond!"

Her head turned from his mouth, avoiding its burn. He kissed her arm, her shoulder, his anger growing, and as he bent, she turned from him, and the two soft ropes of her braids fell apart from her neck and the slave-mark lay revealed, faintly pink in the yellow moon. He pressed his lips there fiercely and his blood pounded through him, pounded against the soft sough of the sirocco and her cries.

He gathered her up as easily as a pillow and turned, with her moving in his arms, to look into the hard eyes of Mihera Falloc.

"Oh!" said Zoë as she was let down upon the flagstones. "Oh, Oh!" she kept saying as without a word the two men closed in the half-light of the room.

"Son-of-a-pig! Whoreson!" Mihera said, deep in his throat as they went at each other in the scuffling dark. Bohemond had fended the first blow by dropping Zoë, and now they exchanged the punishment equally, and Zoë winced each time as the thud of fist on face, on ear, on chin shattered the stillness and seemed, as she watched, to disturb the shadows like rocks thrown into still water. She kept calling their names.

"Bohemond! Mihera! Oh!" She was on her feet and as they moved, great shadows in the dark, she moved with them, calling, "Bohemond! Mihera!" She was crying with despair.

They struggled up against the casement and she could see their faces an instant, Bohemond's calm, looking cold at Mihera as they gripped each other, and Mihera livid, his face red, his stiff hair swinging before his eyes and his veins rising in his neck.

Zoë felt sick. "Oh, stop it, Mihera, Bohemond! *Stop!*" She was wailing it now and the tears coursed down her cheeks. This was hideous, and, as she heard something behind, she turned and saw a shape tall in the door. The guard.

"Oh!" she wailed again, the full import of things dawning now, and as the guard came, others, aroused, came tumbling in and the fight ended in scuffling and holding and a string of oaths from Mihera. She stood by the bed and screamed, "Get out, all of you! *Get out! Get out!*"

Scarcely heeding her, they all moved toward the door, some one holding Mihera and another Bohemond, and through the door an instant the shape of old Berthe showed, her face like death and her old hair blowing stiff in the storm on the wind-swept parapet, and then the door banged to, and there was stillness again. Thoughts raced of the palace buzzing and the Count angry with punishments and the women whispering, and somewhere she heard gleeful laughter as of fiends or women laughing, and she threw herself on the bed. The brand-mark on her neck kept throbbing, and it seemed to her it was being seared again in the light of the yellow moon.

BROTHER BASIL, kneeling by the west transept of St. James, was having difficulties. A midnight chapel-watch, austere, stone-still and striped with a quiet moon is hard on anyone save saints, worried wives, and those who have mortal sins to keep them from natural slumbers. One could pray for all such unfortunates, of course . . . charitable orisons . . . Brother Basil tried.

The great storm had passed, leaving a pall of quietness all about, like a felon who, fleeing, drops a muffling cloak on the thing of his mischief-doing. The dire events that had marred the night before—no sign of them now, here in chapel-peace. Brother Basil dozed.

No thing stirred. The stiff backs of the four young men at vigil-watch were like candle-shafts, their white mantles wrinkleless, their swords upheld. Faint gules of light from the clerestory round, the intermittent song of a restless nightingale hard by the half-open sanctuary door—only with these did the moonlight mingle. Brother Basil slept.

The squire Bohemond was getting tired. Such an exercise was torture after the busy day they had given him. The Count's reprimand had been first, and he had expected that. The stern confessor too he had expected and the prayers recited in the cathedral, for his future mending. But the penance—the penance had completely shaken him. Out in Castletown where the Arabs kept beasts for the *fondaks,* or camel-caravans, was a stable that once had housed a Christian altar-stone, a chapel turned to a camel-stall by the scornful Turk. This he was put to clean, a labor of filth, like the Baron Hercules', but performed less for honor than for shame—a fine spectacle for all Palermo. The thing had appalled Mihera, who, when the tale was out, had nothing but praise for the affair in the tower room. Young Falloc had lingered at the stable door all day, his face contorted in sympathy for his friend, and when it was done, had given Bohemond a marvelous peace-gift, a heavy sword, of Viking origin, with a silver serpent coiled about the hasp. It was very old, very heavy, and re-damascened by an expert armorer in the marts of Castletown. It had been called by its ancient wielder, according to legend, by the name Bayart, Mihera said. Bohemond, thrilled, would have none of the new brand sent down from

Salerno with Borsa's, which, though coming with Guiscard's good wishes, was from the personal armory of the Lombard woman.

Now Bohemond held the serpent brand, pondered the hapless day, and felt his arms grow weary. How tired one became! How could Jordan, with only one arm hale, endure it, even?

Restless, he glanced sidewise at the others. Squire Borsa dozed. Squire Jordan faintly smiled. Squire Mihera looked bored, and a little irritated. So Bohemond turned back again, sighed, and thought his clothes still stank a little.

It was then that he heard the noise. They all heard. Not the snores— Brother Basil had been sounding forth for some time now—but a new sound, bruiting faintly like a small snake. Bohemond turned a stiff neck toward the sanctuary door and frowned. A small hand beckoned there and a pert face peered about the edge. The hand called again, and the face made a face at Bohemond. Three squires chuckled. Bohemond put down his serpent-headed sword.

Continuing snores were an assuring accompaniment to his soft, light-stepping boots as he moved to the sanctuary entrance and slipped, a husky wraith, to the moonlit yard. Three swords shook a little with the muffled tumult on the sanctuary steps.

She stood, breathless and a little tentative, in the sand that was drifted there among the tombs. He thought for a moment she might run away again.

"What are you *doing* here, Zoë? And how did you come?"

She spoke quickly, "None keeps the Bower tonight—all is confusion there. You heard of old Berthe?"

"Dead in her couch this morning? Yes."

"And you heard of *me*, Bohemond? Did you hear what will happen to *me?* A convent, north someplace . . . Near Monte Cassino . . . Awful . . ."

He laughed softly.

"Do you think I'd know *all* the news around here? I with my stable-duties?"

"Oh, Bohemond!" she groaned. "What a night it was, and ours the very worst of it! That's why I came. I'm filled with humility for it, Bohemond, and I'm sorry . . . When I heard of your task . . . Oh, Bohemond. Hideous . . ." She hid her face in her hands, but quickly drawing them away again said, "But it was mostly *your* fault, of course! If you weren't such a beast about it!"

He lifted her face. He saw several things there, but none of them humility. He became quizzical.

"Tell me—what did you want, after such a welcome? That we should sit to a bowl of gingergal and gossip?"

"I won't *talk* about it, Bohemond!"

"You broached it."

"Yes, to say I was sorry. Now don't be beastly."

"And what do you hope for from such a beast but what you get, aye?"

She made as if to go, but he caught at her hand, chuckling.

"All right, minx, we won't talk about it."—But when she was still again—"Though I *do* think the Count shows wisdom in the convent plan. Presently you'll emerge a grand'demoiselle, and catch a fine cock for your night-trysts, respectably as you want it, in the bonds of wedlock!"

She ignored the raillery, for something else was in her craw.

"Oh, Bohemond, you speak as if—as if I won't see you again—as if it were a foregone fact . . ."

"Maia Torre is *quite* a fact, minx."

"Now Bohemond, don't talk like that! *You'll* live, and in time we'll meet again . . . won't we?"

She saw his forehead crease, his eyebrows rise a little in the moonlight.

"I guess it's my ears I can't trust, because my memory's good, and I recall my repulsiveness keenly spoken of lately, here and in the tower room!"

"Oh, don't stiffen your neck!"

She stamped her foot, and in the sand leaves rustled, the mingled residue of the storm and the finished summer. She looked about apprehensively. The old moon caught her gaze a moment and bemused her.

"Well, then," she said to his cool silence, "I wish you fortune at Salerno, and I pray my orisons go with you through the gates of— Won't we be kissing goodbye?"

"I thought it scarcely your custom to ask first, Zoë. Did I scare the sweet method away?"

But she would not kiss that mouth with the proud, closed look on it. She leaned her head instead against his breast—a moment up to his face. Her cheek was cool, and then he felt a warm tear flow between their faces. His arms went up, but she turned and walked quickly through the tombs, her sandals rustling a little in the leaves.

He stood there a moment, then slipped once more to the darkling chapel. With a sidelong look at the slumbering churchman, he knelt, took the sword Bayart in his hands, and turned his eyes to Heaven . . .

Brother Basil stirred by the wall, starting from dreams of rat and busy worm, dreams where old Berthe and other dubious acquaintances he remembered piously had prominently figured. He shivered, suddenly chilled.

The four sword blades, still stiff on the sanctuary steps, glowed faintly pink with the first hint of a busy Sunday morning.

BOOK 3

MONSTERS OF SALERNO

CHAPTER IX

Maia Torre

"HE *CAN'T* GO IN THERE like this! 'Seyes—it's *murder*, Falloc!"

Duke Robert sat his mount at the walls of high, pink-bastioned Salerno and stared at the broad back of Bohemond gradually disappearing up the steep street that led to Salerno Palace and, only some ways further, to Maia Torre.

The great gates banged to. Bohemond was gone. Big Hugh kicked his stallion closer to his liege.

"I don't *understand* you, messire! A fine young fellow like that!" He spat explosively. "Excepting my own Mihera, there's none I've seen fitter to wear a knight's belt—and he'll be dead before it's soft to his ribs, most likely. Why? All because you refuse to let us ride in and *take* the town, and be damned to Prince Gisolf and his firebrands! What if it *is* Lady 'Gaita's birth-town he threatens to raze? What if that plague-pocked brother of hers *does* char to cinders with it? And I doubt if he will!" He snorted in chance unison with his horse. "I doubt if he *will!* Five months sitting at this town—when all we have to do is scale the walls, or sneak through a postern and she's ours . . . God knows the starved dastards inside are good and ready to show the white . . . I tell you, Robert, you're losing prestige over this. Nobody keeps the watches any more, or shines a shield, or edges a brand—nobody.

And Geoffrey Ridelle gets drunk every night now, he's so disgusted! I say it doesn't *lay* right . . . Don't we recall how you were before Palermo? Sweeping the lousy Turk aside like chaff and leading the charge yourself to capture Castletown? What does it signify—this damned delaying, negotiating, playing hostages with your own blood-son, to let fat Gisolf give up like the gentleman he's never been?"

"*You* know what the reason is, Hugh. . . . My wife."

"Hmph! It's time we found out, I think, what kind of army we're fighting in—Norman or Lombard!" Hugh ventured, rolling his huge eyes sidewise at his liege.

Duke Robert shifted in the saddle; he put a lean, hard chin a little wearily in his hand.

"I don't know, Hugh," he said absent-mindedly, "I don't know."

He was silent, gazing at the panorama of the town, at the long beach fronting a dark green stretch of olive trees that ribbed the perfect harbor; at the fertile slopes flanking it, where trees and vines bloomed yearly with the kind Italian sun; at the lofty wild-lands up beyond where the world heaved to heaven and delved to earth in such rugged ways that nothing habited there, save boar, elk and the fierce little black-horned roebuck, dear to the heart of the hunter.

"You see, Hugh," Robert said, "I *like* this town. I don't want it burned by that damned Lombard if we enter by force. I'd half a mind to settle here, make it my capital instead of Melfi, as it's high time to do, away from those murderous vassal-lords of mine. I'd hoped for peace and quiet and a little respectability for my last days . . ."

Last days. Peace and quiet. Hugh smiled in his grizzled grey-blond beard. Guiscard might be sixty-ish, but all said, he looked half-a-score less and had lost none of the insatiability he had beforetime. But Hugh listened respectfully enough.

"I've *tried* to do right," Robert was going on. . . . "I thought I'd earned a little credit . . . I've tried to bring peace and order to my lands and not oppression . . . I've tried to be generous with tithes, go to mass, take the sacraments . . ."

Now Hugh surmised what pricked, and he gave no quarter on it.

"And are you regarded as a just, pious and well-meaning prince, messire, for all these admirable reasons?

Robert snorted. "Hardly! Excommunicated—plague afflict that Hildebrand . . . And now, for this affair, my wife's not speaking to me . . . Bah!" He sighed prodigiously. "Come along, Hugh . . ." Then abruptly, "Did you see what a fine lad he is though?"

"Who?"

"My *son*, Marc Bohemond! Did you see the look of him? Magnificent! My most felicitous achievement, y'might say, and now I'm like to

lose him . . . But by God, *that* I won't! I've got to think of something . . . Come along!"

Out on the sea the Norman navy sat. Stout ships—a thousand gats
and a hundred hulking dromons—all bulging with men-at-arms. Five
months now, sitting out on the glittering sea, stewing like pots of
grunions in the windless Gulf. Guiscard and Falloc boarded the
barge that lay in the shallows like a flat-nosed skate. The bargeman,
without a word, pushed off truculently, as though watching skies he
had once sailed better sea-craft under. Guiscard had dismounted and
stood at the rail. He was frowning about doubtfully. There were
ragged lines in this craft, filthy decks, everything neglected. He
cleared his throat and made plain to the ancient that the barge displeased him.

"Those cables," he said, "they badly need looking to."

The pilot turned, observed the lines, looked at Robert, and spat to
the sea.

"Sometime," he said.

Robert inhaled, sniffed, snorted.

"Mend those lines *today!*" he shouted. *"Now!"*

"Aye, aye, sir," said the bargeman, but not very brisk, and Guiscard
looked at Hugh, who elaborately gazed outward at the still, still sea.

When after a somewhat silent ride they came alongside the flag-ship
Imola, saw the mounts stowed, and scrambled up on deck, Guiscard
tried to feel a little better, tried to think that soon, tonight maybe, the
Salerno tocsin would ring, the gates swing forth and Gisolf walk out
surrendered as the compact was. But even as he looked back, the high,
white-wattled burg of Maia Torre at the heights of Salerno where
the pink walls met struck his eyes like a blow.

Guiscard knit his brow, drew up his bearded lips in a worried
grimace and shuffled down to the hold of the *Imola*.

As he and Hugh walked into the close, smoky cabin-hall, he saw
the ship's company was already at mess—without waiting. His family
—Sigelgaita, his many daughters, his three sons—Guy, little Robert,
and next to his lady the dark, thin Borsa—these sat above the salt, his
Norman retainers below. And this was not a thing of rank. This had
gone on for weeks now, an unspoken feud between his household and
his men, a silent war in the cabin of the *Imola*.

His men looked up respectfully enough as he came, but they all
appeared sullen and unutterably bored. And Geoffrey Ridelle, he
saw, was drunk again, stabbing at the salt-fish on his plate as if it
lived.

At the dais-head the children stared at him, openly hostile. It was
obvious they were taking sides again. Borsa's glance glinted in his thin,
foxy face. Knight's samite scarce improved *him*, Guiscard thought

suddenly. Seeing the look on his wife's face, he attempted no word, but slid to the bench beside her on the dais . . .

Strong-minded women!

Sometimes, Robert thought, playing with his food, child-wives were a good idea. Quite often, lately, he wondered if he had heaped only coals on his head for abandoning Albarada so long beforetime . . . Not that the lady was inarticulate, even now—far from it! Wife to Richard the Seneschal and after his death to the powerful lord, Roger of Pomerada, she nevertheless maintained a sort of mental bigamy, as far as Guiscard could figure. It was awkward, for instance, to sit at mass in Melfi and hear the Chaplain announce new monastery grants, new charters, a new fund granted by Lady Albarada of Melfi and Pomerada, *wife to Duke Robert!* And in other ways the good lady had vengeance, unbeknownst, Robert thought sometimes. For in Sigelgaita he had met his match, in love and in war, but in times like this they were ice and fire, flint and steel, and the two of them seemed blown through hell on the wind of their own vituperousness. Damn. It was getting on his nerves.

The board was spread with a good mess, for sea-fare: mullions, sand-dabs, mead and pulty-cakes. But Robert looked at it and his knife drooped in his hand. The cabin had suddenly become the donjon-hole at Maia Torre. Even the guttering torches, lashed to the bulkheads with stout leather thongs, began to bother him. Smoke, straps and smouldering fire. He watched Borsa sprinkle salt in the cut of fish he had opened with his knife, and his stomach turned. He became fascinated by sounds of gulls at the ship's hull, screaming. The sweat had risen on his face.

Sigelgaita should have been still. She generally was nowadays at times like this. But she unfortunately elected to incline her fine head to Borsa's and to say in a tone passing sweet—"Won't you, son, dear, have some honey for your cakes?"

" 'Steeth!" The Duke roared. "Let me out of here!"

The whole company turned and stared, in time to see the Duke spring up, curse at her ladyship and place the ducal paw in her ladyship's face as she rose in alarm. She sat down again, hard, and, "Robert!" she cried in her strange, harsh voice, "where are you going?"

Her husband, already looking happier, made answer.

"To see to things, my sweet. Battle-lines, charges, and a few of the other niceties—that damned brother-in-law of mine, for instance!"

Under the salt, Hugh Falloc's big bug-eyes were bigger still. His large mouth fell open on its way to a grin. Farther down, Ridelle had risen from his place. "*Aoi, aoi!!!*" he shouted for the first time in months, and the place became bedlam. Men-at-arms reaching for swords, helms and war-pikes, making for the cabin stairs.

Guiscard had stalked to the deck; and in a trice the cabin belonged to Sigelgaita and her brood, with one exception. Geoffrey had been caught incommoded. With his shield-thong about his hips and his baldric on his arm, he nearly sliced the back of his neck with the nose-piece of his helm which he'd put on backwards. He turned at the bulkhead, put his thumb between his teeth and flipped it at her before clambering up the gangway to his brothers-in-arms.

Borsa pulled a piece of half-chewed fish from his mouth to say, "Lord, Madame! The Duke my father *was* perturbed, wasn't he? And all because of Bohemond. It is plain who'll be favored hereabouts from this day on!"

"Zut, Roger, you thistlehead! You don't know what you say!"

The Duchess Sigelgaita was very white, paler than ordinary, and she was breathing hard, like a fine, high-bred Lombard mare, at bay.

"I do not care for chess, Prince Gisolf. I've indifferent skill at the game. I never play it."

Bohemond shifted his knees at the tabouret between them. He felt anger choke off what fear he had, and render him suddenly articulate.

"*Besides,* Prince Gisolf, there was the question, as I came here, of—"

"Surrender?"

Gisolf of Salerno laughed, very pleasantly, but save for that one word, did not deign to touch further on it. He was fat, and except for small, light-colored eyes with black edges about the irises, there was nothing, at first glance, unusual about him. "Is this the young man?" he had said, emerging from behind an iron bowl full of flame-tipped cactus of the south, which, with other green and colorful pot-plantings, filled his airy solarium where Bohemond was presented. "Is this the young man, then?" he had said, and invited him to sit. He spoke excellent French, wore a cream-white, hide-belted robe on his stout frame, and was balding. Here was no madman, no twisted monster, no freak. He looked like a very jolly, and not inappropriately mundane, monk.

It was queer now to think of the starving, suffering town—Bohemond had just now witnessed the horrors of the long-sieged, foodless city as he passed to the palace. It was strange, too, to think of the grim place above and of the Amalfitan prisoners tortured there and driven thence daily to the fields outside to work like oxen, whipped raw against the plow-handles. He sat uneasily on a Greek circule beside the divan.

"Now, young man," Gisolf said, pushing his fat sides deeper into velvet cushions, "I would know more! How came *you* to be the hostage?"

Bohemond skipped the truth for a brief lie. It seemed like a long rigmarole to enter upon; he had not told his father the full details of the thing by preference, and he had no slightest reason to undertake the full truth here. "The winner of the Winter Lists in Sicily," he said merely.

"*Jousting*," said Gisolf with a world of scorn. "Here we prefer to *race* the steeds, not ride them to death in mock war. It is strange to think how even here in our far-removed South you Frenchmen cling to the battle-games, for all the world like continentals. Strange. And all that you find here of the mighty East affects you not. Very strange . . ." He fell to a reverie, his huge jowls working. "But," he resumed with a pudgy finger by his nose, "I find myself highly interested in you second crop of Normans!" He leaned across the tabouret and touched Bohemond delicately. "You are a splendid specimen."

The strange, dark-edged eyes seemed to hypnotize. Bohemond felt like a bright bird held by a serpent's eye in some tropic glade. He had been thinking, too, that the Prince had not inquired for even bare statements of his identity, let alone the seals and proofs-of-hostage he came supplied with.

The Prince smote a clapper.

"Sergex—the board, now, and we'll try a game."

And Bohemond's demurring had been in vain, and his efforts to bring them to the point of issue had produced nothing by the commentary.

"You Normans—loving the tilt and such contests, but under it all more tradesmen than knights, always wanting to get to business! Especially the de Hautevilles. I abhor that in the de Hautevilles, with the other things . . . What pawns, ivory or teak?"

Bohemond felt his neck go hot, and the last sweetmeat felt like dust in his mouth. With his heart pounding he chose the white figures and set them silently.

"You first," invited Gisolf.

Scarcely attending, Bohemond moved his knight to the field. The Prince chuckled.

"Oh, no, young Bohemond . . . I reject and place a counter gambit," he said, duplicating the move from his own side.

The sudden and very casual use of his name so unnerved Bohemond that he had consciously to stiffen his fingers as he made the next play with his rook. So. Gisolf's spies had all the facts scouted, and Gisolf's plans were more carefully laid than this game of chess. The thing that kept going through Bohemond's mind was the part they always related about the case of the son of Maurus. *At first the Monster of Salerno treated him honorably, made him dine with him and often invited him to play at tables. But one night he had retainers tear him from the board* . . . Bohemond felt like an actor in some sort of nightmarish miracle play like ones he had seen at Palermo Cathedral, of devils and their activities in hell. Salutary to the soul only if in the audience, he thought grimly. Like a stage-struck mime, he had eagerly sought the lead in this one . . . Mother of God, what a fool. He chanced on a reflection of himself in one of Gisolf's flower-laden jars. *"A splendid specimen."*

Gisolf had retired to the deep fog of the chess enthusiast. Bohemond studied the room, the possibilities . . . the window-leads, smashed with a vase to let a man through, and a stepping, leaping progress thence to that chest and casement . . . There was a cough. Bohemond, emerging with difficulty from these speculations, applied himself to the game, but was presently thoroughly kinged for his clumsiness and the challenge had apparently vanished for his host.

"Look once more sidewise like that, my boy, to please an old fellow."

Bohemond frowned and turned his head stiffly enough.

"Yes. The head—perfect." He cleared his throat again and suddenly swept the pawns from the table to the floor. They scattered across the flags halfway through the solarium, scudding among the shrubbery with the violence of the gesture. Bohemond stiffened at this first hint of the nobleman's true unbalance. But Gisolf was smiling.

"You must see our town this morning . . . Of course, there's but one place you must visit to see my finest interests in full play. That would be my personal adjunct to Salerno University, which is vested above, in the Citadel. My efforts there have been much slandered, but they do not know . . . Contumely . . . Behindtime . . . The ignorant, you understand, who lay the name of witchcraft to knowledge and of madness to curiosity. Only this year we have found, we surmise, what causes head pains in the region of the right brow and through the cheekbones . . . Obstruction of the humors? Thickening of the blood? No. Away with their pills and cathartics . . . It is a narrowness of the nose . . ."

He leaned across and drew a fine, cool line on Bohemond's features. "There. Especially in fine, high-bridged beaks like your own! By laying such areas exposed, we have been pleased to observe . . . But come, you can't imagine. You don't understand, not seeing, and my chatter . . . Your face, my boy, is only *politely* interested, if *that!* Ah, well, I fatigue the young, lately. But come, you shall see . . . "

The ascent to the Castle was a rather long piece by a narrow path edged with tall, sharp cypresses set a cubit apart. Beside them stood huge, armed cuirasseurs. Above them, the great wattled gate was swinging out.

As Bohemond climbed, aware of the Prince beside him puffing, his legs felt suddenly like water and his spirits began to fail. But not because of Gisolf. Fear, dread of torment, yes. He was painfully aware of these matters, haunted by things he'd heard. He meant to give honorable account, God helping, and die as a knight must. These were known things, things learned and trained for. But to be put to this doom by his own father—that was what crushed.

His mind flashed to the past, to his first and last meeting with Robert Guiscard. No place for him then in his father's city; no welcome for him now but death—a bitter favor. With his thumb he felt the seal-ring on his middle finger. Apparently the ring meant nothing; his hopeful dreams meant nothing. Guiscard's promises—and here he drew the ring off—meant nothing. He heard the small tinkle as he tossed the talisman away.

"What are you about?" cried Gisolf, startled by the move.

Cuirasseurs had stepped forth. Bohemond felt rough hands and the bite of gauntlets. But at the same time, an oath from Gisolf. "Hark!"

A sudden breeze had struck on the heights and with it from somewhere below and far, a strange tumultuous clamor. Gisolf had whirled, and within the hood of the cape he wore, Bohemond saw him whiten. Looking back upon the vista of the sprawling town, Bohemond observed nothing—only the gradual fall of roof-tops toward the shore, and far out, the Gulf with the winter sun hung high and reddish on the Norman navy.

"God help you!" the Prince said. "Your father is droll indeed, to choose this unimaginative moment." His pig eyes flashed. "Damn them! Not one of the dogs would sound the tocsin. They're *all* against me! Ah, but don't smile, boy!" (for Bohemond had not stifled his relieved grin) "here in the Castle it is otherwise! Here are my loyal countrymen. They've held out with me times unnumbered before you were born. And we'll do it again—especially—" he smiled. "Come, Marc Bohemond de Hauteville. The two of us shall instruct your father in the true hues of his folly." Instantly he sobered. "Come!"

A small stiletto showed at his sleeve-tip, and above them the archers had set their shafts. They proceeded between the bows as they had walked between the cypresses. But Bohemond's heart had lifted.

The Prince allowed Bohemond to precede him through the gate. The cuirasseurs, ranked behind, passed after. The gates slid shut, the bolts fell. This was the place they told of, notorious Maia Torre.

As Bohemond stood blinking in the harsh cold sunshine, the Prince resumed his hideous courtesy.

"We are faced to the winds, here—a pleasant place in summer, of course, but chilly on days like this. But we will presently be warmed as things accelerate."

Bohemond said nothing. He was staring at the right wall, to a covered colonnade that ran its full length. Under this eave-like shelter was a profusion of objects. No swords, pikes, maces—none of the usual castaways of castles like these—but instruments, shined to brilliance and hung straight and orderly on iron hooks. Fronting this array was a long table, a wheel and a Spanish arrangement he had heard of, called a *strappado*. It iced the bones to see them. But at the same time he turned to Gisolf and caught the small pig-eyes alertly probing him. *Damn,* he thought hotly, if I'll please his beastly loins by showing anything. He returned the Lombard's glance with a shrug and a stare. But presently, and in spite of steely resolution, he looked to the far side of the court and gasped.

A great barred cage was set out beyond the shelter of the rampart. It was filled, packed, jammed as a fowl-crate, with shivering, unclothed skeletons of men. They all looked ill, and the cage was filthy. The thought came that these must have been like this for some time—through the days and the cold, windy winter nights.

"Recalcitrants," said Gisolf. "The Amalfitan captives. They've been having their spleens cooled."

Bohemond's blood froze and at the same time he felt an overpowering urge to action. What fear he had known was forged to a hot anger, together with an irrepressible desire to help these wretches. He had never felt exactly like this before. It was all very well, for instance, to hear about Turks and how they tortured pilgrims on the way to Bethlehem—but mere hearsay failed to fire. But the Amalfi sufferers brought all such things to focus (the infidel could do no viler), and from this moment Bohemond felt himself alert, strong and ready for anything. *He* was not helpless. He was hale and unfettered, standing in the strong sun. Where were his wits? Where his fine skill and the good-luck-faith of a de Hauteville? He looked at the dull-eyed cuirasseur who stood guarding him, observing the fellow and noting, in his new sharpness, the key-ring hung to his baldric. And then, like Gisolf and the alerted garrison, he stood tensely waiting.

They could not see the Norman army masking the wall—but they could hear it. Shouts, commands, curses, the scrape of horses' hooves as they struck stone on the path about the Castle. And the sounds made Bohemond thrill and at the same time tremble, and he saw that the guard, now, was somewhat paled.

Prince Gisolf had climbed the wall by inside tower stairs. He stood there, his fat thumb hooked in his leathern girdle in which enormous amethysts were set, and these and his bald head glistened in the sun. He was smiling as though officially receiving the enemy, as if he had no fear. Courage or madness?

Then came Guiscard's voice.

"It's a long time, Gisolf, since the day I was flung from your hall. And now Salerno is mine—and it's a shame, since instead of enemies, we should be brothers."

"Salerno's yours, aye?" retorted Gisolf. "Then I take it you prepare yourself for the mortal screams of your son as you consummate this folly!"

There was silence. Then Bohemond heard the Duke say, *"You would not dare . . ."*

Gisolf merely laughed, his head and his huge shoulders bobbing eerily. "Make him ready," he called to the yard.

For some time now the Amalfitans had been gesturing to Bohemond, grimacing, telling him that which had already struck. As the guard with the key-ring came toward him, he lunged, and in one great effort the cuirasseur was on the ground, the key in his hand and himself across the courtyard at the cage with the key poised before the lock, while the prisoners called encouragement through their bars.

"Now!" he called up to the Prince. "Will you use some respect, please, in speaking to my father? Do you prefer his mercy, Gisolf, or the tender ministrations of these eager friends you've made? The first move of your soldiers will find the key turned, the cage opened, and these poor wretches free for a long-owed vengeance . . ."

Gisolf paled.

"Stand back, cuirasseurs," he called, and indeed the men were little inclined to action at this turn. Again there was Gisolf's dagger. Bohemond saw and expected it, and was crouching for the dodge, so that he was astonished to see Gisolf turn and the flash of the blade flying outwards from the wall. The subsequent tumult told him the Prince had struck his father.

But Guiscard called up:

"Don't touch him! Conduct him to the palace."

"Open the gate," cried Bohemond to the guards, "and send out the Prince ahead." And when they lagged, "Hurry!" he snapped. "Look alert there! Bring clothes and nourishment for the Amalfitans."

It was a sad procession that straggled down the hill. The angry warriors milled about Gisolf, pulling him this way and that, while Bohemond walked ahead with the litter-men and Guiscard's close followers who crowded around. Robert rolled and groaned, clutching his bleeding side where the Prince's blade had come out with its point missing. Hugh and Geoffrey were speaking to one another as they trudged down, half-hysterical. Geoffrey had a half-smile on his face and Hugh rebuked him.

"What are you grinning at, fool?"

"I was thinking how it was that time with him in the old days when we had to enter that monastery where the brethren had said us nay. Do you recall? Him on a bier like this with a dead cock under to make the smell of death?"

"Zut," said Hugh. *"This* is no time to think of *that . . ."*

"I do not mean it unseemly," said Geoffrey, his leathery face working to keep back tears, "I was only thinking of the old days and how it was . . ."

"Be still!" snapped Hugh, choking. "Shut thy mouth."

And the long, sad line swung down between the cypresses.

Guiscard should have died that night. That lance-point threatened his life for very labor. He bled so, was so agonized and finally so weak that undoubtedly he was ready to expire. The physicians said so. Guiscard tossed, the knights mourned, Sigelgaita dispatched a post to Rome. She announced his death and claimed the inheritance for Roger Borsa.

But Maurus Piereleone, old sea-lord of Amalfi, called a turn, producing his own bleeder, Jacoppo Poldi, the Italian leech. The leech labored, the knights prayed, and by the time the messenger returned (Hildebrand Gregory VII having embarrassed himself badly with an answering parchment confirming the Duchess' claims), the point was out, the wound closed, and Guiscard was on the mend. Piereleone's Poldi had worked a wonder.

During the time of the convalescence, good will spread among the company like wine. The false death report became a high theme to jest about, especially since Sigelgaita had long been the favorite butt of army humor. Even Gisolf was loosed from his lockup with his skin whole and allowed to escape to Rome, never to be heard of again but in country plays on "Monsteroso."

Bohemond meantime was in his glory. He spent most of his time in Guiscard's presence, and otherwise expanded the knightly joys, tilting, hunting and racing on the new horse Falade which Guiscard had given him. In the offing, when Robert should have sufficiently rested, were campaigns, captaincy and fresh honors, the two of them together. Bohemond rode the crest.

His friend Falloc had definitely chosen the sea. Over Sir Hugh's protests and Bohemond's chaffing, Mihera pressed plans to master a vessel under Piereleone. Bohemond opposed it, did everything possible to prevent it and did not actually believe it, until he was summoned aboard for a farewell meeting.

There, cloaked handsomely in his new white samite, he trailed Mihera over every quarter, young Falloc displaying rib, seam, and spar of the lateen-rigged, high-pooped craft.

"She's a fine ship, Mihera," he told him. "You'll prosper like a doge." But his congratulations held no warmth. He observed Mihera in the thick water-repellent deck-boots and his plain merchant's tunic with its short dirk stuck in a belt of marten-fur, and there seemed already to be worlds between them.

Mihera laughed at him. "Don't fret, Bo. We'll meet again, perhaps for high adventures—you a great lord, and I to transport your Lordliness to far-off places! By the way," he said, blushing for his abrupt and irrelevant change of subject, "has Zoë Ridelle had word of your luck at Maia Torre? I daresay she waits for something."

Bohemond started. "By God, no—but I see what you hint at! Write her, Mihera, with all my blessing!" While Mihera stood blushing, Bohemond tossed back his bright head and laughed. He was more every day his father's image.

"Well, good luck, Falloc," he said. "Good luck in everything."

"Good luck," Mihera rejoined, and as his friend vaulted lightly to the dock, *"Dex ais,"* Mihera called after in the ancient knightly way, but not loudly enough for de Hauteville to hear as he mounted Falade, waved, and spurred to the steep street.

CHAPTER X

The Convent of the Holy Revelation

MIHERA FALLOC proved much more communicative to Zoë by letter than he ever had been in person. Outside of the far-spaced and irregular visits of her father, Mihera's letters became the high moments in three years of exile at Holy Revelation, and she came to wait eagerly for his detailed and lively accounts of his travels and his news of home whenever he harbored there. She preferred his notes from Salerno, for certain reasons, but all of his precise, careful parchments were a welcome addition to the pool of news from the outside world to be added to those of the other young women, daughters of great lords whom these events touched.

"What news, Zoë?" they would say. "Of family? Of wars? Or maybe of love this time, aye?"

The letters had won her an immediate place in their vociferous esteem, and they lost no time in inviting themselves to visit her sometime soon in those romantic Sicilian scenes.

"Where *is* your father's hall?" the fat Walloon girl called Bertha inquired one evening.

"*Lord*, where indeed!" thought Zoë, a new hot emotion suffusing her checks as she swiftly ducked her head to re-read some half-seen reference on one of Mihera's parchments.

Guiscard has pressed on your father for his distinguished services, a castle behind the town, and my own sire and Sir Geoffrey hunt there daily, attempting, it seems to me, to empty the woods of all game around Burg Ughol.

"I think," said Zoë, after what had seemed a moment of judicious indecision, "that you would perhaps enjoy your visits best at our country place, at Burg Ughol . . . " (her tongue faltering as badly over the uncouth Lombard name as theirs did in the myriad intrigued repetitions of it as the rush-lights snuffed out to the convent bell).

Mihera was generous with his parchments then, but this fact did not make up to Zoë for its obverse. There was never a roll from Bohemond—not one word from young de Hauteville. And Zoë was

sixteen, full time, in that age, to begin to acquire the hard sense of
maturity, and be done with feckless dreams. But still, youth is invincible
and sometimes at night when the wind blew warm from the south, the
whisperings of the convent covey became as far-off music and the
shadows beyond the window-square were full of half-remembered pictures of herself and Bohemond—on horseback, in the wood, even (in
some fantastic fantasies) on Mihera's vessel, freed from the haughty
trappings of castles, courtships and ancestral halls.

As the months went on, other facts filtered to the shut-ins. There
was dramatic news from Rome, of Hildebrand Gregory VII and his
terrible quarrels with the German Emperor Henry. Eunice d'Este of
a wealthy Lombard house from the north was in sympathy with the
imperial rebel (it was gathered that her family was being amply reim-
bursed for their weighty alliance), and when Zoë ventured to defend
Hildebrand—

"What are *you* perking up about?" Eunice asked pertly. "You
Sicilians with your excommunicate Duke Robert?"

"Pope Gregory has rejected *Robert*, not Duke Robert *him*," Zoë
retorted. "Duke Robert knows how His Holiness is deceived on all
sides by lies of enemies!"

"And speaking of Duke Robert," winked talkative Bertha, "there
is rumor his first son is a veritable dream-prince and a feast to the eye,
aye, Zoë?"

Zoë knew the minx had taken a chance shot, since never had she let
his name be heard from her lips more often than any other, so that they
expected, and got, no special comment as they snuffed the lights and
continued the gossip about him and other far-famed young champions,
filling the darkness with their leashed enthusiasms and suppressed sighs
like bird-flutterings in the long, dark night.

The hint of war in their letters grew more imminent, until one day
Mihera wrote that Robert had made contact with the deposed Emperor
Michael of Byzantium who had supposedly fled to refuge in Calabria,
following a revolution in the City of Constantine. He had brought him
from his hiding in a Basilian monastery and with a great show of
arms was parading him through southern Italy while recruiting men
and weapons for an expedition to Asia Minor.

"So," said Eunice d'Este, "Duke Robert looks to Constantinople
and the Golden Horn. As my father wrote, he is a land-swallower."

"But listen to this!" said Zoë. "Abbot Desiderius has invited him
to bring his train to Monte Cassino and His Holiness will be there too!
There is to be a reconciliation!"

This was good news, news to cause a stir. For the singers of the
Nuns of the Revelation were often invited to attend the Masses for lay
celebrations like this.

"Do you think we shall really go?" someone asked.

"Indeed," came a voice from the door. It was Mother Superior with the night candle. After a flutter of feet and a snapping of bed-covers saw her charges each in her own couch, she smiled and said, "It is verily a happy day that the forces of Rome and the repentant Duke mend friendships at Monte Cassino. Our Church is in imminent danger from the presumption of the German Emperor and the Abbot is desirous to consummate this reconciliation and asks our prayers. Our choir will be present to sing the service. A great honor, one that you must ready for in all diligence. I must tell you to guard your health too, for that juncture. Just today a girl in the far wing fell ill with pox, a mild spell, such as children get, but I hope it will not indispose you all. Pray God to spare you for that privileged day. *Pax Domini,* ladies."

Zoë Ridelle prepared for the occasion halfway between earth and heaven. What was for the others the mere anticipation of a lark and a holiday and a glimpse of the highly theatrical doings of the war-bent Sicilians was for her condensed and intensified into the one irresistible conjecture that Bohemond would be there. Mirrors were forbidden to the dormitory walls but brief shared glimpses into the smuggled substitutes that appeared nightly in the glow of rush-light told Zoë that she looked some better than beforetime—slimmer-lined, taller and more grown-up. To be more grown-up was the *main* wish. But how could you, in this bevy of convent squealers? Zoë stayed aloof from them as much as possible on the last days before the occasion, as a sort of repeated rehearsal in being sanguine and serene.

And there was another reason. At first she thought it only a spring cold that made her sneezy and filled her eyes with rheum. But she suspected the pox, and sure enough, the very day of departure there were spots on her arms when she made her morning toilet. Her face was yet innocent of pustules, and she quickly put on her shift before the rest noticed. Sir Geoffrey had sent her a new gown whose best feature was the new French-split sleeves, but these she sewed up without a thought. There was a bad moment in the convent yard beside the litters, when Mother Superior glanced hard at her hot face before giving her a place. Between this fright and the fast-mounting fever, Zoë was somewhat dazed so that she landed on the interior cushions quite precipitately and drew "What a clod-foot!" from fat Bertha, whose toes she had crushed. It was a distinct relief when finally the mule-drawn carriages rolled off for the long bumpy climb up Monte Cassino.

The new basilica at Monte Cassino was a magnificent fusion of Greek and Roman art not seen in Italy since the break-up of the Empire. Abbot Desiderius was very proud, and for this occasion had hung the triforium arches with a profusion of banners and sacred tapestries, and in the nave the bier of the founder Benedict was covered with fresh wreaths and surrounded by tapers burning.

It was high noon when finally the great bells set up their iron din and the huge doors opened—those huge, bronze portals brought from Alexandria, with the twin reliefs of Adam and Eve and the Serpent coiled upright between them holding the golden fruit, a design to be seen anywhere in Christendom, yet startlingly graphic when worked out in bronze and silver three times the natural size of man. The Abbot Desiderius entered first between them, carrying a footed tree-cross with branched tapers, then hesitated to allow the stooped, slender Hildebrand Gregory VII to precede him, the Pope clad in a white serge cope with a bronze cross-bar staff and high pointed tiara. A whole massed wave of Benedictines, their black-and-white habits looking crisp and fragile against the magnificence of bronze and stone, swept up after Gregory, escorting him to enthronement on the high pontifical seat.

The clergy ranged itself in the side-stalls bounding the altar, and the lay-congregation filed in.

From the side of the nave in the shadows of the multi-leaded transept, the young noblewomen of the Maidens' Choir of Cisterna sat behind high parclose screens. Here, without being seen, they had a latticed but adequate view of all the ceremonies. Duke Robert de Hauteville, grey, lean and straight as a drawn sabre, led the lay group, escorting a dark-skinned, monkish-looking little man who, from his long, purple-silk tunic and festooned crown was taken to be the deposed Michael. No aspect of his own proclaimed him kingly; Guiscard was minding him diligently, with all the respect and dignity befitting a rightful emperor of New Rome, but it did no good. The little Greek strutted beside Guiscard like a banty-cock beside an eagle.

It was the next comer who attracted notice, the tall officer with the narrow hips and broad shoulders. He affected a Byzantine tunic-and-capelet of golden mesh, whose theatrical lustre stole not one whit of thunder from the young man wearing it. He carried a round Greek shield emblazoned with the Imperial Eye, but his sartorial honor to Michael ended there; for thrust down from his baldric-belt was his own long sword, a weapon already celebrated in local balladry as the brand Bayart. A champion of more feudal skirmishes than many with thrice his years of wars, the young prince was quickly identified in the motley audience as Bohemond de Hauteville.

Hildebrand looked worn. Guiscard, as he knelt before him, though actually his senior by far, looked really younger. The Duke was attired plainly and it was rumored that today he was bearing the link hauberk against his naked skin, a proceeding of great torture tried only by the strong.

Hildebrand spoke out in a careful voice in which his habitual lisp was scarcely to be heard.

"You have conquered all enemies, Robert. You have secured wide lands. But it is not for that reason that we pardon you. The Church concerns itself not with those mighty for the life in time, but with those intending truth for all eternity. Do you pledge yourself henceforth to league with truth, Duke Robert?"

"I do."

"Do you pledge, even to the detriment of your own triumphs, to go to the aid of truth, if need be?"

"I *do*, your Holiness! Should I conquer all the world—I *do!*"

Robert was like a bride. Like a bride full of resolve, he humbled himself at Gregory's feet. Everyone in the basilica was deeply moved to witness the laying of so powerful a sword at the feet of an unearthly Baron.

The one exception to the storm of profound feeling was Hildebrand. From the back of Robert's bronzed neck the Pope raised his black eyes to scan narrowly the aspect of the supposed ex-Emperor Michael. The little Greek also knelt, with his head bowed down, and Hildebrand's sharp glance took in the area behind the crown where the crescent-shaped tonsure worn by Basilian monks was not quite evenly faded into hair. Gregory Hildebrand's severe thin mouth tightened. Was this little creature really the former Basileus of the great city on the Golden Horn or some *new* play-thing of Robert's bag of tricks? The presence of the Holy Spirit, so likely to hover near popes for matters of faith and morals, was in Gregory's case accustomed to illuminate earthly matters also, and he had to hold himself to keep from publicly remonstrating with his sly penitent on this new possibility of a bogus Michael. But to reform Robert in *all* things was a major projection of small hope, and remembering the last raving letter from Henry of Germany, the fiery little Cluniac for once exercised the less towering virtue of prudence over zeal and tendered to Robert the pontifical *absolvo* from his long-borne interdiction.

And though now, from behind the parclose screen, the Maidensingers from Cisterna broke into high, meticulously trained paeans of joy and thanksgiving, poor Zoë Ridelle had long since abandoned the resolve to sing. Her ears rang and her eyes smarted with a veritable torch-breath of fever, and her whole world was becoming more and more strange. She had discovered her father in the group of retainers below; Bohemond was standing directly in front of him, and the ubiquitous lead-glass figure of George-and-the-Dragon was in the central round window over both their heads. All three had commenced to be mixed up and oddly confused in her vision, so that she sometimes ducked her head to stare dazedly at Bertha the Walloon in front of her who was wearing a great beaded girdle of red wool gauded with jewels which spelled out the legend, *"Amor vincit omnia."*

The next time she looked over at Bohemond he seemed to change and wave and tremble as if he were under water. And St. George was sometimes in the window, sometimes not. He— Zoë swayed against Bertha.

"Will you mind yourself!" that young lady snapped.

Once more Zoë referred to St. George. His blue-glass eyes moved, rolled, then deliberately stared down, and his right red gauntlet lifted to his saintly lips, which pursed up and went, "Sh-hhh!"

She must have replied to St. George with something disrespectful, for the Walloon this time poked her in the ribs. She felt herself slip against Bertha's shoulder into sweet, sweet rest.

While the Cisterna maidens' choir was transported back to Divine Revelation, to resume its hum-drum life, while Pope Gregory participated in a great *fête* with Guiscard for the reconciliation and renewed vows, and while Guiscard with his war-train went on gathering lances for the campaign to be later waged against the Byzantine usurper in Asia Minor, Zoë Ridelle lay ill in a private apartment in the infirmary-wing of the monastery, perhaps the first young woman ever to pass a week at Monte Cassino. Felicity, the lay portress from Divine Revelation, had been left here to tend her and to administer dwales and sleeping potions at the direction of Jacoppo Poldi, now chief leech to Guiscard, whom the Duke had lent to Geoffrey Ridelle for his daughter's illness. The two men, together with Hugh Falloc, had absented themselves from Guiscard's retinue for a spell and remained on the wind-swept monastery hill fidgeting out Zoë's pox.

Dr. Poldi had applied as much care and diligence to this matter as he did to his tasks of lance wounds and other battlefield surgery, of which he had had much practice since taking up with the Duke's service. The technique of keeping the patient well drugged (save for certain periods when broth, gruel and other digestives were pressed on the drowsy patient) was in order that she should not claw her face and perhaps mar her beauty, which was much commented upon by Dr. Poldi. This enthusiasm did him no harm in the eyes of the fond Sir Geoffrey.

Dame Felicity indulged in her sourest mood in this exile on the mount, shared as it was with Southern brigands. (The leech was *ipso facto* not included in this category, and was the only one she spoke to for the whole time.) Zoë had risen in Felicity's opinion not one whit, for her connection with the two roughs who watched, quarreled, drank and mooned at the bedside.

About the fifth day of Zoë's session the whole corps bunched at the bed while Messer Jacoppo plied his young patient with spirits. It was naturally some trouble to bring her from the spell.

"What's amiss, Poldi?" breathed Ridelle. "Lord help you, if you've done anything—you won't be leaving here alive!"

"Calm yourself, Sir Geoffrey. It's been a long while. She'll respond presently."

"By God, the girl's pale!" worried Hugh, towering above him. "Why don't she rouse? What's up, you devil-dealing, black-magicking faker!"

Poldi did not deign to reply. "A little of that broth, Felicity."

"She'd be better without *everyone* craning at her, wouldn't she, doctor?" inquired Felicity with acid. Hugh Falloc's breath had been pumping down her neck for some time.

"Bah! Tend your task, woman!" barked Sir Hugh.

"See!" said Poldi. "We have her now!"

Zoë came up from the depths, swirled, went down and drifted up again, and opened her eyes to the circle of faces leaning over her.

"Ho, Father," she said weakly. "What a mess, aye?"

"Silence!" said Geoffrey.

"Yes, quiet, girl!" said Hugh. "Do y'want to strain yourself?"

"Silence nothing!" contradicted Poldi, his round face smiling down at her. "Outside of weakness and a rather short-rationed gullet, she'll *do*, now. *Ave Maria*, to hear you gentlemen talk you'd think she'd been carved with steel, instead of having nothing but a little child-pox!" And to Zoë, "We've kept you as good as asleep, sweetheart, so you'd not spoil that pretty face of yours! And a right winsome beguiler she *is* too, all pert curves and that saucy glance! By God, if I wasn't such a badly confirmed bachelor, Sir Geoffrey, I'd ask leave of you to woo her myself!" The little Italian withdrew from the circle with terse directions to Felicity on feeding, and prepared to go.

"Speaking of such things," asked Geoffrey suddenly, "is it then all right, Dr. Poldi, to discuss certain matters now, in her health, I mean? Will serious talk upset the girl?"

"Oh, no, Signor; go right ahead. I declare her hale. Meantime, while Sir Hugh arranges to escort the ladies again to Cisterna, there's a little matter of a carbuncle-letting for one of the good fathers for which the Abbot asks my services; and then we will join Duke Robert at Campobasso, so?"

"Right, Poldi, and many thanks." Geoffrey made a heartfelt courtly bow to science.

Hugh Falloc meantime was busy helping Zoë to sit up, plumping up pillows and chucking her paternally under the chin. "Now, pretty, mind what your papa says, and when this thing is done with the Emperor Michael or whatever-his-name-is, we'll all be with you at Salerno. It's fine there; there'll be dancing, parties—you'll see, chicken!"

And with a clumsy paw he once more poked her under the jaw-bone
and went to the door. "Mind your sire well!" he repeated mysteriously,
with a tremendous griddle of lines on his sun-blackened forehead, and
a grin on his wide mouth that made him look for all the world like a
giant attempting to ingratiate himself with a mouse.

"*Will* you leave off!" cried Geoffrey. "Give us privacy, will you?"
And finally with a stiff-necked Felicity caught up and propelled before
him, big Hugh disappeared through the oaken door.

Zoë was mightily mystified.

"What *ails* Sir Hugh, Papa?" She was already wolfing the plate
of stew Felicity had left her.

"Don't mind him," Geoffrey told her. His bright eyes had a serious
glint, and he fidgeted back and forth, with his hands locked behind.

"Zoë, my pigeon, listen. It's high time your convent days ended, so
when I return from this expedition, you will leave Cisterna and come
home with me."

"To Salerno?"

"Aye."

This seemed to please, and she went on eating with a look of interest for more he had to tell her. He hesitated with an indrawn breath,
then plunged without prelude.

"Sir Hugh has asked about betrothal arrangements between yourself and Mihera, and since it was agreeable to me he wished that I
should confirm *your* feelings on it."

Zoë pushed the dish aside and frowned up at him.

"Does Mihera know this?"

"No, he's at sea, but according to Maurus, will harbor this month.
I understand there've been letters between you."

She pulled at the counterpane.

"Papa, I've known Mihera all my life. We were children together
at Bull Joy and shared the same lesson-masters in Sicily. You know
that! We're like brother and sister!"

"Sister and brother don't commonly keep parchments between them
for three years running."

"You can *see* his letters if you like, Papa. All in my dormitory
read them . . . Travel, business, politics . . ."

"No love?"

"No love!"

"Poof! The lunk-head!"

"I have never shown reason for words of love . . ."

"Why *should* you! Not *your* place! But *he* loves *you!* No one could
miss it! *Sangre dex*, the boy's sunk!"

"Father!" said Zoë sharply. "I have no intention of wedding Mihera
Falloc!"

Geoffrey sat on the bed-edge and took her two hands in one of his, while with the other he spread her damp curls in a fan on the snowy bolster. "Come, pretty. We're off the subject. I'm speaking of marriage—a good, right marriage, where straightness and kindness is, and love comes later. *Affection*—not this poet-love, that the jongleurs rave about, this thing of songs, moonlight, and wispy nothings . . ."

Zoë pursed her lips and cornered her eyes at him. "But, Papa! You *yourself* have always sung of love as well as battle, no? And what of your *own* case, a short idyl of moonlight and this mad fight to the South, but to which you have been faithful these many years, with only a memory!"

"Now, Zoë! With your mother—that's different—as for the other foolishness, of songs and so forth, all bubbles and talk—and don't be like *me*, mignonne!"

She laughed, and he heard a new, grown-up, delicately arch laugh.

"Oh, but I *am*, Papa, I *am*! Don't you know that in Cisterna, they'll have none but *me* make their ballads and their miracles for feast-days?"

"Stop talking nonsense!" said Geoffrey, and his hard hand on hers came to hurt a little. "This betrothal with Mihera *must be! Think!* Don't you know I've no lands, money, anything to leave you? I am no longer young now, Zoë, and I mean to see you sound and safe. God is good. You've attracted a fine boy, knightly and rich to boot, though with marriage it's hoped he will incline to forgo this thing of trade."

"Oh," said Zoë, her pert mouth held in a straight line and her sea-blue eyes curved up at him in a sharpened glance. "So *Sir Hugh* hopes! And *that's* why he acted the wheedling father-in-law just now, and no doubt sits below biting his fingernails for the outcome of this talk! Well, disenchant yourselves, Father! I've no sheep's eyes for Mihera Falloc—or anyone else!"

"What do you mean, Zoë? If not Mihera, then it must be something else. And before we discuss this further, I have eyes and ears, and from stories out of Sicily, there was something between you and Guiscard's Marc Bohemond once, wasn't there? But of course, you understand . . ."

"I understand *everything*, Father! Three years in that conventical cage of female schemers has taught me a thing or two about love in the chivalry and who must bed with whom, for the good of the fief!"

"Hmph!" grunted Geoffrey, somewhat seared by his daughter's sharpness. "Look here, you lose out to none of 'em, Zoë! Your mother's blood, and mine too, back in Normandy, is as high-placed as anyone's, and both houses, by the way, have several times begged me to send you there . . ."

Zoë's eyes had hardened a little and Geoffrey for the first time sensed a rebellious sort of wild note in his daughter's personality that did not augur well.

"Zoë—the more I think of it, Normandy right now is the answer. I should have done this long ago but I refused altogether to give you up. It was a mistake, I see now, but perhaps we can mend it."

"By packing me off to Normandy?" She was horrified. "Oh no, Papa! Don't do anything as bad as that. Don't send me away!" She threw herself against his chest, preened his grizzled but still dapperly sharp mustache, and covered his scarred cheeks with kisses. "Take me down to Salerno, Papa, and we'll have a fine time together at your new hall, Burg Ughol . . ."

"My new hall—ho!" Geoffrey snorted. "You haven't *seen* Burg Ughol . . . It's not much!" But he was pleased. His voice became merely coaxing again. "You think of the South, sweetheart, as your proper home, since you've known no real anchorage here, where everything's strife, hardship, dog-eat-dog . . . You can't imagine how different it is in Normandy . . . You'll find peace, place and a fine, knightly husband, and a castle with lands to it . . ."

She stiffened.

"Oh no; it's not that, I have no feeling of home, Father . . . One place or the next is good enough . . . It's just that I want Salerno after dull days here . . ."

Geoffrey sprang from the bed. "Where *Bohemond* is, aye? So I thought, you vixen!" He shook his head helplessly and spoke as if to himself. "This is of course how it *would* be! I have been foolish! *Foolish!* Selfish and a fool!"

Zoë returned to Cisterna and prepared for the trip home with her father. And a week later she was indeed returning to Salerno, but alone. The party of three on their way to Campobasso had been ambushed by road barons and Dr. Poldi had been the only one successful in escaping with his life. Zoë was sent for, escorted by spelled horses, and arrived at Salerno narrowly in time for the funeral masses of Hugh Falloc and Geoffrey Ridelle.

CHAPTER XI *Burg Ughol*

IT WAS EARLY AFTERNOON in the summertime, and Burg Ughol and the wood about it seemed to sleep. So quiet did it look and so lonely, it would seem that no one lived there but the timid wild red roebuck and his enemy the wolf. The old hall itself— huge, larched and half-ruined, thrust one high wall of its ashlar-and-oak construction out of the forest's edge. This fragment, open to the sky and hooded by the remaining overhang of black and rotted beam looked on a good day like a troll, with one lidless eye set balefully on the mere below it. The little lake, rush-choked and over-run by the roots of ilexes and cypress, had been a fine thing in more violent days, the sole entry of the hold of Ughol, a Lombard chief whose deeds had long since sunk to the bloody soil of Salerno legendry. Of the wooden block-houses that had guarded it, one still remained, kept whole more by the vines that entwined it than by its own greyed timbers. It stood on the bridge-head beyond, the abode of a hermitess. But to attain to Faustin's Bridge and the hall itself, the mere was navigable to several flat shallops kept beached in the mud, to be rowed precariously across and moored to cracked stone steps where there was a rousing-horn and a row of scummed elephant-trunks to receive the hawser.

Faustin was said to have tolled the Bridge for years, through two generations at least of the Burg's retainers, her pair of round windows facing two ways—one on the wide path that led to the hall, and the second on another more ancient one down through the fen, which, tangled, dark, and wildly beautiful, profusely footed it. As the path wandered, the trees and vines broke here and there into lawn-like meadows, suggesting what were once more cultivated uses, and the tail of the eye would constantly leap to what seemed like human forms darting, leaping or poised in repose in the thick fastness—a mossy god, a minotaur, or a satyr-pair who had cornered a weeping nymph, all enacting their everlasting interludes against some much-carved tree-bole.

In one of these open glades, quite beyond the Bridge, yet not so far that the castle-yard intruded onto it, the path emerged on a deep wide glade, where green-grey pediments of what once had been a small Greek oratory lay fallen in grass. In the center of the temple-space was a tenderly formed, life-size statue of the mortal Psyche, miraculously well-preserved in all this ruin. Psyche once more had life around her, for today a congenial company lounged on her fallen stones. Mihera Falloc, Bohemond de Hauteville and Zoë Ridelle were holding a re-union—impromptu as far as the inclusion of Bo was concerned, since he and his young squire had ostensibly merely chanced to drop in on Mihera's visit to the newly bereaved Zoë on their way to a hunt. The occasion was a farewell too, since Bohemond would march to Illyria with Guiscard, and Mihera was repairing to Amalfi in order to or-ganize his father's lands, making sure that the dead Count's serfs had not made the recent funeral the occasion for revolt. Sir Geoffrey Ridelle's affairs were less complicated. Burg Ughol and a small money dot to be managed by the warder of the Burg was his daughter's sole legacy. The passing of Hugh and Geoffrey had been most felt in their loss to the army. In the present preparation for the Byzantine cam-paign against the usurper Alexius Comnenus, Bohemond had become involved in difficulties the like of which he had never imagined before accruing to the matter of conquest, and tasks he had once considered below the dignity of a knightly rank had kept him hard pressed to eke out a holiday. He had come with his young kinsman, one Tancred de Hauteville, of the same house and name as the great ancestral lord in Normandy. Tancred, a lad of about eighteen years, sat next to Bohe-mond at the picnic-cloth. He had blond curling hair, blue eyes, a high-bridged Norman nose and full red lips with a habitual pout. When sitting he always kept one foot under him, it having healed wrong after a tilting accident. He was extremely fond of his young uncle, even jealous, and in all ways looked and seemed like a pretty girl, except with a lance and a horse under him, hacking a man's war-wood from his hands, when he was said to be deadly. Bohemond was training him as his own equerry.

Right now his handsome, spoiled features proclaimed resentment at the dwindling of the hunting expedition, and his attitude was second in testiness only to Mihera Falloc, who had openly hinted that they had intruded on a picnic planned for two. At the moment only a common interest in Zoë's food-baskets muffled conflict. War, according to Mi-hera's sharp looks, would indeed come later, when the wine and the chilled venison were gone.

Zoë herself looked not out of harmony in this hunters' company. She was dressed in a gown of soft wine-colored wool, low cut above and suggesting through its fine softness her small, hard, upthrust breasts. Round her waist was a broad girdle of wheaten-colored leather, in which was stuck her hall key-ring on one side and at the other a short lady's baselard, making the beholder recall that save for a hallful of stranger-servants, she walked this wilderness alone.

Her small feet were encased in riding-boots of soft red leather. On her head was a green wool round-cap, and a crown of short dark curls (Poldi had advised the shearing following the pox) beset her face. Over her right ear she had stuck a short feather plucked from a peacock's wing. Her expression wore a melancholy look that was likely temporary, a pert rebellious look that would likely grow with the years. The childish appearance, so sweet in her beforetime, had somehow vanished, but her lips, so mobile, shadow-curved, and dented with mischief, and her glance—tilted, blue-green and wild as a woodbird's—made her ten times as fascinating.

The effect of all this was evident in the actions of Mihera and Bohemond, who in the immemorial fashion of males on the preen, were discussing with terrific gusto and masterfulness the detailed problems of making war—Mihera, in spite of his rejection of the company, supplying ways and means, names and quantities as fast as Bohemond could mention his own and Guiscard's difficulties in planning the push-off. To cross the Otranto strait to the Greek coast was no small part of the proceedings, and Mihera was voluble on galley-loads, provisions, and the decking of horses.

"By God, Mihera," cried Bohemond, "you're better than the Genoese! Why don't you lend my Father your transports for the crossing and carry the Duke's command?"

"Not me!" Mihera quickly demurred. "None of your foolhardy quests. I hear Alexius has enlisted the Venetian navy, and small blame to him for it! You think Guiscard fools *everyone* with his bogus Michael? He's waited a long time for an excuse at Byzantium. It has a bad smell!"

"*Bogus Michael! Excuse! Ventre dex,*" exploded Bohemond who, basking in the glow of Guiscard's favor, apparently believed implicitly in his every venture. He was flushed and rising to his feet, and there would have been a scuffle except for Zoë, who had begun to yawn.

"What the devil, gentlemen! Is war all you talk about? I've been shut up in that nunnery, remember! Where's some gossip?"

"Gossip, darling?" subsided Bohemond. Since his first glimpse of Zoë Ridelle at the great double funeral he had lost no time in attempting to resume the old pretty intimacies. "Mihera knows gossip! *I've* been busy!"

"Oh, come now," she rejoined, "I've had enough of Mihera's news in letters these years. I know all about how many leagues distant from the world's edge is Muscovy, and how to transport galleys over dry land, but not one word of a new dance or a new marriage, or an outworn one, which is often more interesting!"

The mention of the letters caused Bohemond to start, looking quickly from Zoë to young Falloc, with a fleeting smile for Mihera, of surprise and grudging admiration.

Bohemond had spent three years in Guiscard's army and at his Salerno court, and both experiences had matured him. He had a bluff, hearty ring to his voice that gave the impression faintly of insincerity, even when as today he was not *pretending* fellowship, and his grey eyes, in spite of their warmth, had a look of keeping his true thoughts remote, giving his whole face an appearance of great subtlety for one his years. He was still but twenty-three years old.

Mihera was going to reply when Zoë unconsciously forestalled him. "What of the Duchess, Bo? My lady Sigelgaita?" But her expression demanded no special answer. The longer she sat there in that glade, with her supple back pressed against the side of the Psyche-statue, the more it seemed that she became aware of Bohemond alone. What she asked and what was replied, what converse went on across their picnic-cloth meant little, except as an underlay of pleasantry to mask and support the warm looks that more and more boldly passed between them—a tautness and hotness of mood that even a stranger could not ignore. And Mihera was not stranger to it. Young Tancred could only stare, fidget and interpose hints on the hunt to his uncle Bohemond—hints that constantly fell flat like the scraped dishes and empty wine cups strewn in the stones.

"Cousin!" Tancred ventured for the last time, "what of the hunt?"

"Aye," said Mihera with a black look, "it grows late for it."

"Aye," repeated Bohemond dreamily, "it grows late."

Zoë sat leaning against the stone, her dark head pressed against the Psyche's thigh, and in her glance was the self-same look which in Psyche spoke forth in tender contours—throat, lips and out-thrust breasts, so that the whole glade, in the warm, westering sun-light, seemed indeed suffused with the ancient incense, and Bohemond said, "Aye, it grows late. Why don't you hunt, Tancred?"

"But I would not know . . ."

"Go to! The woods are *full* of roebuck! Hunt, Tancred, hunt!"

But Tancred stubbornly stayed and Mihera too, the latter glaring from the far side of the Psyche-statue, and the crowded little concourse did not break up until the trees of Burg Ughol had begun to drip dew, and the star-sharp, chill Italian evening had commenced to close in on them.

The next afternoon, though no word had passed between them for a rendezvous, Bohemond led his charger onto one of the shallops and crossed the mere alone. The elms bent in on him and the high, thick osiers brushed against the skiff, but the path of sky straight up was pale and clear and a white, transparent day-time moon appeared in the zenith. An overlay of water-lily leaves coated the lake where the reeds parted, and noisy insects darted in the sedge. The shallop cut a smooth path in the soft green watery wilderness, and as Bohemond guided it past the bend, a branch cast a shower of blooms across his shoulders and on the neck of Falade, and up ahead he could see the jutting overhang of Burg Ughol.

He pushed the boat through mire with a final lunge that careened it to the elephants' trunks where he grasped the stag's horn and put it to lip. Falade's hooves cracked the marbles into new shapes as he spurred him onto the ancient bridge, and at the hole in the blockhouse a long, wan, wrinkled face had appeared, like a much-dripped candle.

"Ho there, youngling!"

Bohemond doubled back and dismounted. There were such odd tales about the hermitess that even a sanguine heart forebore to flout the lady in her dismal kingdom.

"What word, Faustin?"

She talked a sort of half-Greek, half-German jargon that even a multi-tongued South Norman was at pains to understand.

"None for many years has passed without alms to give me! *You* did yesterday with that young one, which was not wise!" The gummy jaws mouthed the syllables like an old she-hound with a piece of gristle.

"Alms?" cried Bohemond, his quick laughter shattering the noontide peace. "What do *you* with alms?"

"Hmph," said Faustin, her collapsed bag-like jaws ballooning. "Think you I don't grease the palms of those niggards at yonder hall? *Misericordia!* Niggards! So a coin, mind you, for tonight's gruel bowl!"

"And what's the recompense?"

"A hunter's blessing, generally, but *you*, with neither bolts nor bow . . ." She smiled and he was shocked at the toothless idiocy. "I'll wish you fortune in love. *Sic alia paliampsit* . . . 'Tis the same charm I made yesterday for the white-head."

"Mihera? Don't *do* that, Faustin. I fear he's already laid up powers, being a prudent sort . . ."

Faustin's old eyes almost disappeared in their crowns of thick wrinkles. "Should I trust looks with luck? The other seemed more honest, and it's a tender maid!"

"Old Jade!" laughed Bohemond. "I'll have vengeance on you for that!" With his two hands on her sill he shook the block-house till it rocked threateningly.

"*Misericordia!* Thou wicked!"

He tossed his coin, grasped Falade's reins and struck into the fen, his bright head bent like a hunter's.

When presently man and horse emerged to the green glade, it appeared empty. Remnants of yesterday, a few cheese rinds, a crust and a half-gone apple lay scattered in the grass. Psyche presided solitary, smiling her young-old smile over memories of things past. But Falade pricked up his ears, snorting softly, and Bohemond stood halfway between joy and caution, hoping it was Zoë's presence the beast sensed and not an interloper, human or otherwise (so powerful was the spell of Burg Ughol that one unconsciously held an open mind to *any* prospect).

"Zoë!"

He peered intently at the bushes, but nothing stirred. There was no sound save a bird-cry or two far back in the fastness that he had just disturbed, or the soft rustle of a hare in the bush foraging. He glanced at Falade, at the perked ears, at the eye-whites showing. Someone was here. And as his eye caught something at the Psyche, his hand crept to his blade, then relaxed. There was, infinitesimally jutting, the tip-end of a blue-green feather, plucked from a peacock's wing.

Halfway to the Psyche a thought struck and he said, "All right, darling! Come! It's Mihera!"

She stepped out pertly. "It is *not* Mihera! It's *you!*"

"Oho!" said Bohemond, taking her two hands in his, "is this place *enchanted,* that you know such things, as who likely comes?"

The sea-blue eyes slanted up at him, and she seemed to be masking a well of secret laughter. "No. No more than the church-yard was enchanted, or the Castle-bower."

She had a small, compact head and she tossed it in her little habitual way, and the crop of short dark curls did not respond as had her once-luxuriant mane. She pulled from his grasp and perched herself on the high pediment under Psyche's feet.

She was dressed in the same gown, though capless. Bohemond reached for the peacock-feather. "This betrayed you," he said.

Now that he was here, the fine hot mood on which he had fed his daring dreams all night betrayed him. The very strength of their current seemed to make him helpless, and he felt with a sort of anger the moments melt unused, all this proximity and the fact that they were finally alone.

Zoë, woman-like, seemed to know. Flaunting and provocative to her heart's fill before, with the security of numbers, today her mood seemed cool, calm, amused at him and even her passion, this side of it, could keep him remote.

He burst out, "You're a *scurvy* witch, Zoë!"

The blue eyes widened as though not privy to all these thoughts that went swinging through his mind like flying sparks, and she questioned him innocently.

"What *ails* you, Bo?"

And without prelude he plunged.

"By God, darling, as long as you're *in* this world and not mine, I'll be wild. There's everything they sing of between us, and so to the devil! Will you be game? Be mine? Marry me?" he added, oddly tentative.

Zoë looked up at him. She lifted her head and laughed.

Bohemond with a quick anger stooped to catch her by the slight, firm shoulders, his hard fingers pressing through the soft wool that covered them, and knelt to kiss her lips, his own hard and hot and his eager mouth demanding her answer to the very summit. And then he saw that she was not really answering, her eyes not slit-closed the way she did when she really kissed him, and that she was watching him with a frown-furrow between her thick dark brows, and she had her eyes wide open.

"You with your fine palace and your plans, how can you bear to come to this horror of a place, even to make love? Have you seen it, Burg Ughol and the half-mad gnomes that serve there, not to speak of Faustin, though she's much the best of it?"

"What has that to do with *us?*" he asked in a flat tone.

"Everything! Don't be feckless!"

Her glance snapped at him and a little dent of anger showed about her lips.

Bohemond was taken aback, but she did not give him a chance to think about it.

"Don't be impetuous, Messire—you with your battle-plans and your father's designs to be King of Byzantium. We must understand each other." She pulled from his arms and resumed coolly, "There is one thing I wish and when I asked after Sigelgaita yesterday I was wishing it then—that I too could go into battle! What is it like, the flesh-cutting and the charge and the breaking of a man's body with a sharp, bright wide-cutting sword? And the stealth and the danger and the scaling of walls?"

She seemed so bloodless, so utterly cold, that Bohemond wished to strike her. But he wanted her. His whole present wish was encompassed by what they did and said here in the Psyche-glade. Battle, court, death, that was one thing. But this was another, this hard, changing demand for achievement that sang in his blood, and by Judas, he meant to have it of her! But she was gamy, he saw now, not that former combination of innocence and fire. What had that damned convent done?

She wheeled out of his reach and wandered down the far side of the glade into yet another fen-path and he followed her.

"Have you shot many roebuck hereabouts, Messire?" she asked in a new mixture of formality and chill through which her latent passion showed, like the undercolor of aroused excitement through her suntouched skin.

"Yes," said Bohemond, playing this odd game that apparently must be played with one who, though none of your cold bargaining chatelaines, was not yet exactly an innocent young maid, nor a bit of your generous country bouncing wenches either. A man could learn . . .

"My father," said Zoë as they made their way through the sweetscented path where the lady-slipper grew and the hares darted and the moist earth gave up odors of flowers and spice and rotting leaf, "my father killed one once, a roebuck, not here, but in Calabria where I was a child, and it turned out to be the intended prey of a wild boar who came out and gored him clean through the thigh. I shall never forget those twittering Calabrian serving-wenches gathered afterwards at my father's tub, he sitting in the tubful of blood, laughing, and they fluttering about him like frightened pea-hens. He never looked so fine and so full of living it seems to me, as after that hunt, sitting and laughing in that firkinful of blood.

"He was a great hunter," she said, "and a great singer too. They used to say that even the trees listened when Sir Geoffrey sang! Lots used to say that he was foolish, reckless, because he was not prudent with lands and money. Prudence is a dismal virtue. He was criminally stupid, they said, not to get lands, though there were rich chances even with Guiscard grabbing everything. Hugh Falloc did it, and most of the rest . . . They said it was grisly that he left no grand bulging *dot*, or made me a fine marriage-troth. Well, I've seen your lords and your dot-furnished daughters and I've seen them led weeping from Cisterna bound for some lord whose fief bordered theirs, some loathsome one, ugly, or who stank or who had a reputation of flogging his first wife to death with a chain, for all your chivalry. And as for chivalry while we speak of it, my father was your true knight—fighting, singing all his life, honoring the dream of his own true love—as fine, as gallant and as merry a lord as ever rode out in company!"

During all this strange and passionate recital, she had walked fast ahead of him down the narrow path. Not for haste, not distraught, but propelled by the surging outpour of all the pent-up thoughts that had welled up in her since Ridelle's death. This was her obsequy to Ridelle and her love-song to her inevitable fate before she met it. She wanted her own and Bohemond's eyes wide open.

But as he followed her and heard and understood every word she poured out to him, his mood melted and changed and a whole new suffusing tenderness entered every nerve. In a wide, grass-matted space on the path where tussocks of osiers scattered their star-shaped blooms, he whirled her about, catching her up with a low, soft cry.

"Zoë, oh Zoë . . . I know, I know. And by God, sweetheart, I'm game for it! I've no high wit like Sir Geoffrey, and I can't sing, but I'm looking to be a fair hand at taking cities! And all I can do will be with the thought to have your love, to see one half of that present light in your eyes when you say my name . . ."

He held her, long after the chest of his light hauberk had dried of her quick, brief tears, long after the afternoon sunlight had gone and the star-filled fragrant Salerno night had come upon them. And when, as they wandered back again toward the Hall, he fetched his cloak from Falade's pannier and wrapped her in it, he felt that never was anyone so dear to him, nor was any moment so satisfyingly full of meaning as this last hour of this strange day they had spent together. Like a fine lord, at the last, he asked, and like a great lady she promised, faithfully, to wait till he returned from Byzantium.

"Someday I'll *give* you Byzantium," he said. "Byzantium's my first song!"

CHAPTER XII

The Flight of the Eagle

BOHEMOND'S TENDER BOAST, made by starlight in the Wood of Ughol, was scarcely an over-extravagant one in the light of events that followed. Guiscard hit the Byzantine coast and with Bohemond captured the strong isle of Corfu. Then by sea and land father and son, subduing all garrisons as they went, approached Durazzo, the western terminus of the ancient Roman highway to Byzantium itself—or Constantinople as it was variably called.

But in late summer while the Normans sieged, the magnificent Venetian fleet appeared.

A terrific embroilment ensued between the Norman and Italian navies, with Bohemond leaping from galley to galley exhorting the knights as the Venetians burned the decks beneath him. On land Alexius ruined Guiscard's engines, so that the timid Apulians and flighty Calabrian foot-troops were all for heading home.

But as they made for the boats, Guiscard burned his own fleet.

Sigelgaita in full battle-armor rode among the ranks with sulphurous language and a long bull whip, and the Norman horse struck again and again with cries of "Guiscard! Guiscard!" so that the end of the day saw complete Byzantine flight (Alexius in the lead), leaving the brave English mercenaries of the famous Varangian Guard to be utterly slaughtered, their final remnant being roasted alive in a little church where they had at last fled.

After but nine months and one pitched battle, the road to Byzantium stood open.

Here simple fate intervened. At Robert's winter camp on a hummock called Devil's Poll which he renamed Mount Guiscard, a messenger arrived with a papal parchment. Henry the German was approaching Rome. Uprisings in the South where Robert had left Borsa in charge were being simultaneously touched off. They and Henry planned a rendezvous. Hildebrand asked Robert, in the name of Christ and Guiscard's renewed fealty, to come to the rescue. Leaving Bohemond in command with instructions to mark time and fortify gains, Guiscard embarked on a galley with sixteen knights and gave the command to row for Italy.

In lower Calabria he was joined by Roger the Great Count, who with picked forces had hurried from his Palermo court, and together the two aging champions embarked on a typical campaign. Such high tales of de Hauteville heroics issued out of it that Hildebrand, now sieged by Henry's army and holed up in the time-honored last refuge of Castel' Sant' Angelo, was reported to have cried out, "What? Is the Vicar of Christ to be left freed by the Prussian Wolf while the de Hauteville brothers hold a tournamental joust?"

And indeed, as Count Roger withdrew to Sicily again, and Guiscard marched with sixty thousand Norman knights and thirty thousand Lombard and Saracen peasants up the Latin Way, the affair retained the contours of a tilting-match. Desiderius of Monte Cassino again played mediator, but in the interests of protecting his own high Benedictine citadel, avoided all unfair appearances, in announcing Guiscard's coming, by simultaneously informing Henry. In fact, Henry, losing his nerve at the prospect of the Terrible Duke, mentioned great affairs demanding immediate attention, and fled, leaving his troops to their fate. Three days later Robert arrived at the Gate of St. John Lateran, pitched camp and tarried sixty-seven hours, examining the City on all sides.

The unwary German forces foolishly deployed about Guiscard's camp. So Robert, of a dark night, secretly marched east and north with a picked thirteen hundred. San Angelo was quickest available from the Flaminian Gate. The bulk he sent there, while with an intimate faction of Norman blood he secretly turned off at the Gate of St. Lawrence (previously observed to be lightly guarded).

A swift skirmish. Swords at work beneath the crumbling aqueduct. Then a ride by obscure avenues across town to the surprised garrison at the North Gate, where the rest of the Normans now gave tongue. Then the whole company up the Latin Way, burning as they went; burning all districts against possible rear-tactics of the aroused German and turn-coat Roman legionaries. Burning, burning, burning.

There was a terrible battle by Hadrian's Bridge on which Hildebrand was able to gaze from his lofty perch. For miles back he saw churches, senate-houses and historic villas, whole neighborhoods going up in smoke. And presently Robert arrived, conducted him to the square of the Lateran Palace, and in the eerie light of two-thirds of Rome burning, the Duke and all his knights threw themselves down with great reverence at the feet of the dazed and horrified pontiff.

There was a painful interlude in which Robert was at difficulty to halt things (Lombards and Saracens having been let loose in the city of a thousand treasures), and all Europe buzzed with the horror of it.

As in many castles, it was the chief topic of conversation on a certain cool spring night in Burg Ughol where three friends sat in the vast hall lit only by a fire burning on the central hearth. One Abbot de

Grentesmil, a notorious hall gossip, was engaged in listing for Mihera Falloc and Zoë Ridelle all items that had come to him on the Roman sack, as well as other side-lights of what meantime transpired at home. He refreshed himself constantly from a great flitch of venison and a horn of *Calvados* or Norman jack. He was a tiresome talker and repeated himself constantly, yet his listeners afforded him full attention here. Mihera was scarcely disposed to dispute the floor, being content to watch the play of firelight on Zoë's hair, and Zoë would promptly have shushed him if he'd tried.

She sat before the great faded arras under the canopy, her slim fingers working delicately with the torn fragments of a string that had snapped in her zithern. The firelight fell blue on her dark, short hair. She commented on the abbot's stories now and then, encouraging him, asking a question or two when the subject touched her. (He had many an anecdote on Bohemond's Illyrian feats.) Now and then a short, square-browed servant, the hall steward, moved briefly among them, replenishing the abbot's refreshments, and supplying Mihera and Zoë with an occasional cup of wine.

In his deep, yet trivial voice de Grentesmil had just remarked that the Duchess Sigelgaita had arrived from the east with her retinue and resumed residence under Maia Torre to await Guiscard.

"Really?" prompted Zoë. "How does she fare?"

"How do *you* think?"

"Ravening!"

"Right! There's Marc Bohemond, perched on the pinnacle, sky-high in Guiscard's command and favor, and here's young Borsa, by his rank stupidity letting this whole *ragout* of mischief boil the minute Guiscard was gone. And know, friends (I'm here to tell you), he acted the dolt! Weak where he should have been firm, and when he should have tempered justice with politics, committing the most blood-thirsty crimes against the most popular *vavasseurs*. Talk about Bloody Gisolf! Know you what Borsa did to old Rouf de Guisseps for falsifying tithes?"

"No," said Zoë, in the expected mode, rubbing the overstrained muscles in her bent neck. "What?"

"Hanged him!"

"No!"

"Yes, indeed," said de Grentesmil, taking a huge chunk from the deer-hock splayed in his fingers. "Roger de Ballive had a go at one of Sigelgaita's stable-studs and was flogged for his pains—in public—a knight, mind you!"

"Oh!"

"And then there was the serf who was behind in his grain-dues, whom Borsa caused to be stood in a firkin of ice till his feet froze."

De Grentesmil wiped his mouth and washed the inside of it with a swallow of jack. "It would seem, friends, that young Borsa had more Lombard in him than Guiscard's vintage of blood!"

A sneer crossed Mihera's features. "Do you call the burning of Rome a tame thing? Last season I carried hides up to England, and while there I heard tales of 'Norman justice' wreaked on the English wretches who objected to being robbed, raped and enslaved by your blooded Normans! Deeds are done there that would turn your stomach and make Borsa look a saint. Incidentally, I heard in Amalfi that our friend Bohemond, who also is Guiscard's son and with no foreign taint in him, has sent home Count Saracen, blinded."

"Well, really, Mihera!" spoke up Zoë. "That *was* a little different. Count Saracen was persuaded to connive with Alexius and attempted to let the Greek troops into the Pass! Bo wrote me about it."

"Oh, excuse me," said Mihera with a wry smile.

"Young Bohemond's up *against* something, all alone there," said Hugh de Grentesmil, taking fresh hold of things. "They say this Alexius is a far different article to be faced than the old usurper."

"At least he's but little over Bo's own age," said Zoë.

"Aye, but the Grand Domestic George Paleologus is a formidable fellow, they say, besides which Alexius himself (according to the Duchess) is an able soldier, an artful diplomat, indomitable of perseverance and fertile of mind."

"Bo encountered him once on horseback," said Zoë. She had laid the zithern by and sat gazing to the fire. "They met on a high tussock of grass by the dunes, and Bohemond swung out with his sword. The Emperor is short in the saddle and his body, though thick, is very agile. So he leaned back, Bo's sword passed over him, and he galloped off. He has a swarthy, bearded face, and he laughed, Bo said, as he made for the dunes."

"Oho!" shouted de Grentesmil. "I see you memorize mêlées—or isn't there aught of love in your *billets-doux* to work with, hey?" And de Grentesmil swayed back, convulsed with his own laughter while Mihera sat unmoved. The steward served silently, replenishing the abbot's venison from a silver plate.

"Well, anyhow," chatted the abbot, "I'm glad to see the boy Marc Bohemond wresting the chance of heirship from Black Borsa. It's bad enough to have to *live* down here among these murderous dastards, let alone to be under their thumbs!"

"Ssh!" motioned Zoë as the steward moved from the hall.

"Oh, Psaltery!" exclaimed de Grentesmil. "I forgot the help! Your pardon, young woman, but your father did wrong to leave this hall chock-full of 'em like this." He grasped his pendulous gullet. "Think you they heard all I said? They're handy as Hades with the poison bottle!" He pushed away trencher and cup. "I swear I've lost my appetite."

Afterward young Falloc lingered on the narrow portcullis that spanned the ancient moat, while de Grentesmil sat patiently on his white mare in the moon-lit courtyard.

"I wish, by God, that he'd go!" Mihera groused. "There'll be more of this the whole way back, the boozy old wind-bag! Well then, fare you well, my little Basilissa!"

"Basilissa!" took up Zoë. "What do you mean by that?" observing the slightly sarcastic curve of his mouth in the moonlight.

He shrugged. "That, soon, is what you'd likely be called, if you'd wed de Hauteville!"

"Hmph, I see what you think—that it could never happen . . . That I'm a fool to wait, dreaming impossibilities . . ." Her little mouth set and he could see the bitterness in her own glance. "At that, you may be right, Mihera. Are you sticking about for the laughter, later?"

He stared down at her, the muscles taut in his hard young jaw. "No. No, Zoë. I stick about because I love you. . . ." And as though the saying of it made him bold, "I love you, Zoë. Does that mean nothing to you?"

She avoided his glance, her arms folded. The little dents of mischief showed at her lips. "How can you love one whom you hold a fool, Mihera?"

Her eyes widened as he coolly answered this.

"Your foolishness will pass with time, Zoë. All this in you will pass . . . It is my hope that then we can take up and go on together."

"*Fichtre!*" Her foot stamped. "My God, I wouldn't think it *possible* for a man to make love one minute and make little the next. *But how you do it!*"

They were thus faced to one another when hoof-sounds echoed from the wood.

"I sent a page for any letters," said Zoë. "But if it is the page he makes quick going, over Faustin's Bridge."

But it *was* the page. He came tearing through the fen and de Grentesmil's mare reared as he crashed through and dismounted.

"No letter m'lady, but ill news! Alexius Comnenus struck a surprise blow at the stronghold of Larissa and contrived to force Bohemond into full retreat. The Prince sails home defeated!"

Perhaps there was no sadder occasion in all Guiscard's career than the day he arrived with the ailing Hildebrand to find Bohemond waiting.

Still Guiscard was not one to give up easily. Why should he? All justification for hopes of an Eastern Empire had been fully supported by his one try. His dreams were even bolder now. His ambitions knew no end and he wasted no time in again promoting them.

He gathered fresh troops, engaged new galleys and sent Borsa, Robert and Guy, the latter his two youngest by Sigelgaita, on ahead. Sigelgaita was to leave last, having waited for other forces, and between-time he and Bohemond were to make a bold and secret sally based on new knowledge of the land. He did not blame Bohemond for the Larissa thing. He was too much the philosopher not to blame fate more. Bohemond had proven brilliant, ruthless and strong, and Robert meant to set his son's feet on the high-road to his proper destiny before—well, he had just had a birthday. Guiscard was sixty-nine!

One evening shortly before they left, Robert and Hugh de Grentesmil were returning at dusk from a day's hunt and passed young Bohemond going the opposite direction over Faustin's Bridge.

Father and son hailed, and Robert watched Falade's shoulders disturbing the thick leaves as the horse left the path and plunged into the fen. A veiled moon hung over the cypresses.

"Oho," said Guiscard as he tossed a coin to the dripped-candle countenance in the window-hole. "So Marc Bohemond rides across the lake! Well, maybe this is what we oldsters fought for, some of it—twilights and misty moons, time for young bloods to dally in the reeds. And yet," he said, his gnarled brown hand rubbing the soft mass of fuzz beneath his charger's mane, "and yet there's danger here! I'll make no bones, de Grentesmil! Much as I loved Geoffrey (may God rest his merry soul) I've got far other plans for the boy's nuptials than Geoffrey Ridelle's daughter . . ." They unlashed the two shallops and stood there a moment talking in the gloom.

"What's she like, de Grentesmil?" The million fine lines and sabre-furrows on Guiscard's face had screwed into the expression that long ago had won for him the sobriquet "The Wary."

"Oh, she's a strange one and rather wild, but she's no trull, that I'll swear," said the abbot.

"All the worse," fussed Guiscard. "Left poor like this and no doubt sufficiently attractive . . ."

"*Very* attractive, Robert!"

"H'm . . . The boy has a vein of chivalry an ell wide. It could trap him in such an idyll!" He shook his head, the tassel of his red hunting-hood going to and fro on his bronzed neck. "No, de Grentesmil." Then as the thought struck, "Where's young Falloc? Didn't Geoffrey use to say . . ."

"Oho!" laughed the churchman with the right mixture of amusement and ruefulness to flatter Robert. "What chance has Mihera against young Bo?"

Guiscard immediately broke into a broad smile, in which his row of strong yellow teeth still showed whole and handsome. "He *is* a fine-looking youngster, aye? . . . Well, Hugh—" he instantly sobered. "Who knows about the future? What will transpire here sometime while I'm gone? And this must not *be*, de Grentesmil! I tell *you*, it must not happen!"

"Marriage?"

"Marriage. I leave it to you. If those two tie up, that's *one* thing I'll never forgive you for. But beware of force in the case of Bohemond. There's as wide a streak of iron in him that resists pressure like a buckler resists steel. You've worked many a sly game in your day, you rascal. Heaven knows you've worked *me!* Now try your fine ecclesiastical wits on *this!*"

And with a short, carefree laugh, Guiscard poled out into the lily-padded mere, and presently the second skiff, bearing the huge and frowning abbot, slid after him.

The recapitulation of gains against Alexius on the Byzantine coast proved this time not long but more difficult, and to Zoë, waiting in Burg Ughol, the winter was drear. She wandered daily in the depths of the wild wood restless and haunted, fearing the possible chance of the future and dreaming of yesterday. Mihera came often to the hall, his eyes wistful and his face pale, but Zoë's eyes were turned inward on her thoughts, and she looked constantly on the gold ring that Bohemond had left her and she did not know that Mihera suffered.

The page brought her constant letters, as usual not of love and of future marriage-plans, but of battles, sieges, and the Venetian fleet, winter-quarters and of Sigelgaita, and how he could fairly feel her hate for him because of the honor and love his father showed. He wrote of misfortunes too, a flux that went through the army, killing five hundred knights in a short time.

In the spring, abruptly, he wrote that he had asked Guiscard's leave to return home, for medicaments for an ill he had, and for a good doctor. Not the flux (he wrote). There was nothing else. The note seemed strangely disturbed, except that since Dr. Poldi was in Salerno attending Hildebrand he had requested him by the same messenger to await him there.

On the morning in June of 1085 when young Bohemond returned to Salerno over-thin, weak and unduly spent by the journey, Hildebrand Gregory VII lay surrounded by leeches and medicos in the huge castle adjoining Guiscard's newly finished St. Andrew's Cathedral. The Pope was dying.

Bohemond paid no heed to this. Without delay he proceeded past the sick-room down to the chambers where they had told him Dr. Poldi stayed. But Bohemond himself could not nowadays walk unnoticed. In spite of the Larissa fiasco (they still talked of how he innocently ate grapes in a Greek vineyard while Alexius demolished his camp), he was still a brilliant prince with a brilliant future, so that though there was today perhaps no busier spot in Europe than St. Andrew's Castle where Hildebrand expired, his reputation and his outstanding appearance gained him buzzing attention among the crowd of messengers, attendants and cardinals on the death-watch.

But on Bohemond de Hauteville the curious stares of the greater and the obsequious vows of the less made no impression. He moved in a sort of nightmare. He was still the youngster who had dreamed of this adulation, but he was very suddenly the covetous and ambitious de Hauteville, seeing future possibilities in the East that were only half a dream. And he was also gripped by the fear of a healthy man for mysterious symptoms that plagued him. Slight pains, strictures of the bowels, followed by weakness and aversion to food, that had, in winter-quarters, recurred every few days. He noticed there had been no actual spell since leaving Cephalu but this fact only increased his anxiety for the interview, glad that in his last seizure he had made certain preparations, saved certain elements, to present to the use of Poldi's retorts. Poldi . . . Poldi would know . . .

"Prince Bohemond!"

He turned to see a sober-faced ecclesiastic beckoning to him. He bowed to the scarlet hue of the churchman's garments. It was Cardinal Ricco Rossi, who had sat at meat with the family the autumn before at Salerno Palace.

"Come, Sir Marc . . . His Holiness has been informed you are in the Castle, and would speak with you."

Hildebrand felt better today. That last rally before the exit. Even his disposition had recalled its old bluff sting.

Well, he thought, as Bohemond approached the high couch, *so this is the new crop.* "How goes the Duke, Sir?"

For one mad moment, young Bohemond, kneeling at his ring, almost replied, "In grave danger, Your Holiness, of being poisoned by the Duchess!"

But it was a wild thought, like those whims one got of leaping out and swinging upon the hanging torcheres from the choir of the cathedral. And he heard himself answer with conventional phrases of battles, engagements, successes with Alexius.

"Your father is a great man," said Gregory.

The statement came as a shock, to think how Hildebrand had suffered at the holocaust of Rome.

"Your father is a great man," repeated Gregory, "and I'm sure he has handed his strength and prudence and his far-sightedness to you. But know you that this present affair is feckless? My hope is he'll forswear it before causing a worse rift among men of Christian thinking. Ah, Sweet Mary! King against Pope, Duke against Emperor, knight against knight—when in Spain and touching to Byzantium itself, the Turk rages. Know you that Alexius has already called good men to aid him against the heathen? It is in that cause that your sire should be bearing arms. The time will come. It will come soon, and remember, Marc Bohemond, that the prize of that quest will figure not in cities, rules, kingdoms, but in the unity of men of good will united at the Cave of Bethlehem. Be sure you are there, lad. It is for this that you possess your gifts. God prepares, points, enlightens, but will not force, He who was so just as to give us souls and wills together. Do then, as God wills it!"

"God wills it," repeated Bohemond. And Cardinal Ricco, seeing Hildebrand getting tired, escorted the Prince from the room.

Bohemond was not thinking of the Pope's words as he emerged from the death-room. It was not that he was incapable of being reached by the cloth. There was, as in the others of his house and time, a deep streak of the spiritual. But it would take another type of priest, a churchman of more colorful stamp, say one of those warrior-bishops so common in that violent day. Such a one might fire him, play on his best side, even humble the de Hauteville heat in him a little. But not an old man, dying in bed. As a matter of fact, Bohemond as he re-took his way, was thinking, "And now *that's* done—to Poldi! And then ho for Sigelgaita! *We'll* fix her! Poldi and I'll fix her—and the devil take what the devil whelped—that three-times accursed Amazonian harpy whom God may damn!"

He remained closeted with the Amalfi physician all afternoon. Blood-lettings, purges and the mysterious alchemy of substances he furnished for the doctor's bottles and bulbous globes. He stayed about, the whole time, asking questions, answering them, watching the little Italian's absorbed face.

Poldi's report sent him flying through the castle, down the steep streets and onto the high-road that led to Tarentum, where he could take the ship and row to Guiscard at his unsuspecting bivouac on the Greek coast.

CHAPTER XIII *Afternoon of an Abbot*

HUGH DE GRENTESMIL did not in any sense possess the attributes of his profession. He did in fact the very opposite. Hard, shallow, worldly, he was the epitome of what Hildebrand had spent a lifetime in trying to pluck from the Roman Church—a parasite whose noble birth had wrung from secular hands a habit he was grossly unfit for. Formerly an intimate of William of Rouen, the Norman courtier had not even *wished* for a monk's mantle. But the love of petty intrigue that had made him a fugitive from the youthful Conqueror had combined with the circumstance of a sister's southern marriage to ensconce him in this orbit of wealthy brigand-barons which he eternally scorned as less lustrous than William's. Yet he must please those who sheltered him and supplied him with rich clothes, fine mares, and plenty of Norman apple-jack. It was a duty owed to his one loyalty, which was Hugh de Grentesmil.

Therefore, one late afternoon three days after Bohemond de Hauteville had fled Salerno as though pursued by a covin of witches, Hugh took a leisurely canter over to Burg Ughol Wood for an interview with Zoë Ridelle. A great stroke of luck had hit him. He had met Bohemond on the gate-road, to be charged by the young lord with a message excusing himself from visiting the Wood. Unchanging love had been mentioned, but not the cause for the headlong haste. Of this last, even de Grentesmil had not been able to inform himself, though he'd pumped Poldi. No matter. The thing was perfect. The opening was there for a clean blow.

As he approached the Hall itself, there was a distant din—the iron tumult of bells throughout Salerno. Gregory VII was dead. It scarcely concerned him, yet he felt chilled. Poldi had mentioned journeying to Amalfi to tend the old Jew, Piereleone, who was also very low. This fact touched him no more than the first—yet what a misery to observe one's contemporaries falling from the tree! He repelled the ill thought and gave the portcullis chain an extra hearty rattle.

"Ho, in the Hall!"

When Zoë sat faced to him beneath the grey shreds of the ancient canopy, it pleased him to study her with the eyes of a connoisseur.

She'd been a fair wench as a child in Sicily. She was lovely now. He approved of her long, tilted eyes, her oval face somewhat full at the jaw, and the half-grown curling hair that pushed from her pointed head-dress. If her glance was too sharp and her full mouth ready to be subtly cynical for one of her years, it was all to the good, since these last were the very elements he meant to play on. While thus reflecting he had already set his campaign, exchanging the amenities and looking as though he dreaded the opening breach of what he had to say.

He was rewarded by her quick frown, observing in her warm skin the swift undercolor of apprehension and the quickened breath that stirred the young curves above her bodice. Three days had been the right interval for this, Hugh told himself. Her long eyes narrowed.

"*Bohemond* sent you, *Pere* Hugh!"

"Yes, demoiselle." With eyes downcast and a suppressed sigh. She was clay in his hands. The engagement half-won, psychologically, and truth not even wounded—yet.

Her voice came tight, low, and shorn of the odd singing timbre that was part of the charm of Ridelle's daughter.

"The page has informed me, Father, that he was in Salerno—that he is come, and gone."

Again Hugh nodded with regret, at the same time adding with enthusiastic bluster, "He's a busy man, rendering high service to his eminent father. A young lord of the highest promise, Prince de Hauteville!"

The fulsome title daunted her too, he saw. Her glance shifted. He leaned forward confidentially, "He tells me there was a secret betrothal!"

"Yes. I—we—"

"Congratulations, child! Congratulations, to have been the first to rouse romance in the heart of so fine, high-minded, and sensitive a princeling! There's no love like the first one, and nothing ever to equal it again! With his father, I recall, it was a certain Albarada, a little thing. But of course, he *married* her and it was quite some trouble to correct. Yet sometimes I think Guiscard . . ."

Zoë had sprung forward from the high-backed chair, her knuckles white on the arms.

"Stop babbling, you trivial old fraud! Out with it! What did you come to tell me?"

Hugh shrugged, his ringed hands flared, his eyebrows meeting on his high brow. "I wished first to make you see that it must *be*, chicken, that—"

"*What* must be?"

"That it is something inevitable and no discredit to you in any sense!" *Name of God*, what a marvelous hot creature she would be when fully matured, the abbot thought.

"You mealy-mouthed rascal! You're trying to tell me Bohemond has broken our troth, hey?"

"What round language!" he said. "And to the *cloth!*"

"Cloth my eyebrow! Come, Sir Hugh! Answer!" She sprang forward as though ready for his throat.

"Well, Lady Zoë, you are right, of course; that's why I'm here—*now don't fly again, my dove!* Hear me! Things go excellently in Asia Minor, much more than you hear. Don't ask for details—Byzantium soon will be sieged, Bohemond was sent to see the Pope . . . don't you get the picture? As I say, you should be proud to have—"

"Don't digress!"

"—to have been the love of a future Emperor! Naturally, Paris has not been blind to this. The young King Philip was quick with legates, and there's a sister of his, Constance, a child now—but later . . . You see, Lady Zoë, it was no trick to expect this. Robert's other children have been allied with Flanders, the house of Este, Byzantium itself. What else to *expect?*"

What else indeed? She had gone white and the full charge of her latent cynicism lay in her rueful smile. *What a fool.* Aye, Mihera—*what a fool.* Come *now*, with your barbed laughter!

De Grentesmil was not even called upon to compose a bogus message. He had improvised the French betrothal, which was enough . . . He'd have to depend now on a long campaign and interception of notes from the palace post to Burg Ughol—a matter of byzants. A matter of cool vigilance, and byzants . . .

De Grentesmil sauntered from the Hall, leaving her standing there with that odd smile, tearless, dry-eyed, bereft of a thousand half-believed-in dreams.

At the mere-head he met Mihera.

"Aye, it's a grave thing with Maurus," Mihera told him in reply to his sympathetic inquiry. "I am arranging to ride out to Amalfi on the morrow."

"To tend matters at the end of which you'll be rich as an Italian sea-lord, no doubt. Ho! What am I talking about? You'll *be* an Italian sea-lord!" He gave the young man a hearty smile.

"I don't know for that," Mihera muttered with an annoyed frown. "How did you find the Lady Zoë?"

"Not too sprightly . . . But messire!" He leaned from the velvet saddle so that Mihera caught his ale-drenched breath. "Press your love-suit constantly! Patience, I think, will know reward, in this case!"

"Why so?" The light eyes bored him.

"Oh—women are changeling things!" said the abbot airily. "And no less, mayhap, Geoffrey Ridelle's daughter!"

Mihera was left to reflect on this as with a flourish the monk's mare capered off.

There are two taking-off places for the sea-crossing to the Greek coast. On the first campaign the de Hautevilles had employed the wide beach of Otranto, the southernmost of the two. But when Guiscard and Bohemond together had rallied troops for the last great strike, they had launched from Tarentum. It was a small harbor but closer and more strongly protected. It was this last that had prompted them to its use, perhaps thinking of the Venetians.

It was at Tarentum that on a blustery fall evening (it had been the first week of the new sirocco), Bohemond appeared, to find gathered, on the acropolis of the ancient seaport, an excited gathering of men. There were flares and torches, shouts, exhortings and battle-cries, all the evidence of some sort of rally. There was much in this to wonder about, especially as Bohemond caught glimpses, through the throng of fishermen, sailors and men of the town, of warhorses pulling at the posts; and up ahead, the flash and glimmer of links and the torch-light striking from conical caps of steel. He had wondered, coming up the rocky sea-road, about the beached vessels moored in the tiny harbor—the dromons and galleys and small gats, their bright paint visible in the ruddy half-light . . . The sight had worried him and he had spurred Falade and broke through the throng, shouting, "Tancred, Tancred, what is it?"

For it was the youngest de Hauteville, surrounded by a remnant of Guiscard's original Norman company, who harangued the crowd.

"*Name of God,* cousin, what—"

He had no need to ask if there was tragic news. The crowd fell back, muttering sympathetically and the fair-haired Tancred was already down from the improvised podium where he had been. He stood wringing Bohemond's hand. His young face in the torch-light was flushed with regret.

"Sir Cousin, thy sire is dead."

"What? Sir Robert—dead?"

"And that's not the end of it. The Duchess and Borsa fled Cephalu before the army, crossing the strait by night, and beached at Otranto, and already a messenger is said to be speeding Romeward to have Borsa declared Duke."

Bohemond would have interrupted, but Tancred silenced him.

"There is more. Word goes that the Duchess has had contact with Count Roger at Palermo ever since Guiscard was first taken."

"Roger! Roger supports Borsa?" So much was there to be digested that Bohemond answered Tancred almost mechanically. Back of it all his brain burned with the one thought, *too late, too late.* . . .

"Aye," Tancred was telling him. "Count Roger fears you, so he supports Borsa. Even now he rides up with thousands to bar Salerno against you!"

Bohemond's face was pale, his eyes two chips of flint in the stormy light. The shoutings and the noise had somewhat ceased and the soldiers and Tarentese listened in a thick collar of silence about them.

"Where is my father's— Where is his body?" he breathed.

"With the Duchess, of course. She will conduct it for burial to the abbey-crypts at Venosa."

"We must get it," said Bohemond, white to the lips. "We must get it, Tancred! I have from Dr. Poldi proof positive that he may be—"

"Poisoned?" asked Tancred sharply. "Then suspicions of your *own* were—" Then, "But *Name of God*, sir, even there I have ill news!"

"What do you mean?"

"I would have spared you these details, but under the circumstances . . ." Tancred shook his blond head and went doggedly on. "When her galley set out from Cephalu a storm came up, a terrible gale, the same I suspect whose fringes plague us here tonight. Duke Robert's body was unlashed, tossed up and washed into the sea. It was this reason, to prevent spoiling after such immersion (the Duchess said), that she had the heart and vitals removed immediately upon reaching port."

"Good God, Tancred, there's *proof* of a monstrous guilt, but also the undoing of our ability to publish it!" He stood there, looking utterly beaten. But Tancred bade him pluck up.

"Look you, Uncle! We have been holding this concourse tonight to inform all the good folk of Tarentum of the evil that has struck the Duke and the Duke's first born. The people here are fully with us. We have troops in every strong place in the town. Come, Messire, your new subjects are waiting to proclaim you, wanting no part of the Lombard domination!" And he pulled Bohemond up on the high place where all might see.

He cupped his hands (this pale-haired, frail-looking youngster who had coolly secured a province this night for his lord and suzerain) and called out, "Rally with us, messires! Make way for future victories, make way for good days with your glorious and just Prince who has been cheated of his birthright by a crime which shrivels the heart. Rally, *chevaliers*, and give a cry. *'Guiscard! Guiscard! Bohemond por Guiscard!'* "

CHAPTER XIV

*The Bridge of
the Hermitess*

IT HAS BEEN SAID, during the Norman campaign of Asia Minor, that Guiscard and his son Bohemond had been called by the young Basileus Alexius, "The eagle and the crocodile." (*What one does not swoop upon, the other gobbles up!*) It was manifestly absurd, therefore, that the son of Guiscard should meekly submit to being bilked of his intended inheritance, especially when from himself and his personal retainers terrible accusations were circuiting concerning the nature of Robert's death. While Bohemond tarried in Tarentum all Italy laid wagers on how soon the fireworks would start.

But with Guiscard's troops scattered far and wide after the retreat from Cephalu and only gradually making their way back to pledge their fealty to either new young liege, and with Roger the Great Count keeping all strongpoints garrisoned with his troops, it was definitely a place to allow discretion to rule above valor, and during the interval Bohemond improved his time. He gave his best energies to the administration of his little realm of Tarentum and immediately won a name for being a wise, just and popular prince. But when, after some months, Count Roger and his cavalade sailed south again he gave over these peaceful pursuits with the swiftness of a thunderbolt, and launched a grim revolt against Black Borsa and the Dowager Duchess.

With a pure-blood Norman army composed, besides his small nucleus of Greeks, of Lombards and traveling adventurers of all types whom a romantic disinherited champion would naturally attract to his red standard (since Cephalu he had taken the device of a striking serpent on a scarlet field), he set out in a wide circle, ravaging fiercely as he went. Straight across the ankle of Italy he conquered, burned and marauded his way, so that in one year he had become chief holder of all places that Guiscard had taken in the old days here. He was marching up the Calabrian sea-road bent for Salerno when a quick offer of peace signed by both Borsa and Sigelgaita reached him in his quarters at the Castle of Rocca Felucca. He could have all he had taken—Bari and the rest, and become the lawful holder of his Apulian possessions from Roger Borsa. He sent back an affirmative paper, naming two stipulations in it—that he not be asked to appear in person in Salerno for the solemnizing of oaths and that he be allowed to comply with a recent written request from Count Mihera in which the young sea-lord had expressed the desire to hold his lands about Catanzara and Bull Joy from himself rather than from Roger Borsa. While negotiations for these things went forward the Prince of Tarentum remained ensconced in Rocca Felucca with Sir Tancred, hunting.

Several weeks were passed here pleasantly while the knights hunted in hidden places where no arrow had yet disturbed the leaves. The castle was rock-bastioned, and so well garrisoned besides, that any stranger daring to penetrate would find himself summarily hanged in the branches of a tree. One day, however, an enemy entered their strong-place in the shape of a small parchment, which Tancred, seeing it first in his duties as equerry, did not immediately show to the Prince. It was a letter from Zoë Ridelle. Young de Hauteville sensed danger in it and also he dreaded to raise the old unhappy associations, since Bohemond after five months of unanswered letters, had given up trying to contact her, deeply hurt, and the name of the young chatelaine of Burg Ughol had ceased to figure in their conversation for some time. Tancred had therefore kept the letter, carrying it hidden in his hunting jacket until one day, when surrounded by the dogs of the hunting-pack, he and Bohemond were squatted together over a dead doe which they had just pursued and killed in the ravine. Bohemond had fallen into one of those silent moods which since his father's death so often beset him.

"Of what are you thinking, Uncle?" Tancred politely asked. He still had the courtly manners and noble air acquired from his first youth in Normandy, but he was otherwise beginning to blend with the hard living and tough world of his new surroundings. A long, welted sabre-cut that would never fade now marked his left cheek, the souvenir of the year's campaigning, and this, combined with his name as a non-pareil fighter, had made it so that never again would he be thought of as a pretty woman, in spite of his blue eyes and corn-silk tresses.

"I was thinking," said Bohemond, after a time, "of the wood of Burg Ughol and the hunts we had there in the first days of your squirehood. Do you recall?"

Tancred smiled, his full lower lip twisting a little where the scar cut into it.

"Aye, I recall! I recall too, that very seldom did we *arrive* at the hunt, together! Many's the doe I chased singly through that fen!"

The hand on the deer-knife tensed, and Tancred looked above the close fitting green hunting costume into his uncle's face. What he saw there removed the last measure of indecision about the letter. He fumbled in his leather *surtout*.

"Here, I'm tired of having this about. But there's peril in it, Sir Bo! It's for that reason alone that I've dreaded to give it!"

"What *is* it, sir?" said Bohemond severely. He had brooked many a presumptive gesture from this youngest de Hauteville . . . Surprise strategy in the field . . . changed plans improvised against his council . . . But the lad was loyal and valiant . . .

"From Lady Zoë," Tancred said hesitantly.

Bohemond snatched the packet. "God of God, you go too far in your meddling, young whoreson!" And in the same movement he sent Tancred sprawling with a swift push of his hand. *"Fichtre! I've* got brains, too, man! Enough to see through this. Now that I'm powerful once more, my lady feints at my favor again, of course! But I'd see her method, anyhow. I may as well *learn* my rote about women— with all the trappings!"

But the bluster did not fool Tancred. Ensconced on his elbow in the leaf strewn ground (it was early September) he watched the big knight's hands tremble as he tore at the seal, bloodying it from the doe's carcass. It sprang apart without tearing.

"Open *too,* by God! Tancred, I'm telling you . . ." But his words left off as he perused the letter, his lips involuntarily forming the words.

Tancred was mystified to see a great grin growing on the Prince's face, and even more mystified when he began to read aloud the end of the paper in a mock-sweet voice, his free hand gesturing mincingly.

" 'I love you! I'll love you always, carissimo. When will you return to me?' *Va! There's* where they slipped up, by God, not to speak of this clumsy copy of milady's hand! Those ardent sentiments would never come from the stubborn lips of my Lady Ridelle, let alone be set on parchment to one she hasn't set eyes on in a year! Do you know what this means, Tancred? This letter's *not* from the Demoiselle Ridelle!"

"No?"

"No."

Tancred was still mystified. "Then what's happy in it?" Bohemond was indeed preparing to desert the half-flayed doe, having wiped off his bloody baselard and gathered his arrows with a happy whistle.

"Because, Tancred, thick-head! There are details in this letter that could only be known to one who has read my notes to Zoë. It means that my own letters in those first days were consistently intercepted." He mounted Falade, and in the first Guiscard-like, happy gesture he had given in months, he kissed his finger-tips crying, "My star's high again, Tancred, in love and war! Come, leave the dead beast for the steward to fetch in! We ride to Salerno!"

"But messire, it's a trap!"

"Then *vive la trappe*, Tancred! I *love* the trap!" And he spurred off toward Rocca Felucca, leaving Tancred to follow with the worst misgivings.

Accordingly, during the same pilgrim-season, two palmers muffled in heavy wool against the sea-winds of the Calabrian coast were to be seen traversing the rocky gale-swept road beside the Tyrrhenian.

They were ostensibly man and wife, the husband huge and stalwart, with his face bearded, and his hair completely hidden beneath a pilgrim's hat. The woman, though quite comely, with wide blue eyes, long blonde tresses, and a sullen pout to her full lips, wore a wool scarf tied about her head so as to obscure her fair cheeks, as though she had toothache or something like.

"By God, Sir," the "wife" muttered in a voice that was well settled in the tones of mature manhood, "had I fully seen all that was *in* this bargain, I'd not have come, and to Hell with *thee!*"

Similar remarks had passed the cherry-stained lips a hundred times, and this one was brought on just after the gatekeep at the north postern of Bull Joy had slyly given the wink behind "her husband's" broad back.

Bohemond laughed deeply. This adventure was one to please him, and he exuded happiness such as he had not shown for many a month. No one rode near them on the road.

"Ho, wife," he told Tancred. "Serves you right for being so blasted *pretty!* But hold out, nephew, your charms give us good stead! There seems to be neither inclination nor time for the dastards to peer at *me*, when you're by, though I'm sure we're watched for. And maybe you think this bear doesn't stink and tickle! Bear up, son, and I'll give you a charter to the tithes of Sant' Claire's monastery in Bari if you like! Meantime, make the best of the game!" At this point a mule caravan was bearing down on them. Bohemond glanced sharply aside.

"Lord, Tancred, I have *some* pride! Don't make it seem that I was bilked into wedding a shrew—take that storm-cloud off your puss!"

Outside of Bocco, the last hamlet fronting the Salerno outlands, they turned off, striking up into the high craggy wilderness that collared the woods behind the town. It was slow punishment, threading the dry gorges and skirting precipitous peaks. On beasts and riders the hot southern sun beat mercilessly whenever they lost the shelter of wooded ravines.

"Holy Chrysostom!" exclaimed Tancred as finally one evening they emerged on the far rim of the glen of Ughol. "It was a fair plan, hitting the Hall from this angle where none of the Duchess's knaves would likely patrol. But what worries *me* is this. How'll we get out as we came in—with Lady Zoë? It would be hell for a woman!"

"You ought to know!" laughed Bohemond, pulling Falade up to

a rearing halt on the edge of the woodland. It was exactly as he recalled it, the shadowy masses of tangled fen, the moonlit glades between, and in the midst of it all the ancient black-timbered castle sprawled like a great ugly beast asleep. Far in the wood that tumbled away at their horses' very feet, there came the deep belling of a stag in the autumnal evening.

As Bohemond looked, the infinitesimal glow of a torch showed at one of the castle's upper window slits, stayed a time like the arrested stare of a red eye, then vanished as though the orb had shut. The steward, doubtless, doing the last night's chore, yet Bohemond's blood leapt.

"Shall we enter tonight, Tancred?" he suddenly suggested, contrary to their previously arranged plan.

But young Tancred, breathing hard from the last climb to this moonlit ridge, demurred vigorously. "Mother of God, Sir! No! Get rest for ourselves and the blown jades!" The breathing of Falade and of Tancred's own destrier were indeed visible in little cloud-puffs in the crisp air.

Bohemond complied, sensing that his young henchman was at his last extremity. So he lay down in his cloak on the matting of leaves, dreaming and waking, planning and mentally conquering all obstacles to be met on the morrow when they must appear from nowhere in their so far successful guise of road-worn pilgrims.

The next morning, a breakfast of salt pig, cheese and wine, with no camp-fire. The sight of a half-score of grey smoke-tongues lying in the wind informed the intruders that Burg Ughol Wood was well spiked with men. There was a veritable banquet of breakers-of-the-fast on bivouac, apparently, down by the mere.

"Well, Tancred," the pilgrim said, replacing the last bread scraps in his saddle-pannier, "put on thy woman's-tire, and let's go!"

A faint breeze stirred the forest as they cantered through it. For once they blessed the dark wood for its density that had so plagued them on the hunt beforetime, and as it goes with hunters, Tancred swore many an oath as several splendid specimens flew startled from their path. Their boots stirred up scents of dead leaves, of soil fermenting and of meadow-saffron flowering in the shade. In the midst of the tall elms there were little wild cherry-trees turned red at the summits where birds, disturbed in their year-end nests, gave off excited squawks. The morning was soft and golden, with just a touch of one of those faint autumn mists that merge with the light of the fading summer whose well-remembered perfumes did little to quiet the wild heat that burned in the blood of Bohemond.

They had come to the threshold of the Wood, and now Tancred, looking to each side, tightened the scarf on his scarred cheek, let back his hood to display his long hair, and limped out boldly to the castle close.

"Good wines, god's-cakes!" he called in a respectable falsetto that Bohemond had practiced him in on the road. *"Acarenza* today!"

The plan was that if he got past the observance of whoever came to the portcullis without alarm being raised, then Bohemond could somehow enter with Tancred standing guard. And it would be a great premium, beyond their best hopes, should the summons be answered by Lady Zoë.

And such was not the case. The square-skulled steward replied to the tumult of the chain. But it was a fair omen that he stood on the lip of the ruined moat-bridge for many minutes, informing the cloaked pedlaress that the lady of the hall did not wish wine.

Bohemond sat his stallion beside the grey trunk of an ancient tree, fidgeting with his spur, and was just getting ready to dash forth, Tancred's signal or no, when a gauntleted husky arm issued from the fustian mantle at last, gesturing affirmatively.

"Come!"

Once in, the plan had been for Bohemond to hide himself within the keep, until such time as he could secretly see Zoë. Tancred was to talk to her over the pedlar-basket, and with some luck (if the steward made himself scarce) to inform Zoë that Bohemond was there. But just as he entered there was suddenly the sound of her voice, talking, and at that longed-for music, all thought of danger faded. A species of madness seized upon Bohemond, and he strode straight to the hall.

Under the canopy, in company with a stout serving woman, she sat at a game of chess. The Lombard steward, at a respectful distance from their low game table, stood murmuring to the pedlar. Bohemond broke up the quiet tableau, scattering the chessmen with the wide sweep of the pilgrim's habit, as he caught up Zoë and swept her to his arms.

She resisted at first, her eyes widening with fright, then recognizing the flushed face above the beard, and seeing the short, bright cap of hair emerge from the hood that fell back, she breathed, "Bohemond!" and for one moment responded with warm demanding ardor as he kissed her—her mouth, her eyes, her face and back again to her swollen lips.

But then she tensed, pulling away from his embraces. In a flash he was facing a different person, her whole body stiff, and her long eyes, so lately green with sudden passion, grown strange to him and cold.

"Well, Bohemond! How is *this,* that you make love to a married woman!"

His arms relaxed, fell.

"This is no time for a jest, sweetheart!"

"No jest! See?" She held up her hand with a strange golden ring on it, not his. "While you dallied with nuptial notes to the French princess, I realized all but too tardily where my true love lay, and made haste to secure that which in my bewitched blindness almost passed me by!"

He snatched at the one word, dizzy with it all.

"Princess! What princess?" Even as he absorbed the news, relief flooded in. She had *not* forsworn him. It was a misunderstanding! As for marriage—marriage was no obstacle to stop him now.

"Abbot Hugh supplied all the details, and conveyed your message with great aplomb . . . A good performance on all sides."

"Stop chattering, Zoë! There *was* no princess! As for that damned abbot I'll see him flayed alive for this. I'll . . ."

"Small chance, Bo," the cool voice interrupted. "He died last twelvemonth in a hunting accident." But she was not actually thinking of her words. Her mind scanned the facts. Odd circumstances that had recently brought her here—and fear for him drove out everything.

"Bohemond—there are men about the hold! I've seen them around here this week past. And now I understand . . . We live in Amalfi, now, naturally, and there was a strange note from Mihera who has been at sea, for me to visit here and wait. I *thought* it strange . . . What is it, Bo? The Duchess?"

But he had gone white.

"You married Mihera Falloc?"

"Yes. Mihera."

"My God, Zoë!" He went to pieces a moment, pacing the width of the hall, roughly tearing off the tow beard and throwing it on the stones. And when he again faced her, there was a look of savage determination that she had never before seen on his face.

"Listen *well* to me, Zoë! You don't think I intend to be tricked out of *you* too, do you—you whose lips on mine just now proclaimed to the high heavens that we still belong together? Blast them! Get your cloak, Zoë! You're coming with me!"

The manner in which she shook her head, ruefully and with a certain dignity that he had never known in her before, daunted him for the first time.

"No, Bohemond. Don't you see? I am wife to Mihera, and there's more . . . I—I haven't felt well lately, and Dr. Poldi says I'll bear Mihera's child within the year . . ."

This last convinced him—this first, strong link in the chain of inevitable circumstances that told him their mutual dream was done. His face darkened.

"It is an ill thing you did, Zoë, flying off at the first rumor that confirmed your own doubts of the trust that I thought was finally strong between us! As for Mihera . . ." He ripped out an obscene oath.

Her lips tightened, the little dents of anger gathering about.

"Mihera is least at fault in all this, Bo. And don't mistake me—I will love him. I will always love him."

"Agh! That, from you, is histrionics. What of your kiss?"

Her glance shifted. "I lost my senses just now, as you fell upon us. But it's truly over, Bo. We must accept what must be . . ."

Chains clanked outside. Bohemond started, looked about.

"Marcelle! Where's the steward?" said Zoë.

"I know not, madame," the fat one answered, half-way between fright and sly pleasure at having witnessed the hot little scene. "He hurried out—"

"To rouse the troops!" cried Zoë.

"If he went by the portcullis," said Bohemond, "he's dead, doubtless. Tancred's there."

"Then why do you tarry? God help us—go!"

There was a scuffling sound in the outer hall. He hesitated.

"Down in the scullery cave," she told him wildly. "There's a rotted place in the west wall beneath the overhang. You can follow the fen-path from there. Oh, hurry!" She was crying now.

"Send Tancred with the mounts—the old woman at the portcochere . . ."

He hesitated and turned back a moment, hard-eyed, grey-lipped, looking like a stranger as he stood there, framed in the sullen shadows. A curse came from his lips.

"God blast you, Zoë, for your fool stubbornness and your small faith!" And he struck out toward the gloom of the castle kitchens.

He waited heartsick and with pulses pounding, until Tancred brought the destriers. He could hear voices roused in the wood.

"We'll take another way then," he improvised. "Now be bold, Tancred," he called, mounting. "Make for Faustin's Bridge!"

They flew through the fen-path, unheeding the briers that flailed cruelly at their horses' hides. Emerging thence, they found luck, for the Bridge was bare and Bohemond pulled up at the hermitage, proffering a coin.

Faustin sat within, reading matins by the light of the dull sun through her eastern window-hole. Looking up, startled, she cried, "Young Bohemond!" and hobbled to the ledge. "They *all* seek you! Borsa has men in the hills that track you as a hunter would a buck, and the Duchess herself commands a whole company down at the mere!"

"Aye, what to do, Faustin?" He seemed to bore into the eyes of the melted old face.

She laid down her psaltery and pointed with a long yellow finger-tip at a point to the left of the road. "There's a way, nearly gone now, that leads far through the forest and emerges through a natural pierce in the mountainside onto meadow by the road. Take thou that. I like not this wolfpack besetting a lad in whom I know no wrong. Fly, Sir, and remember my soul in death!"

The two fugitives had fled, seeing the God-sent cleft in the tangled over-growth. They found it, and presently when they emerged from an obscure cave into open country, the sunlight found Tancred smiling, chattering and caracolling his war-horse in boyish relief. But Bohemond rode after him silent and newly hard-faced, in a deep muse.

BOOK 4

THE WARLOCK PRINCE

CHAPTER XV

At the Wall

WHEN THE DREAMS of the dead Hildebrand and the verve of the young chivalry caught fire for the First Crusade, strange worlds were destined to collide like stars. Alexius the Greek was thoroughly shocked at this flood of Frenchmen, when he had only, most ruefully now, inquired for a few. He extracted oaths, gave gifts, and consigned them to heat, sand, and unimaginable hardships they had never faced before.

But they were game. They took it all with gusto. They had spectacular successes at Nicea and Dorilay. And then they saw Antioch, wanted it, and sat down at its walls like children at some fine, new game.

Alexius, leaving legates and vague words, returned to Byzantium.

This was different. A tired enough outfit when they spread their pavilions for the siege, their aplomb soon faded. Stopped, helpless, their camps raided nightly by marauding sheiks, they were scared, they were getting hungry; and they were naïvely puzzled by Alexius' withdrawn bounty. It was late autumn, 1098.

One night, deep in the French encampment, Lady Falloc woke. Trembling, profoundly shaken from another of those dreams, she pressed her tensed side against her husband's.

"Mihera, are you awake?"

There was no reply. Her glance, half-mused with scenes of Wood and Bridge and jousting field at home, withdrew from the Count's still profile and brushed the interior of their sleeping-tent. The bed half-filled it; a jumble of war things ranged its silken sides. Mihera's longsword, his steel cap, chain *maille*, and the bold round of the Mussulman raider's shield he had taken yesternight. It stood out, this painted pagan thing, like some blasphemous vision, its harsh lines lit by a break in the tent-flap—that reddish wedge of the Syrian sky and a piece of the Wall of Antioch. Toward this presently she moved, slipping from between the ticks and throwing a stiff silk cloak about her nightdress and a veil about her dark, unbraided hair.

The guard moved decorously away at her emergence, and she had the palisade with its guttering watch-flame to herself. She lifted her face from the parabola of warmth with its sharp-sweet scents of sumach and burning bay, and gazed across the sleeping Norman camp. To the north, hard by the silent Wall, night fires illumined Prince Bohemond's new fort on the Mount of Maregat, and opposite this, on the escarpment of St. Paul's Gate, torcheres moved slowly. Westward—silent and white and menacing—streaked the road to Aleppo, the Shiek's highway. It seemed that it rose to the world's edge and into the quarter-orb hung above the sand. Dimly scarlet, wind-whipped and curved as a Saracen scimitar, this moon held her gaze. What was that dream again? The Wood, the field, the Bridge, the old excitement—no! Her smile was rueful. Not *that* again, with all these years between. That old quickening, that very ache . . . Not that *again*, at thirty!

And yet, what a vivid thing, this resurgence of the past—a start, a stir, and a quickening once again—a high renewal . . . zut! A mirage of mockery, this—like that moon. Tonight, in this late autumn time, it *seemed* like the same that hung on Sicily, Salerno—all the places once called home. But it wasn't. It was only a thing of mischief, arousing these dead dreams, visions of half-won heavens, and the bittersweet taste of old goodbyes.

"Zoë!"

"Yes." She started a little. "Are you awake, Mihera?"

"But of course, with this breeze you loosed in here with the coverlets apart . . . Oh . . . Ow! God save us!"

"*What* Mihera?"

"Your zithern by the couch, on the very spot where a man must put his foot down!"

"Don't hurt it, Mihera!"

"Vaugh!"

"I'm sorry, dear!"

Her slight laugh assured him she was merely sleepless, and the bruise from his brush with the instrument had dampened his intent to rise. He pulled back the upper tick. She was restless, fretting on some song, no doubt. The zithern was always the sign. It had appeared again only yesterday, and Zoë was stricken once more—as by a pox—with song-making. Not that one held rancor for this (not when one had married Ridelle's daughter!), it wasn't that. But something—her dead earnestness about it, mayhap—irritated. Too bad there was just one child for all their marriage. It had told on Zoë. It seemed to him, thinking on it now, that she had never come to full-blown, settled matronhood as other women did, had not much changed indeed since the days of their youth together, when she and he himself and Bohemond . . . He suddenly frowned.

"Zoë, why don't you rest?"

"I don't know, Mihera. I think I'm catching an ague."

"You are *not!* You'd be quaking here beside me, not standing about in the night air!"

"It's a *strange* ague, Mihera . . . The symptoms . . ."

"You're *not* catching an ague!"

There was silence.

"Mihera. There's torch-glow in Lady Albarada's tent!"

"So?" His irritation edged his voice.

"She *leaves* soon, you know, with the sick ones, to return to Byzantium and make ship for Italy. All the way home without peace with Bohemond . . . With her *own* son! She told me she turned him away again. She wept. I think she mourns, Mihera. It might be otherwise, with one more interview. Maybe you and I—"

"Should stick *our* noses in?" came dourly from the gloom. "Don't fash yourself, Zoë, she's a hard old woman. De Hauteville's tried thrice to reconcile that I know of. She'll have none of him."

"But Mihera!" She was in dead earnest now. "Such a *shock,* after all these years, seeing him his father's image. Duke Robert broke her heart, you know! If you'd hear her when she speaks of him. I wept . . ."

"Doubtless." He yawned audibly. "Doubtless you did . . . But Robert's long dead and Bohemond's bounden for his *own* sins only, and she'll be dead soon too. So let her mend it with Guiscard in hell . . . I'm sleepy."

"You know, Mihera—" her voice, vibrant with that singing quality came back to him. "You *hit* it, in a way! I think she knows her end's near. Today she said, 'I'll never see the Holy Land with this dallying here, with my son as stubborn as ever Robert was, resolved on the siege. Therefore, I'll go back. I've a certain rendezvous prepared there.' . . . What did she mean?"

"*I don't know,*" cried her husband with almost boyish exasperation. "Save it! Save it for songs or a tale for little Ursule! But now come to sleep, I beg you. Dawn shows already."

He stirred, drowsy beneath the tick and watched her tall, quick silhouette advancing through the tent-slit. He had not intended to come awake and he did not wish to stay so. He closed his eyes. There was much for tomorrow. It would take straight talk to Bohemond, to show him his folly. The brief riotous holiday they had known here after desert rigors would soon be done. The summer was past, the winds rife, those maddening winds called simoon here, but only an eastern version of the savage gale they knew so well—the sirocco. And here, as at home, rains followed. They would have it hard. For within the Wall the governor Yagi Sayan only waited . . .

Zoë stood above him while she let the cape slip off. His light, stiff hair dishevelled on his brow, his strong, straightforward, serious face—how dear he was. Much more than one deserved . . . She climbed to the high couch and bent across him, laying her face on his a time. She felt his lashes brush against her cheek, then fall. He was quite still beneath her warm impulse, and his lips were dry when she brushed them tentatively with her own. But she was not hurt. The passive dismissal was typical of him, when annoyed a little. She even smiled, settling against him for sleep, for there had, besides, been love a little earlier. After all, he was not insatiable . . .

Still, sleep was fugitive. For Mihera too, she suspected, though he lay there breathing quietly. Grave tasks in the Host—dispensing rations, laying stores, keeping contacts with ports as they traveled inland—kept him full of cares. Starvation was a far worse threat, he said, than Saracens.

How the Crusade had wrecked their peace! What a good life it had been at Amalfi Cliff-Hall. Mihera with ships for a thousand places and she serene and still as she had never been before. And then, after nine good years, the Crusade, with Bohemond appearing from no-where, as if on its crest, calling. How he had laughed, Mihera, at the high tale of Bo on some petty battlefield, dramatically slashing his cloak to crosses and riding off with half his relatives' retainers! But only a little later, Mihera too, had come home, acting odd, with a sheep's look on his face, confessing an assignment in the Norman horse, as chief Knight-Seneschal for the barons of the South.

Mihera had regrets. She knew this. He had yielded to Bohemond. He had shattered, for the time, at least, his preferred existence. Hard-headed, successful in business, and long alien to feudal ways, he had left everything, donned armor, and gone riding into unknown worlds, for a dream.

Yet, why not? she thought abruptly. Why not? Had not many a lord and many a sage, and many a king's son, including William the Conqueror's? As for yielding to Bo's persuasion, Mihera was not alone. In *all* this company, deferring to Bohemond was a general thing. In the Greek tricks at Byzantium, in the slews of the desert, in the fighting of Turks and maneuvering of the clumsy western horse, all, amazingly enough, gave ear to the knowledge, judgment and manifest superior skill of the upstart prince from the Sicilian moors.

The army jongleurs, so busy with their war-songs, made ballads of the Host, of the Saracens, and of Antioch—why he who would compass the whole should make a song of Bohemond, and have it done with!

She was struck by this thought. She stirred in the rustling straw. Did these princes and pilgrims, these saints and churchmen know what sort he was—these trusting valiants who sought the Sepulchre as others had the Holy Grail? What a thinking and knowing—what remembering it would take! And who to know it so well as she!

She thought again of the ancient noblewoman, Albarada. She thought of all she had dwelt on yesterday, of the old days, and how it was when she was young there, and of Bohemond, when he was only a babe called Marc, her first-born . . .

And so she mused, half-waked, half-dreaming, while the red wedge paled in the tent-flap, and the torches dwindled on the walls of Antioch.

CHAPTER XVI *Little Ursule*

RISING MUCH LATER than he had planned and wryly blaming Zoë for it, Mihera had gone seeking Bohemond with the sun already mounted, and Zoë had one more desert-hot endless day to fill with her own resources. Tasks in the tent enclosure busied the midday hours and it was not until late afternoon, with the hot, dry breeze rushing in again from a copper sky, that she announced to the nurse her intention of once more seeking Albarada. The meditations and surmisings of the night before had but roused her to find out more on the old theme the baroness had sounded.

Carrying a small pannier with sweet-cakes in it, still warm, she made her way over the high dune that separated the two encampments, holding her head down to keep her veils from whipping unduly, so that she was quite to the spot when she drew up short in surprise and disappointment. The space where the tent had stood, a great, weather-stained mushroom with retainers' pavilions hugged about it in the manner of the wealthy in the Host, was empty. The sandy soil was scraped into little waves where the silk had been dragged across it in the folding, and now that the wind had risen, the pole-holes were gradually filling with small waterfalls of loam. One portable stone oven had been left behind in prodigal impatience, too hot to cart off after a hasty morning breakfast. The Byzantium-bound caravan, leaving at dawn, had carried a last-minute passenger, then. One knew the old one had meant to leave them. Yet the suddenness of this—without a leave-taking at all!

The crotchety, ungrateful old thing, thought Zoë, who had taken for granted that things she had done for her—visits, exotically prepared dishes, other small favors—had insured her a measure of friendship. That she had cultivated the noblewoman's somewhat sour company because of her titillating link with home and the past, a sort of sop for her own carking melancholy, was something scarcely to be admitted. She was piqued. She stamped her sandal in the sand. And after a brisk mounting of the dune, for this, she let herself lean breathless against a large bay, that made with others of its kind a spot of coolness here. The breeze riffled the bay in its topmost fronds and sent an aromatic fragrance downward to where she stood. She sniffed, catching its spicy scent, and slipped a hand beneath the napkin of her hand-basket. She ate, staring through frustrated tears at the remnants of the establishment of the vanished countess.

Suddenly there was a noise, a tumult of galloping, a singing of hooves on sand. Zoë shrank against the bay. Even in the dunes, where Mihera and other chiefs had camped for some measure of privacy, going about alone had danger to it. Stragglers from other camps, spies (though these were few now) and rogues from a certain doubtful company called the Ribalds—half-pilgrims, half-thieves, who had attached themselves to the expedition—thoughts of these gentry made one quail. Still—a mounted knight . . . She looked out, the Wall and the hot landscape swimming through her tears. A heavy, dun-colored gelding had reared on the ridge but even before the nervous animal set hoof to earth again, she knew the rider. Massive shoulders, towering height and a tossed cap of red hair. It brought both relief and panic. For though fear was now needless and flight unthinkable, dignity was much to be desired. For Zoë, with due notice that Bohemond had not once attempted a family call, since the start at Byzantium, had long since planned him a cool reception when they finally met. But now . . . ? Watching him come, his mount still dancing to the tautened reins, she knew, without shift to mend it, that she was all agape like any schoolgirl with a great grin on her face, squinting up against the lowering sun, the sweet-cake suspended halfway to her slightly opened lips.

"Well!" he cried, swinging his great frame to the sand. "What have we here? Disappointment and pleasure together!" He had not known of his mother's going—she saw it on his face a mere moment before he shunted and concealed it, in the old way she knew.

He came, walking lightly, unarmored and with only a short dagger slanting in his sash. A weightless mantle of saffron whipped about his legs. A little heavier, she thought, and more of a dandy, and his face is even more subtle than it once was. He had walked quite through the pavilion-digs, and idly, with his boot-tip, pushed earth into one of the post-holes in a small gesture of finality.

He looked up at her with his old, faint shrug.

"I too meant to visit her," she told him, indicating her burden of sweets. "I spiced these with strange, sweet willows they pluck here by the river-banks; she liked them well."

"Sugar," Bohemond said absently. He was staring beyond her, his face darkened with his thoughts.

"I scarcely thought the caravan would try it," she said, "in this time, with the winds starting up again . . ."

"I myself directed it," he said with a slanted smile. "There was an anxious passenger. The Emperor's man Tacitius—homesick, I daresay, for the Basileus. He insists, of course, that it's help he goes for. But we won't see the Greek again. *He* has heard tales, *too,* I take it. Starvation, simoons, and Saracens . . . All *manner* of dooms, which they say my plan for Antioch will bring to the Host. Don't I scare you, Zoë? I'm a sinister fellow!"

He laughed, and she heard the harsh note and saw the new, hard look about his mouth, and as he came, continuing in this vein, she was slightly unnerved. His voice had always been deep, strong, yet marked by a gentleness and preciseness of speech that came as a pleasant shock in one so forceful. It was a thing she loved to listen to. In the sure privacy of great crowds gathered in the Host, she could hear him with sheer pleasure and, while other barons spoke, could watch him for long spaces of time—his profile, so coin-like, with the high brow, straight nose, the fuller, rounder chin, than she had known of yore, but the same sensitive, chiseled lips that even in repose marked him in that assemblage of princes as truly princely.

But this, at close quarters, was different. She felt the scrutiny of *his* eyes now, and she could scarcely look at him, and wished for very desperation to end the interview. Indeed, she had insensibly moved away and they were walking athwart the dune to her lively pace, with the gelding faintly jingling as he ambled after.

"*Quel miserere!*" she thought in a garbled phrase from childhood. "Am I thirty or thirteen?" The thought somewhat summoned her aplomb.

"Here, Zoë! Where are we bound to?" he inquired, chuckling a little. "Why don't we settle where it's cool and sheltered by the bays?" He began unbuckling his saffron.

"Mind your fine cape," she said. "My own of fustian takes well to desert-places." Her lips dented with mischief and she noted he flushed slightly. With some satisfaction she sank comfortably to the sand, and turning one shoulder from the Wall where the low sun seemed to hurl itself, proffered the basket.

"Well," he said, as though sensing her easier mood, "the lady, my mother, has fled our company, but she left me a nice enough benison for it . . . !" She said nothing to this, not wanting to broach the personal. He saw her reluctance; he laughed. She smelled his sand-and-salty sweating as he knelt beside her for the sticky treat. "My God, Zoë," he exclaimed, his hot-grey, intense eyes quite frankly on her face. "You look superb and the *big* treat is to see you!"

In a great restless movement he rose up and she found herself fearing for a space he was going to leave. But with one hand in his sash he began to pace, talking rapidly between great bites of sugar-cake, his bright hair paled a little against the warm blue glare of the sky.

"What a day it's been!" he mourned, half seriously. "What a time of it they give me, Zoë! You can't imagine!"

"Who?" she asked quietly, glad he turned on other subjects. "The chiefs? Is Raymond about again?" It was well known that Raymond St. Gilles, the old and irascible leader of the Provençals, quarreled hotly with Bohemond on every turn.

"No, not Raymond, nor even Godfrey. They've both a flux. My God, Zoë, now that I think, I'm alone in a command here, with them sick and Tancred scouting and Robert of Normandy whoring himself to ribbons on the Coast! But no—the particular fly in my ale today and always, lately, is Mihera."

He paused momentarily and leaned again to the basket. *"Good,* Zoë! You might sweeten Mihera some on these. It'd do that peppery tongue of his no harm, I tell you! . . . Doesn't *like* my siege!" he went on with his mouth full, propelled by his boundless enthusiasm. *"None* of 'em have the stomach for it. Faint-hearted, gloomy as the Styx . . . *You* know how they talk . . ."

"But after all," she told him mildly, "it would scarcely be sensible to starve here, before ever we see the Holy Places . . ."

"Starve? Who speaks of starving? Why, Falloc is hand in glove with the shippers at Laodicea."

"Laodicea will hardly be reachable once the rains come, he says. Besides, the Venetians are there too, and in Alexius' pay. They would break up the Viking ships like so much beachwood, should Alexius ask it, Mihera says."

He stood, legs apart, half-frowning at her. *"Et tu,* Zoë—against me. The good wife upholding her husband's cause."

"And why not?" she countered. "Especially when common sense is on the side of it. Sarcastic talk does not become you, Bohemond. You were not always thus."

"I don't recall that the way I was *beforetime* had much good favor with you either, Zoë!" He caught his breath then; he shrugged, and broadly smiled. "Do we quarrel already? No matter. It makes the fabric whole at least. Those closest to me ranged on the one side where I can get a good look at what they have to say. You and Mihera and one more—Adhemar the Legate. You know him?"

"The Pope's representative? Yes, as who does not, on this undertaking! A good, wise counsellor. You'd do well to heed what *he* says, Bohemond!"

"I do, ordinarily. We suit each other's company, the Legate and I. Adhemar's a wit, a good trencherman and unequalled in the field, for *all* he's a churchman! But lately I find him troublesome. He too harps on the thing of Antioch. He plagues me, coaxes me—footless obsessions . . ."

"How do you mean?" Zoë asked, as he hesitated, in a frowning study.

"Well," with an agitated flinging of arms, "because of events thus far, the fact that Stephen of Blois, though nominal chief here, is a weakling, and because of the illness of Godfrey and the Provençal, and the doings of Robert Shortshanks at Laodicea—his 'shameful pursuit of passion' as Adhemar piously puts it—the Legate surmises *me* to be the one divinely destined, and says I should therefore scuttle us all straightway to Jerusalem, with no more ado!"

"Well," faltered Zoë, "is that not our goal precisely? To capture the Sepulchre?"

"Yes . . . But also to push the Saracens to their proper limits. Militarily we'd do ill to by-pass Antioch. Here we are, sitting at the oldest town in Syria, Christian always save now for these damned Moslem rag-heads! And we should let it go by? Look at it, Zoë!" He turned with a sudden violence and flung an impatient arm toward distant towers sparkling in the sun. "Do Mihera or Adhemar or the rest of you think to tease me from *this* with your gloom or your silly visions?"

He laughed mockingly. "Even today, as we conferred, Adhemar conjured a phenomenon for me, the very way you'd make fancies for a babe. The sun, by chance, on my sword-hilt, forming the Cross . . . Bah! I quickly disenchanted him. Let the gullible enjoy their holy signals as they did at Clermont and in Europe last spring, falling stars and sky-crosses and the rest of it—sops for the rabble! *I'm* not taking any! Let the Legate and the rest remember that I'm a soldier, not a God-anointed guardian angel for the whole damned Crusade!"

He was quite flushed with emotion. His fingers rattled against his dagger alarmingly. Zoe smiled and quietly reminded him, "You protest much, yet the rôle does suit you! All in the Host speak about it, Bohemond—how you war against the infidel not with war-joy only, but as one endowed and dedicated, so that even the Moslems call you *Maimoun*, little god. And all like to tell that when Peter the Hermit sought recently to leave us, you became a very monument of righteousness against him, the soldier shaming the saint, as the jongleurs put it.

"Look, Bo! That's what carks you, isn't it? Not *their* words, but *your* choice, between this"—she gestured toward the Wall—"and the mighty vision!"

His face held a mixture of things as he heard her outburst—startlement, admiration and a sort of grudging assent. But in his voice was careful mockery as he told her, "Indeed, my friends and enemies should make *you* their legate of dissuasion, Zoë. I should be better moved by you than by Adhemar's fancies or Mihera's nightmares, did I not know you are your father's daughter, with his tongue and his pretty dreams."

She flushed at this. She became quizzical. "There are those *too,* Bohemond, who call you otherwise: a dark prince, whose nature is warlock, whose ways are warlock and whose power comes not from skywards, but more likely from the devil! I have not said which view I hold to . . . I doubt if I know. Do you?"

"That's an old question, Zoë." He leaned toward her, one boot propped on a tree root and his chin in his hand. "I could have wished you not so bothered by the point. Things had gone better for us formerly!" His voice and the raillery in it had suddenly softened. "But I like to see you roused, whatever the cause. When you are angry, as when you love, there's magic in you, Zoë."

His face was close. The edges of his eyes seemed widened, seemed all dark. There was no sound but the rustling of the bays, deepening their sense of aloneness together. He murmured something more. Zoë started, and the mood had suddenly vanished.

A little girl came scampering up the dune, all dark bobbing curls, with outstretched arms. She was reaching them toward her mother.

"Little Ursule!" Zoë caught the youngster breathless and laughing in a quick embrace. "Where's Marcelle?" she cried. "Not *with* you?"

Ursule winked. "Looking for me! She runs about like an old she-bear, puffing and mumbling"—Ursule was minutely grotesque—"but I concealed myself."

"Ursule!" cried Zoë, pale. "That was very naughty—" she frowned —"and unforgivable for Marcelle to allow you off the palisade. For this I shall stripe her!"

"She's the very image of you, Zoë," said Bohemond, beside them. "Your very self!"

Little Ursule gazed up at the fine soldier, much impressed.

"This is Prince Bohemond, Ursule."

Ursule regarded him gravely as, sinking to one knee, he drew her gently on the other. In answer to his own tentative grin she dimpled and faltered, "Bomun."

"What a barbarous name to say, aye, sweetheart? But you do prettily enough!"

Ursule observed him, his splendid silks, his hair. She eyed him. She reached his hair and touched it gingerly. Bohemond laughed, his great voice booming with delight. Ursule, startled, made shift to leave him, but he drew her back, saying softly, "Here, I've scared you, barbarian that I am . . . You're not to be laughed at, I see, no more than your lady mother." He wound a coil of her spring-like curls about his finger.

There was a noise of puffing and expostulating and they all turned. Huge, red-faced, Marcelle came lumbering up the dune, her fat breasts heaving heavily, her tall coif knocked rakishly askew.

"*'Sbody!* What a fright!" she rasped, her wind a wheeze and her hands madly wringing one another. "I've looked and looked . . . For minutes I've been devastated!"

"And well you might!" said Zoë, her voice cold. She advanced. She struck her. "I've told you—*how often* I've told you, Marcelle, that never must you lose her here! Never permit her from your sight, save with me . . ." She struck her again. "Never, save with me!"

"Don't, Mama!" Ursule called from her perch on the knight's knee. "It wasn't her *fault!* I sneaked! I sneaked away." She jumped from his arms and went pulling at Marcelle's skirts. "Come, Marcelle! Mama's angry! It's better to go now!" And she dragged and pushed till the old servant complied, and must half-run, half-slide with the wee one down the dune.

"My word!" said Bohemond with mock concern, "the poor old burd will have a stricture of the heart between you—two such bombastic mistresses!"

"I don't find it humorous!" she snapped, and he saw with surprise how her eyes still watched them, and her voice still trembled with chagrin.

"Without that nurse and Dr. Poldi, without their full attention and constant care, I could never have brought her on this expedition . . ."

"Messer Poldi," Bohemond repeated. "Ursule is in good hands. He was known to my father . . ."

"The best to be found," she said with vehemence. "It could not be otherwise, with all the dangers here . . . Even now, sometimes, I think, if harm should touch her . . ." She trailed off . . .

Bohemond was thoughtful.

"No other?" he said with deference. "She's scarcely of an age to be the first . . ."

Zoë colored, keyed to the scene he recalled.

"She isn't, of course. The first did not live, and even with Ursule I was gravely ill. The doctor did miracles to save us. His measures, apparently, have kept me from further babes . . . So Ursule, you see, is precious beyond the ordinary . . . !"

She waved again, but Ursule had vanished from the dunes.

"She's captivating! I think we'll be comrades!" His smile was genuinely warm.

Zoë was pleased and her eyes, as she answered him, were filled with her old mischief. "Comrades? That were hard, Bohemond, save that you visited us more than you've managed in the past. I've reminded Mihera often for you to take supper with us here but . . ." she shrugged, and, her natural high spirits emerging before she thought, "Even at Byzantium, I thought I was avoided," she said. "You were busy, I know, but still it seemed strange, since you promised me Byzantium once, or don't you remember?"

She stopped, appalled. She had meant to make a jest, but midway it had become a blunder, touched off by a quick huskiness in her voice and the devil waiting in her all these months. The query had escaped her like a flare to light up unknown places she had glimpsed, like a child opening a forbidden casket—or (her eyes dropping to his serpent-chased baselard to avoid his own) like a woman offering some of what she tentatively and in secret tasted . . . She wished the words unsaid now. She would have cut her tongue to make them so.

But he towered close. She could feel his quickened breath on her temple.

"Do I remember!" he breathed. "Zoë, Zoë, tell me," he said urgently, as if in their last moment earthward, "was *that* why you ruined all between us—because I failed that time on the road to Constantinople?"

There was no retreating. She had broached it. She must answer.

"You know better. It was *you* I wanted—not Byzantium—not the world. But I thought I had lost—to Byzantium."

"What a fool," his voice came low and raspingly. "What a fool I was to lose you!" His words, his tone demolished the long years between. With great effort she kept her voice empty of things that might be in it now. She felt him, felt his eyes, but she kept looking down, and blessed the twilight.

"It's late, Bo," she said quickly. "I must go back."

There was noise of laughter at distant supper-boards and small ribbands of smoke were rising everywhere.

"It *is* late," Bohemond repeated. "Aye, it's too late now, and I am an exile for it."

"I'm sorry, Bohemond."

But there was no answer. She looked up. He was not looking at her, but over her head where the final rays of the westering sun had crept like spilled wine across the battlements, beyond the walls of Antioch. All the glory there was in his eyes. He seemed entranced.

Zoë smiled. "My sorrow is scarcely *de rigueur*," she thought. She began to hum:

> *Lord of a city will I be*
> *With lots of glory to cover me*
> *With plenty of gold and plenty of glee*
> *And the Queen of France to marry me.*

Bohemond gazed down at her. He was puzzled, even piqued a little, yet all but drawn to her own quick laughter. He placed his two hands on her shoulders and shook her a little.

"You're still strange, unfathomable," he said. "You haven't altered any."

She sobered. "Don't say *that*, Bo. It must *be* that I've changed." There was an odd silence after that. "Goodbye then . . ."

"May I take you?"

"But no. Just a few steps to the pavilion."

He seemed to be very poised now, and this, in him, was obscurely frightening. His whole aspect as he stood there, his hand on the gelding's saddle, his boot raised to the stirrup beneath his wide cape, somehow crystallized that strange impression, and somewhere deep in her consciousness sounded a bell.

"Till we see each other, Zoë," he said. "I'll mend my ways, I swear, and come often to your board." He mounted and, with a last look that was only half a smile, he turned and sped away.

"Why am I disturbed?" she thought. "Everything's well. Surely I'm free now, when even at this moment I recalled how it was. An old game, to have no more traffic with—my eyes on him and his on some shining city."

She made her way across the dunes, guided by the spiral of smoke from her own pavilion. Her step was determined and she hummed a little tune.

Winter came, with them still bivouacked at the Wall. Mihera's worst warnings came woefully to term. When the simoon ceased, the rains followed, converting the dunes to mud. After hideous endurances in hardships and in war, this drawn-out misery seemed the last extreme. They suffered, they complained, and in disturbingly vast numbers they fled.

Those who stayed were desperate enough. On rare, rainless nights by the damp and smoky tent fires, they would congregate, discussing their chances of survival. Where were their leaders? Where were those fine, pious lords who had led them hither with so much aplomb? They would pick off the captains, one by one, like the leaves of an artichoke.

Not so wonderful, the French barons. It was only the "upstart" Bohemond that could be looked to with real hope. "Inspired!" they said. "Dares all—fears nothing! Not rumor, not bad luck, not Greek, Saracen, nor the manifestations of the very Devil!" It seemed the Sicilian's peculiar genius that he fed, as much as their need of leadership, their spiritual hopes of triumph.

To be sure, some doubted this delay at Antioch. It was hard to fathom, this divergence from the goal. But doubts were shouted down. Because their need was from desperation, their regard was near idolatry. "Faith, have faith!" they cried. "The Prince from Nowhere will lead us to the Prince of Peace!"

The legend grew.

"Wait for the spring!" said Bohemond. "Endure, pilgrims! Endure till the glorious spring!"

He harped on this with all the powers of his ingenuity, and they were endless. He kept religious ardor high—masses, votive displays, song-fests, pilgrimage-like processions in which the faithful could participate. He gathered minstrels, mimes and jongleurs and cast them in strange new entertainments that never had been heard of before, save by those from Paris or Chartres or the more sophisticated towns. Many a night, while the rain beat sodden on the great pavilion he had ordered to be builded for these exercises, the people sat—drenched, pinched with famine, their bodies racked with uncontrollable ague—but happily intent on bizarre depictions. Scenes like their own plight, where trolls, demons, and Saracenic ogres attacked the white-clad pilgrims till the latter overcame them, arriving in a great to-do of music and incense, at the Tomb of Bethlehem.

The Clergy augmented his efforts for religious exercises. Not so for the plays. On these there was a decidedly mixed opinion. Bohemond's "mysteries" were far removed from the European performances (these last being short sequences done on feast days and with all reverence by acolytes and choir-boys). Here, indeed, the great favorite of the day was Tafur, King of the Ribalds, whose bold interpolations on his highly satanic rôles were freely spiced with the questionable humor of his clan. His appearances were attended with high gusto, in spite of bans by certain bishops in the pilgrim-throngs, which for those who patronized lent an added fillip of deviltry indeed!

There was one tale connected with all this that could scarcely be credited. Reports persisted that the wife of the Knight-Seneschal, the Norman Count of Bull Joy and respected lord of the sea, was taking a hand with the plays—making songs and verses at Bohemond's behest.

Base calumny, the more charitable declared. Whoever heard of such a thing? A Christian lady (and a Countess, at *that*) involved in theatrics! Wild talk. Rank, malicious gossip . . .

CHAPTER XVII

The Quarrel

"ALL ILL THINGS PASS, Madame Zoë, and of all things, thanking the good God, the winter weather!"

Marcelle regarded her mistress with a knowing look, where she stood in the patch of late sunshine let under the arras-cloth, her arms filled with stuffs from the bargaining just finished on the palisade with Nepaz, the sutler.

"We've all *wished* for the gentle season, on seeing madame so melancholy!" Marcelle said, making a clumsy obeisance. Her sly glance continued on the Countess's mouth where the faint shadows were, and the new little dents between the dark, slanted brows. "Look, madame! Here at the charcoal pot, I've yesterday's *ragout* and a cupful of wine waiting . . ."

But Zoë refused. Her smile was forced, distraught, uneasy. "Go on with your meal, Marcelle. I find no appetite for it. You were saying, as I came, that the Count is returned now?"

"Aye, but busy in the book-press chamber. He wishes to see you when he's presently done. He said he would speak with you then on an important matter."

"Very well." Zoë tossed her purchases on the low ottoman by the bed, her glance sliding without aim about the room. Her teeth moved tightly on her lower lip.

Missing nothing, Marcelle chattered on. "I'll pour you a bath, Madame, I'll scent it with some of the balsam you had of the craven Nepaz."

She fell on the stuffs, rummaging through cloth-rolls, rugs and a pair of leather taper-holders till she rescued the vial. Sniffing as if she could smell quite through the sealed enamel, "A rare scent," she cried, "and priced by that scoundrel like a ruby, doubtless."

Zoë shrugged. "Food's far rarer than trifles, Marcelle. I had preferred some *wheat* of the Armenian, to make pulty-cakes of mornings, for little Ursule!"

Marcelle beamed. "The Count has remedy for that, Madame. We see already he has seemed to bring the spring. But more than that, a great shipment of Spanish mutton which he fell to from English shippers at the Port will follow him by caravan in but few days."

There was less of a rise to her fine tidings than Marcelle might wish. Lady Zoë nodded, sighed, and asked, not looking at her, "Does my lord seem well?"

She hitched a heavy shoulder. "You know how it is with him; difficult to tell. I fancied him troubled on something." This drawing a frown, she added somewhat tardily, "Doubtless he's tired from travel." She fussed, she bustled, intrigued to scent new tensions between mistress and lord, yet anxious to commiserate. She said, with an air of wisdom and conspiracy, "But do you bathe and coif yourself, madame, and forget all cares! The sight of you fresh and radiant will give him comfort. Also—" her heavy voice sinking to a wheeze—"I'll show you such ways with these ointments as only easterlings know them. *Wise* ways: tricks enabling a good wife to charm, bewitch, mesmerize her master into golden oblivion . . ."

"Lord!" exclaimed Zoë, regarding the creature with frank distaste. "You and your oriental nonsense. Get on with the bath!"

Alone, Zoë unhooked the chatelaine from her belt, let the coins fall to the couch, and ruefully contemplated their fewness after the clash with Nepaz. Then she removed the leathern zone itself and part of her clothing, and moved restlessly about the room. She felt apprehensive, frightened, guilty. All these emotions had suddenly assailed at once, banishing today's new mood which at the outset had been such a happy one. For one thought hammered at her mind—the songs. Mihera's failure to seek her, this strange formality on returning after two long fortnights, could only mean he was displeased. Perhaps already he had heard how in his absence she had fashioned some rhythms for the Easter Play—though he'd been set against it—and was determined now to show this anger. Yet why? What harm was there in it, especially when she avoided the Pavilion herself? A few songs, some sacred, some merry, such as her father had loved to make. Where was the great wrong? True, Mihera had protested, even as Bohemond first broached the subject at their supper-board, but had not Bohemond laughed him out of countenance and banished the question of impropriety altogether? It was Mihera who lay at fault, if any. Why, nowadays *everyone* composed!

Aye, but minstrels, jongleurs and peasant troubadours, and no lady, save with the gypsies.

And her heart said something further. Time was when she would not have dreamed deliberately to press a thing Mihera disapproved of . . .

For that, from the first, had been the pattern of their life together. Mihera had been a rock to Zoë. The Amalfi years had only increased and manifested the essential goodness in him. She had always known them well—those virtues inherent in that integrity of his, which if plain and somewhat lacking in aplomb, were as firmly rooted as a wind-blown cypress on a lofty rock. But Zoë, in love, had somehow expected further overgrowths, nuances, facets of feeling in this, her husband. These were not shown forth. Yet she had sought to answer his simple affection for all the world as though these qualities were someday to be waked, like hidden royalties of some beslumbered prince. And the coin had an obverse. She was immediately apprised of Mihera's far-from-satisfied views about *herself*. He loved her, aye, but he saw, had long seen, and now set about correcting, what he regarded as considerable flaws, giving his own guidance, the common-sense teachings of life, and the passing of an excess of spirits full credit to accomplish his ambitious project.

Chief in these lessons of his was a sense of stewardship in money matters. Descended from Norman nobility on her mother's side and with a soldier-poet for sire, she found husbandry new and tasteless. But Mihera, in spite of his wealth, was so irritable and sharp-tongued about account-keeping in all things, that she hurriedly assumed these neces-sary chores, hugging them jealously to herself to avoid encounters. She counted and sighed and rebelled and counted still, and even was beholden on several occasions to a certain lender. It was not that clash-ing would find her inadequate and meek. Resentment and rebellion, not guilt and repentance, were the sparks he raised. But cold, captious, arbi-trary things that he could calmly say so fired her that she mortally feared to speak. She could hurt him. His genuine affection made him unfair game. Her slightest coolness could wound, without changing him. Her full flame could spoil what kept them attached. So she quenched it. She kept some of her fire and some of her tenderness for-ever hidden. It was the necessary price.

Mihera, meantime, could felicitate himself. He could sometimes compliment *her* on the alterations. He could point with pride to the pattern's goodlier design. Was she not circumspect, sensible, and grave? Was it not a blessing, seeing her diligent at household tasks, careful in husbandry and no more idly occupied at harp or viol? The palace came less and less to be troubled by her footless ways, except for requirements of the small Ursule, who seemed tirelessly hungry for songs, games and endless nonsense in her mother's lively fashion. And who could oppose this?

Mihera of Amalfi had been, at thirty-five, a fulfilled man—prudent, successful and almost happy. His ships were busy, his affairs straight, his love accomplished. What had seemed lacking in this last had been speedily repaired. He had not known the costly, dangerous, continuous payments for his tight design.

He might never have known them, in a whole existence passed in the ordinary way of life. But it was inevitable for most in the turn of this eleventh century that life should change, burgeon, shift in all its aspects, and this alarmingly, and that it should move forth with new and vivid hues. Did not the feudal world itself arise from the flatulent futility of self-struggle and flow forward, its whole long-slumbering splendor suddenly in tide?

On that strange journey into unimaginable worlds, life was in all ways harder. Yet for Zoë, at the outset, it had seemed improved. Adventure was lively, and to be parted from past roots held no fears. She was raised to this. And change, change had the virtue of by-passing those small pesky details that in quietude sorely carked her. She was much less daunted in thin times they encountered here by the necessity of helping to ensnare a bedraggled hare for supper, than formerly to make three last thin byzants endure till Sunday!

There was one flaw—the perils to little Ursule. But the protection of Mihera, the skill of Jacoppo Poldi, precluded these. For the rest, she was well content. Mihera was strong, he was watchful. *Their* little company, if any, could survive here. They were meantime a close part of the mightiest, most nobly inspired quest the world had ever known. And their final peculiar fate—their reunion with Bohemond—made everything perfect.

Friendship, for these three, lived again—warm, comforting, casual, as it had been in Sicily (how long ago!). They became, in the long, dreary winter with the Host stationary and with time for once overplentiful for all, inseparable comrades. Warm fires, old tales, new bonds in the exigencies of the times. Not old love. This did not intrude, or threaten to. Zoë and Bohemond had not referred to it again, since the first impulse that day on the dunes. Mihera, much less, ever. Yet, for Zoë, a strong, sudden, long-needed light had been cast down. She suddenly saw things. She suddenly knew whereof she sought; whence came those secret, unfair demands she made on poor Mihera. Her loyalty to him warmed and waxed, from her own sense of long injustice in it, even though at this precise point she fell out of love a little. Indeed, by some paradoxical alchemy, the strain in their loving dissolved to nothingness, and at long last there came to him her simple passion, unmixed with the vague longings she had shown him that he did not even see, much less satisfy. Mihera, in this aspect, found peace at last, seeing in this subtle change, this final sign, complete possession of his foolish, vagrant, but beloved Zoë.

So Zoë knew herself. The view was too long and too objective for any blindness in it now. There'd been nine years free from the confusing presence of her two beloveds. She knew in a wild flash what ancient fires were merely banked in her affection. Not that there was a question in it. There was the simple fact: her anchorage to little Ursule from which she would never break, and her real affection for Mihera, and especially the need of both of them for her, would outweigh against all odds her wild, wrong, unreasonable longings.

It was a terrifying knowledge. It was a nice, almost an over-nice, balance.

Some of these things she pondered as Marcelle stood at her bath. It was a device, this sifting of thoughts, which she often resorted to, a self-accounting in solitude. By the time she arose, lithe, gleaming, and stepped from the great tub into Marcelle's towels, she felt somewhat restored.

"Aha," cried that sly one. "What did I tell you, madame? The bath! Nothing like it for the welfare of a woman's soul!" Then, having appropriately anointed madame, she proceeded to sprinkle a few drops over the couch, and on the rugs. She was humming, and her whimsical attitude, in Zoë's present mood, was a peculiar irritant.

"Marcelle, what are you about? That ointment cost dearer than a denier, you know! Get on, you scandalous old trull!"

Marcelle, with a satisfied air, and a final glance about the tidied and freshly scented room, waddled out, her tall-coifed head pursued closely by a wadded chamber-towel.

Zoë dressed quickly, savoring the steamy perfume and the twilight hush pervading the sleeping room. The splendor of spring, an eastern spring with all its fresh, mysterious, aromatic overtones, had that day burst on them after the endless winter. It had been a lovely day, for itself alone, but also a special day, unique, and so significant for the pilgrims gathered by the Wall—the feast of Easter. Seemingly from the heart of gloom it had come, full of promise of glory, conquering the heavy, long-overhanging mists of the week before to send them sliding away, leaving the scent of spices to kill in stagnant rain-pools and secret, leaf-rotted places the stench of death.

With light, calm and unhurried fingers, Zoë plaited her hair. She bound the ends with bits of silk and with these thick, dark luxuriant ropes, she was engaged in setting a coronet about her temples.

For the first time in a long time, this day, she had felt completely and inexplicably happy. Not buoyant, not excited, not expectant, there was nothing she waited for, but in tune; in tune with this night of spring. She had been happy as a child is, with a sort of carefree indifference and a soft somnolence of desire. As if years sped away, and she was back in the days before marriage and even before love, when each hour of her life seemed full and perfect, for no particular cause, even in the presence of loneliness and insecurity, just because she was living. Even that feeling was not lacking, that feeling of suspense that used to give her the sensation of running breathlessly on the edge of a magic precipice . . . Secret joys—more hidden than the pulses' beat!

A fat sheaf of lambskins lay on her dressing stand, together with a quill and ink. From time to time she glanced there, picked up the quill and made a mark or two, frowning a little sometimes at the rustling diptych. The only sounds were the tune she was humming, the occasional quill-scratch, and the faint sound of a chorus of voices singing somewhere in the night. Her face, reflected in the long shield and lit by the flame from a cresset burning near, was radiant. She was thinner—the cool, transparent skin lay taut on the high planes of her face. Her eyes were bright and her hair lustrous and curling, and she had taken lately to employing, to aid these things, just a wee touch of the strange salves she had purchased beforetime from the same Armenian sutler. The first taste of the salves had been in Byzantium when the Princess Anna herself, helping her robe for the Emperor's banquet, had insisted on it, and it was hard to forget the bright, defining beauty that blossomed with such assistance. Not that one would ever adopt the painted ways of the doll-like Byzantines! Thinking of this, Zoë suddenly abandoned the cherry-hued stuff she had been thinking to touch to her lips. No, not that. But none, surely, would detect the bit of soot-like salve dotted minutely at the corners of the eyes and the rosy ochre rubbed ever so lightly onto the skin around them. She leaned back and surveyed herself, examining more the effect of these strange usages than her own beauty; but had she been conscious of it, her mirror would have told her that she had never in her life looked better. Over and above her physical well-being (the winter privation being beneficial to one of her sturdiness after years of sluggish living at Amalfi), there was a still, a secret, inexplicable twist to the corners of her lips that lent to her features an anything-might-happen look, a cosmetic thing in a woman!

Suddenly a slight laugh, more like the bubbling chuckle of a girl, came from her throat. For she suddenly thought, where am I going? Why do I preen like this? So the walls may see? So the stars, a little later, when I look at them the time before sleep will look down and wink? But after all, she reflected, not being from the tent for weeks, save for chapel in the pavilion near-by, was conducive to nothing healthful. Perhaps a walk across the dunes, anywhere, on this lovely night, with Mihera, would banish old cares and idle fancies. She rose and left her chamber, thinking to suggest this.

Looking past the heavy arras at the entrance to his study-room, she could see how absorbed he was. She almost retreated. His expression, something hidden on his face as he worked there, sent a warning out, but she shrugged it off, and entered.

Mihera sat barricaded by his books. A band of pale light glowed on his features from the entrance-slit, as he turned and faced her.

"Oh, it's you," he said with his dry, uncertain smile. "I heard you singing," his light-lashed glance brushing her appraisingly. "I like what you've done to your hair. But I *do* remember, Zoë, it reveals your scar, which of course is foolish among strangers here."

Her hand moved to the nape of her neck, touching the mark there. She had been halfway across the room. She stopped.

He said, "Really, Zoë," his face screwing up a little, "I've spoken to Dr. Poldi. He could change it with a plain mark simply obliterating the embossment there, as they do with—"

"Sheep?" she said. She laughed.

"What amuses you?"

"Oh, nothing really, Mihera, just the comparison. Bend to a new brand . . ."

"My God, Zoë . . ."

"Shall it be done now, in the Paschal season? Rather apt."

"Don't be blasphemous! Besides, it's a serious matter. I endlessly fret some trader will espy that thing . . . You are open prey, you know, with the Brand of the Apple . . . You're in no case to be impractical about it."

She smiled. "Practical, Mihera? On a night like this, do we speak of what is practical? You've been away so long!"

He half-started from the chair. "Zoë . . ." his face suffused. But she reached him first, embraced him and leaned away, her cool fingers pulling at his ear.

"I thought to suggest a walk, Mihera, as we used to. None is abroad this hour. I'm a shut-in these last weeks, and now you're here, my shield from stray Egyptians?" She disturbed his hair with a kiss. Then, the corners of her mouth denting, "Or maybe my shepherd, Mihera—since I seem to you as silly and helpless a creature as those lambs you barter for—"

He stiffened. "Don't speak so, Zoë, and twist my words like that! I did *not* say you were silly and the rest. I spoke only of the brand." He looked up at her. "You've changed much since the old days, Zoë. I have often remarked that, and you should no longer be your own disparager." He shrugged. "Carefree, unheedful, but I only admire you for this, even envy you, God knows, to stay so lively in the manifest miseries we're having here!"

Her chin, as she sensed the sarcasm he could not keep from his tone, imperceptibly lifted.

"I have never asked for your admiration, or to be made into something you'd find admirable," she said. "It is for me an impossibility. I often wonder why you did not see that even if I did not!" Her eyes no longer smiled. They tilted upward still, but with bitterness.

"Oh, Zoë, why do you always put me in the wrong like this!" He released her and came to his feet, his boots shuffling a little in the reeds. He had always been taller than Zoë by a foot or more, but the added weight which success and the fullness of years had brought him made him seem even more. He had travelled armored from Laodicea. He still kept his mailed shirt of silver worn over leathern hose with a silver-and-gold-fretted baldric about his somewhat thickened waist. He had been darkened by desert and bitten by wind till his large eyes seemed almost to protrude from his sunburnt face. Yet he was one of those better-favored by middle age than by youth and his voice was not untouched with tenderness as he spoke to Zoë.

She had moved away to the pavilion entrance. Her arm was above her head, the arras held back a little. She was listening, but not to him. In the interval he too heard the faint sound of singing, and a look of anger passed quickly over his face. He seemed torn between impatience and his genuine concern for her.

"You seem touchy with me, Zoë. I do not understand you, or rather I understand you less than before. You seem, I have noticed it lately, to love me better, yet you seem, too, more ready for a quarrel. My God, what *is* it? Tell me," he said, and she started at his sudden grasp. "Before, in Amalfi, we were happy. . . . We were happy, Zoë, were we not?"

His words rushed together, and his hands, laid heavily on her bare arms, were moist.

"Why, yes, Mihera. Of course we were happy."

"Don't 'of course' me, Zoë. I must know!"

She nodded vigorously, for his fingers hurt. "But yes, Mihera!"

"All right—we'll be happy *again*, my dear. We're going back . . ."

"Back! Back home? But surely not for this, that you fancy . . . What d'you mean, Mihera?"

She whirled as he released her.

"Naturally," he said, "my thoughts are not so limited or simple. But I hoped you'd see that it is best in *all* ways, that you would see it right . . ."

He was foundering now, for her face had a cold look.

"Do you mean *deserters?* That you'd abandon the Crusade?"

"There!" he cried, his face flushing again, but this time from anger. "That's how I feared—that's how I *knew* you'd view it!" He sighed. "Listen. Bohemond must make a move soon. He must capture this city or no. The crowd shouts to get on to the Tomb. I have seen him in my particular capacities here through the worst part. He can ill expect more. Now, just now at Laodicea several of my ships were in. I spoke with certain masters, two captains whom I implicitly trust. There is trouble in Amalfi, plots brewing to send me to ruin. I've no other course but to protect my interests."

"Why did you come at *all* then, with vows and solemn promises like the rest?"

"Who has counted on this thing at Antioch? No one, except as I sometimes conjecture, Bohemond himself. I think he thought of Antioch, and acted the zealot till he caught us here. His prayers, plays, those songs that you meekly make for him—I tell you, Zoë, I forbid that! You're getting yourself a light name, for his devices, and this I won't have." He was quite excited.

She quickly capitulated. "Very well . . . But on Bohemond, I think you're unjust. Why *shouldn't* he take Antioch? Is it not to be admired, that purpose? A practical thing? The way things go now, it might be a western city."

"*Bohemond's* city, you mean—and no one else's!"

"Oh, he *couldn't* do that; the barons consent to share it; it would scarcely be honorable . . ."

"I say nothing of honor. I only say that Bohemond wants Antioch . . ."

"And wouldn't *you?*" she cried, "wouldn't you in Bohemond's place? Believe me, had you any interest, any interest at all in Antioch, were they *your* monopolies here rather than Genoa's, you would scarce be loath to try it. . . ."

He grinned dryly. "But I have an interest! You forget, perhaps, how old Maurus, dying, bequeathed the doors, could I recover them—the Alexandrian doors, coin filled, which he lost that time at Bull Joy and which, according to what Bohemond said, were sent to Antioch . . ."

"Well!" she said. "In *that* case, is it not well to wait for what transpires?"

"On the mere thread of finding them in that ancient maze?"

"But maybe we *could!* It would be thrilling to try . . . I could help . . . I recall how they looked, Mihera, from their mates at Monte Cascino . . . Great bronze and silver things . . . The first parents, the serpent and the tree . . . Oh, Mihera!"

Mihera shook his wheaten, ear-length locks.

"Only by luck. They might be gone, sold elsewhere, the gold discovered . . . The secret might have leaked—a thousand things. No, Zoë. My real wealth is my ships." He suddenly swore. "Can't you see? I'm a tradesman. I chose that. I chose its peculiar responsibility and its compromises. To such as these here, the making of wealth thus—carrying things about the earth—seems trivial, I grant you, even base, since none of this ancient fol-de-rol goes with it. None of the old games bolstered by fine sentiments and banners and brilliant caparisons and mouthings of young boys singing of fame."

"Oh, don't bother to justify it!" she snapped. "We are going back. That's the issue, isn't it?"

"But there you are," he agonized. "Closed against me even with consent. I can neither understand nor reach you. You're beyond me, sometimes I think you hate me"—she saw his temple pounding—"sometimes I think you love another. Is that it, Zoë? Do you still love *him?*"

"Oh, no, Mihera!" she cried out, hearing the thickening of his voice. "I love you, you!" She was suddenly panicked. She let fall the arras and moved after him. But he had turned and he did not see her strange, lost gesture, when she should have been crushed in his arms. There was an interval when neither spoke, and still he did not look at her. The singing came faintly in the silence.

"It's the Crusade!" he said. "A madness. All will be better when we are home again. No place for a woman"—turning to her now—"especially a woman as impressionable as you." His voice now took that tone she knew so well. "There are forces here you know nothing at all about —all cloaked in the stripes of glory. Beware, Zoë, with your songs, with your songs and Bohemond! You're not made for such things. In this you're a little *fool*, Zoe . . . !" And even though now his voice suddenly softened, and he added, "but a beloved, a sweet fool I cannot live without," and his arms went about her, she was rigid.

At such times, generally, his arms, his lips demanding and strong, were compelling, his passion-steeped voice soporific. But tonight she could not feel or hear these things, for the sting, indeed the challenge in his words.

If Mihera had really looked, he might have seen the small lines harden a little about his wife's mouth. She pulled from his arms.

"We will go back, Mihera. But here or in Amalfi, I know that nowhere can such as I am make you truly happy. For I am neither a child, a fool, nor an emotional cripple, for all your perspicacity. It is how I am and it will never please you."

"Now what brought *that* on?" he asked in an injured tone. "You are changeable as the weather. I cannot even talk straight with you, before we are off on some theme I neither follow nor trace. Holy saints, Zoë . . . Everywhere is there no peace for me?"

Even as he spoke she had gone to the arras, lifted it and stepped out.

Presently, when Marcelle came lumbering in, he sat once more among his parchments. His face was flushed, his brow knotted in a prodigious frown.

"Lord Mihera, little Ursule wants one of you. She complains of her dreams, and I cannot lull her."

He halfway rose, but looking toward the doorway he said, "Lady Zoë is just on the palisade, I think. You can easily call her in."

The servant Marcelle called several times but in vain. Zoë was already in shadows of bays by the dune. Marcelle for moments dimly caught glimpses of her full, light gown. She was walking rapidly toward the distant sounds. Poor child, thought Marcelle, who had her own ideas about her mistress with her alternate fits of apathy and joy, and her two good ears with which she heard these distressing quarrels with the Lord Mihera. "There she goes. Like some half-mad enchanted child led on by her pretty music. Where will it end?" On the old slave's face, as she watched, there was a mixture of intrigue and pity. At her feet lay two of the camp hounds—big mastiffs—like limp sacks in the twilight, snorting a little in their after-supper naps.

"Lazy louts!" Marcelle told them with a scuff of her sandal at them both. "Why didn't you follow her?" She spoke to the mastiffs but loud enough so the Count, if he wished, could harken to her voice and the warning in it. She waited a few moments, then shook her head, straightened her skirts and re-entered the pavilion.

Twilight slipped down from the reddish sky in broad, oblique bars, thrust from the distant cloud-banks to paint the earth in patches of soft colors. They fell, these many hues, like rain, or like light from cathedral glass, scattering rose on the dunes, amber on the bays and budding myrtle-trees and deep blood scarlet on the dark cedar-tops beyond. Far ahead the music burgeoned, and Zoë became suddenly impatient with the useless windings of the skirts of the sand-hill and began to run across it. It was not alone that she was anxious to go forward, but a sort of panic drove her on. She sped, scarcely knowing that she was actually running, on the multicolored dune.

CHAPTER XVIII *King of the Ribalds*

IT WAS COOL. She shivered a little in her fustian capelet but already her outraged nerves were calmed a bit by the soft air and the peacefulness about. The tents pitched further in the dunes looked draggled and faded out after the hard time here, but small bushes and plants pushed up in the loam about them and green vines crept upon the streaked silk of many, lending these an odd, quasi-permanent air. Before the city, in the cultivated hills, the olives would be grey-green now, and the quickened vines shoot out their first curled tendrils, as in Italy. Home. It had been so long. She frowned. She glanced over at the Wall as at an enemy. The Wall, so rosy, pearl-like and beautiful, looking almost fragile in the softening shadows of the night. Yet one was undeceived. Winding upwards on the breast of the Cassian hills, irregularly sprawled like a moon-basking snake it lay, and it was alive, alert, unsleeping. The Host knew its impregnability as they knew the seven sins. Ramparts of solid stone, double in exposed portions, with towers at short intervals between, all guarded by swart giants pledged by pain of both death and the loss of Heaven to keep unbreached that necklace of stone about the Emir. What use, in the face of it, the brave, cross-blazoned gonfanons, the squat, square donjons, the once-splendid pavilions that paled, tore, crumbled, rusted and were now beginning to be overgrown in the shadows of that immemorial stronghold?

Yet one thing Mihera had said, one hint, had her wondering if there might be on hand some key to the impossible. "Bohemond must decide soon," he had said. Did Bohemond *have* a plan or was it merely that this long-vaunted spring would set a zone on his touted promises?

Zoë had walked far with her swift, agitated thoughts, and louder and louder came the sounds of songs. She was near the river now, already the ground was marshy to her steps and the vegetation waxed full of reeds and lush plants such as luxuriate in the environs of running streams. Finally, upon threading a small last hummock in the vanishing dunes, she came into view of the singers. Clumps of osiers stood about like parclose screens, and by standing on tip-toe she enjoyed a reed-latticed view of the scene below.

Spread out in a semi-round by the north bank of the Orontes was a strange assembly. Not monks, not pilgrims, not mailed crusaders these, but all manner of nondescripts, male and female, and everyone— for the music had suddenly ceased—speaking in rough and various tongues. In their midst was a great fire. A carcass was tautly stretched across the flames, the night was filled with its ripe, amazing stench. The meat had apparently just now been pronounced in the state of edibility and like pads surprising prey in ambush the feasters rushed in. Swords, dirks, knives, all manner of weapons seemed ready to hand, and they cut their shares at random, setting the carcass to quivering as a thing alive on the blackened spit. Behind the osiers, Zoë, watching this, knew nausea. Weird thoughts struck the mind, old tales of black Ethiops hacking steaks from the still-living bullocks and of human offerings on the shores of ancient seas. And suddenly one knew. These were the Ribalds, those followers of the Host who by deed and by custom gave a malodorous air to an otherwise respectable undertaking, like the sphincteral off-throw of a ducal tilting yard.

Zoë squinted toward the fire, her attention held morbidly by the spitted thing. On what did they feast? Mihera's sheep were yet to come, and meat was unheard of now for several weeks. Earlier in winter had occurred an incident of the Ribalds that had mystified most, scandalized all, and colored Zoë's speculations now. For some time Yagi Sayan had been sending spies into the Frankish camp, causing much consternation in the knights' council. It was the height of the winter famine. About the same time, Tafur, King of the Ribalds, was called to the board to give answer for a wild tale of a certain repast he and his crew had reportedly indulged in. It was thought that Tafur would be summarily punished. This did not occur. Instead, fresh tales issuing from the staff of the Norman Bohemond spread wind of a special feast to be held at the city ramparts. Several Moslem spies were at that time in custody. These were beheaded on the site, and great fire burned well into the night in the midst of the merry group of Ribalds, while from the Wall could be heard the loud ululation of the Moslem mobs.

The *odeur* of the affair had pervaded both camps, with Bohemond coming under censure, though nothing actually was ever to be proved. The one sure item was the result. Though sorties, barrages and raids in force continued to plague the siegers, spies from Antioch were thenceforth conspicuously lacking.

These things brushed uneasily through Zoë's mind as she watched the present doing. But being more curious than repulsed, more fascinated than afraid, she surmised the death of some knight's charger as occasion for this untimely feast. There was, besides the music, a note here of home, transporting her to scenes glimpsed from afar on horseback in Italian moorlands.

They had commenced the singing again, and she moved, half

knowing that she did, from her reedy shield behind the osier-bed, and melted unseen into the fringes of the kingdom of the Ribalds.

Though he stood quite in the midst of his noisy subjects, Tafur, King of Ribalds, was not, for once, partaking of their revels. While his long, strong, slightly pointed teeth did full justice to the shin-piece of the defunct cob they had barbecued, his sharp mind ruminated on the latest assignment he had fallen to from the Seigneur Bohemond. Men surmised that if Tafur was not in truth a sprite, his odd, thin frame and his hair growing sharp along his cheekbones imparted the look of one. Others said the muscular slightness of his arms and legs made him more like a half-man from another age. They speculated if his feet were cloven. He and Bohemond had conferred much since the thing of the spies, with Tafur making his varied peculiar talents of much use to the Prince, especially in the winter plays. They were a titillating pair together, the hale and ruddy knight with the bluff ways and noble face, and the swart and subtle rascal in the short cape that fitted him ill as all his other raiment of uncertain age and origin. Most men would say, "There goes Bohemond and his hound of Hell."

This new assignment had intrigued Tafur. It had amused and made him a little curious.

"I have need," the Norman had told him, "of one of your female subjects—a handsome wench, if you please, with a tall, strong frame to her and a meed of theatrics such as you yourself are able to employ . . ."

Tafur had smiled, cracking his broad lips to a satyr-grin.

"Fret not, messire. Your choice of the night-frisking doxies of my tribe is at your instant beck. Indeed, they'll *all* be plaguing me for such an assignation!"

His patron had replied with his roaring gust of laughter. "But no, good Tafur! My motive is war, not love . . ."

"War, messire?" with tilted brows nearly meeting beneath the rat-locks on his brow.

But Bohemond's face had closed. "Forget you I said that. Only send me within a fortnight the appropriate wench whose chiefest requirements I've not yet divulged. A voice, Tafur—she'll have a large, rich voice that will carry upward and for some distance and still please the ear with its tone; a thrilling voice, a voice as of bells, a voice like a lark of Heaven. Know you such?"

Tafur, deftly assured and warmly assuring, gave his pledge, even as his mind skittered doubtfully over the immediate possibilities. Who? Margot had the voice truly, but was ugly as some people thought of sin. Sara, the comely one, croaked like a frog at insect-time and Clothilde was pretty and full of tunes, but of delicate stature and with the shy ways of a woodland finch.

Two weeks proved no time to work the miracle he had rashly pledged. Hours, days, he had spent trying to blend from his various female ingredients a creature of music and charm. Quickly abandoning little Clothilde whose tones rose hopelessly to a pale squeal when forced, he tried and gave up on melodious Margot, whom not all the oils and unguents of Asia Minor could make good to look upon, and placed a desperate hope in the beautiful Sara. He cajoled, begged, coaxed and beat her, trying to garner one true note from that amazing, statuesque form. There was nothing but an uncertain bellow from her ample bosom and the pain of her tuneless stridency. Tafur was stumped. He had worked, he had searched, he had prayed, he had even gone to his sooth-dame who dealt in the occult and had concourse with the souls below. Tafur was not above evoking these. He had. But the darker deities, too, seemed dormant. He cursed. If only the Prince had called for a minstrel, a clown, a jongleur from the masculine performers in his crew! But how could a *lady* of such sorts be found in the midst of the ranks of the Ribalds? Were there such a gem, would the slews of this Crusade contain her?

To be sure there was no lack of talent or enthusiasm in the male contingent. Tafur mused now, listening with lazy pleasure to the sound of their steady singing. They applied themselves to the seasonal anthems with the same pious gusto as any loft-full of cowled choristers. Tafur tossed the shin-bone, stripped, across his shoulder-blade and gave them his full attention, his sharp features pulled to a half-cynical grimace.

They had trailed, with a good show of imitation, through the alleluias of the Paschal Mass, their hearty voices inquiring and replying across the great fire, their motley strains meeting and blending and pleasantly dying in the undertones of the murmuring Orontes.

> *"Make our feet follow on the Christ-way,*
> *Make our hearts' hollow bear the pain . . .*
> *Let us—"*

Not suddenly, for the blend of harmonies on the darkening air was so close that none stood out, but very gradually Tafur became aware of a clear, alien strain in the voices of those immediately near. Someone sang, a woman, whose tones he could swear he had not heretofore remarked. He started with the certainty of it, his quick glance raking the upturned faces in the vicinity where he stood. A strong voice, musical and rather dark, swelling with the quickening chorus as sure and clear as a bell, but softening as the rest faded; a fine, thrilling stream of sound that wove through the rough melody of the others like a thread of silver. By its very ease in burgeoning and fading thus without loss of tone it was teasingly elusive, all but indistinguishable. But alone . . . ? Beneath the faded finery of his gem-embroidered tunic, the heart of the thief Tafur grew quick.

He quietly began to circulate. He frowned and listened and frowned again, straining for some bearing on the thing. Several astonished girls found their mouths clamped shut a moment, or their heads drawn momentarily back by a forelock by the claw of their frantic, mystified chief. At one juncture he lost the sound completely. He halted, cursed softly, and glared viciously at one burly ruffian whose enthusiasm was canceling the efforts of his neighboring choristers. Tafur had leaned athwart him with a hissing exclamation, when he saw that which stopped the blasphemy on his mouth. She had not seen him, she was singing still, completely detached save in harmony from all about. Tafur stood there, staring. Presently he began to smile.

The face was unfamiliar as the voice. A woman not young, but not old either, one of those whose features refuse to become the barometers of time, with a dark mass of lustrous hair piled intricately—woven, plaited, twisted and pinned, into a magnificent coronet. A face at once striking and piquant with long, strange eyes which as she sang seemed full of endless depths in the light of the flickering campfire. He noted the gown she wore, of fustian, plain but well cut, with a cloak to match, its velvet-lined hood falling full on her shoulders and down from the gleaming arrows of her coif as she bowed her head in the momentary pausing of the pilgrim verses . . . Tafur suddenly stiffened, his eyes narrowing as he shifted his stance to station himself behind her. He stepped nearer, his sharp, thin shoulders bending angularly above the kneeling woman . . .

When he straightened again, his eyes had an unbelieving width. The scarlet apple—immemorial mark of the Egyptian prostitute. His eyebrows rose the further he absorbed the fact, and in the midst of the sounds and the singing, again he smiled.

His mind told him here was a prize indeed, one of those highly touted Alexandrian bawds brought by some lonesome and rich seigneur from Seleucia or Laodicea on the coast. His fancy told him more. She was a gift of his own private gods, to whom an effigy must in the morning be burned in thanks for this thing of passing fortune. He reeled with conjecture, all sorts of titillating thoughts aroused in the bizarre realm of his thief's fancy. A witch? A vision? A succubus out of nether-worldly fires? Zut! She was here, but if of such an origin, she might in truth be troublesome as an angel to detain, and naturally much more subtle. Tafur even thought, now that he struck upon it, that he saw other than natural flames darting from those marvelous orbs, and felt more than ordinary heat-gusts from the warmth of the feasting fire itself. One did not question the lambent powers of such incendiary creatures . . .

Tafur stood collecting himself, his fawn-like face pulled oddly to a point, his whole, thin, knobby-legged form arrested in quiet, watching expectance. He had pulled the short, ill-fitting cloak across his folded arms as though to hide in it, while he ruminated. Looking at him, one thought of a minor Lucifer, or of some Pan risen from the far, dark, western wood, out of fashion but potent still, tagging patiently along in the wake of the First Crusade.

Zoë was thinking she must leave. She must make her way from here as she had wandered in—unnoticed and undetained. The general singing had now ceased and at the fire a group with zitherns and a sour sackbut accompanied themselves to new verses, verses that were lively and of a poignant familiarity. She smiled with delight. They were *good* songs, after all one's fretting. One knew, hearing them like this. She thrilled. She thrilled to find that indeed they had caught the essence of these things she had wished to tell of—the free joy, the color, the sheer animal awakening of the coming of this strange, new spring. Adaptations of old Greek lines she had learned in Bull Joy long ago had gone begging for their placement in the Paschal play, she knew. She had felt doubt about including them there. But here in the open by the ragged fire, in the vividness of this night, they were perfect. They spoke of war, old gods, new stirrings of the ancient earth, a strange duality abroad for good or ill, as if oriental myrrh from some old altar-pile were suddenly to rise and mingle with the incense at Cathedral services.

And so she lingered, congenial to the mood of the troubadours, wrapped in a mood of pleasure. She looked up. In the summits of the cedars where the wind breathed, the small shining leaves were mirrors of moonlight, of light from a slim new moon. It was later than she had thought.

With the music still holding them half in thrall, the assembly of feasters was commencing to disperse. It made one pattern, headed on its ways, to its tents and its beds and its nightly diversions there by the murmuring river. Against this Zoë moved athwart, thinking with slight uneasiness of Mihera and of little Ursule who might be restive and missing her nightly lullaby. Several in the stirring multitude stared at her as they passed; so she pulled up her cape to put her face in shadow and began to hurry. But somewhat apart, a form sidled after, the two of them like twin shuttles threading this dark warp of the realm of the Ribalds.

Zoë did not at first take alarm at sight of this thin shadow moving a certain distance from her, half-hidden by the reeds. Some spyer on the Ribalds' revels like myself, she thought. But when presently she changed her course, and struck across to the start of the dunes, he altered his own direction too, and she knew she was stalked. The knowledge immediately colored her picture of the night and her escapade. The darkness, no longer romantic, was highly sinister and even the moonlight seemed suddenly no friend, touching the strange tents and their appendant horse-stalls with a wan, estranging silver.

She struck out in earnest, trying to seem not to run, managing a sort of gliding half-trot in her billowing skirts. She kept to the open pathways, hoping to gain at last some vantage, to take new bearings of this moonlit, unfamiliar land. She could not think to seek the dunes now, with the shadow there. Surely it *was* but shadow, one more miasma of the moon, or even her own reflection thrown by some freak of chance onto far thickets and rock-copses opposite which she passed. An attenuated, weird and lively shadow.

She stumbled a little, and knew with joy that this was because the road was rising from the marsh and it seemed very quickly that she gained to a hummock on the ridge whence she could see about. There was the Wall, Mt. Maregat and the Aleppo road, and between this and the St. Paul's Bridge must be the tent of Bohemond. She gazed with relief and longing at the bright fires she saw burning and she thought she could hear the faint hammering from some late-laboring smith still busy at his forge. She could run now, there was a goal to win, but even as she rejoiced in this, the enemy was there. Where she had paused was a sort of minute theatre in the native rock, a stony copse, collared with clumps of stunted, dwarf-like styrax trees. And there her pursuer stood, rising as though from shadows on the land behind.

A sort of numbness seized upon Zoë, to which her fright, the sudden depth of the darkness, and the eerie aspect of her pursuer all contributed.

Tafur had tossed back the mantle from his spare arms.

He stood, poised on the edge of the copse with his hands stretched to either side of the rocky place. He had, thus poised above Zoë's immediate horizon of the world beyond, a look of having arrived on the spot by other than the way of feet. The two stood gazing at one another, both equally astonished that a close view but augmented the opinions they had entertained at a distance. She was even more striking than he had observed at the fire—and to her he bore yet the air of a shadow, an illusion, a spirit not out of tune with the night, or, more astonishingly, with herself. Viewed thus in the half whimsy of her mood, he seemed like a bogy conjured by Mihera to pursue and punish her, the almost too graphic embodiment of night, of evil at prowl, and the lurking Egyptians . . .

Yet this was no shadow. He was a man and she was trapped. So she said in a tone of contempt, arrogance, and as much calmness as she could muster, "What are you about? I am Countess Zoë, wife of the Seneschal, the Knight Mihera, and if you dare to detain me—"

She did not finish, noting that the words electrified him more. He stared, immensely surprised but without the slightest bit of the fear she had hoped for and indeed expected.

"Lady Zoë?" he said. "Then you are Zoë, the heavenly singer!" He used light, smooth silken tones of one possessed of a thousand tricks of voice and gesture. He suddenly came forward, placing both hands boldly on her shoulders and gazing with a strange expression straight into her face. She gazed back, oddly fascinated by the black depths of the eyes that were bright, intense and large in spite of being cast in shadow under saturnine brows. She felt his thin hands clinging claw-like in her flesh.

He said, "You are real—no smouldering succubus as I at first conjectured."

He had a lewd, hissing laugh. "Fancy, I thought you a gift of the Dark One, sent that I, his favorite, might keep my pledge with the Baron Bohemond. But it is better. It is more! You were not sent; you came. You came yourself, seeking me. I have sung your songs, mimed your miracles, and longed to set my eyes on the maker of these. Your being here proves that you felt this, that you somehow knew us to be akin."

Zoë was in full alarm. His eyes seemed to bore into her and his hold on her shoulders was hard as though she were being seared by thin, strong irons. She shifted suddenly, tore free, but he easily stepped back to the opening of the copse and she saw there was no escape.

He was going on. "And what was more natural than our meeting? I should have seen this, and not been surprised. The only matter of fortune is that *you* chose the time. The one whom you love, as the rumor goes, you know whom I mean, gave me a strange commission for some concealed purpose of his own. And you came, you who alone could satisfy the quest—that is the miracle. As for the rest—zut! How I've dreamed it—but I thought there were worlds between us. Worlds indeed! You heard my name—Tafur the King—and you heard how it was with me, and you knew . . . Ours is the same world. I am the King of it, and you? How—when did you first wear the brand? Before you loved the Prince? Or after? No, don't tell me . . . I like it better this way. We came to each other by devious and unknown ways, and together—of course! I feel utterly renewed. You will come as to a young man, one who will play unutterable music on the thousand pleasures he knows to be waiting in such as you!"

Tafur was now moving about on the very edge of the copse, the moon white on his face and on his mad, gesticulating form. He was doing a sort of dance. She was scared, and at the same time saved by a cold anger. Tafur's identification of himself had brought him to life, and pulled her from her half unbelieving fantasy. That this creature, the chief of the scum of the pilgrimage, should dare to use her thus in speech and action had her full of disdain. Yet, at the same time and worst of all, her conscience stood apart and thoroughly convicted her of carelessness and held forth the amazing price of her vanity for wearing the fatal coronet.

Tardily assuming the trappings of dignity, and deeply wary of her adversary's whim, she again tried firmness. Pointing past him to the blue smoke curling skyward from the pavilion by the Bridge, she told him, "Tafur, I demand you take me to the Prince."

His face changed. He stopped in his fantastic prancing. He was breathing hard and his glance became cool, whimsical, hard, and she felt herself freeze, more alarmed by this than the former frenzy he had indulged in.

"Oh, come now. La Zoë seeking the Prince has surely some time for the King . . ." His voice broke on a thick note, and with a direct and searing smile he approached her. She felt his short sharp beard scrape on her cheek as she struggled backwards. His arm yielded and she staggered, momentarily off-balance, so that Tafur's embrace once more enclosed her, and he moaned with pleasure. She screamed. With one hand on his shoulder and the other straight against his face she flexed her fingers and left the valleys of her nails in a bleeding path from the hair tuft of his right temple downward to his nose. He leaped up, clawing his eye, which she had touched.

"She-cat!" The long hands grasped her shoulders. "*I'll* take you to your Prince, but with a few new tricks in your basket contributed by your proper peer, the King of the Ribalds!" His hands charged with frenzy, he loosened her hair and the torn bodice became a net for her upper arms, and as she twisted and struggled against the edge of the coppice the rocks came cool and cutting to her skin. Suddenly, as she felt herself sinking to the ground, she spied over Tafur's shoulder a glimmer of steel far down the path by which she had left the assembly.

She cried out. Tafur clamped a hand on her mouth, looked back to the road, seemed to hesitate, and said, "Zut! There's no luck in this tonight. I take you to Bohemond." To her utter amazement, he quieted, straightened her frock about her shoulders, rescued her cloak where it had fallen and said, "Look, hold, that I may tie this rope of hair about that noisy vessel of your over-coy protestations. No one, nothing, must interrupt my getting you to the Prince and accomplishing my orders . . . Yield!" he repeated as she stared wide-eyed, with both hands pushing against his grasp on one great soft rope of her fallen coronet with which he meant to gag her. The more she fought the harder the pain came searing in her scalp. He presently won the unequal tug of war and plied his bony fingers to the business at hand . . . Thus securing her, he suddenly heaved her on one shoulder and descending from the copse, began to run at a quick, light lope. She saw the armed stranger she had glimpsed come over the copse and ride off in another path. He obviously had neither heard nor seen. It was a long way to the Bridge. Her head bobbed against his bony shoulder-blade. Her tongue burned to the braid, her stomach hurt, and she wished nothing more than that she had stayed at home that night with Ursule, Marcelle and Count Mihera.

CHAPTER XIX

On the Parapet

TAFUR FLED ON. The road was starlit and there seemed to be myriads of soldiers and strollers in the night, some of whom knew and spoke to her abductor with a word and a jest as he hurried by. What an iniquity, she inwardly raged, when such a one as this moves free as a bishop through the throng of Christians with a woman hung like a sack of millet on his shoulder-blade. Knights indeed! When Bohemond heard . . . But then she quailed on a new tack, to think of the figure she would presently cut before him. She was suddenly queasy at the stomach, both from these wry thoughts and from the upside-down view she had of Tafur's rhythmically trotting sandals. Her eyes went bulging and she shut them tight, waiting in a pale sweat for the last extremity. For indeed she was about to be sick.

On a sudden the rhythm broke, her eyes opened to a wheeling sky and to the earth wheeling, and she teetered dizzily mid the tents and the smithies in the camp of Bohemond where Tafur had, without ceremony, set her down. The de Hauteville gonfanon was visible everywhere and from a spear-pole thrust in the soil atop the palisade, the Prince's own serpented device went whipping to the wind. There was little activity about. In a leather-covered booth hard by the pavilion, a huge forge bloomed its rhythmic fire as a skinny groom pumped it for the smith, and Bohemond's big gray stood quietly by to be tended. Not more than three other horses stood at the rings. One was the still-burdened cob of Nepaz the sutler. Zoë recognized the familiar heap of sundries bulging above his panniers, and she saw the Armenian himself squatted silent by the color-pole. This was strange, for the law of the Host forbade the circuiting of pedlars by night. Nepaz looked weary sitting there, his eye-whites unnaturally visible in the moony dark. The whole place seemed unconscionably still and Zoë, glancing at Tafur, saw him gaze about in an odd way, like a hound sniffing, as if he too felt the strangeness here. He had meantime removed the plaited hair gag from his captive's mouth. He put a bony fist to her arm, and she jerked ahead, running a little to keep measure to his cat-like gait as they climbed the escarpment.

A great arras of dusky silk fanned under the lintels of the pavilion foyer, and from its folds a guard appeared, a brisk, husky fellow, who seconded the careful coldness of his face with a halberd held gullet-ward of Tafur the King.

Tafur paused, but the woman pushed forward, braving the edge of the naked blade, staring him down and demanding in a sharp imperious tone:

"Fetch your lord, sir!"

Tafur tried to push her aside but she would not be pushed. She was now prodigiously scornful of him and of the sentry too, for she heard through the arras the sound of dishes and cutlery and of men laughing and of Bohemond's laughter over all.

The moonlight slid on the young squire's helm as he shook his head in warning. Indeed, he moved sharply forth as though to end the thing without ado when a shaft of light fell through to the foyer from within and Bohemond himself stepped into it, wary but smiling from some merry word inside, and his serviette still in his hand.

"*Well*, Vieuxpont, is it *this* hard to keep beggars and brawling women from my door? Tafur!" Then his expression even more startled as he squinted in the half-light, "Zoë . . . By Christ Risen, what have we here?"

He banished the sentry with a nod, Tafur made an inelegant gesture at the fellow's back, and Zoë assaulted the Prince with a rush of words . . .

"This dirty, impossible peasant approached me on the road . . . He forced . . ."

"But no, Lord Bohemond," cried Tafur hastily, thrusting his face forth till his breath lay fetid on them both. "It was thus: she came to my camp . . . She . . ."

"Wait, but wait!" laughed Bohemond above them. "One at a time only!" His expression struggled between alarm, wonder and high amusement. "Give me the tale straight. Patience, Tafur!"

But Zoë's bravado at this juncture suddenly collapsed. She caught her breath, emitted a soft wail and without ceremony invaded his arms. There was a moment of silence from the two men. Then Bohemond, pulling her head back by a gentle tug of the loosened hair braid, let the light fall on her face, all flushed and warm and now commencing to be streaked with the tears she was shedding on his broad and elegant breast. And though he asked with a husky tenderness that held laughter not far at bay, "What is it, my girl, my Zoë?" it was Tafur who took advantage of her momentary impasse to state his case.

There was not much elegance to the tale as he told it now; he was scared to diffidence by the sight of his erstwhile captive in the embrace of the towering Norman. But he embellished the good and omitted the worst of it, banking on his shrewd surmise that Zoë would scarce expand upon the theme of her indignities, so that Bohemond might see it all as a droll thing at best, and at worst a grave indiscretion on the Countess's part.

Tafur did well. It was Zoë who pulled indignantly from her protector's arms at the initial burst of his explosive mirth. Bohemond leaned against the color-staff, his fingers hooked in his baldric, his head thrown back against the silk, while his guffaws shattered the silence of the tent enclosure. At the forge the stallion snorted as though in answer and stirred impatiently under the ministrations of the smith. The little pedlar at their feet stirred in his swaddlings.

"Excellent, Tafur!" he said when he could. "You are magnificent; you are more, you are inspired! I confess that heretofore I entertained this very possibility myself, for the singing lady of our plot, but—" he wheeled and addressed the back of her head (for she had stiffly turned from them both), "but I seem just short of bold enough, in the thing of this lady; I do not easily learn . . ."

In the silence ensuing, Tafur grew restive. He was chary of this interview, his spurious royalty melting in the highly charged presence of these, his compeers. He looked his relief when Bohemond, tossing him a pouch heavy with coin, said, "Well done, Ribald. You may go. I am well pleased, and you are indeed king in your unique realms."

The thief flashed his satyr grin and vanished. Bohemond turned to Zoë and gently propelled her through the foyer.

She tried to hold aloof. "Where do you take me? I am tired, unkempt and all but ill. I would leave under escort and be quit of this misadventure!"

"What!" cried he elaborately. "After seeking me out with such a difficulty?"

Zoë sighed. One *came*. One *sought them out* . . . She was infinitely weary of the uniform self-esteem of men, of whatever station . . .

"Besides," he was going on, "you might well learn, whether you came or whether you blundered here, of the high affairs going forward this happy night!"

He recalled the guard. "Be sure that blackguard is indeed gone, Vieuxpont. I think he scented something . . . Come, Zoë." He pushed her ahead of him through the arras.

With full expectations of encountering the pack of them—Raymond, the Legate, and the rest who mooted here nightly—she was relieved to face only two across the ruins of the Prince's supper-board. And of these one was unknown to her, one rare to be seen here, a dark-skinned easterling in the white burnoose and striped underrobes such as Nepaz wore. Yet he sat at the salt next to Bohemond's own dais. She noted, but had not time to ponder this thing of the first guest, for the tumult which the second proceeded to create. Young Tancred de Hauteville rose so violently from his place that his wine-cup spilled a ragged stain across the trestle-cloth and his sword clattered against the board itself as he came, plunging his tall frame forward, frowning prodigiously.

"Good God, Uncle! What madness! What do you think of, admitting any here, and worst of all, a woman!"

A fine string of curses enlarged on his theme. It was odd to hear them emanating from that once-so-innocent young mouth. Zoë fleetingly noted how that mouth had changed, no longer beardless as in Salerno wood, but hard and firm now, with a man's firmness, combined with a new sort of sullen look owing mayhap to the limp, to some hidden self-love, or the great place of favor one heard his uncle had continually granted him since the Crusade started.

Now Bohemond gave him a half-indulgent frown.

"Rude, Tancred! But you are *rude* to the lady whose guest you were so oftentimes in the hunt! Forget you the forest, Tancred, and Lady Zoë of the Hall?"

Tancred slightly pursed his lips. "Indeed not." There was a shade of primness in the phrase and there was primness too in his "Good morrow, Lady Falloc." And she saw he had not wholly lost his air of innocence, which quality, combined with his matchless courage, had made him the sinecure of his more worldly uncle's affections. All his guilelessness was in his expression now as he said more mildly, "This is no time, surely . . ."

"Time for what?" asked Bohemond laughing, while Zoë beside him flushed a chagrined crimson.

Then Bohemond grew serious. "Come, Tancred, it's time enough, it's *high* time . . . Besides, we grow careless of our other guest. Lady Zoë, this is His Excellency, Captain Firuz of Antioch, a Christian gentleman and commander of the main barbicans at St. George's Gate." The dark one had risen and stood quietly by while between Arabic and his own tongue the Prince completed the presentations and rendered to Zoë a swift picture of what they had afoot. Tancred had machinated the contact with the willing Armenian; the Wall could thus be breached and Antioch would fall.

The bald telling of the plan seemed to agitate Tancred anew. He cursed explosively, grew quite red, and his blond curls shook about his cheeks.

"Would I had kept it all to myself, by God! It is too late now. But curse me for dog-begotten, if in future I look not to my own benefice, and save myself the sight of my best efforts leaking away through dalliance and ingratitude!"

"Come, come, Tancred," cried Bohemond, half-laughing, half with commiseration for the hot-head. "How could you think that dalliance will be allowed to lose me this I have dreamed of all these many months? As for gratitude, you will learn continually of *that* as our paths go on together!" He clapped a hearty hand on the knight's mailed shoulder. He exuded conviviality. "But the Lady Zoë will *partake* in our *coup*, lad. Remember how we plotted it all? Come, let us pour a new cup, and lay our plans in shrewd council and as trusty friends!"

But Tancred wore his sullen look. He shrugged off Bohemond's gesture and spoke to Commander Firuz. The dark one rose, bowed, and left the board. Then Tancred, with a mixture of resignation and disgust on his serious young face, bestowed a final glare on Bohemond and led the Armenian through the arras. Bohemond shrugged.

"There. Jumpy these nights as a young stallion, my brave Tancred. But for all that, the lad of my own heart—magnificent, all I could wish for had I had a son . . ." He fell silent, looking at Zoë with ill-veiled thoughts in his face, while she, eyeing the littered ruin of the council table with its scribbled maps and spilled wine and the remnants of men's affairs, felt ill at ease and apologetic.

"I am afraid all about this, tonight, is inopportune."

"Rubbish," he deprecated. "My God, Zoë, do you think *I* want this thing solely to myself? Do you doubt I have longed to share it with you and Mihera, as we did everything in the old days? It is very lonely, sometimes, amongst so few friends and so many enemies, keeping one's own solitary council."

But she was remembering some of Mihera's words in their quarrel of the afternoon. "I think Mihera guesses. At least some of it."

"I told him the bones of it, nothing more. I shall inform him closely, presently, of course, now that all is near ready. *Near ready*, Zoë! Come, you shall know how *you* will figure, but not here, with the stink of the Armenian filling this room. Not that I should speak of him thus, that blessed comrade! But out on the bluff it is mild tonight and I shall carry the meat and the vintage with us. We'll broach a new jar, Alexius's own Cyprus, Zoë, which Tacitius was good enough to leave us when he went. Come."

And she, catching his irresistible warmth, smiled and preceded him to the rear of the pavilion.

There were rich divans and low elaborately wrought tables here in the open porch. A barricade of stones, like a baluster, snaked about the parapet. On this he set the casque and tray and the two richly decorated goblets from the supper board, while with his mouth he broached the little casque. She saw his teeth gleam about the stopple, catching a glimmer from the moon, from the white moon which but lately she had thought so sinister, but which now lay like a silver bath upon themselves and the parapet and the far straight ribbon of the Aleppo road beyond . . .

They stood at the baluster discussing the night of treachery that could come to pass with the help of Firuz, with Bohemond full of details about carrying it out, he pulling on the last bones of a roast heron and she sipping slowly at her goblet, which, as he talked, he refilled for her from time to time.

"You see, Zoë, there must be a counter-distraction while we accomplish the deed itself, and for this a spectacle at the Wall is the device. You know how it goes—remember the verses you fashioned for it when we presented it first at Michaelmas? And Tafur is right; only *you* could sing that part as it should be rendered . . ."

She shook her head. "I, Bohemond? Are you mad? A woman in the mystery-pit? Is it not self-evident that when you sought such a one, you looked among gypsies? My God, Bohemond, think what everyone would say!"

"Who cares?" His voice was almost petulant. "Don't you realize that we're not at home, encompassed by all its frame of ceremony? This is a *new* world, Zoë, and we are the makers of it. It is we who will set all rules and ceremony! Besides . . ."

"Save your words, Bo. I should not have protested on those arguable grounds. It is of course Mihera who would not have it, and the thing is thus completely settled." She set down her cup upon the wall and yawned, stretching like a cat. "Let's leave it, Bohemond. It is pleasant here. I am well pleased to stay a moment. It's a long time since we drank a cup together. Let us not spoil it with a quarrel." She gave him a frank, sweet, radiant smile and dropped to the divan. She was feeling something—the wine or his presence or the fact that they were alone together, she could not tell. Bohemond was watching her, alert, careful, expectant.

"Why do you insist on this thing of Mihera?" he said. "You were not so docile concerning the making of songs for my miracles, which, I recall now, he protested *too*." He came and sat on the divan, facing her. Zoë was staring at him, trying to keep her mind upon the issue at hand, trying to say the proper things. But she could feel her blood pounding in her head and at the same time, a sort of lassitude, a weakness and a terrible longing were creeping upon her. She desired him as she never had before. It was maddening to experience this, and to feel simultaneously, that sense of uneasiness, that knowledge that she was glad, *glad* that things were coming about thus. This night seemed suspended in time, and the parapet a thing apart, apart from life, even, and she felt a terrible longing to know for one short moment that was frozen here all that they might have known together. But with one last effort while guilt was still greater than her wild desire, "Mihera is disturbed, Bohemond," she said. "I wouldn't disturb him more. I am sorry for blundering here. I shall forget it all and not even tell him. Do *you* inform him of your plan, Bohemond, but leave me out of it completely. I swear he will desert else. He speaks of it now. Somehow it's torture to him to stay here, Bo; I see it in all ways since we have been together. He knows how I feel—My God, how can I hide it?"

For a moment he sat still, gazing at her with a still expression. His arms reached out and would have drawn her close, but she seized both his hands and sliding from the loggia she stood at the parapet, her eyes looking out and away.

He too stood, then, and they both stayed thus for several moments —he silent, waiting still, and she with her eyes wild and wide, not looking at him.

"Have you forgiven me?" she faltered at last, her voice strained and low.

"Have *I* forgiven *you!* Zoë!"

The expression that habitually crossed his face when he looked at her or any other woman was gone now. There was instead the dearly vulnerable and secret look she had loved in him long ago. His mouth was tender, his eyes luminous and soft, his hard forcefulness melted in ineffable affection.

Zoë shook her head as with sudden wonder at her passion for him. Far from lessening with the years, how it had mounted with the long denial, till just to be near him like this was a happy agony almost too poignant to bear. She lifted her hand and brushed it across his lips and for a moment was powerless to speak.

"My forgiveness, or yours—what does it mean to either of us now? The dream is over, Bohemond. We are committed, we two. I to him and you to—to all this." Then their eyes met, locked, and her words rushed. "But always we will love each other, Bohemond, we will have that . . ."

Bohemond was speechless, almost confounded. He had never expected to hear what he was hearing now. He was breathing heavily and his eyes had grown suddenly hard. They glittered like steel in the moonlight.

"Zoë! We cannot deny it like this, we cannot. You fool. You little fool. Do you think we live forever or more than just this once? *You little fool!*"

His constraint vanished suddenly and he uttered a cry deep in his throat and drew her savagely into his arms. The onslaught of his passion and the touch of him pressed close broke like a frail dam the last shred of her resistance and her whole body on fire for union with his own, she sank back in his arms and bathed his mouth with the warm return of his breathless kiss. She was in no hurry that this kiss should ever end, both for itself and her frantic dread-and-longing for what lay beyond—when she heard a slight sound, somewhere in back of the loggia. She stiffened.

It was the young squire, the sentry, who coughed.

"The Lord Mihera Falloc waits on you, my lord."

"Mihera— Good Lord!" cried Zoë, heaving up against Bohemond's chest. A wave of nausea and shame spread over her even at this instant and she pushed a tight question from her constricted throat with a forced casualness.

"Did you inform him I was here, fellow?"

"I beg pardon, madame?" said the guard expressionlessly, and Bohemond said, "My people are better than *that*, Zoë."

She hesitated only an instant.

"Of course. Thank Heaven. Is it possible to leave by that?" She pointed to a postern-opening in the wall on the bluff.

"Aye, But come here." He caught and held her as she sought to re-arrange her bodice. "Yet one kiss more before you leave me?"

But she turned her face away, avoiding the brush of his lips, avoiding too that edged smile that now had invaded his eyes. "Let me go now, Bohemond. I—I will return. I—don't know. I cannot bear it now!"

She could not have said what filled her with this thing as of a sickness. She did not look back but fled through the way he indicated and waited until the squire brought two mounts and started before her.

Her cheeks burned and her heart felt like lead and the colt's hooves pounding along after Vieuxpont as he led her by an obscure path athwart the dunes was a nerve-jarring accompaniment to her headlong and shameful flight.

CHAPTER XX

The Broken String

ZOE PASSED THROUGH the foyer of her own tent without seeing anyone. But the torches were lighted all about the grounds and she heard voices deep in the pavilion. Mihera's mount had gone from his stanchion and she knew he was looking for her. To her relief she found their sleeping quarters empty. She flung back the arras, went in and began quickly to pull off her clothes. A look in the shield-mirror had confirmed her highest fears about her appearance. She was in disarray from her muddy shoes and the torn sleeve of her bodice to the tumbled mass of her hair. These things were bad enough. Yet her face was what Mihera would judge her by, she feared, for her skin was flushed as though she had swum in a cool pool, her eyes were bright and her whole expression radiant.

She was just climbing upon the high bed when the arras was flung aside and Mihera loomed in the doorway. She knew it was he by the shape of his husky, slightly bent form and the faint outline of his stiff fair hair against the light of the outer torches. She had taken good care to snuff the sconces here, hoping the questions she fully anticipated would be asked in darkness and answered in the snug and pleasant circumstances of their couch together. On the way home, she had wholly recovered command of her ordinary wits, had cursed Bohemond, even placing upon his actions all the blame, and had taken resolution to preserve by whatever means her rightful rapport with her husband. She took vows on all this with much tremulation and with knowledge that his mood of late, and especially since their quarrel, was a delicate one.

Mihera did not care for the darkness of their room.

"My God, is it you?" he said and strode to the coals of the brazier which Marcelle habitually left burning at their bedside, and blew on the embers. His face above them reflected their glow and added to his own bright flush of anger which she knew so well. She turned, and sat facing him on the bed's edge, holding the coverlet modestly to her breasts. The bed was so high that their eyes were on a level. She saw how terrible he looked. She noted his eyes shot with blood and how his face was haggard and drawn with strain.

She was so taken with the obvious distress on his features that she forgot to dissemble a little the various honest emotions that were written plain upon her own. She realized this too late when she saw him smile a little, that sarcastic cracking of his tight, straight-lipped mouth.

"I see you derived a salutary color from your walk about the country."

"No, Mihera." She had suddenly recalled about Tafur and her heart lifted. She had need not to lie, but only to omit a little. Letting the coverlets fall, she placed her two hands on Mihera's shoulders and looked into his eyes. "Mihera, I have changed my mind about the brand. You were right, and almost mystic in your timely prediction. I encountered one Tafur, the chief of those raffish Ribalds and it was just by the luck of Mary that I—"

He laughed soundlessly and without mirth and withdrew from her hands with which she had sought to caress him. "Don't exert yourself to lie to me," he said. "I've looked all over for you, on the dunes, by the river and only as a last resort, wanting to find you anywhere but there, I went to the camp of Bohemond. You had gone by then, indeed he *said* he had not seen you, and I went on till I met your friend Tafur. He was whiling the time for his companions with a song. I have heard it before. It's an old game, one substitutes the name that is appropriate. Have you heard it, Zoë? I am scarcely the singer of the two of us, but I can say words and perhaps refresh your memory. A merry thing.

> *"The horn of the ancient speaks of plenty,*
> *The horn of Artemis cries the game;*
> *The horn of the monger pleads your penny,*
> *And that of the unicorn heals the lame.*
> *But he with a pretty wife, messires,*
> *A frisky wife and hearty,*
> *Acquires a pair of horns, messires,*
> *From quite another party . . ."*

Her hands flew to her mouth. "Oh, *no*, Mihera. You mustn't think —I can explain it *all* if you'll only listen!" She recoiled a little on the tick, for he had come suddenly closer.

"Oh, don't fret, my pretty! I'll not trouble you tonight! I would kill you if I did. *Fric-quenelle!*" His voice rasped on the foul insult.

He leaned across her to the wall sconce by the couch and unhooked his sword. It rattled brassily against the brazier and made her jump. Then without another glance, he turned and strode from the room.

Dismay at the moments just past overwhelmed her so that she slid beneath the tick and lay breathing heavily. Guilt, remorse, and especially humiliation so overwhelmed her that she could not at first think. Then suddenly she sat up as the idea struck. He was seeking out Bohemond: *he will fight him; they will kill each other.* Then her horror found release in tears and she lay back, sobbing in the coverlets.

Through her weeping she could hear a tremendous din as though everything in their pavilion were being moved about. She lay still a moment. There were loud voices too, though she could not make out words, of Mihera and the dame Marcelle and some other. Presently and with a great jingling, she heard several horses ride out of the pavilion close. Her mind reached wildly for some explanation of what transpired. *What is he doing,* she wondered, *taking his whole retinue with him to attack publicly and in a civil brawl the pavilion of Bohemond?*

The thought brought new shame and terror and she lay back and surrendered herself to a storm of weeping. Presently the exertions of the last hours sucked her tired body into a pit of deep exhaustion and she slept as one dead.

She awakened some time later to the noises of Marcelle bustling about the room in her morning business. Instinctively she felt the empty tick beside her to see if it might still be warm from Mihera's body, but her fingers drew back chilled and she sat upright, the whole dread of the last night's evil taking hold of her once again.

"What is it, Marcelle? What happened last night? Where is the Lord Mihera? He was a fool to think of fighting Sir Bohemond."

"Then my Lord is no fool, madame," Marcelle answered, her broad face stiff with a new sort of smug expression. "He gathered his clothes and his ledgers and weapons and left for Laodicea. He means to ship for Italy." She turned and faced Zoë. "He means also never to return."

Zoë started.

"Marcelle, what of *Ursule?*"—her heart nearly stopping.

"I was hard put to keep him from taking her. Only my solemn pledge to be fully responsible and never leave her solely to *your* care, madame, dissuaded him. I absolutely refused to accompany them."

"Them! Who went with him?"

"Two squires and the physician, Messer Poldi."

"The physician!" Zoë was fully aroused now. She swept her tumbled hair back, pushed aside the tick and gave a jump to the rushes.

"How dared he, Marcelle? Leaving us defenseless in this cradle of fevers, this slew of plague!"

She fled through the outer room to the bed-chamber of little Ursule. With the sleepy child in her arms she came out again, and surveyed with horror the wreck of the interior of the tent produced by Mihera's ransacking. A new worry crossed her mind.

"How will we fend? He left monies, Marcelle?"

"Aye, he left ample funds," Marcelle said, this time with an officiousness she did not bother to conceal. "In my safe-keeping."

"In *your* safe-keeping!" Zoë stood there, in chagrin and frustration. She stepped to the arras and looked out upon the dunes. The stanchions were empty, four mounts gone, there were empty fodder bags swinging in the breeze.

She came into the room flushed, her eyes brimming, but angrily, not with fear. Her humility was gone, she was aroused to more positive thoughts. Several emotions followed each other over her mobile face.

She sat on the fire bench, cradling Ursule in her arms and rocking gently.

"Good Lord, Marcelle," she said. Then, with doubtful bravado, "My God, he doesn't mean this. He's not *permanently* gone. It's one of his moods. He means to punish me and make me stew myself to a pulp about it. Which we shall not do!" She rose. "Marcelle, give Ursule her breakfast while I set this mess to rights. And do not fret. Mihera will be back directly, when he feels I am sufficiently chastised. Damn that Tafur!" she added as an after-thought.

Marcelle raised her brows, and pursed her lips as she watched her mistress make herself busy. She still had her night-dress on and her hair was wildly tossed about as she set to her tasks like any cottage-wife.

But Mihera did not return. And now, as days dragged to weeks, Zoë learned, in ways she had never suspected, how much Mihera had meant to her. She missed his returnings after trips and after days of conferring with the stewards of the Host. She missed spending evenings with him over his ledger-books or listening to his talk of business while she plied the loom. She missed his companionship and his rare dry humor, and even his irritable blustering at her for countless little things. And in the lonely nights, she missed his virile presence beside her under the ticks. And not these things only. She missed his warm, sure love and the utter dependability of his nature which had sheltered and stabilized her whole existence. She had, at the Mass and in prayer, given thanks for the blessing of him many times. And when, in the months past, she had dwelt too much upon the thoughts of Bohemond, allowing her memories to kindle her senses to dangerous excitement, she had ended always by telling herself what a fool she would be to forfeit, for whatever reason, Mihera's rock-like affection. As the dreary weeks passed and Mihera did not return, it began to look as if she had done just that. She cursed him. She cursed herself over and over. But also, and many times, she cursed her sheer ill luck.

"Great Michael," she said to Marcelle one day, "many a wife strays from the manor as a constant pastime. Recall you at home the Baroness of Bull Joy? She used to lie with her page each time the lord was absent; and Melanie de Laie, who prayed each day that the bellicose Duke would involve himself in yet another border war so she could sample her varied assortment . . . While I, vaugh! for one doubtful moment and that scarcely my fault," she put in with a pout, "I am come to this!"

"*This whole pot de ragout for one kiss*," she added to herself but not for Marcelle's hearing. Marcelle was out of hand as it was; she held to the purse Mihera had consigned her like a dog with a bone, and Zoë wished she knew its hiding place. This being under the thumb of a servant, in a most real sense, was very humiliating and something she would never forgive Mihera for. It would be the main theme of her diatribe against him when he returned.

"And, moreover, it's the fault of men that women suffer so," she went on in this vein, "and not the wicked ones either. Mind you, Marcelle, at home it was the docile good wives and not the philandering cockatoos that found themselves girdled with iron belts while their righteous sires rode off to the wars with the key-ring in their baldrics . . ."

Marcelle looked up from her sewing.

"The Lord Mihera did not do likewise to *madame* when he departed yestermonth . . . did he?" Marcelle asked with the faint flicker of a more-than-idle question.

"But of course not, you fat pea-goose!" snapped Zoë. "But by Sant' George in these reverse circumstances he might have done me a service if he had. I dread to go abroad at all, of late, Marcelle." Her forehead gathered in worry. "Do we have *ample* funds?"

"Aye," said Marcelle. "Some eight hundred byzants which should see us through the year, and by then we should be to the Holy Land. But madame, you will not consider going home?" she asked for the hundredth time. "We should not remain, it is dangerous here for us and for little Ursule."

Zoë frowned.

"Ursule is my real worry," she said, "and the worst of Mihera's deed. But I will *not* go home, Marcelle; I will *not* give in to this quirk of his ill-nature, for I'm sure he will return. He is only in Laodicea, trading or settling business there. He will be back. We must stay here and be well content, just as we are now, when he does."

Marcelle shook her head. "In the meantime, madame, what is to become of you? I, too, am afraid every time you go to the Mass or to the markets, for your very life."

"Don't fret," said her mistress, "I can look to myself."

And so she did, but in a gingerly sort of way, and it was half bravado. She felt lost, afraid, and in a different world.

For though Zoë was prepared for some of the things that were to happen to her now, still she was shocked at the changed aspect of her world, and especially in regard to the spread of the word of her altercation with Tafur and the Prince. It deprived her at one fell blow of the various aspects of her previous respectable status. It had been threefold before—as a noblewoman, as a wealthy person (for Mihera's affluence was legend among this host of debtors), and lastly, and importantly enough, as a happily married woman. As all these things she had known the knights of the expedition as good friends of her husband's, respectful of herself for those reasons, and for their considerable rank and power. She had thought of them all as gallant noblemen, brave knights and pious Christians, for all of the wild rumors of debauchery among them. There were always a few wretches in every large gathering of soldiers. But now she could not go to the market place at St. Paul's Gate without being flirted with by these same barons, maliciously ignored by their wives and made sport of by knaves of the peasant infantry in the public gathering places. She had never much mingled with the women of the Host; it was not her nature to go gossiping with them at the looms about babies and high prices, and she had grown up with and always preferred male company anyway. So this did not bother her. But it was disconcerting to be making her way home with provisions for the household and to be accosted on the dunes by one of these—the Count of Cantanzaro, the Lord of Treapani, even some of the French knights who had oftentimes been guests at Mihera's board. It was in all ways unpleasant and humiliating to see them dismount, come plucking after her stirrup like ill-mannered boys and in various unsubtle ways ask for an assignation as though they paid her the time of day. It did no good to show them their place with hauteur (which they took to be coyness) or anger (which they took to be a show of fine spirit), or flight—she had tried this once and the old Duc de Meniens, his sword rattling and his plumed helm bobbing, had taken off and pursued her as if he were charging in the lists!

It was not only frightening and humiliating, this sort of thing. It was terribly disillusioning, it was dulling the edge of one's sense of the order of things. She had always imagined the noble gentlemen *kept* the vows they had made for their potential journey to the Holy Land. Had not Robert Guiscard, in spite of his dearly indulged vanity, endured a beard on his face all during the campaign of Asia Minor? She thought, now, that Robert Guiscard would have kept a vow of *chastity* too, had he made it. But this was a different world. And these men who made fun of the rough, Italian-bred Normans with their barbaric ways, a different species, for all their elegance! *Fichtre*, the world she had seen that night from the peculiar vantage-place of the shoulders of Tafur was the *real* world here—and she was as much a part of it now as Tafur! And like him, she had a spurious distinction. She was sought after by the gentlemen, damned and obliquely envied by the good wives, and was watched by everyone. For by guess and by gossip she was at least beloved by, and most likely the mistress of, the mighty Bohemond!

As for the Norman Prince, the thing had in no way touched him, as far as one could tell. At the outset, when news of the thing, thanks to Tafur and the busy jongleurs, had spread through the camp, it was readily believed, elaborated and embellished, because of tales and snatches of tales that had gone before. Of their youth, of their reunion here, of Zoë's dallying with the miracles. It was a delightful thing to wag the tongue upon, a welcome distraction from the everlasting worry over what might become of them here at the Wall of Antioch.

Bohemond, through his bachelorhood and the discretion with which he lived his private life before, and because of the legends of almost god-hood that had grown about him, might have lost something by the thing, especially among the lower classes. Among the great lords, there were no illusions as to the varicolored motives behind this crusade. They had all of them captured towns and castles for themselves on the way here; they had with greedy hands taken booty and women with equal relish and conducted themselves like Turks. And now that Bohemond, up to the affair of Antioch so single-minded, high-souled and straight-aiming, had insisted upon sieging here, they had few illusions left as to what *his* plans were also. They merely, as it later proved, were underestimating them. But the pilgrims, the palmers, the priests, the peasants, and all the lower contingent of the Host, who had come on this arduous journey with no purpose but the plenary expiations of their sins and to see Christ's birthplace, were somewhat puzzled by the pieces of gossip on Bohemond that now fell even to their lowly portion. For to them the brave Prince had been Solomon in Byzantium, Moses in the desert, Michael in the fray, and a sort of Job here. They were ready to follow him anywhere, and to wait and watch with him under any circumstances. They wrote home glowing accounts of his prowess that was rivaled alone by his purity of heart, and the jongleurs made many a verse about the Prince of the Normans who shared many characteristics with the Prince of Peace. They did not mean to blaspheme; they really looked upon him as a sort of Christ.

So he might have fallen a little from his perch, but for the fact that almost before they had time to listen to the smirchers of their saint, far more significant news was bruited through the Host. In the fears they had harbored all through the season here, this one carked them worst—that somewhere to the north a great emir, Kerboga by name, was gathering all upper Islam, and would presently descend upon them thousands strong. Compared to this, the peril they had borne of Rudwan and his Aleppan raids had been but a tilt. This would be the end, the finish. Kerboga was ready—Kerboga was started south—Kerboga was coming!

And yet Prince Bohemond had no fear. So they kept their faith in him. They watched, they prayed, they gazed each dawn at the emptiness of the Aleppo road. They stood about his faded tent, waiting to hear what miracle he would work for their deliverance.

Meantime he kept from the lords the workings of his plan, telling them only that he could capture Antioch, that he *would,* telling them too, that if he did, it must be his. Old Raymond, count of Toulouse, stood in the council-tent and reminded the others that they had oaths to Alexius, that their sole hope lay in the Emperor's coming; they must conquer it for *him,* enfeoff it to *him,* and go on to the Holy Land. But Bohemond told them that since Alexius forbore to come, their feudal pledge was void and the city belonged to whoever contrived to take it. In all this young Tancred de Hauteville supported him. Old Raymond had risen up, shaken his sword in Bohemond's very face, pulled his gonfanon from the council color-pole, and led the Provençals from the pavilion. The rest, the French, the Flemings, the Germans and Walloons, though they favored the Prince to old St. Gilles, demurred at Bohemond's high-handed stand. At this the Prince had ordered them all out and had stayed in his tent like a Greek, sulking. Meantime the lowly ones prayed and watched and pled with the mighty ones to cease their quarrels and to save them from a pagan death. For Kerboga was coming. Kerboga was coming. KERBOGA WAS COMING!!!

It was during the period of his final quarrel with the leaders over the right to Antioch that Zoë was visited by Bohemond. It was warming to summer and Zoë was seated outside the shelter on a dais at her loom. She was feeling miserable. As she saw his dun-colored stallion approach her palisade, she lowered her eyes quickly to her loom, and though her heart gave the old uncontrollable lunge, she determined to be short. She had been conning her troubles, and he had made an unfortunate entrance as she was thinking to herself, *My God if Mihera comes back I swear I'd be everything he ever wanted me to be and more, and I'd beg him to take me back to Amalfi with him this very minute!*

So Bohemond's reception was cool. He saw her mood at once, apparently, for he dismounted in silence, meekly climbed to where she sat and she felt his hand lie light on her shoulder an instant before he murmured in a sympathetic voice, "By Sant' George's right arm, I'm sorry, Zoë."

She thought she heard something in his tone—did he think *this* situation was funny?—and quickly glanced up to give him a sharp look. But his whole expression was perfectly sober, even sad, and true sympathy seemed to show from his grey, sable-edged eyes.

"It was an unfortunate thing for all of us. If I had seen Mihera before he went—"

"Don't *mention* Mihera!" she said with a lighting change in attitude and a vicious stab at the embroidery. "A wife shouldn't need a spokesman for her honor, if that's what you mean! Let him, with his foul mind and his over-active imagination, go to the devil!"

Bohemond stared at her; a look of amusement passed across his face. But Zoë was bending to a cloth, a tapestry depicting Ruth in the Corn, and sewing the beads with fury as though she had but the next few seconds to see it done.

"Besides," she added, "I don't need your sympathy. I do very well, and I find it pleasant to be without a soul to answer to. There are many making this pilgrimage alone. Mihera was discontented anyhow—I told you so that night, and everything is better as it is." She gave him a defiant look as though he were the whole disapproving world, her chin tilting and the corners of her eyes lifting a moment before they plunged once more to the shelter of her lashes that were still black as soot.

This time Bohemond openly grinned and she heard him give a sound, almost like a sigh of satisfaction. "Well . . . ! You are brave! You are sensible! You are truly the stuff I wish my officers were made of! Now look you, in a fortnight perhaps, we're going over."

"What of the Provençals, Bohemond? I hear Raymond balks, and what of the Saracens, ready to fall upon us all?"

"You've even *said* it, Zoë! The one takes care of the other. Do you think St. Gilles or the rest can hold against me with Kerboga marching?"

"Is it true he will come soon? How do you *know* there's a fortnight to tarry?"

"Never mind, sweetheart. The Armenians are thieves, with their usury and their high prices, but they serve rather handily and they keep in good touch with things from Artah to my own pavilion."

"You have it all your way. Very clever, Bohemond."

"Yes, I have. I have it all my way. Now all I hope is that Yagi Sayan doesn't guess about Firuz and scuttle the whole." He had lowered his voice.

"Don't fret. Marcelle has gone to the Bridge. Besides, she would scarcely spoil a plan to get us out of here. She hates it as much as any," she told him.

"Aye, but she's a talker. Is it true she's custodian of monies he left you, Zoë?"

She gasped. "But yes. How did you know?"

"She bragged in the market."

"That cabbage-head! I'll lash her for it!"

"I know nothing of your discipline. Only take care about her. You've said nothing of the plan?"

"No."

"Good. I was afraid you would, at least *your* portion of it."

"What do you mean, *my* portion?"

He threw himself onto the parapet, crossing his legs. They were smooth in blue hose that matched his tunic and both made his eyes seem deeper and made his hair flamboyantly red.

She sat looking at him a moment, acutely aware of the old charm, but also convinced that it was deliberately being exercised upon her now.

"I did not accept the 'portion' in your scheme, Bohemond."

He frowned, almost a pout pursing his strongly formed lips. He is all tricks, thought Zoë. He has used them long and well, and one is almost willingly his dupe, just to see him machinating in full career. "Disenchant yourself, Bohemond," she declared. "My case is bad enough. I have no intention of further making a spectacle of myself— for *you!*"

"For *me!* A *spectacle!* Zoë, don't you see? This will be deliverance! They will be grateful to everyone, to *all* who take part in that happy night! My word, you'd be their idol, you'd be a sensation, and it would be fully shown in such heroic action how Mihera wronged you! Up near the Wall, Zoë, masking the barbicans for us all, giving a chance for us to breach it while they watch the play! This makes a niggard of propriety, Zoë. Ruth in Israel, Judith in the tent—can't you see?"

"No. I can't. Mihera said I was gaining a loose name for some songs. What do you think *this* would do? A mime, an actress, flouting herself in the mystery-pit, for the eyes of the pagans . . ."

An expression of impatience touched Bohemond's features. Sarcasm hardened in his voice.

"My God, I did not, until just this minute, know how truly you've changed! I can recall, without troubling my memory overmuch, when *you* were the one to scoff at gossip . . . But now, what a vane—a stiff-backed matron quaking at every whisper that might cross the manor fence. Pardon me, I grow boresome. Why should I linger here, to tread on the tussocks of your respectability! Let me but take the hint. Farewell, Zoë."

And abruptly he turned and left her.

She was surprised. She paused for the first time in her needle-work to observe his expression as he threw his silken, heavy-thewed leg

across the charger. He was not red with anger, nor sad with disappointment. His face was a cold mask. Tired, bored, disgusted. For
a moment mixed feelings assailed her and she felt a twinge of fright
in her throat. Had she actually been tiresome? But instantly her usual
determination revived and as she saw his mount's tail switch about
the distant bays and disappear, she rose, stamped her foot and strode,
angrier than she could give any reason for, into the pavilion.

Marcelle did not come from the markets at the usual time. Zoë
made supper for little Ursule, then waited, strangely restive, for the
first sign of the nurse's palfry to appear on the dunes. She was worried,
the sun was low, and she had sent for a groom with the notion to take
him as link-boy on a search, when she saw the old one come at a brisk
canter from the direction of the Wall.

"Where have you been?" she asked as the woman dismounted and
waddled through the dust. "I've been frantic, waiting."

"Oh, oh, madame." She stood, wringing her hands and Zoë stared
at her clothes, in disarray from dusty hem to torn wimple, and saw
how her fat frame sagged with exhaustion and how her heavy face
was crumpled in despair.

"Marcelle. . . . What *is* it!"

The groom was unloading the panniers from the blowing jade and
Marcelle turned to caution him with strange words.

"Take some pains with those foodstuffs, Panturge. They are all we
may see for long."

Panturge, a hunch-backed youth with a swarm of festering pimples
on his face, gave her a puzzled look and then peered at the Lady Zoë
as if he expected her to explain the cryptic cue. Marcelle looked utterly
devastated.

Zoë frowned. "What mean you, Marcelle, 'all we may see'? Not
famine again! Lord, we should have stocked against it."

"No, madame, not famine, not for anybody *else,* that is." Her eyes
dilated as she plunged. "*Just for us!*"

Zoë took her by both shoulders. "What are you prattling of, gossip!" shaking her as if to make her eyeballs loose. But Marcelle stood
immobile on her post-like legs and stolidly said, "Madame, we were
robbed today."

"Robbed!" Zoë released her, stood back and eyed her in disgust.
"La! Let that be your lesson. I thought of the lash but I see now that
fate has punished you well enough for your jowliness. From now on *I*
shall go to market, since I must, and have henceforth full charge of
all our monies!"

"All our monies," repeated Marcelle dully and as though the words
strangled. "All our monies, madame, are gone."

"Gone . . . My God, no!"

"But yes! I carried it *all* today, the whole eight hundred byzants!" She wagged her head, her eyes wide with woe.

"Oh, no! Oh, no, Marcelle!" Zoë sagged against the hitch-post. "What will become of us? How will we fend?" Her voice rising, " 'Sbody, Marcelle, what will happen to little Ursule? You? Me? All of us?"

Then she turned on a new tack. "It's my fault. I should have taken that money if I had to flog you for it . . . Holy Chrysostom, we've got it now!"

"Calm yourself, madame!" Marcelle, since no lash-o'-leather was raising its ugly head, was relaxing a little. "Don't blame yourself. Your lord charged *me* with full responsibility, seeking protection for us through my more experienced husbandry. Oh, oh," she wailed, the full significance of her failure once more overwhelming her. "What have I done?" She fell heavily to her knees by the stanchion and scooping a handful of horse-dung, sprinkled it on her head.

Zoë ignored her, switching her skirts away as though she found her leprous, and went up on the palisade. "There! *Now* he has done it, crediting with more sense than me that blowsy old hag!" She cursed again roundly and kicked the loom viciously against the balustrade where its crewel-staff snapped against the stone and broke in a dozen pieces. "My God, how did I stand it all those years? How I hate him. I *hate* him!" She turned to Marcelle, her full cloak swirling.

"Where, when, how was it taken, Marcelle? Tell me all! We must plan its recovery if we can!"

Marcelle, kneeling in the dust with the filth sticking about her veils, spread out her fat hands.

"As for the first, it was snatched by some devil-whelped knave— pulled from that pouch that I hang to my chatelaine, as I bartered with those Armenians in the place of poultry. I felt a small tug, a lank, nondescript creature darted through the crowd, and la! it was gone. I screamed, shouted 'Thief,' and some of the younger women gave full cry against his heels, but he vanished. I have since been engaged everywhere, trying to get help from the authorities. I caused it to be cried. I went to some of the officials your lord knew who govern these things, I even sought the Seigneur Bohemond—"

"Marcelle!"

"The Seigneur Bohemond, but he was gone. A message was promised to be delivered by the sentry, Vieuxpont. But there is great confusion in the camp now, madame. The streets buzz with the talk that Kerboga will come. I doubt if it matters now, for our byzants. I doubt if we'll care. Before long we'll be rotting to dust like those bones we saw beforetime from that venture of the Hermit Peter and Walter

Sans Avoir, whose followers fell to the swords of just such heathens!"
And she lapsed into noisy blubbering tears.

Zoë felt dizzy, ready to burst with fury and despair. Devil! On top
of everything that creature had cried their plight to the whole camp.
Tears of rage and impotence stood in her eyes.

Panturge the horse-boy had left off fussing with the sacks and
watched what was going forward with interest. His lady stood tall,
angry and soul-shakingly beautiful in the full light of the setting sun.
Its rays bronzed her hair and turned the tears to diamonds in her
lovely eyes. He could not contain himself. He leapt upon the porch,
fell to his knees and took the hem of her great-cloak and pressed it to
his lips.

"Madame!" he cried, his pimpled face purpling, "let me take you
away! Let me hide you in the hills somewhere behind the city. Then,
sometime later, we could flee across the hills to Laodicea! Madame . . ."

She frowned down. She could smell his foul jerkin wet with his
nervous sweat. Revulsion and disgust distorted her face. She pushed
her knee against him, toppling him off-balance to the stones, and
rescued her cloak as though stung.

" 'Steeth, Panturge! Get to your tent!" He had unnerved her. She
stood, her whole body shivering with revulsion and a sudden fear.
Not for the imminence of Kerboga, this seemed the least of it now.
There were other possibilities of doom, and in the face of these she
could feel a distinct indifference to the sword of the Sultan of Mosul.

CHAPTER XXI

The Bishop and Beelzebub

THE DEPARTURE OF MIHERA had been misfortune in the abstract; the loss of the money was disaster imminent and real. For the next few days Zoë stayed closeted in her pavilion, taking stock of their meager stores, and trying to decide what to do next. Mihera would of course come back for her; he must, for little Ursule's sake if nothing else. It was merely that she must husband what they had and make it do. But what a boon would a little help be! Crusaders' women bearing tithes of their larders to someone in straits—how often she had seen it done for a fallen knight's lady, a squire's goodwife, or a pilgrim's ailing *dame*. She had never done alms of the kind herself, for Mihera had assigned such shares of goods as part of his duties here. How she wished she had made friends, had gossiped and held their babies and been neighbor to them all. The only kindnesses she could recall were certain overtures to the old Countess Albarada, and these had been oblique favors, tinged with other motives than sincere friendship . . . For the first time she realized how narrowly she had lived here, caring for Ursule, for Mihera's household, and in reality interested only in them—and in Bohemond. How he had warped, compassed and dominated her life, not only here, but the whole of it, without giving anything of himself. Right now, for instance, when she needed him most, there was no sign he knew she existed. He had been conspicuously missing since that last visit and she took it as a dismissal from his life. (Why not, damn him, with a new world to conquer?)

This was the sorest spot of all. Inwardly she mourned him. She went over every word of their last encounter, conning each phrase and expression for a key. Like a vane swinging to the weather, she lived again each moment since they met here, and by turns dreamed of his love and his possible defection. Like a vane . . . what was his final cut? "I had not thought you were such a vane, Zoë, a stiff-backed matron . . ."

Was that the reason for his outburst? It must be. It was not that she had lost attraction. Her mirror told her that. She was full blown, glowing, and she knew it well. Her body was slim, her hair glossy and lustrous as it ever was, and she was still young and lovely. Love these last months, with the loved one newly near and yet titillatingly unobtainable, with the heart reaching to be assuaged, had refired her whole being. She was experiencing a second youth, more full, more richly glowing than her first. A lone and arid blooming.

But if Bohemond stayed scarce and the women ignored her, certain gentlemen of the camp did not. In her plight, with this strange combination of the name of a jade and the fame of a beauty in distress, she was assailed by a following of odd hue, so that she needs must hold her tents untenable to guests. Marcelle was instructed, and the rule precisely kept, so that it came as a surprise when Marcelle announced one day that out in the main chamber a visitor had asked for madame, had been admitted, and now awaited her.

"Who is it?" Zoë had asked peremptorily. She was closely engaged with Ursule's hair, and did not look up. Even so she could feel the servant's obvious delight.

"The Duke of Normandy, madame."

"Who?" The title confused her and she was distracted too by the tone of Marcelle's voice. It had a sort of reverence in it, for both the guest and herself to whom this overture was being rendered. Marcelle had viewed her mistress's withdrawal with some distress. The attempted flirtations, the biddings that had come to join this noble knight and that, at entertainments and wine, had impressed her mightily and she failed to understand this seeming reluctance to advantage oneself of all this glow of popularity. She could recall her own good days . . . Besides, would not all of them, sometime soon, be hungry?

"Do you mean Robert?" her mistress asked her now.

"Aye, madame. He is finely dressed and smells like a garden and seems all of a fire for a visit with yourself. Did you expect him?"

Zoë made a face. "*Expect* him! I have never so much as had the occasion to meet him, until now." She frowned, flushing a little, thinking of his reputation which was known to all—his flamboyant "pursuit of passion" as the Legate had aptly phrased it to Bohemond. She went on plaiting Ursule's hair.

"Who is that man? Is he Papa's friend?" asked the little girl.

"I think not." Her mother suppressed a slight wry smile.

"Who, then?" insisted Ursule.

Almost absently Zoë replied. "He is Duke of Normandy. His father was William the Conqueror and his brother is Rufus, King of England. His cousin is Philip, King of France, to whom he mortgaged his dukedom to come on this Crusade."

"He sounds like a nice man, Mama."

Zoë laughed. "Little snob! Mind thee, my darling, nobility is as nobility does . . . What notions has Marcelle been putting in thy small head?"

"Aren't you coming now, madame?" interrupted Marcelle, who could scarcely stand it.

"Presently!" her voice swelling to an edge.

But Marcelle shifted her great frame from one foot to the other. She put out her hands. "Here. Here, my lady. I will do for the child. Your own veils should be looked to, they are quite disarranged."

"Silence!" snapped Zoë, her patience at an end. Her nerves were frayed, and every word the jade said scraped like a nicked blade across her feelings. "Contain yourself, woman, or I'll send you to Laodicea where your obvious leanings will be usable as the fat procuress for some Egyptian bordel!"

But Marcelle was not daunted. Her jowls flapped and her small eyes seemed to sink in a little while she tossed her telling shaft.

"Duke Robert tarries continually at the ports. Does it hit you he brings some word of the Lord Mihera?"

The effect was completely satisfying. She found herself charged with the tidying of Ursule while without prelude for wimple-fixing or anything else, Zoë hurried to leave her for the outer room. Marcelle smiled, taking extra pains with Ursule's little coiffure, and hummed a bawdy tune.

It was with a definite sense of breathlessness that Zoë approached the interview. As a Norman she shared with her countrymen of the South a certain awe and curiosity concerning her compeers at home. Besides, Marcelle's surmise of possible news was not too badly taken. On the wings of these thoughts she sailed into the room and at first saw no one and thought for a moment that the visitor had gone. Then she heard his slight cough and turned about, her stiff silk pelisse swirling about her hips. He was standing by the iron coal-cradle which in this weather had been pushed from the center of the room and left unlighted. Was there news? her expression asked him. But the Duke of Normandy smiled, bowed, with nothing but admiration in his eyes, and her hopes passed from her mind.

Robert Shortshanks, for all the grotesqueness of his famous bandy-legs, was well-favored, and in his smile was a generous inkling of his jovial personality. His attire passed the gaudy. Above his *pantalons* of steel (which had been rubbed till their flat discs shone like the skin of a mackerel) he affected a parti-colored tunic, something akin to the tabard of a page, of fine silk, such as dandies wore (but fashioned of plain homespun) on the upper continent. He combined these not too incongruously with a pair of red pelt, gold-laced buskins which he had no doubt come by on one of his pleasure jaunts to the Seleucian coast. His shoulder-length, straight brown hair was without covering. He had a well-met, convivial look—it was easy to see his popularity withal; but there were also, in eye and mouth and in his pitted skin, the marks of dissipation which added a good decade to the prime of his manhood. His fame as a fighter *nonpareil* was backed by numerous sword cuts on both heavy jaws.

"My respects, Countess! Forgive me, but long have I wished to be presented to your grace, for the fame of your loveliness has travelled far, and not that only; the glory of your art has been bruited clean to Normandy, I hear tell. It is hard to credit being actually *with* you!"

The compliment, extravagant but deft, had Zoë falling instantly to the role of a *grand'dame*, cool, distant, and a little condescending.

"Your Excellency surprises me at an inopportune moment. I have been indisposed, the fevers here," she lied, "and I am not attired to receive such a guest."

Robert's dark eyes glinted, and a slight hollow came to his shaven cheeks where his breath was sucked in to suppress his grin.

"Indeed! I am sorry to trouble your recovery, but let me declare, madame, that if it be true you can appear lovelier than you are this morning, these eyes could not bear the dazzle."

Zoë stiffened at his tone, which by the minute was changing.

"You have lately returned from the Coast?" she coolly inquired.

"But yes," with a Gallic shrug. "I have spent much leisure there while we stop in this swamp. I have absented myself from my fellows overmuch, I suspect, but I thought that life held nothing interesting here, and life is short; so I pandered my boredom on Asia Minor. I know now I was mistaken."

Robert had a charming, if impertinent, smile.

"But speaking of the Coast," he went on, "I managed a good trade there recently. I thought it would interest you peculiarly and it is my acceptable excuse to present myself to your presence." He clapped short, soldierly hands together twice, while Zoë stood there feeling bitterly let down, her scarce-admitted certainty of a message from Mihera withered by his words.

Through the arras pushed, rather than stepped, a little fat behind draped in striped wool, then the back of a turban wound toweringly to a high cone on which an incredible bright gaud was perched. When he turned, she saw a black chubbed face, round eyes and a bare black stomach, like that of a doll she had won once in a Greek fair at Palermo in the days gone by. His fat arms were filled with an irregular bulk wound in lapis-colored silk, of which Robert immediately relieved him. As the Duke, grasping it by its narrow neck unwound the shroudings, Zoë knew, long before the last revolving of the silk, that it was a lute, of rare workmanship, and, she immediately guessed, of tone; a beautiful instrument, such as she had never laid eyes on before. Its back was grained like a peacock's tail and its ornate, Oriental-looking bowl was decorated with minute, numberless, airily executed arabesques, picked out in pearl, ivory and multi-hued majolica luster. She swept her fingers, trembling a little, across the quintet of polished strings as he handed it to her, evoking a stream of exquisite sound like a burst from the throat of *bulbul,* the oriental thrush.

"My faith—matchless, is it not?" Robert said, his voice tight and his breath quick upon her.

"The loveliest I've seen," she said and plucked several notes from its pear-shaped belly.

"But the lute is an accompanist," he said, "lacking its fullest existence without a matching song. There is one of your own people's, a thing of the conflict of love and war, that I dote on. Would you do me the boon? Surely, madame," Robert said earnestly, his eyes soft and true entreaty in his pleasant husky voice, "but one song?"

She could not resist. She seated herself in a fur-covered high-backed chair, and with the instrument cradled in her lap and her foot upon the edge of the unlit brazier, she began:

> *"The trumpets call beside my wall—*
> *Love hears them chide,*
> *Love leaves my side,*
> *Love . . . flies.*
>
> *"Another spies my lonely eyes—*
> *Love cannot wait,*
> *Love is too late.*
> *Love . . . dies.*
>
> *"But then the old love comes to my heart still*
> *And makes my poor life all a-woe*
> *Till all my days are blighted*
> *To know that my heart's still plighted*
> *To love;*
> *Come, love; come back, love—*
> *Oh, pity my plight . . . love!"*

The music, the instrument, and especially Geoffrey's favorite tune, had sped her back to happy days she had known on the Italian moors. Through his song, Geoffrey's sympathy and tenderness for her, his prescient visions of what his carefree improvidence would one day bring her to, seemed to rush from the years, and her father, half-laughing, half-rueful for his self-known sins, seemed lingering near, with his handsome face and his oiled mustache, smiling at her through her sudden mist of tears.

Thus Zoë, completely absorbed, gazing unseeing through a cleft in the arras to the dunes beyond, had nearly forgotten Robert, so that when she glanced at him at the ballad's end, she was utterly startled to catch the eager look with which his dark eyes had apparently been raking her. He grinned as he met her gaze, and with a slight pause and no embarrassment at all, he remarked, "A loveliness that is without peer. Not the instrument, madame—your voice! In that the lute has found its only rival, and come off loser."

But Zoë was not deceived. She rose, handing the instrument to the boy who stood restlessly beside the Duke, scratching his black ribs.

"Oh, but it's yours!" cried Robert. "Why should I bring it else? Do you not care? I saw in your eyes that never have you sung to lovelier. True?"

"True. But, of course, as a gift . . . Out of the question, Excellency."

"How would you have it else?"

"Buy it," she parried, flushing red. She did not want the thing; she could not think why she spoke thus—except for a sort of pride, fending his certain knowledge of her precarious plight.

"Come now, madame!" Robert seated himself in the opposite chair, leaned back in its furs and tapped his ringed thumbs on its elevated hand-newels. "You'd give a hundred denarii, I suppose, if you had the notion. That's what *I* gave for it, Zoë!" Then he leaned forward, and looked her straight in the eyes, his coarse hair falling about his silken shoulders and the cords showing in his muscular neck. "Listen, *ma belle chanteuse*. Let us be straight with one another! I know what has befallen—Mihera fled, your purse gone, and the one you might fancy too occupied with things of war to relish the silken fetters of love. Well, don't let it bother you, pretty! We both know what *he* is made of—grand ideas, enormous visions. Too bad, too bad! He would have enjoyed high birth and taken advantage of it more than I! That's life! But to come to the point. You know me, my life, and all about it. We have no mysteries about each other. I am tired of my wanderings, sick of loneliness and I long to settle down to a companionable existence. I came here today on a whim, intrigued by the idle tales, and by assurances of your wit and beauty that have come to me from various sources. It was a calm-blooded tentative thing, if you will—until we faced each other." He rose and began to pace, while she sat staring at him, a thousand thoughts shooting through her head like fireflies.

Zoë had no illusions. It did not even occur to her to mistake this for a bid to be Duchess of Normandy. He wanted her for his mistress, baldly this, in spite of the silken words and the extravagant couching of his suit. She wondered how many had heard these skilled sentiments —country trollops, city jades. It all struck home. Pride. Hurt. The old resentment. The recollection that in Normandy her mother's house was as brilliant as his own. And something further.

For some time now, as he talked, she had found herself comparing him with Bohemond. Robert, first-born of the Conqueror, should be the first man here. But he was not. Inevitably she played with a few if's. What if Guiscard had been a first son too? Would Bohemond have squandered his sire's regard with futile quarreling? Would Bohemond have left his lands mortgaged and fled to his feckless adventuring under cover of crusade? *Fichtre!* If the son of Tancred the Forester had been heir, like the bastard of his hunting companion, the Magnificent Duke, who would be the King of England now? Within her the question sang: does this weak wastrel dream to aspire to one who has known the love of such as Bohemond?

Shortshanks, who sat like a necromancer compelling the answer of her eyes, saw them full of contempt, saw with outraged vanity the lifting of this pretty gypy's chin. As for Zoë, it did not occur to her to note the significance of her reverie, much less to recognize how much she had slipped her defenses in the last months. Such thoughts, the heralds of her spirit's metamorphosis by her graceless fate, merely brushed through her consciousness like the rush of a swift's wings. In reality she admitted in her act only simple, outraged virtue, when in a cool dudgeon she ordered the Duke of Normandy from her pavilion.

The next day it turned to rain. A low mist drizzled against the tents and made the dwellers by the Wall remember their trials of the winter before. Zoë had stayed abed, feeling depressed, and being a little low in energy from doing without much food that it all might be husbanded for little Ursule. Marcelle had prevailed upon her to take a little broth made of lambs' hooves which would otherwise have been ignored, but which was assumed to have properties of strength, though vicious-tasting. Zoë mentally instructed herself to sip the stuff without making a face, when Marcelle came in with an announcement.

"The Sieur Bohemond," she began, and was not allowed to finish. Madame jumped from the bed, spilling the broth across the counterpane. She snatched her bed-robe and hastened from the room. She had made her decision instantly. She would dispense with ceremony, ask Bohemond for funds and ride out with the very next caravan to the coast. She would pay him back somehow once she was safe in Italy. Her one question was the caravan. But with fear of Kerboga giving desertion once more a spurt of fashion, surely she could shift for passage. It were better to endure the company of oath-breakers and cowards—one's sentiments to the contrary notwithstanding—than to stay here and starve. Besides, was there a choice, with little Ursule?

But Zoë gave a start of disappointment as she entered the reception chamber. For Tafur stood by the arras.

"What are you doing here!"

Tafur bowed. "Prince Bohemond commissions me, madame—your tiring-habit."

"My tiring—What is this?" The word which indicated the costume for a mime in a mystery fell strange on her ears. But there was no doubt of that which Tafur was speaking as he hauled a bundle off his shoulder-blade (familiar gesture!) and set it in the reeds. For he drew from it fold after fold of a lovely flamboyant robe, at which Zoë must gasp for the ingeniousness of its style and the sheer bold beauty of its colors. There was a long, sleeveless, multi-folding chiton of diaphanous white silk which flowed like water through his folded hand but which expanded to a multi-paneled cloud when spread. For the shoulders and head there was an enormous aureole, which would stand like a sun-burst, flashing with gold thread and faceted emeralds. And from this to the feet, a delicate veil would fall, to sweep against little gold cassikins of soft leather such as patrician ladies wore in Constantinople.

"A former gift to the Prince from Alexius for his oath of fealty," explained Tafur with a wry smile, "the official habit of the Virgins of the Grail."

Zoë gave him a hateful look from the corners of her eyes, glancing first at the costume and then at the mime, as if both were tainted, and said coldly:

"I have given the Seigneur my decision on the play."

"Indeed?" said Tafur, his long, prehensile hands smoothing the pomegranates on the veil. "I know naught of that. He is counting on it. I know not what we could otherwise do, since tonight is the time."

"Tonight! Tafur, is there a caravan leaving at the last?"

"Aye, with tomorrow's sun-up for the old ones, the sick, and those who feign one of these to escape the solemnity of their vows. But why?"

"Tafur. Take me to the Prince."

"No, madame. He is engaged—in many things and in divers places today, and I know not how we could reach him."

"Tafur! You must *find* him! You *must!*" She stamped her foot.

"Why, pray?" said Tafur. It was not a question, there was pure insolence in it, implying her helplessness. He had seemingly lost all interest in the interview, and was gathering the costume in the bag. "I know not whom we can fetch at the last like this . . ." As he leaned over, busy with the aureole whose shape gave him some trouble to en-compass in the bag, a full pouch of coins fell out, dropped open and spread in a silver pool among the rushes. Zoë stiffened.

"What have you there?"

"Tithes for the actors' embursement. Since afterwards all may be confusion, when the thing is done, Lord Bohemond thought well to pay us previous."

"Then what of mine!" said Zoë. She was flushed and breathing heavily.

"Eh?"

"What of mine?"

"Well, madame, I did not seek to insult you as a common player . . ."

"Don't let it cark you, Tafur. My only distinction in it is that I get *more*. *I'll* play the mime with you, but for thrice the tithing. In fact, all you have in your pouch."

"H'm. In the circumstances, the Prince might fancy a blow to honor!"

"Pother his honor. Don't fret for that! The gold and the habit, Tafur, and let us have done!"

She saw nothing but deference on that satyr-face as he handed her both.

There was at this point a tumult on the palisade. She investigated through the arras, then turned to the beggar king. "What a paradoxical roster we have today! First you and now my lord, the Legate Adhemar."

Tafur's nose twitched. "The Bishop?"

She nodded.

"Christ's blood!" whined Tafur. "Let me out! I cannot abide that person! Release me!"

She laughed. She was feeling better, with the pouch in her belt. "Go on, you wicked! Take you the scullery hall and thence by the rear tent onto the dune."

"Farewell, Madame," he said hastily. "Till tonight."

As the creature's cloak snapped after him through the passage it came to Zoë that with no great troubling of the imagination at all one might perceive the essence of sulphur still in the air.

As she watched Panturge assisting the Legate to dismount, something about his coming rang a tocsin in Zoë's mind. If he had come some previously, before she could feel the pouch of silver bulging in her chatelaine, she would have named it a rare chance. For she had thought of seeking him, not spiritually (so clouded and confused by these latter events, she had from pride long shunned the comfort of the confessional), but to beg of him a loan to expedite her passage home. Several times, after matins in the mass pavilion, she had determined to broach her purpose. But she had never sat with him at the board, and when she encountered him in the faithfuls' dispersement once or twice, he had stared at her with such a severe expression on his rugged face that she had been afraid. Somehow she feared him now, though for no cause she could touch on, and fleetingly she wondered at it. Was her spirit so darkling and her faith so paled in the cool blast she was experiencing in the real world of man that she shied at the sight of orthodox goodness as did Tafur? In all ways, she could think, Mihera should see her now—alert, wary and full of inimical reserve as she stood and waited.

Marcelle, however, was engaged in an official welcome on the palisade, fluttering and ducking, her gross carcass jellying with every bow, "My Lord and Your Grace! The Countess, myself, all of us are in all ways honored by the visitation of your High Eminence!"

He bowed sanguinely. Adhemar was at home a landed French feudatory in his own right as well as papal envoy here, and was accustomed to be taken on these grounds, both of nobility and reverence. It was his habit neither to deny the one nor play down the other. Adhemar de Puy was a man of parts. Not waiting to see if he must be announced, he stalked on past Marcelle and into the pavilion, seeming to fill and certainly to dominate it with his bluff bulk. Siege rigors had left him hale. He filled out a red cassock and appendant cape to heroic tightness, and a small round of brushed marten rested on his tonsured, magnificent head. He wore withal a severe brisk air today and, as he talked from the tall chair on the dais where she bade him rest, Zoë fancied he appraised her closely, as a general might weigh an underling whom he had not before met but who was well known to him for his peculiarly bold infractions.

"Well," he began, his voice unnaturally hearty, like a schoolmaster with new tasks, "now that the amenities are done we can speak to one another plainly." The gold cross on his breast was crusted with garnets and in the center a gaud shone like a great eye in the sunbeams that shot through the blowing arras.

"Speak plain?" The words, an unfortunate echo of the Duke of Normandy's the day before, had a connotation to make her start. The bishop has a pot to cook *too*, at my hearthstone, she thought, and yet she knew that in that sense she was completely wrong. She could find nothing but admiration for him in her innermost thoughts. Looking at him, she wondered why he had confined himself to holy orders. He liked life, she knew, the whole of it, in spite of his stringent air. One heard how he was with the knights at banquet—jocose, hearty, convivial. And how he was on the battle-field—brave, fertile in strategy, dangerous as a lion. Bohemond rode with him in the charge by preference. She wished she had seen the thing at Dorilay near that swamp called Boziujuk in the desert at close range, instead of hearing the din of it only, shivering in the baggage train with the other women, when Adhemar himself had speared a flanking run and routed the Moslems in his first contact. Bohemond had later told her all. He had sat here in the light of that charcoal bowl with the room full of flame and smoke and wine-fumes and with Mihera sitting by modifying the narrative in his dry way and filling Bo's goblet, while she listened to them both and was happy here in the winter lull. Bohemond had sat describing with high words the deeds of Adhemar that day, admitting how he himself had been panicky after the first sweep of their light horse had thrown back his lances, even his own veterans, from Janina and the rest. And how he had called Raymond and Godfrey and they had drawn up a new line and how Adhemar, whooping like a hashish-crazed Turk himself, had put it to the charge so that they had hit the Suljukian wedges like a wolf-pack on their own terms and scattered them through the swamp. And so she wondered now, with these things before her, how such a one could be encompassed by the life of the cloth and dedicated to religion, which, now that she was uncompelled by her former kind of naïve faith and filled instead gradually with a bitter mist, seemed in the realities of death and battle, and even gold, and certainly the excitement of life itself, phantoms and trumped-up intangibles, signifying nothing.

"Attend, Countess!" Adhemar commanded her now, throwing his red cloak away from his shoulders and stretching his legs, booted beneath the cassock, on the dais's foot-rest. "I am, here in the Host, the voice of Urban, our Holy Sire. I am pledged to guide the Barons steadfast to the Tomb. As the thing goes on, I see quarreling, greed, venality, ill-nature, and even military weakness itself endangering our cause. Let us see . . . It is two years now, no?"

"Aye, your Grace." Yes, one had the unmistakable feeling of a coming lecture when this preface was done.

He cleared his throat noisily. "I will recall the skepticism of Gregory VII, our departed greatness the sainted Hildebrand, on this. True, he also dreamed of a great Quest, a magnificent rising against the encroaching Turk, but I recall how uncannily he predicted much that has occurred here. He knew men, and he could smell out the weaknesses in their very souls. And he used to say, then, that there was one man who could lead such a march if any—the knight Guiscard. He was unmatched in war, experienced with Moslems and had first-hand knowledge of what must be met with in Asia Minor from his skirmish with Alexius there. And then there was the major thing—devotion to his pledged oath, incontestably proved when he turned his back on Durazzo and a certain victory to rescue the Pope from Castel' Sant' Angelo. That was an act of honor, no mistake. And so I have not been too surprised to mark the self-same qualities emerge in his son. But there is a flaw, Countess. There was in him, there is in Bohemond."

"Indeed," said Zoë. She had risen during the Bishop's recital, her knuckles white with tension on the back of her own chair. "A hunger to be invested of the whole world . . ."

"How acutely you put it," said Adhemar, regarding her sharply a moment from his intense eyes, before he went on. "De Hautevilles want power, but power crowned with respectable sanction, like boys who steal cakes and afterwards seek the maternal nod. Guiscard from duty sloughed his personal gain when he went to Rome, madame. But will Bohemond when the test comes? Like affairs at home, this whole thing rests on the sacredness of the oath. If he does not keep his in the thing now, well . . ."

"Well, indeed!" said Zoë, aroused. "And what has this to do with *me?*"

"Much, unfortunately," said Adhemar. "Look you, daughter. We are seeing the trembling birth of a new age in conditions here in which all deeds turn on the individual. In this we are blessed. Times change in intrinsic virtue. In some times, as in Egypt and old Rome, it is the mass, the driver and the whip, and these times are bad, no matter how great the structure. The structure has little to do with it, mind you, else the Acropolis must be proved more impressive than the Pyramid of Cos. But then there are other times when it is man, his free cause, and his free, gifted leaders, and these times are good, working to the betterment of all in spite of areas of corruption, which will always be. In these good times, there is, in spite of bungling, discouragement and abuses, a sense of ability to give all—one's gifts, efforts, one's life itself if need be, with freedom of will, to a thing that is worthy, like a cathedral, or a chain of lighthouses, or—or this Crusade. Take the cathedral. Is it the master and the lash that raise these structures of no peer? Rather not. The individual; fellow-feeling; freedom and faith. Faith, Countess! It is what Hildebrand lived for, nay died for too. Attempting to cleanse the church of those hazards which would break men's faith. This Crusade, Countess, is an undertaking more vast, difficult and even more spiritual than those cathedrals. Men have eschewed family, friends and fortunes, all, to partake of it. True, the weak keep sloughing from the stream, but the bulk are faithful. And great keepers-of-the-faith are here to lead them—Godfrey, Raymond, young Tancred and the greatest of these, Prince Bohemond, who becomes a legend. I feared, watching this grow. I rejoiced since he was son to Guiscard. I feared and rejoiced together. You can see why. If he runs along the flaw, if in his high place he stumbles, and gives soul-shaking scandal to the mass below, he could scatter the structure to barn-straw!"

Adhemar paused, a troubled sigh stirring the pendant on his breast. "He is on dangerous ground in this thing of Antioch. I regret this here. Yet we cannot expect him to act the saint. Alexius's promises are long since smashed—food, help, men, he sends none of these. Therefore we owe him nothing. I can see the side of Bohemond in this, and Bohemond tells me, if he takes Antioch, that he will secure

it with dispatch, and continue to the Holy Land. We can only hope
for this."

He leaned forward, huge, captious, formidable in scarlet. "But now,
Countess, know you this. Another tale burgeons and that not salutary
to the cause. You will acknowledge what I point to, without my
broaching it more, and save your feelings . . . I refer to yourself and
the Prince and the word of it spreading in the Host."

"But it is all false!" cried Zoë, prodigiously outraged. "How can you
give such insult to a poor wife left stranded here among your chivalry-
with-a-high-cause whose actions prove neither chivalrous nor high!"

"I can guess whereof you speak," he said gravely. "The venality of
men uprooted. I have cajoled, prayed, chastized and given terrible
penances for such instances I knew of. These matters are bad. But they
cannot, of themselves in singular circumstances and on sparse occasions,
undermine the whole. But this I say!" growing red as his habit, "I
cannot allow on the part of the Baron Bohemond, an out-and-out
scandal with a common adultress!"

Zoë stepped toward him, her eyes flashing, her fists clenched. "My
God, priest, mind your manners, or I'll forget your cloth!"

Adhemar made a gruff, clumsy gesture, and went doggedly on.
"You do not relish the plainness of my way, Madame Falloc. Well, perhaps I *am* hard. Nor do I say that your case is not to be sympathized
with, in a measure. It is common, for those who do not know, to question how we, parted by vows from the human world ourselves, can be
judges in matters such as this of love. How wrong they are! For we
see all sides, are told all circumstances, are charged with the inmost
secrets of those who live, love, die, and fight and can advise more freely
than if we were daily involved in our own narrow segment of these.
We know, then, the myriad woes that can beset, in innocence or in
sin, the hearts of lovers. I know of your love, madame. And I think I
can guess what transpires in your poor heart. How to deny, for that,
the beauty of Beelzebub? When the world is a dark wood and the
heart is dark, he shines in the dark wood and blooms in the dark
heart like a radiant star, setting all aflame with his poisonous splendor!
Say we no more. You need help. I am giving you passage and the funds
to get to Italy. You must leave immediately, because of events which I
cannot mention now. I adjure you, Lady Falloc, go with the caravan
tomorrow."

"With the company of cowards?" she asked him, her voice tight. "I
have made vows too, remember."

"Aye, but before those, another. You cannot stretch yourself between
Amalfi and the Tomb. God is reasonable. You're a mother and a wife.
Your place is with Count Mihera!"

There was a long time when neither spoke, when Adhemar looked at Zoë and she at the cold black empty charcoal-bowl, beside the dais.

"I will go, your Grace," she said. "Soon, but not just yet. We breach the Wall tonight; you need not be cryptic with me; I know . . . And I will take my leave when the time is more feasible than this. And I thank you for your proffered assistance, Bishop, but I have sufficient funds, it falls out."

The prelate was silent, unsatisfied and a little puzzled as he ended the interview. But Zoë had in this hour made up her mind. She would sing at the Wall, go into the city, and see Bohemond once more, if only for a last good-bye. A pact of procrastination.

She stood by the arras and listened to Adhemar's departure and to the faint din of preparation astir in the surrounding camps. Then she gave a little run of excitement, swept up the tiring-robe from the bench and called to Marcelle.

"Here, Marcelle, fetch your reticule with the flax-thread in it. I think this gown is over-large about the waist!"

CHAPTER XXII *The Miracle*

THAT NIGHT, WHILE the heavens moved sluggishly from the Lion towards the Crab, the Emir Yagi Sayan could not sleep. For some time now he had been restless in his black palace of obsidian and basalt, ranging about it day and night like a caged jackal. His courtiers, more than usually sympathizing to his face and smiling at his back, were busy as ants laying their individual plans for nest-feathering for the inevitable new regime. For Kerboga was coming— long flourish Kerboga!

Yagi Sayan knew their fidgety perfidy. He had but to read it in their foxy eyes and he could but wait. He could but haunt his astrologer, restive and bemused, reading woe in the very shades of the gnomons of his sun-dials, and dream his horrific visions.

About moonset a messenger came, bringing a report of strange things seen from the Tower of the Dog at the Bridge Gate hard by the Orchard of the Mosque.

"The Franks ride north, O Dear to Allah, and in their van is *Maimoun* the rascally one, accompanied by old Senghils and others of the cursed *gaiours*. They take the bend of the river and strike out, bound for foraging, it is thought, as they have done oftentimes before."

The Turk had been abed. He pushed back the silken coverlets savagely, striking with a fretful elbow the slave who cooled the imperial slumbers with an agitating phalanx of rustling papyri.

"Why do you gnaw my brain with maggots like this? Have these Franks not slithered about like crocodiles below us, lo these many months? Unless—" his petulant features lighted as he swung his thighs forth and perched like a fat, expectant doll on the couch's edge. "Did it seem like a general exodus, O Son of Hashim?" The small eyes dark with hope for the first time in weeks . . . If the Franks gave up, it would obviate Kerboga . . .

But, "No, One of Might," the slave assured him. "Their tents still stand, and more, they hold a revel by the Wall disporting their foulness even now with a depraved spectacle. At the Place of the Mosque, O High, with coarse merry-making and a plethora of food . . ."

"*Food.*" The spectre of Kerboga receded a little before the rage that swept through the gross-bodied Turk at this titillating news. The siegers with fresh stores again! It was more than one could bear. The bins, jars, bottles in the houses of Antioch were well nigh finished, and the great granaries in the Citadel must be kept for last resort. Oh, for the good days, thought Yagi, when the Orontes was full, colorful, teaming with sails . . .

Yagi groaned and cursed. Curse Christians! Curse Kerboga! Curse the Franks and their little God! Might *Maimoun's* entrails be some day exposed, and gnawed upon daily by El Jahn, the Sea-Eagle, sent from the edges of the world!

On the ivory couch, strewn with pillows and decorated with beryls, jacinths, and many other precious stones indigenous to the region, the emir lay back and napped fitfully. Once more he was accosted by a carking vision.

It was *Maimoun,* of the hulking stature and the red hair, whom Yagi had observed from the Wall. And this time he came with his entrails indeed dislodged as Yagi had wished them. But, lo, how they writhed, weaving themselves about *Maimoun* like a suit of chain, with one great gut a zone about his waist and his hair a deep vermilion and his hands fisted and dripping blood. He was riding the beast Al Borak, on which Mohammed once had fled to Heaven.

The Turk awoke in a cold sweat, and fled to the sleeping room of his favorite, Amaya. He did not seek her favors, he had not the strength for them tonight, but he shook her awake and asked her to give a reading of his dream. For Amaya confessed an occult power. Amaya, awaking from exotic muse, would tell him nothing, but rose from her bed and gazed on him sympathetically and said with a soothing inflection in her tones, "Come, Lordly One. Your heart is fearful and your humors awry from all this fretting. Let us go forth as we are wont, and view the city and the night-stirrings there—and forget our troubles!"

She was a fine-figured creature, tall and well made. She had worn a chamber-gown to sleep in, a coat of stiff silk from the webs of Yagi's own mulberries in the Vale, with a deep slash to the waist that was tufted in gems. This she cast off and stood before him naked, her body gleaming with costly oils and her skin breathing the elixirs of a thousand flowers of the East, while her handwoman went fetching more suitable dress.

"See, Most Blessed of the High Ones, Yagi," she reminded him, stretching like a voluptuous cat. "You still have me, and you still have your splendid city. Your fears are but evil dreams!"

Amaya and the Emir took a pole-car down the broad, colonnaded street that led to the northern wall, where Yagi had a mind to wander.

Near the Bridge of the Gate where the sentry had reported the spectacle to be afoot, they bade the runners pause and sat in the litter a long time watching a full moon rise above the Cassians and silver the roofs and tree-tops of the teeming city. Amaya hummed softly, diverting him. She seemed to be sincere in her anxiety for his mood; she looked surpassingly beautiful, and her bright sallies and silvery laughter displayed themselves lavishly just for him. But tonight, for the Emir, there was a chill in the contemplation of her loveliness and of that of Antioch. For he was prey to the full impact of realization of his insignificance. He had this heavenly *houri* for his cushioned couch because he was Emir. She belonged to whoever was Emir and he knew that Antioch was his who breached the Wall. So tomorrow or the next tomorrow, when Kerboga came?

As they descended from the car, they could hear the River. They would soon walk above it on the Wall. He allowed himself to conjecture for a time how good it would be to assume the kibleh and gesture to the East, then fall swift as a thought into the obliterating tide. The guards, following perfunctorily at his sandals, how could they stop him? But even the idea was a weak surmise, a swift dream, of the duration of a breath. He knew he could never do it. He tore his gaze from the beauty beside him and looked back up the length of the broad carriageway, to the fierce and impregnable Citadel on the Cleft of Silpius where the flares of the watch-turrets were just being kindled. Somehow this gave him courage. Then he and Amaya began the steep ascent to the North Wall near the Tower of the Dog.

From their improvised thrones on the bridge barbican, the Emir Yagi Sayan and the courtesan Amaya could stare down without fear of press from the rest of the watchers or chance arrows from the Christian host at the sights before them. Down by the Bridge an egg-shaped space had been cleared at the fortress of *Ramoun Senghils*. The tower itself was scarce to be recognized tonight. It was indeed no longer a tower but the horrific black head of a creature never to be seen in this world, with pointed ears, eyes that were blazing torches, a gaping mouth with terrible tongue lolled out, and with the apparent property of emitting fire at regular intervals. The moat-bridge of the fort itself was the hollow of its mouth. From this dominating apex little rounds ran down on either side—painted, hung with pennons, small carousels illumined with torches or with bonfires lighted near. There were seven of these. Within the rounds could be seen a profusion of players—gaily dressed mimes, both men and boys who were dressed as females, each engaged in a pantomime of action—fighting, love-making, dancing, or eating, drinking and rioting in full carouse. On the sides of the oval space stood pillars, with large odd-shaped urns stationed on their tops; and about these, and in and out among the carousel, a number of red devils danced—mummers in orange, scarlet

and yellow parti-colored tights, with close-fitting caps that had horns
upon them. These bore faggots which they agitated wildly as they
danced, and from the Wall they seemed like quick-darting night-sprites
among the more stationary flames of the torches, the bonfires and the
occasional puffs darting horrendously from the great beast's mouth.
Hard by that terrible aperture, and emphasizing the bulk of the
grotesque by showing himself to be of a height with one of the ogre's
teeth, was surely Beelzebub himself. He was attired no differently from
the rest, and refrained from the mad frolic in which they were engaged; but even in his quietude, with arms folded and a long whip
twining about his feet, he seemed indeed like the Prince of Devils.

Above this djinn and above the beast, and utterly contrasting with
them both, stood a woman; indeed a female and no young boy
attired for the masquerade. The night was warm, the sky behind
her purple and inky black in which the low stars mingled, blowing bright and faint with the ebb and flow of the torchy umbers.
A soft breeze took possession of the upper air, setting her garments
close against her and casting her long hair in a swirling cloud upon
the aureole framing her painted face. And like the stars, the sound
of her voice blew loud and soft, as she stood on the beast's head singing, with a lute in her arms. There was something about her song,
something in the richness and power of her strangely expressive voice,
that gave a sense and meaning to the hodge-podge of activity going
forward below.

Yagi Sayan itched to know the meaning of the nonsense. He leaned
to Amaya. "Do you know what they do?"

"No." Amaya looked bored, her eyes sultry on the actress.

Yagi nodded at her glance. "Full blown like a Sharon rose, aye?"
he mused, his big lips working a little between the mountains of his
jowls. "Such must the minstrel-queen have been, the Egyptian Can-
dace . . .

"By Allah, where is one who can *tell* us this fiery business?" he
complained, and told his chair-boy: "Fetch me that pedlar who squatted
by the arch, that hooded one from the hills." Then he sat, his eyes on
Amaya, his face flushing with pleasure to think that his praise of the
singing *gaiour* had aroused her instant jealousy. It was balm to his
shaken soul.

"Most High."

It was the little Armenian. He stood in a meek pose, with a great
wool cloak wrapped close about him though the night was warm, and
his sleeves seemed far too long and hung like empty sockets below his
fingers.

"Come!" said the Emir, waggling a fat fore-digit. "Squat you here,
and make clear to me what the depraved are doing!"

"You see, Most High," said the little man falling to his knees beside the Emir's chair, "the space before the fortress represents the world, and all the mimes the people in it. The pennoned rounds are the dwelling-halls of sin, or *Togrut*, as you yourself would say, and within them are souls partaking of things forbidden."

"Forbidden!" said Amaya, mystified. "I see nothing but happy things they do! See how they eat, drink and seem in all ways gay, and there is a woman decking herself in beautiful veilings, with a haughty air . . ."

"Aye," said Yagi. "Here, in this scarlet round, a man running his fingers through heaps of monies—a pleasurable thing, in anybody's tongue! And another takes happy leisure on a silken couch! And so they go—all activities that please! Give me their 'dwellings of sin' . . . Ah! But say"—glancing side-wise at Amaya, his mouth folded back in a flaccid smile—"who is that woman, peasant? A gypsy? A mountebank?"

"But none of these," said the pedlar. "A great lady and a friend of—"

Yagi started. "Aye, hillman, a friend of whom? Why don't you finish? You know too much of this, not only their language and their cult, but you name names when the tongue begins to slip. Don't fub me, Armenian. You accompany me palaceward when this farce is through. There is questioning to be done to inquire of you further. Blanch not yet. I will not bother to inquire of you here. At the Citadel there are scientists in this, who have quick and subtle physics for the truth. But your name!"

"Nepaz."

"Well, Nepaz, continue!"

"And now, Most High," the Armenian went on, pale, "we have the Judgment. See!"

In fact such manifestations developed in the pit below that it seemed indeed like a Second Coming, with the devils in rout, their throwing of torches in the air, and a blossoming flame that vomited from each of the urns atop the pillars.

"Greek fire!" gasped the Emir, as great spurts of liquid (from the small store which Alexius had given the Franks as a gift and reminder of his potential might) burst forth and arced across the oval, hissing, to spend themselves harmlessly on the stone walls of the granite fort.

Nepaz spoke out once more with an odd, hurried urgency. "Look, Highest, the climax of the play! Watch the sinners doomed!" The mimes, with much confusion and a great deal of realistic wailing and lamenting, were all being pushed into the maw of the predatory moat-bridge, while aloft the singer struck a mournful tune.

Yagi was contemptuous. "The seven sins, is it? More than *ever* am I glad to know Allah! For the sports and pleasures they indulged in here, the Great One will reward us believers in paradise. Allah be bowed to forever!"

"Amen," agreed the jaded Amaya, who thought the whole performance a holy horror.

Nepaz had been more and more nervous as the miracle ended. He was just beginning to vision himself at the Citadel being questioned under most unpleasant circumstances for his foolish tongue, when a pair of guards came running along the Wall and thrust themselves into the barbican.

"Most High!" one shouted, not bothering to prostrate himself. "The Wall is breached, the Gate is opened, *Maimoun* is in the city!"

Nepaz slithered along in the confused mob that flowed about the fleeing Emir. He looked back, a smile growing in his bead-like eyes. Up on the far terrace, and all along the ridge road leading from St. George's postern to the Silpian cleft, could be seen the Christian progress. It glistened and glowed, a glittering war-car, the flares of the Christian horses repeated in the running stream of light that fled their bucklers. He looked for Yagi. The fat one had turned also, and for a moment, apparently fascinated by what might seem a fragment of his awful dream, he stood—grey, frustrated, lone.

And now there was Nepaz, tossing the too-big cloak. Flopping it from his skinny shoulders, freeing his arms and letting forth his hands, with which he held, as though it were far too much for him, a great curved Saracenic blade.

Yagi fell to his knees, his eyes bulged, his big lips blubbering. The Armenian came on. One blow glanced, but the next dispatched him. The head rolled elliptically along the Wall.

"There now, Most High," cried Nepaz, nimble at rescue, and grasping it tightly by its perfumed hair. "Go to your perfect dwellings, O friend of Allah! And do not fret for me. These lips of yours will plead many a byzant from the panniers of *Maimoun!*"

He ran once more along the Wall, but the opposite way—shouted at, thought to be mad, while his fresh burden spilled its paltry news among the pattering sandals.

CHAPTER XXIII

*The Tower of
the Two Sisters*

TAFUR SOUGHT ZOË, after the *miracle*, at the improvised tiring-chamber in what had been the guard-room of the
Fortress of the Mosque. He was not alone. Players lounged in the hallways, lesser Beelzebubs, puffing and red from their lively dance; young
boys daubed with the fard that had made them female; a couple of
children with burned-out torches in their hands—all watched with
friendly enchantment the Lady Zoë. She ignored them, being utterly
engaged, like a trouper born, in the grease-pots.

Tafur told her that he and his tribe were now to enter Antioch.

"Under whose protection?" she asked, not stopping in her work.

"Sant' George's, Sant' Michael's and Sant' Jacques de Campostelle's!"
minced Tafur, in high spirits mocking the perfervid Frenchmen and
eliciting from Zoë a small smile. And he added, "But more than all
these, at the express request of the conqueror Bohemond, we have a
herald!"

She could see the herald in the shield's reflection. He had patently
partaken in the sack, for he sported an oriental baldric trimmed with
gems and his *maille* hood was wound with a silken zone of softness
and high hue, dyed with sea-purple in the secret formula of the East.
He made a handsome show. The Ribald women were flirting with
him openly, even fingering his belt and his head-dress, till Tafur called
them to task, reminding them time was short and that anyhow a herald
was a knight and not to be treated with immodesty of any sort.

But the herald seemed not incommoded. He stood among them, re-
counting the breaching of the Wall to many a shout of "Bravo" and
"Vive Bohemond" from the Ribalds, whose taste the accomplishment
suited to the last, since it smacked of a knavery of their own color. The
herald, flushed, drunk with war-madness and with wine, showed them
his jewelled estoc with a darkish moisture on it, half-congealed.

"The blood of the infidel!" he cried, and the place became bedlam.

Among those who cheered most robustly was the nurse, Marcelle.
Little Ursule, wide-eyed and somewhat pale, stood clinging to her
skirts, amazed at this assembly. Zoë spied them, sprang from her chair,
and rescued her daughter from the press of stomping sandals. But

Ursule became presently more mystified than ever, for Zoë, harkening to the man's tale as well as any, had removed but little of the make-up after all, and Ursule clamped her eyes on her, fascinated.

Marcelle, herself well muffled against the coolness of dawn, handed her mistress a fur cape, and indicated two large bundles lumped at her feet.

"The mules are ready," she said. "We have everything possible to take, and there is nothing to be seen to further."

But Zoë now hesitated, unnerved and fearful between the herald and Ursule. She laid her cheek against Ursule's face.

Marcelle frowned. "There is no turning now," she said gruffly, guessing Zoë's thoughts. "Be sensible. The Wall is breached, the camp breaking, and the Turks will be out with vengeance for any who are found here. Be wise, make friends of these resourceful people! For they seem to do much better for themselves than we; they are able, inventive and strong to survive . . . Come—we shall follow them to the conquered city!"

The Ribalds cheered this, and blew kisses at her, while she stood, stout, glowering, stern as an admiral, and the delighted Tafur conveyed her a great wink. Ursule, entranced, fairly dancing with impatience now, cried, "Mama, oh Mama, let's *go* with these wonderful devils!"

As the Ribalds, led by the herald, endeavored to pass in by the Bridge Gate, they found the Wall there newly bristled with breastworks—and abatis with sharp spikes pointed toward the enemy. At first they took this to be Christian and thought that the abatis was a preparation against Kerboga. But a shower of javelins made them change their minds. A blade caught the herald, smiting him through the breast, and Tafur, his face paint shiny in the dawn, made sure the man was dead, then placed his foot upon him and addressed the Ribalds.

"Now we have lost our guide, the north portion seems still to the heathen, and we must go by the same way as Bohemond if we can. Stand by, get weapons out and do not loiter on the way. I stress this, knowing you will surely see tents abandoned, household objects left behind, much that will speak to you of adequate loot. But desist, friends! Remember Kerboga! You will not wish to be caught here when that gentleman arrives! Besides," laying a thumb to nose, "remember, riches such as you have never dreamed of await you inside the city! Now obey me, keep weapons handy, and make haste!" And mounting the herald's horse, he spurred away. Whereat Zoë, seeing that the cob he abandoned bested her own mount by far, made the exchange deftly, before any of her diabolical companions had time to think. There was a shocked murmur—surprise, anger, and finally a grudging cheer. Then they formed their ranks behind her, and fell in.

It took them all of that day of June 3rd, 1098, to circumvent the northeast ramparts. Looking back, Zoë could see the whole of the company stringing out behind—most afoot, a few on mules and some isolated fortunates on skeleton chargers too old, maimed or otherwise afflicted to be used in war. They all stayed approximately in tow, ambling along in a formation of queer sorts. They were happy, thinking of delights in the mysterious rich town; so they sang, quarreled good-naturedly and in general enjoyed to the utmost all the aspects of this, their private invasion. Zoë rode with Tafur in the van, closely heeled by the nurse and child, and Panturge who had tardily joined them. She felt caught in a dream. The sky brightened, the Orontes sparkled in the sun, a crane flapped by, golden and white, with a limp fish in its bill, and suddenly they rounded the last barbican of the west escarpment and were looking ahead to St. George's Postern with its high iron gate and its fortified flankings—on one side an old Greek monastery long since garrisoned by Tancred, and on the other the Tower of the Two Sisters which Commander Firuz had that night betrayed to the Christians.

The Ribalds clustered at the bridge-head and set up a tumult in their eagerness to proceed. Tafur, caught by their urge, waved a gay greeting to the guard in the monastery tower and began to cross. The guard stared down, shook his halberd and gave the command to stand. The Ribalds, sobered by the fate of the herald, drew up muttering. Tafur silenced them, advanced alone and explained, shouting across the width of the river that they were authorized entrance by the Baron Bohemond. The guard would still have stopped them. He was joined by other knights who, all disgruntled at being garrisoned here instead of in Antioch, were for wreaking their ill-nature on these late ones by forbidding them entrance. But just then, from within the Two Sisters on the Wall, a voice shouted down, and presently a squire riding a brown stallion at a brisk speed came clattering across the bridge-planks.

It was the Norman, Vieuxpont.

"You are to go to the Emir's Castle," he said, glancing at Zoë with a smile. "There the Prince will presently quarter, having repaired there even this night past to dress a thigh-wound sustained in the mêlée. The Prince has rejoined activities at the Citadel, but he wishes his good friend safe-taken, and to be lodged until other arrangements can be made." He turned to Tafur. "We hold the terraces and the Vale, the fall of the whole is imminent, and you will find your path cleared by Christian victory all the way to the Palace. Proceed down the Great Way, past the square to the Hall of the Lions and turn on your right hand. Will you pass in now?"

"I will that!" said Tafur, feeling like a lord himself, and fully ignoring the fact that this solicitude came for the presence of Zoë.

"Come, Ribalds!" he cried. "Shall we proceed?" And turning to Vieuxpont, "It's an honor to make entry in your company, squire, and an adequate protection against insults from barbarians, some of whom show as little respect for a Prince's envoy as they would to a black wench in a harem . . ." And he made a great face at the monastery garrison.

Antioch was not much changed from twelve years of Seljuk occupation. It had changed little enough in the past ten centuries. Militarily it was still a Byzantine engineering miracle, physically magnificent, and morally full of rot. The glamorous peculiar vices that St. Paul had once preached against in the "glorious city" were still hers, and she wore them proudly, like an incontrovertible harlot her ill-won jewels. It had been mid-day when the Ribalds threaded the terraces of the Vale. It was near sun-down as they entered up into Antioch itself. Down the wide, multi-columned street where Tafur led them, life seemed at first near normal. The motley population swarmed the streets—merchants, wives, slaves and dancing girls; students, athletes, priests. The sun sent its last rays across the western wall and at one point Zoë turned and had a momentary panoramic view of the far Citadel, where Christian banners proclaimed its concentrated siege, and behind it the Cassian mountains, girdled with cypress, myrtle and evergreen and splashed with bright colors of oleanders and the vivid strange flowers of the East. Then the multitudes closed her in. Here waves of color rolled in the hot streets, streams of purple and russet and peculiar bright scarlet washed from the vats of cinnebar in the Vale, all showing vividly in comparison with the hue of nearly every structure in the town—a dazzling bright white. White of the flat and level houses; the courtyards, bursting with figs and vines, their dusty leaves touching their shoulders as they ambled by. White of temples and mosques and on this hot day, even of the quai that jutted into the Orontes, usually dark with activity but now a still sign of the presence of conquest. Antioch, lazy, luxurious, had long lacked those things available to her only by bireme—wheat, vegetables, lime pottery, wines, honey, ores, stone, wood, and even charcoal, so that of necessity many of the shops were shut. Down the alleys where one glanced could be seen booths and stalls—bare, or covered with canvas and branches of trees. And the idle goldsmiths, coppersmiths, potters, weavers and sellers of food stood in the open streets, grumbling, or speculating hopefully now that the siege was lifted. A young boy in a short chiton stood idle by a wine-press listening to his father talk of bad days and dire events to the elders near him. But these faces, these costumes and these tongues—none of them Moslem. Syrians, Jews, Egyptians, Copts, Byzantines—with the conquered conspicuously scarce. It was slightly irritating not to see them. It would certainly be irritating to the victorious men-at-arms. The faces of knights passing singly in the crowded streets showed this, a disgruntlement of sorts. They looked hoodwinked, taken in.

Tafur had not been able to control his Ribalds, once they were in the city. Too much to see, too many things to be busy at, among the stalls and in pleasant courtyards with their doors ajar. And so, at the Forum of Statues on the Great Way, the last of them parted company with their king, and Tafur and Zoë with her retinue went on alone. The city, somehow, was becoming noisier; it seemed that distantly came the sound of tumult, and Zoë could wish for the presence of the whole troupe of the roistering crew. Comic and strange, they had carried a peculiar immunity to harm. But Tafur apparently was not thinking of this. He merely grumbled as they rode.

"Prince Bohemond, if I see him now, will doubtless set me some new task. I am too good, that is my trouble. But I will balk at this. I will say, 'No, Seigneur,' and I will flee to the streets. How can he catch me? I could take *you*, if it pleased me to now, and disappear! And who would know to find me?"

Zoë gave him a look of scorn, no longer afraid of him, since she knew his nature. She was lost in her own misery, aware of how she seemed, dressed in gaudy, filmy stuff, her own clothes clinging with perspiration and dirt and her face raddled with paint like one of the sore-ridden drabs who followed their immemorial trade in all the streets here. She was utterly fatigued and each time she looked at small Ursule asleep in Marcelle's arms she wanted to cry with rage and with indignation at all this that they were being subjected to.

Meanwhile the roar of the city grew. With the sun's setting, torches and oil flares blew in the streets. More soldiers ranged through the crowd like freed bulls, seemingly unorganized. Everywhere, their byrnies blue-flashing in the dusk, yellow in the torchlight, roamed the Franks, roistering and wild. Scuffles broke out. They could be seen breaking into low-walled houses and emerging with arms full. There was a still sultriness in the dusk and their faces sweated in the hot atmosphere. Zoë saw a tall man-at-arms with a young girl under the awnings, ripping off her white garments in the shifting shadows as she shrilly screamed.

Zoë drew her veil about her face. She was thoroughly scared now, and when she saw two enormous painted stone lions guarding a square Syrian façade, she shouted, "Here, Tafur!" and they plunged to their right, away from the teeming thoroughfare.

The whole of the narrow, alley-like street down which they rode was parallel to a high wall, over which they could see the crenelated roof-work of a Turkish palace. Black, forbidding, it was hard to believe this was indeed the Castle of the Emir. Tafur told her to wait, indicating a space in the recessed shadows beside a mulberry tree.

Marcelle snivelled in a kerchief. Ursule, awake now, clung to her skirts. Panturge, thoroughly subdued by all about him, slunk in the shadows, hunched and still.

Just then a troop of soldiers, galloping on the high street, paused and glanced down the alley.

"What have we here?" one shouted, and they spurred in.

Zoë picked up her draggled skirts and hid herself deep in shadows of the lowering tree, but too late.

"Come here, sweetheart," one of the knights called, jumping from his charger. They were all great husky fellows, Fleming to judge from the charges blazed on their shirts and from their coarse accents. The one who had called grabbed Zoë with one gauntlet and drew her from the shifting shadows. "A painted beauty, if you please, and a sound one too, from the feel of her!"

"Wait!" shouted Zoë. "I am a Christian woman." Then desperately, "Dare not to touch me! I am a Norman noble!"

The Flemings guffawed at this. "And I am a liege lord," the first one said. "Come!" And though she clawed and struggled and pounded frantically, they all closed in. Terrified, outraged for her own safety as she was, the main thought uppermost in her mind was of little Ursule standing helpless in the street, and as she thought of all that might happen to the child alone she clawed and bit and scratched like a wild thing, till one of the men swore and dealt her a hard blow that sent her staggering, blinded, against the further wall. They all advanced once more, one saying, "Don't spoil our catch altogether, Curtes," and she crouched before them helpless, thinking, *this is the end*.

Just then a grotesque figure inserted himself in the space between them, dancing, nimble, diabolical and quick.

"Be gone, mime! What are you about?" the big one queried, puzzled, angry and about to run him through with his drawn estoc. But Tafur dodged away and with a great snorting and to-do stampeded the chargers, who reared, wheeled about and went plummeting down the alley. The soldiers, dismayed, pursued them, and Tafur propelled his retinue through the courtyard gate he had meantime opened, shutting them into a lovely garden, rich, tiled and planted in intricate designs, where the sharp-sweet odors of myrtle and bay and cypress filled the air. Zoë slumped against the wall.

But Tafur was impatient. "Come, Madame Zoë. I wish not to linger here all night. The place is deserted, as far as I see; you can have your choice of its many chambers."

They followed him into a broad tessellated hall, where Zoë even in her fright and exhaustion could not help but exclaim at its weird and costly beauty. Rare marbles, worked and carved in stylized forms of flowers and birds, glowed everywhere, and the floors were carpeted in silent grandeur. From this central room a broad stair of lustrous scarlet stone—long, graceful, seeming to curve into nothingness—led apparently to upper chambers. Tafur gestured to the rest to follow as he took these two at a time.

At the summit of the shining balustrade was a plain square marble hall with several doors opening off it, all ajar. Pieces of clothing lay dropped on the marbles—one sandal, a silver comb . . . Tafur picked up this last, storing it in his cape, and said:

"Here, at the end chamber, I think, is where Prince Bohemond stopped last night."

They looked in. Zoë saw immediately what Tafur meant, the chair with his cape thrown over it, bloody rags about, and his *maille* hood with the red serpent embossed upon the nose-piece up-ended on the tiles. She had a quick picture of him, up by the Citadel, likely, still fighting, with his wound and his bared head . . .

"Such magnificence!" gushed Marcelle, panting beside them, staring round-eyed all about.

The room might be four ells long and two wide, its painted ceilings seeming to be supported by plain pillars without fluting of any kind—shining polished monoliths of dark green stone. The floor, a blood-violet marble, granular and rich, was strewn with deep rugs; and a battery of braziers of tawny copper trimmed with rubies, ivory, amber and Persian turquoise stood everywhere about. The wide, luxuriously cushioned couch was coated with gold leaf, and decorated with intricate carvings in geometrical Syrian designs.

In the middle of the room and sunk flush with the floor was a great square bathing pool with a lining of silver that made the water sparkle coolly blue. The only brazier that was lighted stood at its edge. The chair that Bohemond had used was beside this. One wall of the room was completely covered with thin steel, damascene-edged and polished to a shine so that it reflected the whole of the dim-lit chamber. Before it a thin-legged delicate table held phials of perfume and pots of nard and numberless ointments and creams. The whole place was redolent of these; it was obviously the room of a woman. Zoë, tired, soiled and itching from the greasy remains of paint, felt her whole body drawn to the luxury of this place. But they went on to another chamber, with several couches in it and a table piled with half-touched food, and Zoë began to comfort and wash the small, tired, hungry Ursule.

Panturge squatted, nodding outside the door. Meantime Tafur had gone, plunging down the great staircase, his arms balancing his flight, his great devil's tail leaping on behind him.

Some time later Zoë sat beside Ursule, gently stroking the forehead of the sleeping child. A basin of perfumed water stood at her hand. This and a small meal had soothed the tot into easy rest. Marcelle nodded in a deep-cushioned chair. Zoë felt terribly restless and her face was now one intolerable itch. She was recalling the marble pool, the table full of oils and ointments. Below, somewhere, was the roar of the streets. She could hear shouts and snatches of tumult, but here everything was peace. She was gradually losing her fear, gradually recovering from the idea of staying huddled here in this one room. She got up, unlocked the door and stepped out, again locking it from the outside with its golden key. At the same time she indicated to Panturge that he must still stand guard. She could not quite believe the utter emptiness of the place. She went down the hall, her foot-steps echoing weirdly, so that she walked tip-toe as she entered the other chamber.

She closed the door and looked for the same golden key as there was for the first, but since there was none she contented herself with a chair against it. Quickly she threw aside her clothes and stepped into the sunken bath. It was wonderfully cool. She lingered long, allowing the chill and perfumed luxuriance of it to engulf her with utter relief. Then she bathed completely, even her long hair. Climbing from the pool by its silver steps, she dried by the brazier and approached the mirror steel. Her face showed the paleness of fatigue and she found herself dipping into the cherry-powder jar and rubbing a bit of it onto her white skin, laughing to herself a little. "For sure," she thought, "it is difficult to shake off the ways of the theatre."

She moved from the nard-table, still unclothed, and went to the opened closet where numerous rich gowns peeked out from their scented coverings. She tried on this one and that, watching their effect lazily in the enormous mirror. But this was strenuous, taking the last drop of her ebbed energy. That gold-colored gown sprawled on the coverlets of the couch—it seemed the plainest and best for comfort, in spite of its jewelled tuftings . . . She put this on, feeling with pleasure the soft silk against her skin. Turning to the low ottoman by the bed that had a food tray poised upon it, she sampled some delicate dark caviar and sweet red grapes, washing her parched mouth with great draughts of wine from the eared costrel standing by. Then she sank amongst the pillows, her eyes falling upon the chair where Bohemond had sat. There was something so intimate in his cloak tossed upon the back, still bearing the imprint of his great body, that she almost felt him there, and this brought a curious comfort. And withal a wonderful drowsy warmth was growing in her limbs and through all her being. A small thought came to her that she should get back to see Ursule, to see if they were still all right. But this was a vague urge which took, in her lassitude, almost a precise effort. Then her head fell back into the depths of the soft velvets and letting her tired body sink into the deep luxury of the peacock down, she slept.

CHAPTER XXIV   These Mighty Dwellings...

THE HIGH CITADEL on the foothills of Mt. Silpius was alive with light from thick, square towering torcheres, and in this glow great groups of people milled about. The Citadel, composed of many buildings attached to one another at various periods of time, was a vast place, but the Turks who had fled there found it not large enough for their frantic numbers. They were like bees swarming, tumbling one on the next to find a place of shelter. In the Vale below and all about the towers and barbicans of the south Wall could be seen the tents and pennants, the chargers and the spreading pavilions of the Crusaders.

Just below the frowning Oriental façade of the huge donjon, on the first ridge of the steep path that led to it, a Greek temple of Pan was slowly disappearing to the earth. Its white scattered weathering shards were being lifted by men-at-arms and carried to the next ridge down, where a rough and precarious-looking rampart slowly grew. Of the temple itself, a few shafts still stood among the crumbling columns. The night had come, the moon had risen, and the taper-like ruins set great, graceful shadows on the wooded ridge like ghosts of their ancient beauty. Against one of these, nursing with one hand his wounded thigh and gazing moodily before him into the milling mass of the malestrom above, sat Bohemond. Beside him lay the head of Yagi Sayan, oozing its black vileness on the pediment of snowy stone.

A weighted wind had risen from the south, and somewhere not far distant dry lightning slashed at the sky. A storm sat in the hills of Lebanon, waiting. There was no sound from the lightning, for the ominous low rumble of noises from the town beyond the terraces was drowning everything. Dark masses of sandy dust sped along the road and, moving dimly in these, a great heavy destrier could be seen pounding through the Vale. Bohemond idly watched as the figure emerged and hesitated at the half-piled rampart, then went on, stopping here and there as though for directions. There was a great deal familiar in the large, swaying dark bulk of the rider, and several moments before he actually saw his face, Bohemond realized it was the Legate Adhemar. Rearing his mount to a violent stop before him, the churchman dismounted and advancing up the steps like a perambulant bastion in the pale light of the stormy moon, he fixed upon Bohemond his confessional stare: sharp, bitter, stony.

Bohemond did not speak. Depressed, gloomy, from the depth of his melancholy funk, he fetched his accuser a black look.

"Well, Messire?" said the Bishop.

"Well, your Grace?" returned the knight with a note of understanding mockery. He surmised what was going to be said. He had listened with growing distaste to the din of the city. He knew it was being sacked. He might ordinarily have prevented it; he had elsewhere, at Janina, Nicea and the rest. But the madness of this thing now would have taken his full faculties and uninterrupted mastery to prevent or to dissipate. Contrabands . . . rallies . . . and exhorting through all the ranks . . . There had been loosened control while he was helpless under the probe that early hour, and things had gone badly since, with the unlucky injury preventing him even from command. He felt Adhemar staring at him—his bloody mail, his shredded hose and his hair all matted and tangled with Turkish excrement and with sweat he had shed while they sought the lance-point, and with his usual sensitivity to the moods of others he could almost read the Bishop's thoughts. They had been friends, colleagues-in-arms, these months past. But also, because Adhemar had cared to keep it so, they were yet priest and man, and suddenly, as he watched the tall, imposing prelate glance about him, at the Citadel and the rampart and up to the height of Silpius, gathering his big thoughts, Bohemond could feel his transgressions spread about him like a nest of serpents. He had insisted on this conquest. He had repeatedly promised that all would go well. And now in that terrible town there was rape, murder and heinous other crimes being done by Christian men in the hot muggy Oriental night. Urban's embattled pilgrims, groveling in blood and slime: he knew this was how Adhemar saw it, and the charge was his.

The Bishop wheeled, cinching his baldric to his heavy waist in a familiar gesture. The two men looked at each other, and their minds met. Adhemar let out his breath in a great gust of relief for the tacit complete understanding in their mutual sharing of woe.

"How is it?" Bohemond asked.

"Almost as bad it was that time your father went to Rome . . . Though not a real sack, just one great, roaring to-the-devil-with-the-hindmost orgy! My God Almighty, what a bordel-brawl! That sky, look at it, full of thunder! Why won't it bring the storm to drench them? They say there are often quakes in Antioch . . . Why not now? Let it crack the earth, swallow us up in the wrath of the Mighty! Christ, Victim of sins, Thy wounds are flowing now!"

Bohemond was amazed at the real contortions of Adhemar's face, as if indeed he saw the Master hung on the cross of this night's iniquities . . .

"Come!" he said. "Bohemond, I want you to look at it! You and your promises for your shining city! Come!" Like a great bulky schoolmaster he hustled Bohemond to his feet, pushed him up on the big grey who cropped in the stones nearby, and waved him to follow up the gust-swept ridge.

Back on the temple steps the Emir's head lay utterly forgotten, its small puffy mouth pursed, its bulged, surprised eyes transfixing the sky over Antioch with a glassy stare.

The Prince and Adhemar rode slowly down the colonnaded street by which Zoë, Tafur and their retinues had come. The riot was far advanced and on every side were signs of the night's abandonment. The storm brewing behind the city had weighted the atmosphere and formed a still theatre of air in the region about that seemed to put everything in hard, merciless, unforgettable focus. It clarified even the colors—the white of most houses, the bright pink or orange or green stucco of the Moslem palaces with their intricate wrought-iron balconies, their deep arched doors and their tall, sharply turreted minarets. Individual faces in the streets loomed up in the moonlight visible in every lineament for a time, before being merged in the noisy milling maelstrom around them. The din itself seemed magnified, so much so that a man shouting could not hear himself, only feel it in his throat. Even the varied and fetid smells seemed heightened, that fog-like stench of sweat, blood and slime and the indefinable odor of a thousand nights of teeming habitation in luxuriance underlaid with filth.

Suddenly Adhemar plucked at the sleeve of Bohemond's sweaty shirt, bawling through a cupped hand:

"There's another!"

"Another what?"

"A Moslem."

Men-at-arms had a Turk. He was apparently of the rich class, jewels twinkling in his turban as he ran, but this was all he wore. The soldiers had stripped him and were pursuing him down the street in high glee, sending him reeling from one to the next with short, vicious pokes of their misericordias which they used in the fray to hack the throats of enemies. He was a mass of wounds running, and his cries for simple pity mingled with their raucous mocking shouts of "Allah! For the honor of your Allah! Get on!"

Prostitutes showed themselves everywhere. Antioch was the very cradle for this trade, and tonight they were in the streets, in hallways, in the recesses of high arched doorways of the Turkish mosques, their skins dappled with moonlight as they sported with the conquerors under the stormy skies. The door of a green stucco palace had been ripped from its newels and through the gap could be seen the court strewn with furniture, and dishes and dropped clothing and two bodies, apparently of the residents, face down on the ornate tile.

As they approached the ancient Forum Square, the pair on horse-back must halt, since the way was congested by a large crowd about a bonfire which had been lighted at the intersection of the principal ways. All about this a sort of spontaneous al fresco orgy was going on. Bohemond, with the Bishop glaring at him from the round of his mailed hood, stopped, fascinated by the scenes here, as someone would stare at the writhing hideousness of the life on an upturned stone. The Bishop sat his destrier, livid in the guttering light, looking his expressed wish for the elements to strike this place and to grind those in it to the womb of the modifying earth, as if it seemed to him nothing like this had been known in Gomorrah or Sodom, in Nineveh or Tyre.

Bohemond had forgotten the Bishop. He was beyond reproach from any quarter but his own soul. He was filled with disgust, filled with a sickness for the thing itself, and not only this. The thought of his father was with him all at once. He could summon his image with clarity as of a vivid exact portrait from a bad murky dream—at the taking of Bari where he had first encountered him in youth. He could recall the old guard speaking to him of that city, where none would be touched, his father's yoke being sweet and therefore gladly taken, and where no man would feel the Norman sword, save traitors . . . The years fell away and longing for Duke Robert came over him like a wave, and in the midst of this maelstrom by the fire, he became a young man again, mourning . . .

"God have mercy," said the Bishop beside him. "What do we do? We desired but Holy Places, to free His Tomb from pagan mocks—not to make war, to take evil cities for ourselves and be drowned in their iniquities . . . God have mercy!" His was a disembodied cry, howling the torment of his outraged soul in this horrific wilderness . . .

Suddenly the group at the fire was joined by a husky squire-at-arms who pulled a struggling screaming child to the light of the flames. The dark mass of her hair was tumbled down, her clothing torn and there was a wild light of pleading and pure horror in her eyes. She was about twelve. The big youth's face was a mass of scratches apparently from her nails and his expression was full of hatred and thwarted lust. As he flung her down on the pavement, Bohemond recognized him and called out his name in a voice of thunder. It was

Vieuxpont, his own squire, and heedless of his wound, he slid from the saddle and fell on him, pulling him from the girl and beating him to his knees by the spitting fire. Vieuxpont, regaining his feet, gave battle and they fought savagely, Bohemond venting all his grief, disgust and frustration on the sturdy boy until he had him pinioned. The men about had stopped in their dalliance to watch the fight, urging on one and the other with coarse shouts. Now Vieuxpont for the first time really looked at his assailant, and cried out in a startled, shocked voice, "Prince Bohemond!" his hands falling, and would not have defended himself further even until death. But Bohemond ceased and sat back on the squire's cuirass resting a moment, his leg searing, the object of silent stares from those about. "The Prince!" one after the next repeated, at pains to know this bloody, dishevelled, swollen-veined one as the supreme of all the Barons.

Bohemond stood up, his chest heaving, all the anger drained away, leaving him weak and helpless as when he had been hit that day. Only with much effort did he remount, catching as he did a look of questioning resentment in the crouched Vieuxpont's eyes. He felt debased, humiliated, spent. The girl had of course managed her escape in the brief brawl and with his silent, stern-faced, noncommittal companion, Bohemond rode off.

Why? Why had he done that feckless non-consequential thing? He knew it was something about that child, when his own thought had been folding back the years . . . The beach, the fire, the struggling young captives, Mihera and little Zoë . . .

Zoë!

In the tremendous events of the last hours he had completely forgotten her. It came now with a jarring flash—the knowledge that he had left her, to be brought in through this vicious chaos by that knave Tafur. Hell, this was like Hell itself and search for her would be as seeking one soul in that very sub-orbital conflagration (for he had no doubt that all this here was truly the shadow of the horrid reality as friezed and pictured in charm-books and on walls of vast cathedrals). And for this also the charge was his. The straits that had brought her here, like those that had led to the seizure of the town, were his own machinations. Her distress following Mihera's flight; how he had watched it, augmenting it when he could, even setting Tafur to picking the belt of her nurse the beldame! And when, at the last, Robert of Normandy had returned from the coast with the news of Mihera's quick illness and how he was sped to Salerno for the knife, Bohemond had adjured his silence concerning it to Zoë.

And later, Mihera's commissioned message for her to be sent for and taken home, this too he had throttled, sending a written note by return vessel that was vague, circumventing, hinting of her previous departure. Here was the whole pregnant secret. In the high tide of his enthusiasm to breach the Wall, all this had seemed to him not so heinous, but something of cooperation at last with his true fate. Thwarted, buffeted so long in both conquest and love, Zoë, like Antioch, seemed his proper due. But now, at this hour, the reality of it met and merged with the hard dose that Adhemar was ministering to him, for all his silence, and these things, with his throbbing hurt and the fact that he had not slept for thirty hours, all smote him with one blow, so that, leaning from the saddle, he vomited with a mighty tearing, wracking wrench that spewed his sickness profusely among the passersby crowded in the little alley-like street down which they had just turned. Adhemar, coldly and with no sympathy said, "Go to your bed and sleep, Bohemond, and in the morning we shall see what can be done to bring order from this terrible black night . . ."

They rode into the garden, their heavy horses cracking the tiles, and dismounted. Bohemond's nausea had cleared and refreshed him slightly and as he and Adhemar parted at the broad stairs' foot, he saw with a sort of dull thrill the magnificence of this mighty dwelling.

Taking some time to achieve the red polished stone steps, his spurs clinking, he started from his exhausted torpor when, as he fitted his key within the lock, the door of his chosen apartment gave slightly to. Then, feeling the resistance of the chair that Zoë had set behind, and thinking that human weight disputed his entrance, he lunged, setting the door ajar from its brazen hinge. The chair crashed before it, the carved delicate gilt legs flying to kindling-sticks amongst the scattered rugs.

On the great bed Zoë woke. She stared at him, shocked to wakefulness by the crash but with no touch of nervousness when she saw who it was. The wine-jar, empty beside her on the counterpane, she rescued, and set it beside the food-tray on the ottoman table. Then she sat up. She was utterly poised, the sleep had perfectly refreshed her and she looked, in Amaya's silk gown, completely beguiling.

"Why, Bohemond! It's you!"

Bohemond stood rooted, his boots wide apart and his legs trembling a little from the encounter with the door and his own weakness. Zoë seemed to him now like something in a dream. Her face, instead of being flushed from sleeping, was like wax against the moist, curling dark mane that beset it. Her lips were red, but their expression indefinably cold, and her eyes stared out at him—dark, bright, large and almost frightening in their directness. Frank coquetry, with no pretense to be deceived. From her voice he sensed her bitterness, as though, while ready to his lot (he could not be mistaken in this), she was yet aware of his machinations and their guilt, his and hers. The prize challenged him in the very victory and it bothered him some. He wished for wine. He wished for obliteration of some of his faculties, for the stare of her knowledgeable eyes was almost too much. But this thought was nothing, only a candle-spark, compared to the blinding surge of his pent-up passion. He could not want less or more of anything, and her guiltiness would be in fact the crowning touch.

She rose from the bed. "They say that opposites attract and we are at this moment certainly that." She tossed her damp hair upward in a fan-like cloud, raking it with her finger-tips. "Look at you! Look in that mirror, Bo! You are of the very depths, while I—what have I been doing? Decking myself to please you!" She swayed in a sort of dance before him, weaving and pivoting slowly, the stiff jewels of the Oriental breast-sashes opening and closing with the ebb and rush of her quickened breath. "Look at me, Bohemond!"

Indeed he looked. Even as she approached him now, smiling, he stood stock-still, completely fascinated by the heaven-and-hell look from those ochre-rimmed, sea-blue eyes. With her slender hands, small against his shoulder-plates, she pushed, pivoting him off balance with the unexpectedness of what she was about. He staggered back, swayed and finally must half-jump, turning in mid-air to land in the silver pool, churning it to foam as he roared his chagrin to her explosive laughter.

"You devil!" he called to her, panting, instantly exhilarated by the clean chill seeping through his mail, and moving to free himself of the whole mess—links, linens and sweaty swathes, throwing them all to the splashed tiles as Zoë, still laughing like a child, went over and pushed the great door shut again . . .

"Now I've destroyed our difference!" she said. "But oh, let me think . . ." She leaned on the end of a great gilt couch that stood by the pool-rim, its two ends arched like necks of ibises; she was smiling down at him, her hair falling loose about her shoulders. "Our opposite-ness goes deeper than that! An abandoned goodwife—what more degrading?—while you . . . Why Bohemond, *you* are the Prince of Antioch! Did I forget it? Then congratulations! All turned out as you made it, didn't it? As if charmed, war-lock, done with magic. All!" She stopped and a dismayed look came upon her face. "Bohemond! Your wound! The water!"

He looked about him. The pinkish tinge circled his naked waist in a spreading cloud. "It is nothing," he told her. "From my clothes. The blood of the heathen!"

"No! Your *own*, Bo . . . It is like my father's bath was once, when he was gored by a boar . . ."

Her solicitude pierced his trance-like mood, and summoned his unwished-for tenderness. This was Zoë. He remembered her. She went for bindings from the closets in the wall and while she tore some of

Amaya's gear into white ribbands he watched her, struck by a momentary desperate panic. He emerged, dried, and wound the strips she brought about the torn flesh quickly so that she would not quite see how it still oozed. It pained him, but otherwise he felt hale, tingling, renewed, as a god, as he wrapped his great frame in the soft wool night-coat she had fetched him from his panniers that were spilled on the floor.

"Oh, Bohemond," Zoë whispered. She was removed from him, watching him, and her banter was gone now; there were tears wet upon her eyes. She seemed consumed at once by excitement, tenderness and a sort of Iphigenian mourning for their certain fate. But this was a flash only. Passion went up once more, sweeping away thoughts, tears, and everything.

"I love you," she said, her voice low and soft, yet powerful as a shout; and she stood tiptoe to bite him with a kiss. She was up to him and away, he was too late to catch her then, or else he forbore to. He stood looking at her a moment, a great cord swollen in his powerful neck. The single lighted brazier died as he leaned to it with his swift breath. It caught them in momentary dark, but Zoë was at the one great window, pushing the panels outward and letting the sky-glow fill the room. It was raining at last, a warm rain upon the warm earth, the air above Antioch being filled with its thick steam. A low rumble played about the sky, the hint of the coming thunder. Bohemond stood by the smoking brazier, his breath held, waiting. He saw her turn in the half-light, and then, strangely clear from the shadows by the casement frame, her voice came.

"Don't *look* so, Bohemond! I have gone with you nightly in my numberless dreams, so what does it matter if you melt in them with me now?"

She stood before the casement. He saw her, a vibrant form against the rising blue vapors of the summer storm. She called his name and he hers, and starting one to the other at the selfsame time, they met, with the crash of the thunder-bolt, in each other's arms.

BOOK 5

THE INCENSE AND THE WINE

CHAPTER XXV

Death in the Dunes

THE STORM BROKE and swept away on that morning of June 4. Under the north barbicans, thick odorous vapors lifted to the sun, revealing in a white crescent splayed on the plain the newly pitched tents of the advance guard of the army of Kerboga. For seven days then, to the horror of all watchers from the Wall, the Syrian earth teemed, whitened and finally was hid by the numberless hordes of the heathen laying to. From numerous little posterns Kerboga introduced a corps of his crack battalions, black-turbaned turcopoles under Achmed ibn Merwan, into the Citadel.

The Crusaders toiled. While Raymond, Godfrey and the two Roberts raised the rest of the rampart before Silpius, equipping it with monstrous hurling-engines (which Achmed by numerous sallies endeavored to destroy), Bohemond and the Legate Adhemar were everywhere, renewing vows, rationing stores, garrisoning the Wall. The absence of great blocks of manpower, hidden in dissolute living in houses about the town, could not be tolerated. Fire was set to the whole of the quarter about the Emir's Palace and the laggards smoked out, eight hundred palaces being destroyed in the risen wind. But when the soldiery saw Bohemond appear on the Bridge Tower black against the flames, there was a great revival of pristine enthusiasm, and rowdily they roared down at the embattled Turks. All, in the exigency, rallied to Bohemond. All but Raymond of Toulouse, who stood firm against him, crippling all plans and lording it over the assembled Barons whenever he could. At one juncture St. Gilles caused a stir with a dream-ridden peasant-boy troubled by visions of a Holy Lance, which (as St. Andrew informed him) might be found in the crypt of the Church of Peter. There was a certain skepticism, even from Bishop Adhemar's direction, though the Lance was indeed presently disinterred. And though it produced a renaissance of piety in the Host that rendered them absolutely fanatical to get out of Antioch and complete the Quest, it altered Raymond's personal standing not at all, for when the time came, they delegated supreme command against Kerboga to him who had breached the Wall, fired the palaces, led the spontaneous rally—Bohemond de Hauteville.

Bohemond lost no time. After three days' fast, and when Peter the Hermit had been sent quaking to Kerboga with a token peace-plan and returned with his skin whole but with the expected refusal in scrip, they cast down the gauntlet and girded for the gamble of pitched conflict.

The Host was in four great double divisions: the French with the Roberts and Hugh of Vermandois; the Walloons and Lotharingians under Godfrey; and since Raymond was pleading an ague again and thought he should therefore mask the Citadel in the town, Adhemar assumed the standard of the Provençals. Bohemond with his mounted South Normans and his heterogeneous Italian foot, stood back in reserve as was his custom.

In fine order they fanned out and deployed under cover of pre-dawn into the Syrian plain, the French forming a right flange on the bank of the Orontes and the Provençals planted against the low hills some thousand paces north. Bohemond sat behind, waiting.

There was an alarming preliminary skirmish, the Turks riding in sharply to the right wing of the Provençal foot. But Bohemond did not stir; Adhemar commanded there; and he observed with a thumping breast the instantaneous magnificent reversal of the whole howling crew; saw them utterly confused by the savage thrust of the French horse plummeting off the slopes like swift djinns in the murky light; saw them scattered through the dunes screaming like eagles—balked, separated, hampered by the grey, ghost-like clumps of bays before the sun came over his right shoulder and the Orontes stabbed in his eyes.

Presently, when the Provençals, chattering happily, noisily boastful, had re-formed, Bohemond gave a low word to Tancred sitting by, and ordered the ready-for-charge to be trumpeted. He sat the big grey, vaguely smiling, his eyes luminous and glowing, trained on the arched withers and hooded helms of the Turk cavalry spreading row upon row upon crowded row in the glimmering plain beyond. Around him the Latin knights, their restless fidgeting chinking the steel, their links heating to their skins in the eastern light, hoisted the bright, brave, scarcely stirring banderoles, puny before the pagan hordes, and stood ready.

Bohemond was aware of them all, the alert ranks with their French, Italian, Germanic countenances turned to him in a vague blur. And, on raised hummocks where they had stationed themselves to spark the charge, the Barons sat, their stern stares waiting on him too. He could see these well. Godfrey, his noble face alight, his great brown charger restive, stomping for the fray; Robert of Normandy, his high stirrups making his mount grotesquely tall, looking almost child-like at this distance, erect in his rewel-bone saddle; Robert of Flanders, young, brave, champing at the bit like his frisky stallion; the Bishop, his broad face crowded in his link cap, looking puffed and red from his late exertions; and, slightly to rearward, Hugh de Vermandois, haughty, blustering, pompous in manner and gear and sure to mar the sally for his unmistakable aura of cowardice, but ranking, since he was brother to the King of France.

"God support us," breathed Bohemond, and repeated it in a loud shout. "But wait!" He left his hand in mid-air, hesitating, and a great rattle of false-starting sounded through the Host as they pulled in and rallied. Bohemond frowned. He could no longer see the enemy; the heath, dried by the rising sun, had been fired, and orange flames licked obliquely like coiled snakes toward their deployment on a western breeze. The hum of dismay quickened as the others saw it. His own horse snorted, reared and nervously commenced to neigh.

"Peace, Volcan!" he murmured, caressing the arched neck. Then, in a loud voice, "Peace, comrades! It is nothing! Only a bit of smoke, a piece of Purgatory—nothing compared to the complete Hell we will give them now! So, then, gentlemen, to the close—charge!"

There would be in this thing no use for after-thrusts, he saw. And so, raising his well-ripped, red-painted serpent to the breeze, he again yelled, "Charge!" and spurred Volcan to a start. In full stride he whipped straight down the center of the four flanges, while with a great roaring tumult, heeling in a wedge behind and about him and his billowing gonfanon, the Crusaders began the journey.

As they sped across the scorched earth the wind of their passing diverted the tongued flames till they seemed to be twisting after them, seeking to lick the fugitive hooves. The destriers neighed but did not hesitate. The Host poured into the packed division waiting in a marshy spot beside the river and the battle was joined on the edge of the bank. The Turk always hoped to hamper the Christian mounts— bog them, trip them, cut their hooves—anything to rob the knights of the terrible force generated by the huge animals who not only bore them but flung themselves onto the foe with the enthusiasm of mastiffs; who could rear on two legs and fight like strange, savage, primordial monsters if need be; who seemed to the light-weight Moslems to impart the whole of their own massive muscular weight to the sword-arm of their riders as they wielded those hellish swords.

But the cavalry did not bog. Things had been done since the near-débâcle in the swamp near Dorilay. Christian smiths, inventive at their plastic fires, had forged iron shields which were fitted to the hooves like minute snowshoes, made wide as possible within the limits of unhampered speed. So the hapless heathen, planted in that unsupportable position for decoy, died quickly and in vain, screaming their martyrdom to the Antiochan sky.

The Christians now fanned out, the foot-archers by this time deployed and stationed behind their mantelets, ready with swift doses for Saracen throats as the latter began their own peculiar mode of charge. The Turks, with full confidence in the advantage of their ridiculously large numbers, were playing the old game, swooping in, dashing out—their curved ranks whipping at the enemy like the tongues of serpents, and backing the spitting sharp shower of their mounted bowmen with quick swipes of their curved falchions, singing, jewel-flashing in the morning sun. It was a maddening process, a war-way to addle the brain with its constant, confusing, almost musically measured movement—a tremendous death-lance before which the adversary could put peck and heckle and then gradually retreat or be cut back upon itself like flimsy wood battlements before a swinging ram.

Indeed, the Christians did fall back. In twice-seven thrusts of the Turkish horse they were gradually reversed until whole companies were pushed by their own men into the steaming river; until in many places the bowmen on foot were left without cavalry-cover and heaps of them lay where they had crouched, helpless for the kill, or were felled as they scampered in vain before the whooping hordes. It was a not-to-be-coped-with thing. That awful swooping rhythm beating upon the Host was irresistible, almost dream-like in its repetitive force. The Barons fighting in the front ranks—all save the Duc de Vermandois (Sir Hugh was busy behind somewhere)—kept together in united corps. Tancred was one more exception in the thing. He rushed about, wielding and swinging on all sides, achieving in each swipe enough deaths to satisfy the most aspirant knight for his whole escutcheon. But the rest of the captains, wholly one in a sharp awareness of their critical plight, fought diligently and in an orderly manner, sparking the main Christian forces teeming at their flanks. Holding their shields up and sitting their horses close-ranked for a wall, the knights hacked desperately, too busy for war-cries, too scared for prayer, thrusting and parrying and swinging from one swift-riding adversary to the next, determined to give death a rousing competition for their indomitable persons to the last.

For moments Bohemond had been caught in the profitless ecstasy, laying out right and left, crushing heads, shoulders, ribs with his leaded mace, dealing terrible instant death with Mihera's gift-sword. But now he drew out of it some, giving his bursting lungs sufficient breath to yell to those who fought near him, "Charge! Charge! We must breach the line-of-run! Oie, Oie! Eee-Yah!" The ancient Viking rouser broke unbidden from his lips as he found himself in company with Adhemar, Godfrey, Robert of Normandy and the young squire Vieuxpont, crashing through the Turk cordon and bursting into the vast tent-strewn area of the Turkish camp behind, the knights rushing after through the quick breach. The attack was broken, but just as the enemy horse scattered too close for hand-to-hand mêlée at last, Bohemond saw, standing before an enormous purple-and-yellow silk tent, a blaze-white Arab stallion, and poised upon it, a handsome, fierce-featured commanding-browed Turk, looking angry and surprised. Then the maelstrom closed in and broiled between them. "Kerboga!" young Vieuxpont had yelled and the others beyond him took it up. Kerboga! Kerboga! And as the battle once more joined, the name roared through the whole Host, heartening it like a war-cry.

An unnamable frenzy now seized upon Bohemond, having nothing to do with the hope of success. And, though he felt with a sure instinct the burgeoning of that mysterious invincible power that had always somehow invested the horridly outnumbered Crusaders in worse places than this, his fanatical lusty hackings of enemy flesh had little to do with *esprit de corps*. Only vaguely did he know of Adhemar laying about him like a huge bear, of Godfrey wielding his broad war-brand like a multi-bladed mill. And it was not until later that he would even recall Vieuxpont protecting him for minutes when, his own bloody weapon wedged in the hip-bone of a big turcopole, he was for a time helpless and needs must deliver the howling Bedouin with a great kick to recover Bayart. He kept thinking of Kerboga, of that split second when he and the huge Turk saw each other, looked in each other's eyes, like two wild animals meeting in a midnight fen, and he burned to be at him; he fought coolly and steadily up toward the great pavilion whose gem-gauded tent-poles could be glimpsed fitfully between the split heads and slumped shoulders of his adversaries as they fell or fled away.

But the whole mass of the enemy had suddenly resorted to direct flight, and, as the bulk of the cavalry took after them, wanting some more of the bloody business on the next ridge, Bohemond sat panting before the great, gently billowing multi-colored tent, cursing. Vieuxpont lingered near.

"He's gone! The damned heathen's gone—lucky for him! But by

Christ's Little Sandals—this tent is a pretty prize. We shall not neglect it. Call helpers, Vieuxpont; prepare to strike it, but carefully, pay you mind. And prevent looting; I desire it all!"

"Prince Bohemond's man, Vieuxpont, is here to see you, Sire," said Sir Jean de Jaen to Raymond St. Gilles later that day in the Provençals' field-tent at the Silpian rampart.

"He is, is he!" muttered Raymond crankily, shrugging into the fur capelet he wore when the fever was at him. "What does he want?"

"An important message, Sire, he says."

"Aye, I can guess it. At least a score have told me already. Victory—which was naturally to be expected. And don't keep calling de Haute-bille by that purloined title, Prince of Tarentum . . . Which I've seen . . . Been there . . . A garbage strewn, pest-ridden Italian village. A high-flown name for the likes . . . Makes the rabble forget where true aristocracy starts and deviltry takes over. Your link-boy has better blood, de Jaen!" he grunted, fumbling with buckles.

But de Jaen plunged on, drunk with hero-worship.

"But Sire, now for *sure*, he's Prince of Antioch! Borne on their shields across the Bridge, Sire, with Kerboga's tent held over for a canopy. All—"

"Silence, de Jaen! You chatter like a daw, and my head aches as it is; where's Vieuxpont?"

"Before the tent, Sire."

Vieuxpont was brisk, obviously anxious to repair to celebrations. He jerked his helmed head toward the Citadel.

"Word must be sent to Ibn Ben Merwan that he yield and take a choice of imprisonment or the Faith."

"Hmph, a soft thing . . . Baptize 'im with the blade, why not? Keeping the grain stores from us all these days . . ."

Vieuxpont nodded, tersely, cursing the garrulous old man. "Sir Bohemond will presently repair here for negotiations."

But Raymond did not dismiss him. A still, set look had come over his face, and he glanced upwards once or twice to the ranked numbers of his own garrisons stationed about the strong-places at the fort. Then, "De Jaen!" he called. "De Jaen!" And as the knight appeared, "Detain Vieuxpont!"

"Detain him, Sire?"

"Detain me!" yelled Vieuxpont, alarmed, his husky legs lifting in a tentative backward retreat. He could not believe his ears. But as he went to mount, de Jaen pulled him down and felled him with a mailed fist. Raymond, a mite lame this season from an old wound, limped over to him, grinning in his grey, grizzled mustache.

"Don't be awkward, Vieuxpont; we are directly sending for Emir

Merwan. But we cannot leave the fortress unmanned, can we? We ourselves, therefore, will invest it. The Citadel," he turned to de Jaen. "The Bridge Gate and the Palace . . . Get busy, Jean . . . and stop gaping like a boy!" He turned back to the squire who was nursing a smashed nose, his eyes full of involuntary tears of pain . . . "By the way, is that Sicilian baggage of Bohemond's still on the premises?"

He nudged Vieuxpont with his boot for a prompt answer.

"No, Sire. She's taken lodgings in the Italian quarter."

"Good, that is less complicated. My own sweet household could ill abide to share apartments with such ilk. And now, Vieuxpont, employ yourself . . . Say your beads . . . Con your conscience . . . Anything you desire . . . for we here have a busy afternoon!"

Zoë did not like her apartments in the Italian quarter. They depressed her. The Quarter lay on the edge of the burned-out palace section, and was tenanted by those of the wealthy merchant class, whose fleets had for years enjoyed commercial privileges in Antioch.

Several meetings with these worthies were held in Zoë's great chamber, Bohemond saying that with Raymond usurping the Black Palace he was at a loss for time to establish himself officially elsewhere yet. Zoë was in a touchy, easily hurt mood, restive under her indefinite new status, and urged him to avoid the practice of meeting the merchant-princes here. It was not that they looked ill on her connection with the Prince or acted in any way to offend her in their visits there. They were a class too used to customs in the East and too cynical, and above all, too shrewd in business-protocol for that—but for these very reasons Zoë had never been able to abide the *genre* even in Amalfi, and the association with them brought her thoughts too much to the old life at home. She was in no mood for such recollections. It was at this time, in fact, that she learned in casual conversation with Messer Pietro Dondalo, an old rival of Amalfi shippers, that Mihera had gone home ill to Amalfi and but now was getting well again. The old man thought she knew about it, and she gave no sign that it was otherwise until he left . . . Seeing at once the truth of matters during the siege, she confronted Bohemond with it, and they experienced their first quarrel. Bohemond, under great strain, was in no mood for subtleties with her. He answered her shortly, admitting all.

"Well, what did you expect? I knew from that night on the parapet that only your scruples kept us separated, and so—" he shrugged—"I did you the favor of helping you *lose* them in righteous female indignation."

His bluntness piqued her, and she stood looking down at him without speaking. He had removed his heavy baldric and sat down with a tired sigh. The brazier-light lay there on baldric and sheath, lighting up damascened glories on the hilt of Bayart, and troubled her memory with pictures of friendship in happier days.

"You let me think he *left* me, Bo," she said at last. "You let me blame him for it . . . Why, he might have died!" Her voice was low in her throat, and for some reason she thought of Ursule asleep in the trundle in her own room, and she wanted to cry. Her emotions welled up so that she had to move to the window and open it to feel the rough wind fresh on her face and on the cord pulsing in her throat.

"What do you want, Zoë?" she heard Bohemond ask behind her. She had not seen him look quickly up, and struck by her silence and by her pale, genuinely stricken expression, give her a sharp look and go quickly to her. She started a little at his voice, so close.

He did not touch her, but stood there behind, his breath on her hair and the not-unpleasant leather-and-sweat aura of him in her nostrils as she looked out over the flat, sleeping roofs of Antioch. "What do you want, Zoë?" he repeated more softly but in a firm tone. "If you wish to go home now, if you are unhappy here, you know I will certainly arrange it."

She stiffened in spite of herself.

"Perhaps, Bohemond, it would be best . . ." But her last word had an upward questioning tilt to it and he recognized this and grinned silently in the semi-darkness.

"I think it would *not* be best," he said positively but carefully, with no lightness, "for two reasons. I'll give you the selfish one first—that if you did—Oh, Christ, Zoë! Can't you see? I need you!"

She felt without seeing it the movement of his hand to his hair in a distracted gesture, raking the coarse curls the way he always did when genuinely moved.

"And secondly, Zoe," he went on, "you know Mihera. He was always stiff-necked about us before when there was really nothing . . . And now . . ."

She bridled. "Now, you're telling me I'm stranded anyhow!"

She turned and faced him, angry, but he was relieved at the passing of the other more dangerous mood, and he told her eagerly, "I don't know, Zoë; God, I don't know. I only know you can't leave me now and there's an end to it. Look, I have been careless of you. I've been so pushed . . . Did you know that now there's a plague starting? The famine of the siege, of course, and Provence, damn him, sits on those grain barrels like a dog-in-a-manger! And even the Genoese can't get enough to us without it—I think Alexius is holding things up somewhere also, although the Italians of course are too politic to say so . . . . But that's neither here nor there, Zoë, with us, except that you must have patience with me now . . . This is only the beginning; we've a magnificent future . . . a new life ahead of us . . . Meantime, no more conferences here. I have finally settled my belongings in some barracks down by the Dock, and this will be all yours to do with as you will, and we will have happy times here in the Via d'Oro. Street of Gold, indeed! I rename it Rue de Gloire. You'll see! First, we'll deck this gloomy place all new, however you wish. I'll send pedlars here with stuffs in the morning. Ursule's room too." But he saw her eyes darken at the name and he could bite his tongue for it, so he quickly took his leave, instinctively not even seeking to kiss her good night.

Some three days later, Zoë was directing Panturge in the hanging of new draperies in the apartments when Adhemar de Puy was announced by Marcelle. Rich-colored silks, painted Damascus linens, swatches of beautiful materials were strewn everywhere. The down-stuffed, luxurious chairs, couches, and ottomans, their old coverings ripped off, stood nakedly about, placed helter-skelter about the great central room. Little Ursule sat in a corner on the rug trying remnants of ribbons and silks judiciously on an old doll.

The name of Adhemar brought only an utterance of exasperation from Zoë and she hoped to be rid of him quickly, for she was truly enjoying herself in this project, indulging every exciting, extravagant, luxurious idea she ever had in these apartments.

When Adhemar entered the room, he seemed to lumber tiredly, rather than stride in with his usual all-pervading vigor, and she thought, "He's getting old—even he. The thing of Kerboga must have been his last great effort." For she had heard, even in the markets, shopping, his name prominent in the gossip of heroes on that fabulous day.

He settled himself on one of the high-backed chairs she offered, one with heavy carved legs, for his bulk, it seemed to her, would bring some of the daintier pieces there to quick disaster. He came to the point after the briefest of preliminaries and a merry word for Ursule, who peeked at him from her fringe of chestnut curls and went on dressing her doll. Panturge was sent off.

"Madame Zoë," he said. "I shall not name names with the child by—but, let us be short, and frank with one another—" He seemed highly nervous and, she thought, almost feverish, as he sucked in his breath and said explosively, "I implore you, do not remain here in Antioch. Return to Amalfi!"

"Come, come," she said coolly, for she had gone over the whole of it these past days in her mind. "You think to order me where to go?" She stopped his attempt to interrupt. "I know what you are going to say. You are the Church. I shall be cut off from it and its benefits for my flagrant disobedience. Well," she finished, not looking at him, "be it so!"

"Now, look you, Zoë," Adhemar said, lapsing to the familiar in his dead earnestness. "I didn't come here to order—I value human nature a little more than that; God knows I've scuffled with it all these years, though sometimes, as with you and the Prince, I seem to be less than successful . . . I do not order, mind; I *beg*. My reasons I pointed out to you before, as if there were need for further reasons, Lord help us, besides the salvation of your two selves! Listen, the truth is, I thought *before* that you were deliberately abandoned here, but now I know otherwise; did *you* know, all this time?"

"No, but what of that?" she said, nervously running her words together, put suddenly on the defensive for the probing of the fresh wound.

"For one thing," he answered, "it gives hope to my basic confidence in you, in your right intentions. You are implemented with a living conscience, Zoë; and now you know the truth. What further cause therefore, to cling to error? Make no mistake about it—and I wish not to seem to lack romance—it is less a question of undying love that prompts you, madame, than stiffness of neck!"

She bridled at him, untouched by humor or shame, her hands easily on her hips, several emotions crowding in and being abandoned for the one answer she could cling to.

"What makes you imagine, even if I thought to give up my life here, that Mihera would take me back?" They had both forgotten Ursule.

The Bishop mistook her intention, and hope flared in his eyes.

"I think he would. He is of difficult temper, but in the long run, his need for you rules. Aye, *Mihera* would. Were it reversed, mind you, I would not wager on Bohemond. Bohemond has your fancy, has always had, and knows it. If he were dealt with as Mihera was, and knew you loved elsewhere, he would simply put you from his mind. Whereas Mihera . . . Aye, *he* would take you!"

Her face became cynical, almost unattractive in the cold, fleeting look she cast him.

"Now come, Bishop, you don't say. By Christ's Thorns, if things were opposite, *I* would not!"

He shrugged.

"Wives won't, so readily, contrary to gossip, being less patient with frailties than their sires in every way, though they seem so docile."

She did not smile.

"What do you know about it!"

He shrugged again, elaborately.

"Have you not heard of the man-eating monsters, twin trolls of the Uninhabitable Antipodes? Chichevache, who feeds only on patient wives, madame, is lean, thin, oh very poorly. But Bicorne is fat, goodly, merrily rotund, his peculiar and only diet consisting of long-suffering, put-upon husbands!"

"Lord! What dogma is this?"

"As dogma, it fails like your wit, madame . . . Ah, welaway." He sighed, rising with peculiar difficulty from his chair. "It is a never-to-be-missed characteristic of sin—the flight of life's good humor . . . Oh, by the Blue Robe of the Maid," he cried suddenly, reeling and pale, "I have caught something; I thought it for the past hours . . . Help me to my horse, madame. I am ill . . ."

An expression of horror passed across her face. She recoiled.

"What madness is this? Suspecting your illness, yet coming here!" Ursule had risen from her play and would have gone to the Bishop, intrigued by his unnatural posture.

"Ursule!" her mother cried in a loud, panicked voice. "Don't touch him! Come, take yourself from this house!"

And when she had helped the Legate to his palfrey and saw him weakly ride off, she came into the room, her eyes wide and wild, her stare trained on Ursule.

"Ursule!" she cried. "Come here!" but then thinking, she directed her off. "Don't touch me. Marcelle!"

And when the fat one came, "Take her, get her clothes off, bathe her in warm wine with a garlic clove in it, everything, even her hair, and then wash that chair—no, Marcelle, take the thing out and burn it!" In horror she glanced down at the palm of her hand, feeling moisture where sweat was on it from the Bishop's feverish clasp.

"Mama!" cried Ursule disturbed by the name she had heard repeatedly between them. "Where *is* Papa? Mama, why won't he come to us any more?"

Zoë became terribly angry, and would have struck her but refrained, thinking of how her hand was contaminated. "Go to Marcelle, Ursule, or Mama will whip you!" And holding her hand out as if it were a fester, she fled from the room.

CHAPTER XXVI *Maarat*

THE SICKNESS IN ANTIOCH that late summer of 1098 did not long fuss with its victims. Adhemar de Puy for three days tossed on his bed in torment, his huge body raddled with hot festering pustules that bathed him in molten fire. For a time thereafter, while warm winds from the Orontes-irrigated hillsides brought fresh scents of grapes and olives burgeoning and the nutty odor of yellow pistachios coming to term, he seemed to rally some, buoyed by his splendid strength.

The knights fidgeted with new plans, awaiting his assured recovery. While Bohemond wrangled with Raymond of Provence, a desperate call had come from Count Baldwin, brother to Godfrey de Bouillon, concerning certain raids. The Christian state he had founded by breaking from the main pilgrimage before the siege of Antioch had been thought of as a bad thing at the time, but opinion on these matters seemed now to be changed, so that with great promptness they organized a force, with Godfrey to go to Baldwin at Edessa direct, and Bohemond to head into neighboring Cilicia to aid strongholds secured by Tancred, specifically to break a Turk siege at the walled village of Ezaz.

These places were opposite from Jericho and the Tomb.

Suddenly, one late afternoon while the long shadows fell purple and gold on Antioch, the call went out that the Legate was indeed dying. Bohemond and Godfrey had not yet departed. They were found in conference with Raymond of Provence, and all three rushed to the Palace of the Greek Patriarch where the Bishop was lodged.

In the death-place, fat tapers were already ranked about the bed, bier-like, and the smell of oil and incense from last ceremonies still lingered in the close upstairs chamber room. A small ruby vigil-light glowed at the tortured feet of an ivory crucifix pendant on the wall. Adhemar, though his cheeks were sunken and his ruddy countenance was smeared with fearful sores, opened his sunken eyes and smiled at them in comradely fashion.

"Don't weep for me," he said, the hearty, jocose accents lighting up the ruin of his face with the essence of his old self so that they forgot the shock of the ravagement they viewed there; his calm eyes seemed indeed to mock their sadness, as the blood-brightness of the setting sun outside seemed to mock the mournful candles.

"I am happy," he said. "So much so that it is a temptation, here at the last. Peace, so alluring . . . Arrival at the Walls, already, with the gates opening . . . I am besting you all, you see, short-cutting it . . ." He sighed, returning to old cares.

"Listen, comrades-in-arms! I have been busy with my soul, and I find worries, unfinished business with you. Certain ones will have found me too patient with you all this time; Urban perhaps, perhaps God! . . . But let me be chary of thinking of old sins who am so newly anointed. Yet, I can attempt amends. It lies with you to answer my intentions . . . Hear them, therefore . . . Go, go, go! Be daring— do not be prudent, making elaborate preparations for calamities that may not occur. We have felt the softness of the flesh of evil on our actual blades. Be not fearful, then, of their would-be terrifying sallies, little pin-pricks, like hounds yapping on all sides . . . Go! You are wearing the colors of Christ for the truth of the Western World. This is the trial—the *Carousel*. It is not the Tomb so much as how you get there. Give the Dark One not fuel for his pot to boil on—scandals . . . strifes . . . unknightly intentions . . . so that you win the trophy but in vain . . . Go!!"

Godfrey de Bouillon lingered at the foot of the high couch, his eyes luminous with faith, child-like and eager, transfigured, so that the prelate's waning glance rested on him fondly, even as he spoke to the two others, who from either side of him stared across the bed. "If only you would find harmony, brothers! If only—"

Raymond glared at the younger baron balefully, whether from actual intent or the natural look of his battle-beaten face. Bohemond glanced back at him coolly, expressing nothing. Not that he was not moved in this hour, for he was. Adhemar had his love and his admiration as no one had before, save his own dead father. Some movement brought their eyes to Godfrey. He knelt now in the deep-piled rugs, his gauntleted hands joined, his handsome, pale face lifted to the crucifix. Its vigil-flame threw faint sheen on his mailed arms, his gauntlet-tips and his shoulder-length hair. . . .

Presently there was strained movement on the bed and Adhemar said, very softly, "God wills it, gentlemen!" and his eyes closed.

Godfrey de Bouillon was scarcely returned to Antioch when a council was held at the Church of Peter. The knights would have awaited Bohemond who was late from the Cilician expedition, but Raymond herded them in, proposing without delay his Pax Discors in which the question of Antioch should hang fire until after the

Jerusalem conquest. "Get on!" cried Raymond in a rasping echo of the dead Legate. And yet when questioned on his holding of the towers and the wheat away from Antioch, he stiffened, growled, and would not discuss it.

Bohemond turned up late the second day of the discourse looking thinned, with a new sabre-welt sustained in the mêlée at Ezaz. Sulky about the Pax, he suggested delay till spring, Easter perhaps, when there'd be decent weather. But Adhemar's spirit was vividly rife in the conclave, by reason of his sincerely mourned recent passing, and seeing this, Bohemond fell silent, assenting in apparent good grace, and renewed his vows with the rest.

He had briefly visited Zoë before the concourse and now he hurried to return there. The Barons, inimical to his real plans, were not his confidants. Even to Tancred he did not feel like expanding much on his future schemes. Tancred was an outstanding fighter, a taker of forts and a doer of deeds, but he was inclined to be a trifle mixed up and alternately saw his uncle as his hero and his *bête-noir*. And so Bohemond had quickly acquired the habit of laying his laurels at Zoë's feet, and enjoyed more than all things his long hours of talk across her compote table. Long custom, her sympathy, and his loneliness prompted this; also his burning, headlong infatuation. Reckless, heedless, headlong in war, he was wary and close in council, but it was his battle-temper that matched his ways in love. It was Zoë who, when he was announced as she entertained ladies of the Host who visited her, sat lady-like and ceremonious in her sumptuous stiff silks, while Bohemond fidgeted, obviously bored, resentful of their betrayed privacy until the ladies, slightly insulted and more than a little suspecting things, left them at last. But when the door had once slipped to, it was another matter.

"Where have you been!"

"At the conference."

"Always away!" she cried. "I wait and wait. Your poor face, that damned heathen . . . Not that you are not much handsomer for it . . . But it scares me so . . . A shade deeper. . . ."

She flew, utterly unchecked, from one subject to the next; wild, passionate, utterly like a storm. Their love had unleashed in her all the latent incendiary humors and the lively, natural impulsiveness, and she was irradiated, brilliant. A lesser man than Bohemond would have found her too much. But instead she fascinated him. He now knew the reason why, aside from occasional casual affairs, he had instinctively eschewed all women, having once known Zoë. She was at times as irascible as she was ordinarily full of cheer. But her very upbraiding aroused him, as though he were caressed with claws, and her angry whisperings to him (so that Ursule would not hear) were an erotic storm. In a younger woman these things had been unbeguiling, merely hysterical or undisciplined, but she was full-conscious, poised, sophisticated, knowledgeable and in her prime.

They were perfectly matched. She was even as tanned as he was, not white like the other women there of Western blood. In the warm weeks at Antioch they rode and hunted, going swift after crane and hare and coursing with tame cheetahs on leashes into brambled impossible passes for the fallow deer and the ibexes with their curved horns. Her hair grew lustrous, her eyes bright and her body quickened in every sinew, glowing with the prime health, so that one could almost see the blood coursing rich beneath the tawny skin. One afternoon in her apartments, curtained in silence (for the windy weather they had stayed indoors), Bohemond twitted her for it.

"Arms, thighs, everything golden, my dear! Marcelle must wonder that you are turning such a nutty hue . . ."

"Marcelle *indeed* wonders, and is not silent about it! I would have her out of my personal service and confine her to tending Ursule. She is in certain ways a jade."

He chuckled, remembering those hours far ridden from the town, in some warm nook in the Cassian foothills, hare, deer and crane forgotten as they played in the long sunshine of the sunny afternoons.

A jade indeed . . . He hated to see the summer go . . . He hated to think of Jerusalem; he would miss her.

Moving into the great, soft, multi-curtained bed beside him, she saw the look pass across his face . . .

"What's amiss, my lord? Do I displease you in some way?" It was coquettish, said with impudence, for she had full confidence of her constant, instantaneous, powerful attraction for him.

"God no, Zoë! I was just wishing, on the contrary, it were feasible to take you to Jerusalem."

"Jerusalem!" She jumped as though stung, her breasts quivering in the bodice of her thin shirt, her cheeks flushing beneath the young, delicate-lace caul she wore on her low-knotted hair. "Just back, and you talk Jerusalem. I thought you had given that up, indeed!"

"Did I ever say it, Zoë!"

"No, but I thought . . . You seemed not to wish it . . . it seemed logical . . ."

"My vow . . . ," he reminded her, thinking not of his obligation but that Raymond at present had him cornered.

"Ah, yes, I had forgotten. Oh, Bohemond, this summer I have forgotten everything!" She threw herself back amongst the cushions, stretching, revelling in contentment. "Wonderful Elysian forgetting! Heaven! It's been Heaven itself!"

His voice roughened watching her, aroused. "Yes, Zoë. I had dreamed of it like this. What is it? Magic . . ."

"Don't analyze it; don't think about it; don't talk it all away, Bo," she whispered, running her hands across the crisp, coarse brightness of his hair, on the strong, noble lineaments of his face; and on that marvelous firm chiseled mouth she put first her finger-tips, and then her eager, burning mouth.

But soon, on St. John's Day, the Host must march again. Masses, mock pilgrimages, old Raymond waxing bountiful with his guarded stores. To good wives some grain and oil and sacks of pure wheaten flour for cakes of pandemaine when news should come of Jerusalem successes. To Bohemond's Italian and Greek footmen, jars of honeymead, conserves and sheaves of wonderful tasting willow stalks called *sucra*, sugar. Bohemond's lances would support the rear, leaving later in case of a Turk surprise. They would meet at a large walled town previously scouted by Tancred, called Maarat-en-Numan.

As in the first rank Raymond proceeded out of Antioch, he even clasped hands with Bohemond and called him *bon ami*, smiling down at him from his one good eye. But "Plague take that pompous old donkey; I'll give him something to grin about!" Bohemond said to Tancred as soon at the Provençal's back was turned.

A breeze blew from the south, with a faint sting in it. Bohemond warned Godfrey when Raymond's retinue was passed. He was standing at the Mosque-end of the Bridge and he tugged at the Burgundian's knee, arresting him. "See that you pitch camp immediately when this storm nears peak," he told him, shouting above the din of the cavalcade. "It will abate in two days, but meantime marching at it will put eye-boils on every decent cob you've got and have the face-hide off your men too, if you try to bear on. I feared this. It's the season for it. Now all you can do is respect it as you go." Godfrey nodded in acknowledgment, and, directing his massive chestnut to the mailed ranks, rode on.

The storm came the second day. They had struck east. They had already hit the sand. They no longer saw trees nor green spots anywhere. Encamped so long in coastly Antioch, they had forgotten desert ways. They soon remembered. The far wind, raising its veil of grit, seemed at first but to spit at them, as a preliminary. By the second evening they were flung the whole dose. Grey sky closed in; they could not with certainty know their course; their only means of plotting it was the cloaked sun.

Godfrey de Bouillon, urged by the rest and mindful of Bohemond's advice, suggested the halt. But Raymond opposed it. He pulled his mustache, squinted his scar-ribbed face and gestured. "On, gentlemen! Bear on!"

As the sun sank, the simoon broke on them fully, swooping like a storm of arrows—cruel, sharp, penetrating everywhere. The soldiery, especially the ill-protected foot, were so buffeted and whipped that they could scarce sink their tent-poles in the ground. Exhausted, spent, many of them merely rolled themselves in the cloth itself and slept where they fell, in ranks.

The next morning, the phenomenon had fled in its quick, mysterious fashion and Raymond was at them again. He was up with the ruined sun, his good eye glittering in the bleak light, his leathery face grimacing as he mounted before they were half arranged.

"Fanatical!" the Duke of Flanders complained to Robert Shortshanks. "I swear the old goat's crazy as a loon!"

So they rode on, and before noon they sighted before them some high, square towers, all crenelated, with curves and pointings in the Oriental style.

"That will be Maarat. I think we'd best rest," again suggested Godfrey. "The foot are exhausted."

But "Surprise is wise," said Raymond. "*Leave* the foot! We barons will ride ahead—we'll appear at the ramparts in force and give them full alarm!"

And this they did (those who had it covering their horses in body-mail) and marched in deliberate but fast formation to a place beneath the northern walls. Deploying in sparse ranks to make themselves seem numerous, they stood in the stirrups yelling, "Yield! Yield!"—the French, Italians and Burgundians screaming like sea-birds, the Walloons and Flemish baying like dogs.

For a time nothing happened. The Crusaders sat their pawing mounts, their faces expectantly thrust up, and all was unchanged on the quiet ramparts. Everything silent with a queer vacancy too, so that a lone crane winging leisurely across the sky past the central barbican was seen by them all.

They fidgeted, the joined fesses of their head-and-shoulder mail rippling like lustrous necks of roosters as they twisted in the creaking saddles, shrugging at one another.

Then at the great moat of slightly moving water that was doubtless fed by the same spring that had prompted habitation in this Syrian wasteland, a bridge began to fall. And as it banged down spewing jets of sand from the tongue-like escarpment, a solitary horseman shot out from it—a bright form in Christian mail, with a tattered gonfanon red-dyed and sporting a serpent.

"Holy Chrysostom!" yelled Normandy to Flanders. "It's Bohemond de Hauteville!"

Various exclamations swept the assembled horse like wind gusts through a stand of wheat. They were all eyes as Bohemond approached Count Raymond.

Provence raked his beard as Bohemond drew up before him and they heard him say, "What clown play is *this*, de Hauteville! Where's your army?"

"Stationed about, you may well wager!" answered Bohemond with his grin. "A forced march, a quick thing, a good job, you see, being bloodless. My nephew quite reasonably convinced the townsmen of possible results from Franks in combined force. Of my *own* benignities with those at Antioch, of my kind of treatment of Emir ben Merwan whom they knew about, they were wisely reminded, and they chose *me*, rather than risk débâcle."

Raymond trembled with rage, but he said with an unaccustomed coolness, feeling a supporting sentiment all about him now, "Why deceive us this way, Bohemond? Why place shameful blemish on the Western cause? A knave's trick, Sicilian! Why was it done?"

Bohemond returned his stare, bested it; on either side of the serpent-embossed nose-piece the grey eyes grew incredibly hard.

"Maarat's in Antioch's feudal limits, Provence. No more will you help yourself to my posts! Meantime," turning to the barons with a lightening smile, "I *know* you're tired; inside there's rest and feasting. Enter then, brothers, and partake!"

But from the knights, nothing. The destriers snorted, reared, jingled the links. But nothing from the knights, nothing but the narrow, unbelieving stare which, as one man, they had turned on Bohemond.

It was finally Raymond who said, quietly for once, "Let us go in then, gentlemen."

The Latin cavalry filed through Maarat amid friendly hubbub in the littered alleyways. Confidence in *Maimoun's* promises appeared complete. No evidence of fear was anywhere. It was only a gesture that Bohemond had rounded up three hundred men and boys and held them in friendly custody at the Mosque el-Rhan.

The Barons repaired there and sat down to a banquet, Bohemond adding wine to the savory Moslem dishes from his own stores. A veiled maiden, a daughter of the governor himself, played the *rehab* for them, a viol-like instrument on which she had dainty skill.

But it was no good, and when Bohemond commenced parley by declaring withdrawal from the pilgrimage unless Raymond gave up posts at Antioch, the pretense was completely shattered. Raymond laughed, Bohemond scuffled with him at the banquet-board and it ended, while they prevented Bohemond from pommeling the old knight, with Raymond throwing wine in his face.

Godfrey de Bouillon at this point emerged from his usual reserve. He stood to a long speech. He expressed with candor what all of them felt about the day's event. They'd been played cheap; they'd been made fools of, and Godfrey, with a new cup, pledged fealty to Raymond of Provence as their new leader.

Bohemond stood there, his darkened cheeks wet and streaming with Raymond's wine.

"All right, friends," he said tersely, "you can *have* old Dry Veins with his withering ague, and be damned to you all. You can have Maarat too. As for me, three hundred Moslem slaves will imburse me well enough, in Antioch."

He proceeded to the broad corridor. At the rooms where the hostages were lodged, he rapped on every door, shouting, "Out, men of Maarat!"

Tancred remonstrated with him. Godfrey confronted him as he went. To the one, he said, "Secure that talented fine wench, Tancred! Lady Zoë desires new service!" And to Godfrey, "Time to be chasing after Raymond, my noble de Bouillon! Why do you delay?"

He was completely wild. He hustled the old, he struck the stubborn, he cremated thirty in a small mosque where unfortunately they had hidden to escape. And when in three hours he had gathered his followers and proceeded out of town, a long line of ululating wretches rode manacled after him up to Antioch.

The knights were resolute to carry on. But when they returned to the infantry still resting in the desert camp, the latter protested their too-hard suffering and refused to budge.

As one young squire put it (he had lost his destrier in the Antioch charge and was too poor and unlucky to commandeer heathen horse-flesh as some others had), "If it's *thus* far so terrible, what will it be when the winter comes? It was bad enough last year, even stationary . . ."

"The wretches are right," Robert of Normandy told the rest. "It's against sense! Caesar himself always *wintered* somewhere! *Caesar hiemavit. Hiemavit* here; *hiemavit* there; are we cleverer than Caesar?"

So they fell in reverse ranks and straggled back. All except Provence. Sir Raymond remained at Maarat, outraged, immovable, set as a mastiff.

CHAPTER XXVII *Broken Idols*

THE DAY THE CRUSADERS came back to Antioch, Zoë was at her draperess, a Greek woman named Mary Alanoe, having a gown fitted. It was a fashionable first-level salon at the lower end of the Great Way, frequented by rich wives of the woman's own race, and by Armenian ladies and Jewesses who found their way here from the Ghetto on the other side of town. The thick-rugged showing-room gave onto a shuttered balcony where Mary was accustomed to serve dainty collations of ginger tea and small breads with pats of Kiev caviar when her patrons grew tired from the long sessions with bodkins and metering-sticks.

Today Mary had collapsed the painted shutters, giving those who sat there a plain view of the high street where it swung around from the last of the country terraces. Protected from the thoroughfare by a thin grille, and achieving some further privacy with veils, several customers lounged in padded settees, prepared to observe the knightly entourage as it bore up to Antioch.

It was hot and windy and Zoë felt a strange, stabbing tenseness as she listened to the murmurous bruiting of the street-crowd that was close packed even to the grille. Every snatch of talk concerning the thing at Maarat made her wince. She had wept, not a week gone, for Bohemond's departure which she dreaded so, and he was suddenly far from gone, and she should be very happy. Beside her chair, ribbon-encased and ready to give Panturge to bear home, was a lovely new gown to be worn on their very next evening together. There would be convivial companions, and they would have a party. Reunion. Joy. Oddly she was chilled at the thought. She kept returning to the thing at Maarat as the heralds had told it—the Prince's day of wrath. Murder of hostages . . . Taking of slaves . . . She could not encompass it. Surely it was one of those wild tales which people attached to every exploit that Bohemond had a hand in. An idle excrescence to heighten the heady gossip . . .

The crowd had thickened. Quite through the grille, Zoë could catch the overpowering odors of garlic, leeks, and sour wine, and of a big Greek peasant who stood in front of it. She veered, only to meet the glittering eye of a tall, emaciated monk whose glance slid deftly off as she encountered it. The look of him tugged, oddly familiar, but he kept his cowled head turned and stood fingering his beads in the shade there with the rest.

And, presently, up the steep curved street from the terraces they came, the knights on their nervous horses.

The Burgundians were first and Godfrey at their head showed no emotion in his youthful face, nor did his ranks curvet spiritedly behind him as they were wont, but rode up and passed through the watching masses silently. No trumpets, no garlands, no huzzahs, though the steeds pranced handsomely and the byrnies and bucklers blazed fine as ever in the pale November sun.

The Burgundians' last remnants trickled past and presently the Norman hues began to show, and then she saw Bohemond rounding the bend. He rode tall in the saddle with Volcan's bridle pulled so close that his neck was arched almost to his shoulders and his eyes showed red from the strain of it, and foam stood on the animal's velvet lips. His hooves raised high, sparking on the round cobbles, and his mane flew free in the windy sunshine. There were admiring remarks on horse and rider and her cheeks burned with shame and for once she did not look at him, her eyes seeking instead the captives lashed in various ways to the horses that came on behind. A young, comely girl rode at the head of the line. Her hair was disarranged and her eyes red from weeping, but her veils were proudly pulled to her face to protect her as much as possible from the stares of the crowd. She rode alone. Then came the men, not soldiers, at first, but older-looking men, of much dignity, riding two to a horse in a double column. The young men rode last, some in the booted pantaloons and belted garments of the Turk soldiery. But there were few of these, many having apparently resisted . . .

Zoë felt her face grow hot and sweat start from her armpits. She had never been moved to ecstasies as others were when the Host rode off to conquest or to the fray. In those inspired departures and victorious returnings she had thinly shared. She had always been absorbed in some private thinking. Would he perish this time? A chance sword-bite . . . Oh, God, would he return? Thoughts of herself, alone, without him, somewhere adrift . . . But now, strangely, she was filled with a pounding emotion at the sight of Godfrey and his splendid men. There was a hideousness to their being cheaply tricked like this, being false-started and led back in shame. Zoë felt their shame peculiarly, in full force. This she believed in, the truth of the embattled chivalry. The concept of their strength and fineness had been so familiarly certain that she had never been moved by its splendid manifestations. But she mourned for its show of weakness now, and almost unconsciously she began to pray.

It was a thing one *could* pray for without exactly feeling worthy to, as with little Ursule at bedtime.

She did not see a certain tall monk move after her as she presently rose, left Mary Alanoe's, and escaped from the main thoroughfare.

Traversing a side street in the windy sun, Zoë felt better. She walked fast, picking her way mechanically through the litter underfoot. It seemed that the motion of her legs relieved a part of the tension that had mounted. The packet with the new gown was a weight, but still she was glad that, anticipating the crowded main street, she had directed Panturge to wait for her at the Market Jeromid at the Square. She hurried on; she kept on praying, in a sort of made-up soliloquy, dodging, shifting, trying to drive out the dark thoughts that crowded her mind like the dusty heads of serpents.

"My God, what *is* this? This is not good that he is doing, I almost hate him! God, what is wrong with me actually to feel this?"

Suddenly, from close behind, she was challenged. A sharp, thin, familiar voice. She twisted about.

"It is I," he said smiling, "Tafur."

"Oh," she said, at first surprised, then frightened, and then somehow glad that someone was here to talk to, even such.

"What are you doing in that garb, familiar of Satan? Not orders!"

"In *that* you are right, madame, no," Tafur answered. "But piety is in style at the moment, as the result of this last deed of our mutual patron's, and I find welcome everywhere this way (if I'm careful to go where not known), and great opportunity for my peculiar talents!"

"I dare say."

He gave her a side-wise impudent smile, and inquired, "You've heard of the thing at Maarat?" the two of them walking together past stalls and market-spreads, incongruous in the sunshine, their full clothes billowing behind them like sails at the lively pace she set.

"Why not? Haven't all?"

Tafur clucked briskly, his long face homelier than ever in the clinging cowl. "A good trick, a splendid move. At last they know who's master! Not by his bravery, pay you mind, nor his wisdom in council, nor his customary clemency to foes, was it done! No, but by quick-moving them, challenging them, and facing them down. Pht—like that—the supremacy! Now they hate him, Godfrey and the rest, but still they came back; they will not oppose him and they will give him Antioch. Even now his men hustle the Provençals from the Silpian Fortress . . . They *all* thumb under! That of the hostages was a good touch."

"A barbarous thing!" she cried.

"Aye, barbarous, but a good touch!"

She made a face, and he caught at the look of distaste he discovered there.

"Countess! Is that less than pride in him I see?" and she flared back, ready as tinder.

"You *know,* you *know,* Tafur! It was inexcusable!" She tossed her veils, thin, costly veils, which did not wholly discipline the dark, lustrous masses of her hair in their silken fillets.

Tafur shrugged, tossing his long palms. "Strange, madame! I thought you had *chosen* your idol, and followed his every fascinating move with admiration! By my faith, I cannot ravel you"—laying thumb to nose. "What are you like? A false pagan who steals his favorite image with much risk from the oratory, then lays it aside, refusing to fall and worship!"

His bitterness, feigned though she knew it to be, now struck her direct. She felt he was holding her to a cup of gall. She felt choked and buffeted as though forced with rough, mocking hands.

It was with relief that she saw the painted awnings of the Market Jeromid, and the hunch-back Panturge, stationed where she had left him with her caparisoned mare. She gave him the packets, mounted the palfrey and left Tafur rocking on his sandals, grinning after her, with no farewells.

CHAPTER XXVIII

The Dilemma and the Dream

THE RIFT BETWEEN Bohemond and the Barons after Maarat soon passed away. Time and the weather (whose inclemency made them, snug in Antioch, recall how it was in that bad time at the Wall) assisted the resumption of amity on every side. Another matter moderated feelings too—Alexius's desertion.

For some time now they had been writing home to wife, suzerain and bishop that the more they dealt with the heathen Moor, the more did they think the Greeks more perfidious than Seljuks. And when in the spring, they set out again for the Holy Places, they took strength at the thought of Antioch behind them—a mighty bastion masked by a strong knight whose faithful Italian vavasseurs sent fresh new pilgrimages of soldiers for his service every season, and whose heartening knowledge of Alexius's nature by this time was unquestionably attested. In such wise did they console themselves for the fact that he did not continue on.

Meantime in Antioch the Prince improved his time. He entrenched his influence by all means, making his remarkable personality felt by the lowly and great, the powerful and the enthusiastic. He wrote notes everywhere. To Pope Urban, begging him for release from all vows connected with the faithless Alexius; to his sub-vassals at home, touching on affairs at Tarentum and Bari and calling for new youth from the Calabrian hills; to Borsa, even—tentative, teasing letters to his half-brother where he presided at Salerno Castle. But Roger was coldly uncommunicative since the first days after Claremont when Bohemond had absconded with half his vassal knights, and did not reply. He corresponded with Baldwin at Edessa and with Godfrey on the march, and with Kogh Vasil at Kasun, the Armenian lord of Cilicia who was his fast friend. In all these dealings he was eminently, characteristically successful.

And so he sought the world, few even guessing that he was other than whole-heartedly engaged in the Christian project. He was too far ahead. His plans, to the heretofore land-bound barons, were inconceivable; to the clergy, delighted with this mighty pilgrimage of consecrated knights, they were a concept too much of the world. Bohemond, as acquisitive, as able, and far more ambitious than the Conqueror had been, now dreamed definitely of an Eastern Empire. It was for this he began to think of courting the West.

From the West one thing was needful to him—money. Always impoverished, he was now more than ever. He meant presently to mend this. But there were castles to build, towns to subdue, and a vow of pilgrimage to be made good, before he might show his face in Europe. He did not worry about Jerusalem. He had no doubts the knights could make it theirs. Nor did he doubt the rest of the sprawling master plan. He was entirely confident of his destiny in this life and considerably sanguine about the next. Ostensibly fervid as a Frenchman, inwardly calculating as an Italian and dexterous as a Greek, he was more than modern, certainly not a man of his age. He was far more the prototype of a new one not yet seen.

As usual he sought Zoë in the Rue de Gloire. With no sense of binding, but with renewed anticipation and verve he sought her, for far from palling, their relationship presented to him an ever-fresh intrigue. At forty-five Bohemond was bold, jaded, and subtle as a cheetah, and it was an exercise that pleased him well to manage his intrigue with the Italian countess *sub rosa* as much as possible and if not that, under the high noses of his scandalized colleagues, both secular and of the cloth. She presided in her apartments, making each of his exploits in the field an excuse for fetes which they celebrated in gay fashion with a picked few. Inevitably they must take care. At certain times by tacit agreement they avoided each other, in the exigency of a visiting envoy of the See or even some special visitor from the western barony itself. In Zoë's attitude at times like this, he saw her essential conflict present itself repeatedly; he could observe how only her unshakable attachment to himself kept her drastic reaction to it unprecipitated. She might talk incessantly of their necessity to part, and then, encountering him in groups where they must not show their close rapport, she would watch him surreptitiously, feeding on every stolen glance her way, as if they had not a few hours previous been together. And when they must talk amid smiling strange notables in state, he observed her peculiarly panicked; in his cold, bright, loud, meaningless pleasantries to her—for indeed he delighted to tease—her mind seemed to shift and falter. "Of what were we speaking? Oh, but yes, Seigneur!"

She who could ordinarily be so utterly composed, under his elaborately cool eye would babble like a bedlam thing, and he knew that even then she was wondering if indeed he loved her still, and he guessed she would wait—petulant, irascible, moody, till their next private hours.

For faced in reality, her position was insupportable, and none knew it more than she. Divorce was not to be thought of in honor. The taking of Antioch had been a momentous season, a bright noon of achievement and joy that allowed small exigencies of personal life to cast no shadow. But when things settled down and life once more was real, Zoë in the worst times felt as if she were really alone.

Again and again Zoë told him she must leave. Sometimes she really frightened him with the intensity and persistence of these resolutions, for now less than ever, he imagined, could he be without her. She was in his blood. Yet he did not much fear her actual flight away, and the mere fact of this war in her nature made her dear, for it challenged him. She was sensitive to his betrayals, and in that fact provided the worst kind of indulgence of his ethical crimes. He took to looking to *her* reactions to them instead of his own conscience; to see them recognized, appraised, and, in the plain fact of her continued love, forgiven.

Maarat had been the worst. In the first weeks after Maarat, she had been so alienated that he needs must impose himself on her company by force. The presentation of the daughter of the Turk governor as a gift did not help matters; what she heard of his doings on that day from the lips of the mourning child but increased her distaste. In vain he reasoned with her, deprecating his lapse. Could not she, who knew his violence in love, conceive how his violence in war could explode to murder? But she remained unconscionably cool, and for a time he by turns ignored, mocked and was rough with her, even taking her by force. There was one night the Antiochians told of: how Bohemond chased a bireme that had sailed from the Quay; how he boarded it after swimming half-way across the Orontes on the back of Volcan, to fetch her back to Antioch. They could not be sure of this. It was only one of the tales that crossed the wine-bowls concerning the colorful pair. When Bohemond did not march with the rest to the Holy Places, the cleavage of his move from the common cause seemed to heighten the hue of her own personal alienation from society in their relationship; and there came a period when she herself seemed to change, become hard, brittle and fecklessly gay, and their love lived feverishly in a strange climate of passion, conflict, guilt and abandonment that left them both exhausted.

But this time, on returning from Laodicea, he found her radiant. The announcement of success at Jerusalem had something to do with this; he grasped that subtle thread and made the most of it. If they had known defeat, she'd have blamed him. She had mentioned it often enough while the Barons struggled through. But now all was well. Even the news of his own projected pilgrimage had no power to cloud her serenity. That first night she was dressed in a new gown he had never seen, from the Greek seamstress Mary Alanoe.

"I bought it last spring," she told him over their shared platter of little Greek cakes called *palacountas*, served with a tart green conserve of Malaga grapes. Little Ursule had fallen asleep on Bohemond's lap and had been carried to bed. "I have never felt like wearing it till tonight."

"When I'm going away!" rebuked Bohemond in mock distress. "I think that speaks ill for my standing in the Rue de Gloire!"

She rose, laughing like a young girl showing off. The gown was far different from the thick, rough clothes of the west, which were heavily jewelled and furred to make up for what they lacked in richness of material. This was fashioned entirely in the Byzantine way, graceful and light and flowing, with a simple antique cut, but of silk, and colored exquisitely. It had tri-colored panels whose hues were a rare yellow-pink like melon, cinnamon brown, and dark amethyst. Bohemond had seen such dyes made in Sicily, in the vats of Castletown. He knew that their bases were powdered gold. He whistled.

"Have a care there, madame! You well know I scrape for byzants as it is!"

"Why, Bo!" she cried. "You talk like an Italian husband!" She whirled before him, laughing, and he noted how fresh her face was under the severe close caul on her nearly hidden hair. From the front of the golden cap one bright jewel was dangled on her brow.

"Why do you stare at me so?" she asked him. "Did the Greek cheat me d'y'think?"

"'Sblood, no, Zoë!" he said, pulling her almost roughly to the divan. "I was just thinking that soon, now, I'll be growing older; there is grey in the hair; that whelp of a page Gillfried informed me as much this morning. I trust you will oblige me then, sweetheart, by looking a bit more staid than you presently do . . . else I'll be laughed at, called that old man of Antioch who has a white head and a green tail, like an onion! Since they well know it's not for my money you stick about me, more's the pity!"

And while for his pains she kissed him, murmuring, "Flatterer! Rogue! *Fripon!*" into his ear, he drew a letter from the folds of his satin surtout.

"And speaking of our poverty, feast your eyes on *this*." He held it from her, half-teasing, while she attempted to read, guessing the identity of the seal with the fleur-de-lis. "A paper from France, from Philip!" he announced boastfully.

Zoë gasped. She settled herself and read it.

Penned on fine lambskin with the regal crest, it was a declaration of admiration and respect for the "Baron Bohemond." It was more than that. No touch of patronage for the erstwhile "Sicilian upstart." She read on, trembling against his arm.

"My brother, your acquaintance, Duc de Vermondois, came home full of praises and affection for you" (wrote Philip), "and we see in future a rapport in French holdings extending from the Seine to the Middle Sea and on to the Jordan. My sister Constance has been separated from her unfortunate too-close connection in marriage by consent of Holy See. I dare to think a more romantic fate might soon await her, sealing new amities with new nuptials at Chartres. We await your eventual visit.

"Philip Plantagenet
"Paris"

Zoë sat quite still, the panels of the new gown crushed between her hands.

"It's all coming true, the song I made for you," she murmured softly. "Even the kingly wedding . . ."

Bohemond had been re-reading the letter, avid as a boy, but now he looked at her and laughed. "My God, sweetheart, do you think I'd be led by the nose to a second-hand princess? Homely, no doubt!"

"You haven't seen her!" she joked lamely, not looking at him, for her eyes were dark with fear.

"No, but they always are . . . And yet . . ." he teased. Then seeing her pallor, his voice roughened with a mixture of tenderness and impatience. "Look, Zoë, forget princesses or whatever you find in this. Observe the tone! Don't you see what it assures? Philip's palpable support!" He rose, pacing in the beautiful peaceful room. "To the devil with his sister, his cousins and the rest of his female connections, but by Heaven, I welcome his good French coin!"

Woman-like, some core of determination hardened in Zoë as she watched him pacing there, knowing the great dreams that were shadowed in his eyes. His extravagant dreams must be abetted. If only, at this difficult time, he could be kept going, then later on, what riches would there *not* be waiting to his hand? Bagdad, Kalkut, the bazaars of Khorostan; the fur-filled steppes of Igor, the mighty jewel-studded palaces of Ind, the fabulous undreamed-of glories of old Cathay . . . the wonderful realms he knew of reeled in her mind, entirely credible . . . Yet if he went to Europe now . . .

"Bohemond," she said casually while he reached for a *palacounta* from the silver tray, "do you recall that somewhere here in Antioch there is likely a sizable fortune to our hands?"

"H'm," he frowned at her, his mouth filled with the paste.

The stolen doors of Amalfi, But It is yourself who gave rise to the old rumor that they came to Antioch. Did you dissemble in this?"

He laughed a little ruefully. "No, Zoë. Who more than you could know I had not learned to be versed in it then?" He did not offer to pursue the subject, apparently not even attending.

Her color returned a little, for she was piqued. "Night after night, you've sat here casting about for possibilities of wealth ... Everything from kidnapping a Sultan to piracy and raiding the Jews! Why not discuss *this?*"

He shrugged and pulled her up from the divan by both hands. "Darling, if I thought they were here, and still with their lively secret locked within ... I'd have long ago sent troops through every street and alley ..."

"And give it advertisement?" she cried, pulling from his embrace. "Oh, no, Bo! Gold-thirst is not exclusive to *us* in this pack of noble thieves! Listen, I have thought this much, that they could not reside in a Moslem structure since the bronze depicts Nature which the Moors abhor ..."

He shook his head, interrupting her.

"I've neither time nor patience for obscure treasure-hunts, Zoë!"

"Well, *I* have!" she challenged him.

"Then try it, my dear, and have done!"

"You mean you'd loose me in this fantastic maze unprotected? Knave! There are subtler ways of dropping a tiresome friend!"

He put up his hands in mock defense. "Permission, protection, my good wishes—all—you will *have* them, Zoë. Only don't beshrew me! I need my fortitude for the journey to the Tomb!"

The next week, when Bohemond rode out of Antioch, Zoë received, crated in copper and with Bohemond's expressed love, a huge trained cheetah with a jewel-gauded silver chain.

CHAPTER XXIX *The Search*

IN THE LONG WEEKS that followed (Bohemond would need three fortnights, at least, to reach Jerusalem for the Christmastide) Zoë had much opportunity to pursue her search. The task was a lonely one, provocative of melancholy by its very nature. She could scarcely escape unsummoned meditation on her whole demesne, on this life of hers that was tawny, spotted with good and ill, bright, lustrous, sensuously fascinating as the coat of the cheetah. The glare of notoriety was on her full, and if, deep under, had lived some wish to be notable among her kind, it was now more than nourished. Bohemond was lavish with gifts. She had beautiful clothes and distinguished jewelry—thick barbaric gold torcs for her throat and arms acquired through Emir ben Merwan from the Copts of Egypt, and numerous bangles and rings, including a pair of ruby ear-pieces such as were worn by Muscovian chiefs. There were few knights' ladies here who did not envy Zoë; nothing she wore which they did not try to copy. The Latin *dames*, heretofore vain of their milky complexions, now coaxed a certain swarthiness to their necks and arms, spending uncomfortable hours on the flat roofs of their Turkish palaces.

Whether at large Holy Day affairs which on rare occasions she attended, or glimpsed on continual mysterious wanderings through the town, mounted on her rich-caparisoned horse with its gemmed poitrel, and heeled by Panturge and the cheetah straining at leash, she was the object of all eyes.

"By the faith!" Marcelle told her one late afternoon, "you are magnificent, madame! Would that seigneurs and great folks of the homeland could see my mistress now!"

Zoë's smile was a shade bitter as she pinned her towering white headdress over a gold lace caul. "Can't you imagine, Marcelle, the wonder we would cause in a triumphal journey home, my companions and I?" The hunch-backed page and the great cat stood ready for today's jaunt in the bright sunlight of the window-square. "The Prince's Saracen bucklers, his golden round-swords, even the spread tent of Kerboga, would scarcely be seen, I think, among us!" Said in jest seemingly light-hearted, the thought lay deep. She was still isolated, marked as ever. The times here and the mode of existence pursued by the transplanted barony which was paced by Bohemond himself had cast an unique fabric in which Zoë emerged the very essence of the dazzling design, but as exclusively indigenous to life here as was her brawny half-tamed beast to the jungle. It was untenable ever to think of departing from this particular domain, and she hoped against hope that Bohemond would never leave it, for only in this peculiar element could she stay in his ken.

A mysterious vintage, their love, the wine of a strange tree, so all-fulfilled, so much more marvelous than her dream of it, but with still so much in it troubling that sometimes she no longer caught at its essential wonder. Insecurity, dread of the loss of him, these *must* be the causes of her clamoring un-stillness, inescapable counterparts of so great a glory. This *must* be so and must thus be defended, even to the bold, disturbingly impressive stranger who one day remonstrated with her on these very matters.

With her protective retinue she had half-covered the district outside the Wall, a bowl in the wooded hills called the Vale of Daphne. It was a place filled with ruins of once-magnificent villa-palaces where the rich had spent their leisure time, and now tenanted by shepherds and the poor because of its dangerous location beyond the pale. The reasons for its pristine popularity were still here; its wild flower-beds and its shady groves with their sounds of swift springs rushing between the hillocks; rich scents of olives black on the slopes, of figs and of grapes dusty on the vines, the odor of pine and the murmur of turning wheels, and the brilliance of gold-and-russet blooms on the plumy pistachios.

There was nothing distinguished about the place where, with her seal-of-admittance from Bohemond, Zoë sought entrance on that quiet afternoon. It was a long, low, multi-corridored stone structure in the Graeco-Roman style like many another she had visited that month, and she only tried this for the fact that attached to it was a large church of late construction, whose high-vaulted style might well accommodate massive portals like the ones she sought. From the near-dwelling peasants she had learned that it sheltered certain priests, comparative recent comers, a reform branch of Cluny, called Cistercians, and after one more disappointment, she hurried to leave it, as she did all the rest of these holy houses where her appearance could be awkward as well as mysterious and a bit of a scandal. But here at St. Jean-de-Marie she was accosted with perfect aplomb by the house's abbot and engaged in quite an interlude of conversation in the rectory hall. Without knowing quite how it came about (she had been thus far successfully elusive) she found herself seated by the dais-end of the long oaken board with a tray of simple breads called God's-cakes set before her and a tumbler of mulled wine. She felt trapped, oddly frightened and as though alone, though Panturge and the cheetah had been offered places with her on the bench nearby. They had accepted after their insolent fashion,

Panturge slipping to the stones beside the bench and the cheetah lying close beneath her feet.

She looked at her host and was caught with interest. Father Domini was pushing the sweet things from his place, as if he had allowed himself served for courtesy but meant not to eat. He had strong but fine-boned hands, and they were ringless, which was an uncommon thing among even obscurest clerics in that day, and he used them rarely, permitting them to lie composed on the newels of the stiff-backed chair. He had a high, unlined brow, dark eyes, well-cut lips, and eyebrows that were naturally of a lofty arch, thick but not bushy. Zoë realized with a slight shock two things: that this face, sun-dark above the fall of the white Cistercian robe, was the handsomest she had ever seen, and that he was probably precisely her own age.

Or was he? Compared with Bohemond, whom unconsciously she had called to mind, his look was young, guileless, direct, and his eyes were warm. Irresistibly she thought of Bohemond as a young knight, flashes of him in the cathedral praying at the Tomb, brave in the tourney and eager in the wood, and she thought with a shock of his altered aspect. Beside Father Domini he would measure almost coarse. There it was, not age, but just that the Prince had somewhere lost that rare, fine, indefinably precious quality shown in this abbot's face. She checked herself. It was confusing to be thinking this; it obscured one's consciousness to what the man was saying. She could not be accused of inattention, it wasn't that. On the contrary her ears heard eagerly every inflection of his voice, which was soft, unstilted, but boldly pitched. He was obviously a noble, and she was strongly aware of the rich suffusion of his whole personality which yet did not intrude on the awesome quietness in this huge room where the soft afternoon sunshine fell in a pearly glow from the high arched window set in the wall above.

A middle-aged, rather fine-looking monk had been moving back and forth as they sat there, serving them, taking away the dishes which Father Domini did not touch. It seemed to Zoë that when he neared the abbot's chair, he paused there briefly, as though wishing to remain, and she watched him alertly as he shuffled out, wondering at this, and it was then that Father Domini asked her a question. She heard the upward swing of his inflection in her crowding thoughts.

"I—begging your pardon, Father," she said, surprised to be blushing, a thing she had not been accused of for a long time.

"I said," he paraphrased, "that you are probably thinking our servant somewhat oldish for a novice here. He is a layman, bound to the abbey for the time of his own self-taken vow, which happens, in his case, to be two years. It is not known, except to his confessor, why he came here, whether for sin or as offering for a loved relation, as pious widows sometimes do, with trentals for their time in life. Some serve here in this way, while others, bound by our rule and robed in our habit, take pilgrim-papers, reporting for releasement upon return. This is our work, madame, providing a method of salvation for lay sinners."

The calm, poised voice now paused a moment, then swept on again, oddly intimate.

"Sin, especially here, where we westerners come upon a new and dazzling world, is vivid and sensational, and we have sensational sinners. Some indeed need years to free themselves of strong, well-nourished burdens that ride them. Such must labor, fight, pray, until sometimes, maybe at life's very end, the enemy weakens, slips off, and finally lets them free."

This talk was embarrassing Zoë. This man was handsome, lively, obviously of the world in spite of his disconcerting directness and his simple robes, yet he spoke of sin as if he spoke of battle, using the old-fashioned word rather irritatingly in his every phrase. She, who could laugh so lightly over the tales of war, who could encourage the friends of Bohemond in their suave anecdotes of harlotry and blood, now felt discomfited.

The Legate Adhemar, though cut of the same cloth, had not so discomfited. He had warned and blustered. Father Domini conversed. Father Domini was commiserate, calm, completely courteous. She felt defenseless. She felt he was ruthless, that he might ask her anything that struck his mind, that in his courteous way he could calmly invade her soul. In the next moments he did just that.

"What," he inquired now, "what is it you seek? I confess my curiosity in it."

And she found herself telling him, sharing with Father Domini the secret of the doors, omitting the sole factor of Maurus's hidden money in the sides, and Father Domini accepted the tale, though it was plain he suspected a further exposition would be needed fully to explain her diligence in the search.

"Perhaps if you made petition to your patron sanctities," he now proposed.

And Zoë found herself announcing with a shrug that she was in poor straits for favors from on high.

Father Domini shrugged too. "Why do you not correct this matter, madame, *then* inquire?"

Zoë smiled a little crookedly. "You speak now as if you had not the instant previous intimated considerable understanding of sin. It so happens too that one would obviate the other. If I gave up my trespass there would be no pressing need for my diligence in this."

The abbot leaned forward, his smile intimate, his dark eyes pleading a cause.

"I see," he said gently. "You seek these certain portals for some end of the Prince, Bohemond."

"Well, yes," said Zoë, surprised to admission, and thinking that this was becoming too much. She would quickly take her leave.

But Father Domini bore on, leaving her no chance to interpose.

"Attend, madame. Have you once thought of the Prince's returning from the Holy Places, when he is cleansed, renewed, sanctified from powerful contacts there? Would you revivify his old lapse, become liable for both eventual everlasting deaths?" His face now darkened a little. "And there is another side to this. Selfishness, deception, importunate example, spread from themselves to the far edges of their orbit, like stones thrown in a pool. Prince Bohemond is a leader, not only in Antioch, but of the whole Crusade."

"Aren't you ascribing too much to one man—things that can better be laid to chance, fortuity? Even the weather?"

He shook his head. "Not more so than the individual's determination."

"What of the determination of God?"

Again he denied. "Haven't you observed that justice and good is not *forced* to be done? Else Prince Bohemond had been stricken dead, perhaps, at Maarat."

"What of our cry, then, 'God wills it!'?"

He smiled. "A mite presumptuous. Really we mean, 'We will what is good and may God permit our fortune!'—but that would be cumbrous at trumpet-time . . . We must snatch at mottoes . . ."

Zoë had had enough.

"What do you know of it, Father? What would you have me do? Drive him away? We *love* each other! He is my life!"

"And your death. You must know that we cannot grasp at all that seems desirable in this life. You are a singer, you must know!"

"Good Lord," cried Zoë. She rose, pushed back the bench, and paced the long boards before the dais. The cheetah followed her with tentative, cat-like complaints; a bright pair, lighting the shadows like flames. "I cannot live on songs; I am no callow, yearning girl; I have *known* him!"

"Of course, it is worse that way," said Father Domini calmly, watching her.

Zoë returned his scrutiny, feeling that she could not lose by flight now this contest of look, thought, and word which rendered her thus uneasy. She stood her ground, aroused and unconsciously intrigued. He had caught at her imagination, and the atmosphere tugged. It was a long season since she had looked upon a concept that challenged. Cast so long in a semi-world, held in a forge of indecision and self-deceit, she had escaped to the wayward realm of her stubborn will in Antioch. Such a course had been a form of freedom, as well as unimaginable happiness. But here was the obverse of the coin. Reason, truth, discipline. If she had been ignorant or cheap, she would have fled or deprecated it. But being neither, and well schooled in the elements here exposed, she meant to face it down. She was seeing herself in true focus and not from the sneers of the half-envious, nor the rantings of the fanatical, but from her own sort, taking a look at her from an all-too-understandable view. It was almost a relief, as of a boil bursting.

But it burned too. In her blazing green silken chiton with the Russian amethysts in her ears, she felt suddenly silly. The cheetah whined against her legs. She looked down, grimaced, and kicked him with her sharp-toed Persian boot. His beauty jarred; he was inappropriate, bizarre, and only comically bestial, the very grandeur of his brutishness rendered grotesque.

Father Domini was relentless, catching at her trend of feelings like a hound on the scent.

"Now this I believe of you, madame. You are not encompassed by ordinariness. You could well dispense with your fine clothes, your fair palfrey so costly and fat, and the services of that vicious knave who tends you!" (Panturge looked up at this, glaring.) "Anger, envy, gluttony in the usual sense do not confine you. It is a wanting, a covetousness, a beating of clipped wings. Confess it, madame!"

"That I shall not!" cried Zoë. She was breathing hard.

Father Domini waited. In the basilica the bells for vesper-time were sounding; there was a vague stir as of footsteps through the colonnaded halls.

"I shall pray for you, then," said the abbot, and in his eyes, luminous on the woman's face, there was no hauteur, only deep, commiserate understanding, and an abiding pity. And the humanity between them was so strong that Zoë resented this last with all her being.

"Don't hope too *much*," she said wryly. "It's as hopeless as I begin to think my quest for the doors is."

Father Domini smiled, a mixture of optimism and regret. "I shall pray for your doors, also, madame. Matins by our chapel limiter for your quest."

"Thank you, Father. Should I find them, I'll try your dose. I'll make a pilgrimage to some holy place myself, alone . . ."

Father Domini frowned. "Do not say such words, for mere sociability."

"No. I mean it, Father. And I'll add, to the general good of it, your own intention for my erring soul."

For the first time the splendid hands stirred.

"This is not lightly said?"

"*Far* from lightly, Father." By Sweet Christ's Tree, thought Zoë, I am not light on the finding of those doors!

But, though she crossed thereafter many more consecrated thresholds in the town of Antioch, the doors were fugitive, the prayers of Father Domini apparently not availing in this realm. At least Zoë caught at this, and proceeded to push from mind the strange salutary emotions she had been prey to at the abbot's hands. Only one thing he had said really daunted her: the idea of Bohemond and the effect of the pilgrimage. It was foolish, knowing his sanguine attitude to such things . . . yet, would there *be* such a thing that he would turn from her? Or, even for expediency, feel obliged to give her up? There were dreams from which she awoke sweating, where he sent her to Italy on the next vessel.

But, with the spring, Bohemond returned, heralded by messages to her. From the bank of the Jordan, from Valonia, from Laodicea . . . And finally one bright golden afternoon, he stood in the doorway of the Rue de Gloire.

Panturge flushed, hatred filling his eyes; the cheetah snarled without recognition; and it was small Ursule skipping across the rugs, vaulting into his arms and assaulting him with kisses, who made him know how he had been missed in Glory Street. Zoë, who had been mending a little frock, stood up so suddenly that the cloth, the bodkin and the thread fell in a small heap at her sandals.

He looked a little tired and she saw now that indeed the bright hair had grey showing, but the sight of him after four months produced in her the same shock of pure happiness, and she simply stood and looked at him, as though paralyzed with joy. He was gay and elated, telling her over Ursule's head how in Jerusalem all had gone well and how he had been received with a thunderous and triumphal ovation. He bore gifts for them all. Ursule was so taken with hers, especially the life-like doll with the odd slant-eyes which, he told her, had come by camel-train from far Cathay, that she rallied completely from the unwonted apathy that Zoë had seen in her in the previous hours. By the time, some two hours later, she was spirited from the scene by a coaxing Marcelle, she was still chattering, laughing and throwing a thousand kisses at "Bomun." She was overwrought—hysterical, really, and Marcelle, running her knotted fingers across the little brow, turned to inform Lady Zoë of what she thought. But seeing the tension growing there in the toy-strewn room, where their eyes were already fixed on each other with burning eagerness, the old nurse shrugged, smiled and retreated, resolving to ply her little charge with her own remedies; a bowl of distilled hellebore, and a dwale for sleeping, and a spurge, for the incipient fever. She listened awhile at the arras.

In the quiet luxurious chamber Panturge and the cheetah had been quickly scuttled out. There was a stirring among the rugs, which the gossip heard; the clink of armor and the swish of silk; and, at the last, the hushed, ardent, breathless exclamation and the long, drawn sigh . . .

CHAPTER XXX

Death into Dawning

IT HAD TURNED TO MIST on that next morning, that pale January day that Ursule lay in her high trundle and called "Mama! Mama! Oh, Mama!"

The sodden light lay prone across her coverlets in long grey bars, and the fog, blown from some storm-gust on the not far distant sea, seemed to pierce, chill, dampen everything it touched, mocking the great brass brazier they kept glowing there. Yet Ursule was not cold, but burning. She felt the wools hot on her back and the fever in her cheeks and she had in her throat a sort of choking fire, so that it hurt very much each time she cried out, "Mama! Mama!"

But oh, how she wanted her! How she longed to jump from bed and run to her, wherever she was! But some big weight-thing, something fearfully insistent seemed to press her down, seemed to blast her with warm waves of weakness when she tried to stir. Long since, she had yielded to the ogre-hand and lay quite flat upon the tossed and torn-up trundle, her little head hung from the edge of it, being terribly sick. Vague hurts, involuntary whimpers, racking shiverings of her whole small frame. Where, in all this, was the cool, bright, sweet-smelling, cuddling presence?

"Mama!"

Suddenly the arras-rings at her bed knocked together with a sharp, metallic click and Zoë stood there looking down. She was dressed in something shiny-bright, like wet sunshine, and a tight golden cap, and she had never looked so pretty.

"What is it, my darling?"

"Mama . . . I can't . . . Oh, Mama!" the tears welled and torrented.

Zoë's smile vanished. She sat on the trundle pulling the baby to her arms, running searching, experimental hands across the small body, the crumpled little face . . . She found the cold spurge on the swollen abdomen, pulled it out and threw it on the floor. There was the odor of sickness in the silky curls . . .

Ursule had stopped weeping. It felt so good to be pressed thus, to be nestled close and to feel that cool smooth cheek on one's burning one. But Mamma was excited or angry or both, because her heart was beating hard beneath the shimmering golden stuff, and she jerked at sheets and pulled things and pressed one back beneath the blankets with strange cries of "Sweet, my sweet! Stay warm now . . . Be quiet and still . . . O dear God . . . Marcelle!"

The old one came running, her eyes puffed with sleep.

"What is the meaning of this?"

"I *know*, madame. Is it not to weep? Lord, all night—packings and physics and packings again . . . Here's another. What d'you suppose she ate?"

Zoë knocked the dripping hot poultice to the floor. "Don't touch her with that! It's no good and it's not something she ate. My God, all night . . . Why didn't you tell me!"

Marcelle stood with her baggy jowls ajar, eloquently nonplussed, so that there were several reasons for the resounding hard blow on the ear which Zoë administered to her. In her own cheeks were bright flags of fear, outrage and something like not-to-be-looked-at shame.

"Now, trull! Get me a sponge and basin!"

Bohemond loomed in the door. She did not look at him and her voice was one she might use to a stranger as she said, "It's—it's that swollen worm-thing in the side that Messer Poldi knew of." Then, pleadingly, directly to him, "Bo, my God! What shall I *do?*"

Bohemond had already hurried to the trundle and sat holding Ursule's little head while she was once more sick on the floor beside it. "Poldi lanced those, didn't he? Then it must be lanced. Send the hunchback for my physician and we'll meantime make a dwale from those gilly-bloom powders in my saddle-bags. We've used them to deaden wounds. Hurry. There's precious little time, I suspect, as it is!" Indeed, Ursule was now crying aloud with pain, and once while they waited, she sent out a piercing shriek that seemed to scatter the daylight, and Zoë and Bohemond looked at each other, tight-lipped with fear.

And when the leeches came, physicians he had called, both Frank and Moslem, they consulted and murmured with one another and shook their heads, the swelling in the little abdomen being meantime significantly vanished. One of the bleeders, a little Syrian, dared to give hope because of this, at which Bohemond shouted at him in a terrible voice, pointing out to him the pain, the sweat and the terrible pallor on the tossing little face and in a high rage dismissed him. For all along they knew the fatal tale. It was too late. Zoë had moved among them doing the necessary things mechanically, and then on the second day, she settled down on the end of the trundle in a quiet paralysis of grief, with no further move save for a slight rocking of her body as she watched; and sometimes a voice came from her that was unrecognizable, dead-toned and bitter, saying, "Messer Poldi knows how to save her. Even now, Poldi would know. Messer Poldi of Amalfi . . ."

Marcelle was huddled in a gross heap at the bed-foot, desolated, and Mohanna of Maarat, the governor's captive daughter, sat quietly by, her pretty eyes on Lady Zoë, suffering along with her, for Zoë and she had never been but good, close friends.

Bohemond stood looking from the window-square out over the flat white rooftops, as he had stood for the greater part of two days now, all his activities suspended and a guard posted at the door below to fend interruptions. But he had not approached the bed for some time. The last move he had attempted, meaning to give some word of comfort and a hand-pat to the child, Zoë had leapt to the head of the trundle like some distracted animal and the white hot-eyed face she had turned to him wore an indescribable expression of anguish, jealousy and despair, so that the whole effect was the look of madness. It was not Zoë's face, but mask-like and almost bestial. And when, at about the ninth hour, the little one stirred no more, he must look again upon that terrible mask-like visage as she turned to them and uttered hoarse and deep in her throat the words: "Out! Out! Get out!"

She had seemed not to mark Mohanna the Mohammedan girl. Therefore Bohemond signed her to remain, and his last sight of Zoë was her slim form prone across the trundle.

Pictures of Zoë thus, pictures of her sorrowful and anguished, mingled with pictures of Ursule as the little one had been—dear to him indeed for her own sweet presence and for sheer pleasure he had snatched with her from busy days, when over dragon-books and bestiaries their two heads had bent in a mingling of the dark and golden, tormented Bohemond in those after-days; kept him melancholy by day and haunted in dreams by night; and gave him thoughts that he did not care for. He was not cold, nor did he wish to be unaffected. He suffered the same sorrow that a father would know and more—a panicked sensation at the break-up of those happy days which for three years now had been a part of himself. Now, he knew, neither for himself nor Zoë would it be the same. Ursule had been the part of their relationship that was at once the sweetest and worst, and this insight produced in him a terrible dread. There was a new fear intrinsic in it which he did not admit to himself, until one day after the funeral, he went to the apartments in the Rue de Gloire and found her gone. She had vanished, traceless and with no word.

He walked through the rich rooms, the key faintly jingling against his hand-ring and his spurs harsh between the rugs until, hearing a slight creature-noise between a snarl and a growl, he turned, to see the cheetah poised beneath the arras of the great main chamber. He stopped still as though commanded by the sensitive twitching maw and the restive tail, feeling all too well the animal's inexpressible aura of danger. Then the big cat walked silent and stately into the next room, ignoring him, and flopped down with a prodigious yawn on the low table. Bohemond sank down upon the plush ottoman, weak from a sense of desolation, even of fear, and nursed his jaw where the pain of a rotten tooth had been stabbing him for some days past. He watched the cat with annoyance. It somehow angered and disgusted him that the silly animal could look so potent one minute and so undignified the next. This and the silence beating upon him with its peculiar clamor made him hasten to leave.

But the new feeling of loneliness and nameless dread was most difficult to shake. He mourned still for Ursule and languished for Zoë, even disinterestedly, for his nature was sensitive and naturally vicarious and he wished to find her just so that he could comfort her. And also, he thought very much of Mihera for the first time. He found himself actually being angry with Mihera for leaving his dear ones, then must needs catch himself up short, recalling with a new sting his own maneuverings. He tried to forget the dull uneasiness all this brought, like the sore tooth. But unlike the tooth, he could not get rid of it, and if occasionally he did, the very fact was worrying to him, insistent on certain facts about himself, commentaries that he was something less than formerly.

He could look in polished surfaces and see a splendid man, still handsome, imposing, princely. But impelled by tooth-gaps and silver hairs that others might not see, even an ache or two from old wounds that had not heretofore complained, his attention was called to the fragility of this changing self in which he was placing so much of dreams and hopes for in-the-future projects. The unwonted introspection had come because he had planned that private paradise for himself and Zoë—and for his city, but Ursule was suddenly no more, and Zoë was faded into Antioch and its labyrinthine ways; he had lost them, and he could lose Antioch itself if he did not take care; and against this final eventuality he now threw all his formidable strength.

In North Syria the Turks were menacing the towns of his Armenian ally, Kogh Vasil. The fort of Melatia was being sieged by hordes of raiders under the rich, famous and powerful Emir Ibn Danishmend, lord of Siva. For Melatia Bohemond now planned a masterful campaign that was said to be the peer of his best. But then one day his army straggled back to Antioch with a stupefying tale.

Bohemond had been celebrating in his late profligate fashion in the slums of the town of Artah. Next morning was to be the sally. He turned up late, looking as though he had raked the pits of Hell itself, and rode out with a force much smaller than his advisers had counted on; Danishmend was waiting in a mountain cleft and Bohemond was taken, sped away in the midst of the howling Mohammedan army, and was now held in a mountain fortress for unspeakable ransom.

Now to the court of Antioch in that same week had come a delegation from Jerusalem with a bid for Bohemond to come and be King, for Godfrey had lately died. But the priest Morellus and his plenipotentiaries found themselves summarily split in two and sent on the high roads; one mission to Edessa to get Baldwin to go to Palestine, the other to Palestine to tell Tancred to ride up to Antioch with all dispatch.

CHAPTER XXXI

Out of the Shadows

"AND NOW BY your good leave, Sire," said the ancient knight Longveult, "there are two letters this morning that should be tended to at once."

"Whose, pray?" asked Tancred testily, all silver and silk where he sat in the sunlight at the writing-board in the Room of the Throne. From his turned-up tasseled slippers to his artificially curled hair he was attired most richly in the eastern mode; breeches of soft saffron-dyed leather, and a stiff silk tabard of purple and blue, held in place by a jewel-trimmed baldric. He still looked incredibly young, but in these three unwilling years as regent for the captive Bohemond, his sulky under-lip had become more pronounced and habitual, and pointed up the pampered, yet put-upon quality of his golden looks.

"There's one from Palestine and one from Sir Bohemond," Longveult irresistibly added, involuntarily extending the one with the Prince's seal.

"Indeed," said Tancred, leaning from his chair, "give me the first, and lay Sir Bohemond's on the table there—it contains doubtless nothing but his usual complaints—and then you may go."

There was a slight maliciousness in the rude dismissal, but his haste was for more than that. The green parchment from Palestine had Baldwin's ribbons on it and he rose, ripped it, read and threw it to the floor with a flood of obscenities. " 'Sblood!" he exploded. "There goes Bethlehem!"

Longveult had quietly remained. Tancred now turned to him. "You should see, Longveult, the sweet row of lands I had—vineyards and olive groves and Saracen castles all the way from David's tower to the Tomb. Baldwin's been aching to seize them and now that the two years of absence-from-fiefs are more than gone, he rightly reminds me that they are confiscate. You see before you a baron *sans* barony, a lord without lands, a churl no better off than your own hired lances."

"Begging your pardon, young Sir," said Longveult, "but no sooner will the Prince return than he'll give you ample feudatories for your service here."

Tancred whirled and paced, his silver shoes a swishing whisper on the polished mosaics. "Aye, a few towns, a couple of castles, a slight sop for *me* and a safeguard for the borders of his own domains! Don't you know how he functions! Christ, what a fool I've been." He stood a moment looking up at the great central throne which Bohemond had seldom used, as if in its golden emptiness he had caught the shadow of his captive uncle.

"Come, Sire," again ventured Longveult, "without Antioch or with Antioch in Moslem or Greek hands there would *be* no Palestinian fiefs! Even now we are hard-pressed. All about us the Greeks prowl, and the great Turk chiefs, Rudwan, Kilij Arslan and the rest, are stirring again, like beasts after winter sleep. I am an old man, Sir Tancred, and will not live to see the rest of it, but mark me well—to fetch the Prince from exile is the hope of our eastern sovereignty. Your own fine armies have thus far banked the flood, but then, should I show you the new map being drawn this very fortnight by Thibault the cartographer, it would jolt you to see how the orbit shrinks. Beware, Tancred. Be not disparaging of that powerful hand. It is indispensable, especially when even our own inveigh against us." The old counselor spoke not as an adviser to haughty regent, but as venerable knighthood to young, with all the authority which under the old code this implied.

Tancred was truculent, even impudent. "Baldwin produces fifty thousand gold pieces, the Patriarch of Antioch upwards of 40,000. But that, Sir, does not add up to the terrible sum that Kumishtakin demands!"

"Then gather it here," cried Longveult. "Publish placards, send criers, pinch the Jews! Use all the variety of method not heretofore thought of. We must deliver the Prince!"

Tancred shrugged calmly. "Very well, Longveult. I hereby place the charge to you; try your luck, Sir, and see how far you get!"

And Longveult left him plucking a hair from his saffron breeches.

How long Zoë had been sitting there in the black ruin she did not know. It was near sunset and the other lay-portress, if she meant to obtain the last comforts for this dying man, should be back by now with Father Domini. The old almsman, lying on the rush-pile in the hideous disorder of the burned-out sanctuary, was long past conversation, and Zoë merely sat in his vicinity where he might obtain some comfort from a human presence if indeed he could see her any longer through those rheum-filled eyes.

She had visited so many such in the past months as lay-portress among the poor of Antioch that she was inured to hardship and trouble and death and all their neighborhood, and she could derive tranquility of sorts in these very presences. Indeed, she had found these

scenes of desolation easier to live with than certain other aspects of
the convent life she had found herself caught in, for they seemed like
a genuine part of nature rather than what seemed to her a constant
escape from it. A type of that wintry happiness had been able to over-
take her such as she had known in the dreariest hours in Burg Ughol
Wood. Even as then, when she lived in an alien world of stark, un-
softened reality, so she lived now, for no remnant remained of the false-
bright days she had fled except Panturge, who had hung about half-
starving, determined to stay near her like some faithful beast, until
they had allowed him to make his way in the monastery scullery.

Yet now, and for some weeks past, that blessedly restful peace had
been trying to elude her. As she sat here on the stone flight of steps
that once had mounted belfrywards but which now arrived at
nothing, and held her restless gaze on the jagged horizon, and on the
liquid fiery sky, even now and for the hundredth time the instinct of
escape attacked her, the feeling that she wished to break from this
oblivion like a condemned man fleeing the gallows. The peaceful
though desolate scene, the aura of quiet death inherent in it, and even
her own appearance, nun-habited and closely veiled, was exactly opposite to the way she felt, that irresistible yearning for exciting avenues
which also she had felt at the Salerno hall. So far she had hidden,
indeed stifled, the feeling. All her days in the Cistercian convent neighboring the monastery hall were helpful to this, and she clung to the
company of the silent, self-mortifying nuns and the occasional counsel
of Father Domini as a drowning man to a raft.

For stronger yet than the desire for another life was the memory
of the first and indeed second year following Ursule's death, when
she had so intimately known remorse and self-condemnation that she
had tasted not only a physical debility, but the hell of madness. The
fragility of her own nature had been made so manifest in that time
that she feared to try herself unanchored, even in her natural desire
for a more congenial existence than this—like a child who, once fallen
painfully from a forbidden fence-top, fears to tread the curb in the
street.

For a long time, while the sun lowered, Zoë gazed at the round
red bowl as it swam behind the pointed black pinnacles of these palaces and sanctuaries that Bohemond had once ordered burned to rout
an army. There was no sound but an occasional labored sigh from the
old man. No bird sang in the ruined sky. The language of the night
was color. The rays from that dying crimson eye had painted the clouds
swept up to it, had stained the earth before it, and even here in the
drab rubble laid fringes of splendor on the far standing wall of the
church. It burnished what marble was left, searing it so that
pillars stood out with momentary restored luster, so that on the altar-

dome the blistered paints could blaze for a happy instant with a pristine glory. And there where the soot clung and the scorch had stained the metal a brassy red, the lofty pointed doors . . . the doors . . .

She sat there looking up at the brazen portals and at the lineaments revealed where she had rubbed away the soot with her mantle-hem, long after the riotous lights in the west had vanished, long after the stars had come and the blue mist filled with hints and half-shapes of the upper firmament had slid into the almost roofless temple and lay about it. When Father Domini at last appeared with the younger nun and administered final sanctified comforts to the now-unconscious ancient, Zoë was unable to keep her eyes from the huge forms standing upright in the vast fragmentary transept. Almost before the Cistercian had replaced the consecrated objects in his leathern pyx, she approached him with incredible tidings.

She could see the other nun's slim form moving dimly in the ruined garden. In watches like this she said her devotional offices peripatetically, pacing with the great restlessness of the very young. Zoë beckoned to the priest and almost with cunning extended a trembling pale hand to show him the doors. She showed him the figures, the first man and Eve, and the serpent posed coiled yet upright between the two, with the fruit held daintily in his fanged jaws, blue in moonlight. She tapped the metal for Father Domini, unable to hide here the ineffable thrill that they still contained the fabulous burden that made them seem truly dense.

Then she seated herself before him, her head held high and almost haughtily, and her eyes held that mocking gleam that lent to her wimpled face an alive, reaching, almost singing expression and lighted her outwardly resigned and even sad features.

"You see," she said, "how really unfortunate my luck is! And especially unfortunate for *you*, Father! With all your traps set to keep me from traveling on the outward road. I have felt you setting them even when you sat for hours with the others at my bed, and I scarcely knew you were there, for the enveloping sickness that tore me in that awful season. I heard the beads clicking and felt your prayers, and I am not ungrateful. But if you thought that like a burned child I would turn chastened and with permanent resolution to conventical calm, you were wrong! I'm a rebel in your midst, and my inevitable outbreak would outrage those vows should I ever take them. Let me be truthful. As God is my witness, Father, I am sick of this. It seems like death, as nothing-like as death is. I keep thinking that everywhere in the world but in our walls—everywhere but among us—things are happening. I cannot keep these pictures from my mind. The Crusades, new kingdoms . . . I dream about them. And now, cut off, set free as I am, I have crazy aspirations—joining an army and fighting just as Sigelgaita did when we were all young . . . When we were all young, Father! To think how all has been lost and misdirected and come to misery since then, even the Crusade . . . My dream is to ride everywhere, Father, among those cheated, corrupted, led-astray peoples and tell them how it was in the old days and how it was meant to be now; how Hildebrand and Urban meant it to be—valor, unity, loyalty, not greed and chaos . . . In songs, perhaps, as my father used to do."

Father Domini, listening to the end, had been at first concerned, for indeed he thought she might be going mad, but now he sank down on the shards of the chapel wreckage, his graceful mantle spread about him in a pool, and laughed.

"My dear Lady Zoë . . ." (She started a little at the use of her name for the first time in months, since before she was addressed as Sister Esme.) "My dear Lady," said Father Domini, "you are mistaken in two things. First, that we of the rule had designs to bind you, and secondly that you are cut off, as you phrase it—set adrift. I am overjoyed to see you returned to your own spirits, which we know as well as you are not congenial to our cloistered ways. If I had known you were chafing thus, I'd have sent you forth long since. But not, Lady Zoë, to your own meanderings—to lose yourself on some insupportable tangent as you did before. In a fortnight, or as short a time as it will require to arrange it, we shall send you and your brazen portals home."

"Home!"

"Yes, madame. Home to Count Mihera. With Mihera of Amalfi we have been in closest correspondence for some time. He is most anxious to receive you as soon as the recovery from your illness, which he has been most concerned about, permits. His own ships, indeed, would be here for you but for altercations now going forth—Pisans, Genoese and your own Amalfitans—for rights on the Middle Sea. All that, too, will be righted, now that the Barons have ransomed the Prince Bohemond. There will be peace once more . . . Strengthened outposts . . . Security . . ."

He mentioned the name Bohemond carefully, but when Zoë spoke again it was not of him, and her words hinted at a new outlook that her latter experience must have brought, which gladdened the heart of Father Domini, for he mistook them.

"Mihera," she said. "I would be loath to look into the face of my Lord Mihera." Momentarily the mocking gleam left her eyes but then he saw the look that he, so knowing of the ways of sinners, passionately dreaded—the set defiance. For in recalling that spirit which she had for so long not thought of, she remembered the overtones of proud, unassailable righteous thinking, the dogmatic enforcement that went with it, all characteristically administered for the good of the order for a long, long time, and she balked. It seemed that this would indeed be the epitome of punishment, all the more so since it was mightily deserved.

"I shall not go back! Indeed, I shall remain here, become a nun or an almswoman or a beggar like this poor devil here, first!"

"I see that you are not actually prepared," he said, "and in that case you are more than welcome to remain till you come about." She cast him a look full of commentary on his own brand of stubbornness. "You know, Lady Zoë, I love your name, and I like to say it, for Zoë in the Greek is 'invitation to life,' to that true life which is come by only in surrender to His way, which is the essence of freedom itself . . . But you are not listening, I see . . . You gaze upon the doors . . . Then let us speak of them. They, if not you, can be immediately transported home. They can be sent as a sort of promising precursor, if you please."

Unfortunately this touched broadly one more facet of Mihera's remembered ways, and Zoë laughed outright, a weird sound in the moonlit ruins which made the other nun look inward. The nun heard her companion say to Father Domini, "I myself would indeed be an anticlimax to the contents of those!" And she saw Father Domini cast Sister Esme such a severe look, while he mumbled a harsh exclamation under his breath, that she hastily took to her beads again, thinking she had interrupted a grave confession of some sort.

They were both aroused now, fully antagonistic, almost as they had been on that occasion when Zoë had first encountered Father Domini. She knew he was after her, and his very posture, calm and serene as it had been on that other day, made her angry.

The Cistercian broke first, or seemed to. He seemed to have slipped his calm defenses for the first time.

"Bohemond!" he said. "You think of Bohemond. You think to send the doors home as a way of payment, and to remain . . . Is that it, Lady Zoë?"

She saw his eyes plead, his forehead furrow in an expression of unworded entreaty, which, though rendering her drunk with a real sense of her actual freedom, inclined her suddenly in natural swift sympathy to wish to make him happy.

"Don't fret," she said. "On that score I would not *wish* to tease you, Father, were it even possible. All that is truly over. Even in the thinking of it—all I must do is remember those last days when little Ursule lay wanting attendance by the one man who alone could have saved her, of whom she was cheated by that very wish . . ."

And Zoë sat quietly before Father Domini and wept.

But presently one day, when from other errands of charity she traveled down Antioch's suburbs to the Vale, she smiled to think of Father Domini's planning for her strong, new life. She suspected her-

self. She could conjure up Father Domini as she could conjure up
Bohemond, recall every look, action and word that he had said, in the
long course of spiritual instruction that he had given her. She could
recall and be swept away on a tide of all-fulfilling experience she
could scarcely resist. She suspected herself, but for one thing: What
Father Domini *said,* commanded, exhorted her to do bore more weight
than the actual personality of the man himself. Her thoughts continually turned as they had not turned for many seasons to Mihera.

There were still wrong feelings when she thought of him—guilt,
fear, rebellion, dread—but always now, she veered from these thoughts
and made herself think less perilously. Of his face, Mihera's face when
actually he saw those thousands of pieces of gold, and she laughed
outright, until she saw some Antiochians looking, and she reminded
herself of how she must appear, a nun traversing Antioch on a mule,
laughing . . . But then, she thought, three years, six ago, I did not
think Mihera's tightness droll, his tightness and his sharpness and
the rest. But they are! No more than droll, and not matters to break
up peace, home and rightful marriage over! Perhaps that means I'm
free, beginning to be *really* free, of rebellion, and passion and all those
plagues . . .

And she rode along in the brilliant Antioch sunshine feeling
light and healthful and full of a new spring-like joy, and delighted in
everything she saw; the bright striped awnings of the street, the
markets and the beautiful swarthy children and later in Daphne the
shepherds tending their flocks on the little hills. For the first time in
long she desired a lute, a zithern, anything to aid in a little song, for
titillating phrases rose to her mind like bubbles in a fresh clear pool.
But for propriety she stopped her humming as she cantered through
the gates of St. Jean-de-Marie.

And yet, as she dismounted, a small glance into the bird-bath, standing still and crystal-clear, let her see without vanity that her face, this
evening, was very beautiful.

CHAPTER XXXII *The Gauntlet*

BOHEMOND FOUND IT HARD to get back to the swing of Antioch. All was changed, all was difficult; there was a feeling of desperateness. He saw at once these things with his characteristic immediacy. He missed the Crusaders and the old, genuine spirit that he shared with them and it made him restive. A Crusade, a new one against Alexius would be the answer to his own troubles as well as those of the Christian world. A new Crusade.

But to plan this, for a year there was nothing but work and battle. He rarely saw Antioch save on quick occasions when he bargained and chaffered with the Venetians and Pisans and the sanguine Genoese, till he was weary and disgusted (what terms the rascals asked!). Then he was off again to Valania or Laodicea or Ezas to break a siege. Alexius now hounded his outposts with his imperial armies frankly and in full cry.

But in one year, by colossal efforts and frantic concentration of his still matchless powers, he achieved the renewal and enforcing of the entire province, so that presently, in the late fall, he could think of the run to Europe. This was no child's play. He must thread the sea-way past the very eyes of Constantinople and it was wide knowledge now that every soldier, pilgrim and priest, every cut-purse and beggar on the west-bound road was being stripped, searched and questioned, and ships and vehicles ransacked by the border lords of Alexius Comnenus for signs of the Prince of Antioch.

Therefore he planned a strange and daring thing. He told no one. He spent his time on the Quay, quietly seeing his galleys loaded, spending days at what had taken only hours to do in the hands of his equerries. One morning at the docks, engaged in this mysterious business, he observed a strange sight, one which produced in him that odd feeling that this had happened before: enormous bronze doors—they shone in the sunlight—being carried by beasts to the maw of a waiting vessel. A score of mules were dragging at the thongs. There was nothing strange about it. Crosses for monasteries, enormous lead-filled windows, objects of every size and contour found their way here and were daily discharged or loaded on this dock that was ancient in the time of the Seleucids. But Bohemond felt his hackles rise as he watched this, and then the sight of a hunch-backed, deformed frame among the porters sent him forth like a bolt from a bow.

"*Where is she,* dog?"

Panturge howled in the steely grip.

"*Where is she? Take me, you foul and misbegotten troll, before I twist the hide from your skinny carcass!*"

Two nights later, when the thirteen vessels sailed, the night was noisy and the sky restless with swift scudding clouds. Bohemond stood in the stern-lee of his own huge black-painted bireme, making his farewells to the knights. Above him voices barked and sail fluttered. The wind was ready.

He drew a deep breath, stretched forth his gauntlet and crossed forearms with all. There were only four—Tancred, old Longveult, Gerald d'Avesnes, and young Vieuxpont, his steel cap blazed with the arms of fresh-dubbed knighthood.

They stood about, these new-made Syrian barons, these lords of outlandish places, and cast about for enough to say to him. It was so much because of him, handsome, cordial, huge in the moonlight, that they had had the incredible adventure, the new power, and the yet-to-be-dreamed-of wealth . . . Even the sheer novelty of stabling their destriers at the Inn of Bethlehem! They stood about and looked at him, with no words to express the things they felt.

Bohemond was all business. "Is the tale well spread?"

"Like jam on a god's-cake, Sir!" cried young Vieuxpont, his stout face shining with his emotions.

"The pennons on the Five Gates are hung a-droop, and the ladies of the thousand palaces all weep in their pretty veils," said old Longveult, grinning nobly through his senile tears.

Bohemond looked at them, unconsciously missing faces like Godfrey and Adhemar and the rest, and thinking that none here would truly miss him. Longveult's was the sentiment of age, and Vieuxpont's of youth, and Tancred had God-knew-what dirty little schemes waiting to be fixed up as soon as his back was turned. He lifted his eyes above them to the Wall of Antioch, its turrets and bastions purple in the night, and his gesture was to these much more than to those who watched, as he raised his arm and cried, "Good-bye, good luck, rest happy, gentlemen. I shall return with ten thousand lances!" And with the litheness of a much younger man, he bounded up the gangway.

Her head heavy, filled with a strange dull ache, Zoë slowly awakened on the narrow bunk. It *seemed* like her own small pallet in the convent cell—hard, unroomy, yet oddly conducive to rest when one had grown used to it. But it seemed also to be rolling, and the roof to be flickering; all seemed astir in a new kind of mysterious motion.

Then, as she gazed, the flicker became space and the space a hatchment oblique in the wall through which a sail showed. A sail! Pictures of pirates, *latrons,* of Egyptian slavers raced in her brain. "God-a-mercy!" She sprang up in terror.

"Please, Lady!" a soft voice said. "We bear towards your home-land in a ship from Antioch."

"Mohanna!" The sight of the slave-girl brought thoughts that were no less terrifying. She sank back to the pallet. Madness finally? "Home! I had passage home, to be sure, but what . . . ?"

"It's *all right,* madame," repeated Mohanna soothingly. "You were apprehended, stolen by night from the house in Daphne . . ."

"Stolen! And you . . . ?"

Mohanna smiled. "Many of us were gathered, willing or not, be-neath these thirteen sails. *Maimoun* commands."

Shock, relief, then anger. "Mother of God. Where are we now?"

"They say we hold a fair wind between Cyprus and the Land of Rum." As she talked she proffered huge spoonfuls of acrid mutton broth, long mulling on the brazier. This and the smells of oil, cheese, wine and fish-oil that wafted through the hole in the bulk-head nigh ruined Zoë's appetite, but she sipped obediently.

"Three days since they administered the wart-dwale, Lady. *Maimoun* feared it was overmuch . . ."

"Three days? I should think *so.*" Hot indignation buoyed her against the dragging weakness. Footsteps sounded above.

"Is that, now, the gentleman?" she asked with savage emphasis.

"I daresay, madame."

"No, don't call him. I can quite manage." She stood up. She found herself adequately dressed in yellow wool, her hair well-brushed and neatly filleted, and her feet clad in soft red leather sandals. "Thank you, my dear," she acknowledged, leaning on the Moslem girl a mo-ment to be helped with a cloak. Then kicking the small train of the gown behind her, she essayed the hatchway, taking as she went great breaths of the same good air that filled the canvas above.

Above-decks a strange, new, and macabre setting met her eyes. Fresh-painted boards rocked gently beneath her tentative footsteps, and she saw that the whole thing was a superstructure built on the prow-end of a long, low scull-of-war. Far forward, directly behind the jagged hackles of the brow-beast itself, was a huge, carved, ebony sarcophagus, flanked by laurel-wreathed catafalques with thick tow-brands in them, not yet lighted. No one was to be seen. Bohemond, if indeed it had been he, must have meantime gone below, and she gave her intrigued attention to the sea-view ranged about. Some dozen large vessels, most of them short, thick-bellied merchant-barks called roundships, came on behind, flying Genoese crown-and-tritons with the scarlet de Hauteville pennants sub-imposed. Between the double rows of oarsmen in the wide deck-waist were vast, chattering sea-sick mêlées: black slaves, pale dancing women, tents, war-chariots, captive sheiks clad in purple and gold. On each ship, staked in its very center, were large objects: pavilions or war-engines; and in one a white dromedary with trappings of ivory and blue. Rows of bucklers hung on the fat prows like precious girdles—long shields, round ones, even Greek shields taken from warrior eunuchs in Cilicia with golden eyes painted in golden circles. The East was advancing on Paris.

From an amazed survey of all these and certain other strange cargo Zoë's gaze returned to the huge black artifact on their own ship, and she smiled. It did not occur to her to think Mohanna dissembled, that the oriflamme dipped might indeed mean Bohemond's demise, and that he was cached between the catafalques. This broad vista of gigantic buffoonery displayed his unmistakable stamp. It was his kind of show. He *must* be about, somewhere, running it.

A warm feeling of unconscious pleasure, completely innocent, engulfed her, to think that her homing was to be like this—not drear and lonely as she had planned it in Daphne, but in the midst of lively company with a lively friend. So, now, she could view it, and gladness brushed her mind with the soft rush of a swift's wings, leaving her utterly serene as she stood there above the hatchment scenting the wind. Just then there was movement at the stern, beyond the sarcophagus, and Bohemond strode out from the other side.

He stood at the far end of the sarcophagus, his bright sunlit head poised against its depthless shadows. Suddenly in the sun she saw the hard contours of his face—a half-frown, with his lips tightened, the grey eyes narrowed to slits, giving the impression that he was in throes of silent and gloating laughter, and for a small moment she was afraid. "Zoë!"

He covered the deck between them in two strides, and with a sound of deep laughter caught her up and set her down again as he would a child. It washed through her mind that his person was never so powerful as now in the height of crisis, so crested with the triple surges of ambition, lust and greed. It came from him like the dry fumes of a heady wine.

"I was beginning to doubt the dose!" he told her. "I'd have put back to Antioch to help peel off that apothecary's hide . . . Here!" He leaned to the lee-bench where he had a bowl of wine half finished. "I've been calming my nerves . . ."

"*Your* nerves!" she remarked coolly, taking a long draught from the cupful he proffered her. "'Body, can I have no peace? I was already set for home; Mihera sent monies, had obtained my passage . . . It was my aim, purpose and pleasure. Do you understand? Why all this business of potions and apothecaries and footpads in the night? Don't think you'll add *me* to this parcel of wonders to drag through

Europe! I'm bound for Amalfi, *ami,* for the good life and uncompli-
cated love!"

Zoë tossed off the remainder of the cup and stood looking up at
him.

She stood there in the sea-cape and the soft wool gown, dangling
the wine-cup in her hand, her sunburned features denting to little lines
that were piquant rather than hard. She stood there incredibly young
and vital, it seemed to him, but sharp-tempered and bold, not lush-
eyed and half-coquettish as befitted her; not regal and passionate as
he wished. She, in fact, looked untidy in spite of Mohanna's care. But
it was indifference to her own surface appearance before him, and no
lack of beauty itself, that once more angered him. The mention of
Mihera in those cool tones she used seemed to conjure up the half-
Englishman, and Bohemond found his tones as stiff as if Mihera were
actually here, as he said, warily, "How could I know your plan? You
seemed set on getting lost, lately . . . I made sure you wouldn't.
Therefore Mihera would owe me thanks, no? Besides, good friendship on the voyage home . . . Do you grudge me?"

Her chin lifted in delight. "No!" she said, happy as a child. "I
share your happiness in it, Bo! I complained of your *methods,* not your
company!" A small grin told him she was not taken in, accepting
the bargain to be fanciful for him, a small smile, impudent, and insolent too, with no archness in it. The sea-blue eyes, narrowed in the
sun, were brilliant and full of a kind of joy, and suddenly he almost
hated her. He hated, yet wished to possess. Not only to possess (his
knuckles whitening on the rail), but to destroy; to destroy that bright,
secret, insolent joy in the blazing storm of their embrace.

Zoë was walking about the deck, in her free way, in spite of weakness and the wine, not mincing a step, examining the catafalques, the
tow-sconces and the black sarcophagus, running her sunburnt hands
over the shining patina of its surface.

"So this is your death-box?" she asked him lightly.

"Yes." The very casualness of her question piqued him. Faced with
danger and shadowed by death, he could not brook her lightness,
though he himself could make a joke about it.

"Alexius would not suffer me alive, so I present myself for his
inspection—dead," he said, half-consciously courting her concern.

"But what if they board us, Bo?" She threw out her hands. "How
could they possibly resist to have a last look at your thunder-striking
face?"

"Never fret," he said dryly. "They will look, but not long. Live
men do not care for the actual contours of the charnel-house and the
stink of the grave."

"Oh!" she speculated. "Stink-pots, as in a siege?"

"Nothing so clumsy. But even then it's a long gamble. We cannot reckon too confidently, of course. They may *really* inspect, in which case—la!—the end of me . . ."

She laughed—laughed like a child let in on a wonderful game. He could not abide it. His mouth was a tight line.

"Why do you laugh?"

"*You die?*" she said. "Ridiculous! If Alexius Comnenus caught you, *you* would not die! Alexius has Chinese conjurers and star-glasses and even a sun clock that signals him from the hills, and other wonders. He would keep *you* as the first prize in his whole collection!"

She was standing before him now, and before he knew, his hand had reached out and struck her.

"Stop talking rot!"

He had her by both shoulders, glaring savagely, while she with one hand at the welted cheek glanced up at him, not so much with hurt or anger, but a questioning appeal. It flashed to his mind that she had never looked so appealing, yet so completely untouchable, since Sicily. He roughly released her and stalked down the deck.

The fleet flew on, its square sails bellied with the abiding wind, with the long jutting spurs of Rum on one side and those scattered little isles called Naxia to port, making more headway by night than day, and traveling fully fifteen miles each hour of sunlight. And then one day the wind veered, sails were lashed up, the oarsmen strained forward, and the hot gale began to hiss at them from Africa. It was a thing they had feared. In the shipping-world no galley was scheduled east from April on, for none might sail west safely between September and January. They were bearing west in late November. The whole flotilla tightened with a new tensity, whipped up by the sirocco and pointed by the disturbing knowledge that, no longer borne by a God-sent breeze, they were kept solely by human arms, however husky, from blowing straight up the channel to the alerted harbor-cordon of Alexius Comnenus. As it was, they veered ever closer to the time when, like a procession of proud women pushed through a jail yard, their vessels must run the gauntlet of the Emperor's crack galleys stretched taut and far stronger than the Byzantine harbor-chain itself, from Chios clean to the Isle of Crete. By rights, they had a rendezvous with death, with nothing to cheat it but its own cheating image propped on the long-ship *Falcona*.

The storm took its course, abating on that last night before the Byzantine sea-way must be crossed. The gale ceased to make mountains in the sea, the night sky was cleared for the pageant of Cassiopeia and the Bear, and the sea-path lighted eerily by a lambent moon.

On the deck of the *Falcona* Bohemond gave a little banquet. Besides the small company of knights that had staked their chances to reach home on the sham funeral fleet, the deck-board was shared by Daimbert, an Apulian bishop who had fled Jerusalem and the strifes there, by Countess Zoë and Mohanna the Moslem princess. All sat on cushions about the meat-filled trenchers in the Oriental way. The page Panturge, between his duties of service, squatted against the bulk-head, picking his teeth, whistling, and watching Bohemond. There is no bond like shared danger, and between these two, the knight and the hunch-backed page, a truce had been set. Bohemond still badgered him—*dolt, jester, wind-pushing toad* being the least of his nicknames, but he had taken to employing him in small tasks, having him row the skiff which was lowered and launched from the long-ship for quick conferences on the other vessels. Bohemond's usual vigilance in all his ventures was never more exercised than now. Keeping from sight of the captive menagerie which would far too gladly broadcast the talk of the bogus sarcophagus if they knew, he nevertheless informed himself nightly on every illness, riot, or altercation in the thirteen ships.

At this strange ship-board feast, shadowed as it was by finality and death, the mulled wine and the meat went around in an atmosphere of jollity and jest, which by his own mood alone Bohemond was able to generate. Bravery of a sort seemed to sprout even in the timid breast of Daimbert, and many a discreet ecclesiastical dinner-tale dropped from his timid lips. No mention was made of the dreaded gauntlet of the Greek galleys that awaited them at dawn. The wine, sent round repeatedly in generous portions indeed, produced such a well-being and plucking-up of heart that when they were finally breaking up it came as a slight shock—Bohemond's sudden reminder as he rose from his own silk bolster.

"Now courage, men. Everyone's clear on orders, but I know it will be hard. A cold tilt this time; no help from the stallion or the lance. Good acting's your weapon, friends! Wry faces! Tears! Imagining *me* defunct is too pale for the game, I know!" He grinned at them. "But think of your *own* heads, gentlemen, fouling the pikes at Marmora Arsenal if it isn't pulled off!"

He softened the last with a gesture of geniality, but anyone could see the suspenseful stiffening of the barons, the blanching of Daimbert's jowls, even by light of the flaring torches. Then Bohemond called for Panturge and strode onto the companionway. He had a last conference scheduled with the Genoese sea-lords.

That night in the hot, close hatchment chamber, Zoë slept but once, a short troubled spell in which there was a dream. The Wood, the fen below Burg Ughol, the Psyche-statue, and the creeping moss, bright green at midnight. Someone was there on the moss-bed, sleeping and smiling, his arms spread out. Footsteps; men rushing in, laughter and heavy spurs. And when they had finished, the delicate little Psyche-statue had been blemished, chipped and hideously maimed as though kicked by a thousand boots, and nothing was left of her little temple but fallen pediment-posts, and they were bloodied.

Zoë woke, stifling a cry. She had not known of actual footsteps, and she thought Mohanna slept, but as she leaned across her, grasping a cloak, she heard the girl whisper, "*Maimoun* has returned."

She saw him standing at the prow-bird, looking out on the silent sea, and all about him seemed treacherously serene. The swish of oars, the running, rhythmic pattern of the waters from the prow, the slow creak, creak, of the lateen yard cocked up on the mast. Behind them flares on the masthead were licking the quiet night, and on the deck below them an Italian sailor was bawling a sea-chant with obscene words, apparently drunk on remains of the Antiochan wine.

The ship lurched, plunged, and she steadied herself against the sudden roll, grasping the smooth warm wood of the starboard rail. The movement caught Bohemond, and he whirled, his mantle flung outward from his silver spurs. He was fully armored—costumed, it came to her, for death.

He smiled, huge and fair-headed, his links all glowing in the lambent moon. She had thought herself proof against delight, but in her dream and in his smile now, all in her life and what had been best in it rushed together. Lived things, but dreamed things too; things seen in a misty glass, a dusty river, a thousand sharp inklings of ulti-mate unending delights, which he alone could conjure. Not reality, she knew now it wasn't that, but a heady dose, a powerful essence, like incense or wine or a remembered melody.

His voice startled her.

"Will you watch with me, Zoë?"

His link-clad right arm flung out the mantle like a sail, and she walked into it.

All night long the roundships rolled on, past gulfs, bays and light-houses where they knew Greek eyes looked out and marked them. At dawn they were drifting northwestward past the first spur that led to the Hellespont.

The officers gathered on the *Falcona*, Mass was said, and they hastened to assume their places in the well-rehearsed tableau. Lady Zoë, in her pilgrim-cape and the wide-wimpled hat which they had brought to her, stood at the port rail, and watched and listened to the jittery by-play of the nervous barons. It was a queer enough confer-ence for them all, these lords of many a bold endeavor, and as for the Patriarch Daimbert, they could scarce calm the scared little prelate hunched in his hierarchal robes sufficiently to hold the psalter without trembling, and someone made shift to fetch him a movable ship's capstan to use as a rostrum on last notice. All they could see of their central player was his chest and shoulders dressed in their tight skin of linked steel, and of course, his face, for he sat upright in the sarcophagus. The sight of him did nothing to cheer. The carefully chalked face beneath the suddenly unreal-looking straight-cut red thatch was transformed to a spine-chilling grey-white mask whenever he laughed.

All about them was the dawn-time fog. They knew, assured by the Genoese captains who had seen things in the night, that somewhere beyond that misty wall or muffled in it, the Bzyantine biremes drifted at anchor. It iced the bones to think that soon official purple-laced Greek buskins would be treading the false fore-deck of the *Falcona*. They chattered at Bohemond, urging him to bestir himself for the completion of the play. A white-haired seaman bore tinder and resin-dust about the catafalques, lighting their bowls of tow. But Bohemond seemed to prolong these last terrible moments, more poised than any of them, remembering last details.

"D'Avesnes!" he shouted. "Where's your chanticleer?" And when the two-weeks-defunct rooster was fetched and hidden at his hip in the silk depths of the coffin-box, he jested. "It's a scurvy trick on *me*," he cried, "but I think this old master will smell-up the game enough!"

He was not pretending, thought Zoë, answering a grin he spared her. He was obviously enjoying this, unfeignedly gay. This was his very element. "Good fortune," she whispered. Then, the others growing profane with him, urging him down at last, he lowered his head, still smiling, the heavy lid dropped, the box slammed shut. Daimbert jumped sharply as they heard from the death-box a muffled but still lively guffaw.

Zoë's smile faded. She collared Panturge. "Come, churl, come quick, step lively—and no questions now!"

White-faced and silent, the Countess directed the hunch-back down the companionway to the lower deck. There, with the roofed darkness and the low mist not yet penetrated by a hint of sun, the long-ship seemed caught in a cloud. The forty oar-woods slapped slow and faint as though somewhere distant.

"Where is the boat?"

"Eh?"

"The skiff, troll . . . Look lively!" Her small jeweled misericordia was a cold gleam in the bodiless atmosphere.

"Hard ahead, m'lady," Panturge answered promptly, "across the rail . . . There's a hooded companionway that walls off the rowers."

"Then deal with it!"

"*Qu'est-ce-que . . .?*"

"I said, lower the skiff!" she hissed at him. "Wait. Someone . . ."

A seaman stood drowsily at the rail and turned, hearing footsteps on the wet deck.

"Captain!" The black Italian eyes popped a little at the pale wimpled face confronting him from the fog.

"Have you a flambeau, Messire?" she asked civilly.

"A flambeau?" the merchant-pilot repeated stupidly, not displeased with the morning vision of nun-like beauty. Beside it the dwarfish countenance of the page had loomed viciously.

"Flambeau—*torcia*," she translated with patience, knowing full well the churl was not dull to port-tongues. "A rush-light for my page to bear while I read my psalter."

She extended an opened volume in the morning dusk.

A chill struck her as the insolent Italian eyes glinted and she caught his wine-soaked breath. "What is your meditation today, fair pilgrim? I've need for prayer . . ."

"What? Oh, why, I study the wise words of the Prophet who tells us, 'Contend not with dragons that bid fair to overwhelm thee. Flee their breath as you would the fumes of hell.' "

The seaman frowned in the fog. "I do not recall—that text escapes me . . ." He turned to go. "Very well, madame, a torch . . ."

Zoë (who had indeed embroidered Scripture) stood there a small moment observing the retreating tar as the mist closed in on him, and thanking her lucky stars that she had been able to paraphrase so glibly the colorful counsel of Father Domini. Panturge had meantime gone to his task. She peered down at the ugly spider-like presence working in the fog and she cringed a little with a dread chill.

"Cut them, dullard," she said to the bristly head, and presented the hilt of her misericordia. A few more soft curses and the skiff had careened down the scant four feet and smote the sea. Zoë climbed over and down, hung a moment on the cut halyard, and then dropped into it. Panturge then cut the last thick towline by which it was secured.

Just then, there was a noise of thunder. Or so at first it seemed. But the thunder had a hiss, too, and was rhythmic. Steady, terrible, it rolled on the Middle Sea like giant fire-works and lit up the distant spaces of fog-like fire through a curtain.

"What is it?" cried Panturge, cringing over the oar-locks. "*Mere de Dex*, what is *that?*"

"Greek syphon-guns," said Zoë, "signalling a halt to the Franks."

"What a misery of a noise!"

"Aye, head for it." She recovered her baselard from his belt in a flashing gesture. "Head for it, Panturge."

"Madame, for the love of God . . ."

"Row!" She pricked his knuckles with the blade. "Row, thou abortion of nature . . ."

Panturge bent to his work and struck out in a wide swathe, avoiding the stiff, stopped oars of the *Falcona*.

CHAPTER XXXIII

Alexius

AS A MILD NOVEMBER sun slid low on the surface of the Aegean sea-way, the royal Greek navy could be seen drawn up in battle array: gay painted gats and gleaming galleys; huge, high dromons with silver prows; and surrounding these, a small, deadly swarm of raiding feluccas from the Isle of Crete, manned by two hundred huge Ethiopians. On high poops the war-tubes jutted— long syphons with dirigible metallic nozzles that at dawn had shot out liquid flame for two hundred yards. About these the sun struck diamond-like flashes from the glistening gold helmets and shoulder-pieces of the Byzantine officers.

The awaited celebration was touched off when the triarch of the flagship *Justiana* was seen to return from his brief and satisfied inspection of the barbarian funeral fleet which now, 'twixt navy and mainland, slid slowly by. They had watched for the homing bird panniered on the huge trireme flying Paleologus's blue, and when they saw the pigeon dart, knowing it was clamped with papyrus-lead smeared with pig-blood, there had arisen the great roar: *BOHEMOND IS DEAD!*

The din was tremendous. Besides the fire-tubes spitting their bright venom into the sea, there was the clash of cymbals, wild strumming of zitherns, and the raucous banging of the bronze tambours, as the *Hagiatra*, the Byzantine war-hymn, roared out across the bay.

The Frank fleet slid slowly on westward hard below the high poops and canopied forecastles of the imperial triremes, the falcon-prowed long-ship looking weak and helpless, with its dread sarcophagus and its flaring fire-bowls, pale in the brilliant day, and its knot of priests, knights and other mourners gathered about it. Indeed, the fat-bellied merchant-foists drew much more comment with their heterogeneous cargo of everything under the eastern sun, from African pack-camels to a tribe of ragglety gypsies, one of whom swung his lean shanks across the port rail and bit his thumb. On the last ship, a high-pooped, lateen-rigged Turkish caravel, two great shining rectangular objects caught the climbing sun and flashed it uncomfortably into the wind-ribbed eyes of the Greek Admiral, George Paleologus. He lounged on the forecastle of the *Justiana*, a husky, pensive figure in the midst of the jubilation going on around him.

"It would seem, Excellency," said the gilt-helmeted triarch standing next to him, "that they carry a great deal of stuff. Will they bury him do y'think with all that, like they say is done to certain ancients in the cities of Cathay? Seems like a rich cargo, by Mary, to allow them to drag west. My fingers itch for the syphon, to give them a singe!"

"Calm yourself, Theox," said George Paleologus, his tanned, muscular arms crossed before him on the high rail. "To see that fellow passing out of the Empire a corpse is worth anything. I'd let 'em transport the whole of Antioch. For there, Theox, goes half the trouble of my lifetime . . . Seems queer to think that there's nothing now but a bad smell."

"We'll miss 'im, you might say," rejoined the other. "Even the Emperor will. There wasn't room for two in the world like Alexius and the Sicilian tyrant."

"I wouldn't say that, Theox," mildly rebuked the Admiral. "And I wouldn't *ever* say it for other ears than mine, which feel particularly blissful this morning. It's not healthy, or even intelligent of course, Theox, to compare the petty Lord of Tarentum to the Purple Heart of the World."

Theox flushed, and withdrew on a new tack, pertaining to line-of-duty. "The mate on the *Theodora* informs me they fished that skiff from the sea. An Italian woman and her page."

"You know what to do with such vagrants, Theox. It's common enough for those pilgrims to leave their party for one last look at the City of a Thousand Sights. Keep her under vigilance until inquiries can be made . . . But Theox, if it's one of title, take care. You know how diplomacy will turn now. Relations with the West will take on possibilities never to be chanced before."

Bohemond is dead.

The Byzantine fleet, bearer of fine tidings, sailed up the dark-blue waters of the Marmora to be met by little rainbow-tinted barques trailing yard-long festoons of purple-and-gold brocade. Along the coast, on the great Wall built in the fifth century against the Huns, the Seven Speaking Towers rolled out the news.

Bohemond is dead.

There would be parades in the Forum, fireworks in the Hippodrome, and a night feast at the Triclinium of the Nineteen Tables, with masques, concerts of flutes and the official thanks extended to Michael, Mary, and St. George.

Bohemond is dead.

Meantime parchments hung with Alexius's golden bull had gone speeding to Venice, Rome, Paris, all the meeting-places of the barbarian world, reading:

I now have no quarrel with the Western man. If he wills to pass through my gates from his farms to the Holy Places, he will find me kind, for I am just and merciful. But I am the Hub of the World, and the tyrant Bohemond dared to covet me.

The Italian Countess and the hunch-back were confined in comfortable quarters in the Abramite monastery. And within the month, when the pilgrim's interesting connections had been verified, a purple-edged parchment arrived from Alexius Comnenus himself, inviting the lady to become the guest of his daughter Anna.

Zoë did not find it strange, this polite extending of the royal hand. Companies of knights returning from the Holy Land were feted, impressed and showered with rich gifts, before being set loose to advertise Alexius's good works among the Westerners. But when one evening she sat at dinner with Anna herself, she was indeed mystified. Fear of this new kindness was added to all the fears she had entertained since being apprehended. She was well fed, well treated; but not for a moment, in all this poisonous luxury, had there been one small chance to escape.

And so she sat tensely at that strange, exotic board, and opposite her little Anna Comnena fussily picked at her roast fowl and *palacountas*. They were served by a page with night-shade eyes; his hair was dyed red and sprinkled with golden dust; he was dressed in a short chiton all gathered to a shoulder-buckle on which a black parrot whetted its beak.

Byzantine women had a mode of holding their backbones absolutely stiff, giving them a look that recalled those long, thin, owl-eyed creatures on the walls of their basilicas. Anna was the epitome of this, with eyes so large, dark and lustrous that their full look, from the painted pallor of that doll-like face, was most upsetting. She was dressed in stiffened silk like a cornucopia sheath, and her face was beset with black artificial curls and framed in a jeweled aureole.

Zoë, watching her, wondered why Anna had sought *her* out. Certainly not for information. . . . Equerries, secretaries, officials of all sorts had questioned her for weeks, and she had withheld nothing. One inquiry had not been made, having obviously not been thought of, and Zoë's inventions to hide it had been deft and plausible. When the truth was known . . . But she had left off thinking of that. It was too terrifying to be admitted.

When dessert had been proffered by that nightmare of a page (beside whom, thought Zoë, the honest, beast-like ugliness of Panturge was a benediction), the Princess Anna regarded her directly with those oval eyes. "Will you please," she said, "accompany me on a short walk to accelerate digestion?"

They wandered in soft light (it was late afternoon) through the palace gardens with their conservatories, music-pavilions, peacocks, monkeys and chambers of love. They passed through them all in the same long silences which Zoë was finding both curious and disconcerting, since at its every breaking the high-pitched voice and the iciness of Anna had a power to render her dumb. The princess spoke at length but twice. First, when they passed through the Purple Room, the lying-in chamber of all the ladies of the royal house. As they stood on the ingeniously lighted floor where one had the impression of being in a field of purple crystal blooms, Anna had turned with a strange, stiff, elegant movement, and said, "Here, Zoë of Sicily, the Empress lay struggling for three days to retain me in her womb, till my father could return from battle. From the field where the tyrant Bohemond was defeated signally for the first time, he rushed home by spelled mounts of Patchenak cavalry and was standing by in full armor when the royal physicians called him, and with his own hands he pressed the imperial coronet on my pulsing fontanelles."

Zoë was hard put for an adequate reply to this momentous revelation, and merely stood looking at the purple silk birth-couch, attempting to regard it with the appropriate awe for the high-points of history.

In the Royal Library, Anna became even more garrulous.

"We have only three sections to the library, you understand, since there are of course but three cultures—the thoughts of those persons who have nothing to do with the things which lower beasts, Turks, and the barbarians of the West covet. They are our co-imperials of Bagdad and Persia, who style themselves, wisely, as brothers of the moon, the sun, and the Basileus. My father the Basileus is of course the Purple Heart of the Universe, but like other descended prophets, he is also a man—brave, just and merciful. His praises as Christopator are adequately sounded at Hagia Sophia and in every last small basilica on the edge of the Indivisible Empire. But as a man, his excellences could slip through the future ages unknown. To prevent which I have bent the full employment of my scholarly powers (which are not held inconsiderable here and abroad) to the authoring of a great book which I called *The Alexiad*." She had preceded Zoë into a severely furnished, though rich and book-filled room, whose center was consumed by a huge, lion-legged table with neat piles on it, apparently of notes.

Anna signed Zoë to one of the straight-back chairs, and laid hold of a sheaf of skins which evidently had been previously selected, and Zoë realized that in this walk through the book-filled halls smelling spicily of resin lay the heart of the reason for Anna's frigid friendship. For she now turned upon Zoë an expression compounded of hope, pride, and a sort of pleading, the look of an author begging for an ear to her latest try, and without prelude she began to read:

"Bohemond the Frank was such, to speak briefly, as no one in the Empire had at that time seen—neither Greek nor barbarian—a spectacle for the eyes and a face that surpassed all others. In detail: he was so tall that he surpassed all men by nearly a cubit; slender of waist and flat of flank, and of shoulder broad and full. His whole body was white and very muscular, neither thin nor fat, but shaped, so to speak, to the mold of Praxiteles. His hands were active (like all Franks!), his step firm and he seemed to stoop a little. His hair was a shade of dark yellow cut up to his ears (not long like other barbarians) and his face was cleanly shaved, seeming smooth as gypsum. His eyes, bluish-grey, gave evidence of dignity and wrath together.

"Do you mark" (she interrupted herself, almost breathless) "how his nose and nostrils gave vent—I do not know; it seemed that his chest and his nostrils were always together expanded, as though elixirs of his heart might *burst* through his nostrils?"

"Ah, yes—*yes*, you might say," said Zoë judiciously, endeavoring to rise to this new role.

"Then mark, as I read," said Anna, with another of those black, lustrous stares. "The whole man gave out a certain sweetness, but such as was cloaked by terrors he could see on every side. There was something untamed, inexorable, it seems to me . . . Accurate?" she shot at Zoë, who countered with a nod.

"Tell me, Excellency, how *old* were you, when the Crusade came through?"

"Fourteen."

And as her amazed audience struggled with a raised brow, the princess read on.

"He was such in mind and body that love and war seemed always to be bearing arms in him, together . . ."

In the expectant pause, Zoë told her with a sincerity that this time was completely genuine, "*That*, Excellency, is not only a learned observation, it is the life . . ."

At this, an author's most coveted appraisal, the little princess allowed her thin painted lips to part in a smile, revealing an even row of tiny, seed-like teeth. "This is how I end it," she said, not looking at the text. "He was in fortune, eloquence and in natural gifts inferior to the Emperor alone."

"Chrysostom!" exclaimed Zoë. "Your Excellency's opinion would mightily please him could he know."

"*Could he know!*" said Anna. "Do you imagine that to him it would signify, where he screams now for mercy in the bottom-most pit of Hell? Tell me, Tritoness of Tarentum" (her expression was an indescribable mixture of cruelty, curiosity and her own half-glimpsed peculiar passion that was like fire in ice) "how did he look in death?"

But before Zoë could frame a reply, before she had time for the first invention, there appeared at the entrance to the study two of those savage-looking giants with which Alexius Comnenus was pleased to surround himself; huge Russians with rubies in their ears, gold torcs on their arms and two-edged ax-bills in their fists, who announced in rough accents, "The woman of Italy is summoned by the Lord of Micklagard."

Anna appeared as much surprised as Zoë. She stiffened, whirled and faced completely about to look at her, with the full, round attention of those agate-like eyes.

A rumor which had been growing all day in the city had become a tumultuous buzz. Some sea merchant from Corfu had arrived with a certain paper and was being held at Bucelon Palace till investigation could be made. Meantime the tales got wilder and more authoritative. A great crowd had formed about the palace.

Through this mob at about the seventh hour, according to the clepsydra or water-clock on the top-most dome of Marmora arsenal, Tycho, the Basileus's favorite silentiary, pushed his way. He was returning from his weekly visit to the baths of Blachernae, where, on every Friday at the sixth hour, the ancient goddess miraculously lifted her long stone veil. A refusal meant ill luck to the future of the Empire. As the eunuch struggled for gangway, his wide white sleeve beplucked by the mob and his curled beard pulled askew, snatches of news that were threatened out of him set new alarums churning. The Persian seeress who presided over the ancient shrine had had strange visions, never before seen in the time of Christians; djinns and spirits coming together in the black night and producing their kind; old gods risen, sacrificing youths to Helios, maidens to Athene, men to Pluto, and strangled foreigners to the goddess Hecate; and in the midst of all, a risen Satan who shone like a golden flower, wearing a jewelled diadem and fiery garments, his arms sparkling like flames—and when he stirred, the Empire shook . . .

Alexius was off the throne when Tycho entered. Tycho held his wing-like sleeves before his eyes and began to speak: "O Cosmos in midst of Chaos, Lord of the Chosen ones—"

"Yes, yes," Alexius interrupted him, "Blachernae didn't come through! You see, George," he turned to Paleologus, "the damned witch gets the rumor even before *we* have wind of it! That paper from Corfu is neither forged nor faked. It's from Bohemund . . . Hear that mob . . . There's laughter . . ."

Paleologus, striking in scarlet and his gilt helm, shrugged. "You must admit there's point to the jest."

"*You* talk of point! You, beneath whose nose the thrice damned

renegade sailed by . . . 'Dead,' you said. 'Stinking!' Va! It was your
own stupidity that smelled to highest Heaven . . ." Alexius was livid,
but the Admiral did not flinch. He was of a great clan, the favorite son
of the powerful Paleologi, rich feudal tritons who could rise from the
soil in one night, like Medea's dragon-teeth in their golden armor. So
he smiled at Alexius.

Peeking from his sleeves, the eunuch Tycho was shocked and discomfited. He did not like to see his Emperor thus—a squat dark figure
walking round and round, the tips of his purple shoes slapping noisily
on the marble-veined floor, the festoons of his diadem waggling crazily
from his stiff uncurled coiffure. Alexius on the throne was god-like, his
great barrel chest, bull neck and heavy, bearded face appearing to
advantage. Even in a hallful of tall, giant-like barbarian Crusaders he
continued regal, his purple shoes resting on a porphyry pedestal, two
feet higher than any in the room. Thus exposed, motionless and urbane,
he was a spectacle which Tycho could gaze on for hours and be fulfilled. But Alexius afoot was another matter.

So Tycho held his wings before his painted eyebrows, and peeked
out only once when the Varangians appeared with the Frankish
woman.

Alexius threw back his filleted head, gave a great, deep, huffing
sound like a bull, and ascended the throne.

"Bring in the other prisoners."

Although bearing herself boldly between the burly Russians in spite
of the hand chains which now secured her, Zoë was experiencing an
ice-like paralysis of terror. They crossed the golden chamber, stood at
the throne and the long indictment was read by the eunuch silentiary.
It confirmed all fears.

She cursed herself. She had cursed herself often in the long sleepless
nights for getting herself caught in this treacherous well of luxury. She
had called herself fool. It was all the worse to think it had not been *him*
she fled from, in that dim dawn five weeks ago, but herself. Why had
she not more thoroughly weighed the consequences?

How easy, beside this maddening terror, had been a firm, strong,
prayerful battle with fired blood and wayward will, and at the end of
it safe, warm joys of home-coming—strong arms and heartfelt welcome
in Amalfi! And while the sham trial went on, while they formally
read to her the taunt that Bohemond had penned at Corfu, she cursed
him too. But within the next hour all other thoughts gave place to stark,
immediate, unadulterated horror.

Three other individuals in chains had been brought to the room.
But they were in far different condition from Zoë. Two were men, the
first a wealthy old Greek from the look of him; his hair showed signs
of having been habitually curled but now hung thin and wispy about

his neck. The second was young; a handsome soldier who darted his fine eyes boldly about the room. The third was fair, slight, a young woman, lovely perhaps without the filth of prison on her. She clung to the arms of the huge, fair-headed brutes who held her, as if in her actual gaolers she sought desperate solace.

Alexius indeed, his eyes two chips of onyx between his beard and his black hair, seemed to lose all semblance of humanity and sat drawn within himself. There was a tall, muscular officer in scarlet and gilt, whom Zoë did not know, and from the tail of her eye she saw standing in the dappled shadows of late sunshine that sought the casement-square, the Princess Anna—a little black-eyed ikon, motionless in her stiff clothes, the vivid jewels of her high aureole glittering in the sun. It was that late, peaceful hour that Zoë had known in the convent of Daphne as evensong, and she recalled that picture now, of sunlit beauty and quiet worship, and this alone brought first tears of a sharp regret that verged upon self-pity, and she rejected it, and prayed for the strength of anger.

The prisoners were placed in three different spots in the large room with certain instruments arranged, and with tarpaulins spread beneath them on the rich marbles. By this time Zoë was actually surprised when she was not thus similarly dealt with, but was ordered by the long-sleeved silentiary to remain near the throne. Then, over the noises of apparatus being set up, Alexius spoke.

"It is not the custom, woman of the Franks, for things to be done here in such a fashion. It is too much the barbarian way. But in this case, since my aim is always to be just, it may answer a purpose. The elder there is a landed triton, an owner of broad lands, who for years withheld tithes to my treasury—financial trespass, you see. He finds death by garroting. The boy fell asleep at watch, a mistake that in soldiers we do not tolerate. He will lose his sight in a manner which you will presently know. The woman aided her lover in the assassination of one of my best legionaries and it will be seen to that she leads no other man astray." He turned to the huge stranger at the side of his golden chair. "We are ready, George. You may give the sign."

The handsome official hesitated, not palpably for mercy, but as though wandering in some reverie of his own. Then he lifted a well groomed, perfunctory hand.

The inferno which was instantaneously created in that place was a sight from which Zoë wanted to tear her vision but could not. There was actually not much tumult save for the young woman who writhed and screamed pitifully as the torturers placed red-hot brands against her forehead and both cheeks and upon the whole of her bared back, whereupon she mercifully fainted. The old man died quickly under the twisting of knotted cords about his neck, and the young soldier bound in the chair sat with the muscles knotted in his straining arms and his mouth pulled down in a hideous grimace of horror as the soldiers drew back his head so that the physicians could extract the humerous liquids from the balls of his eyes.

Zoë's body was one great writhing of nerves. She had tried to escape that hell by looking everywhere, but in all the room there seemed nothing but the three unfortunate wretches, nothing but their cries and their pain, and the terrible dank stench of sweat that had spread like a thin cloud through the room from the travail of their suffering. As the three were dragged off, she was aware that she had been pulling from side to side, straining her arm-muscles against the firm grip of the huge implacable Russians.

The silence was such a relief that she stood there panting, yet her eyes still wandered from one spot to the next where the prisoners had been, as if held by some horrible after-image.

Alexius Comnenus once more spoke.

"As I said, madame, my intention is always to be just, and my one fear here is a punishment that might be inappropriate. But living within my hospitable precincts you have for three fortnights committed a continuous betrayal, compounded of *many* treacheries so diverse that the mind would hesitate to name them. The *main* one, of course, madame, is unforgivable, that you aided in causing to be held up in ridicule the One and Indivisible Empire, with a boldness conceived alone in the well-known accursed stratagems of the upstart himself. Inevitably I will be avenged, though in your case with incredible mercy. I have been just and clement. I am offering you the *choice* of your own repayment."

"What?"

"Choose, I say, from what you have witnessed here—death, a comparatively easy one, you will observe, blinding, or the brand. Which shall it be? Prepare to ready her, Tycho." Then, turning to George Paleologus, flushing with the vehemence of his instant decision, "Recall the legions from Cilicia. Raise the Iron Chain in the Hellespont; and above all, refortify Durazzo. Constantinople is from this day forward closed to the West."

Zoë stood sagging between the bare arms of her two gaolers. It was with great effort that she stayed upright at all.

"Well, madame!" said Alexius. "Your choice?"

"I don't know!" she cried. *"My God—I don't know!"*

CHAPTER XXXIV *And Remembered Melodies*

ON A FINE AUTUMN DAY some ten years after these events, in the year 1111, a man astride a heavy stallion traveled down the sea-road leading from Salerno to Amalfi. Although cloaked in a shroud of sandy white dust, the rider would have earned regard from any passer-by. He was obviously noble, and to judge by his fair reddish hair encased in a conical iron helmet and the massive great sword he wore, he was a Norman. But a knightly bearing was not sufficient to merit awe, nor was the small red-painted cross he wore on the left breast of his steel pauldron. As highly honored as Crusaders were by the inhabitants of South Italy, they were now quite numerous all across Europe.

Since that first mighty armed pilgrimage there had been three other highly touted, spectacularly advertised and expertly prepared attempts on Asia Minor, and though all had been thwarted by the one who was now considered the West's arch-enemy, Alexius Comnenus, still the knights participating in these star-crossed romantic endeavors were accorded the respect and could bear the self-same emblem as the earlier heroes. It was not merely *this* distinction, then, that marked the knight, nor his towering stature. It was rather his bearing, neither haughty nor proud, yet unmistakably a great lord's, and the aura of magnificent vigor in one who from his wind-seamed swarthy face and heavy shoulders must be far toward middle-age; it was, too, the dark-rimmed bluish-grey eyes which flashed courage and cunning and were at the same time overlaid with a certain pensiveness that is coupled with philosophers, lovers, or the very lonely.

Yet Bohemond, though he traveled single today, was far from lonely. He had for ten years been honored, wined, feted, the most famous knight in all Europe. He had been Philip's intimate, and the recipient from him of hearty purses for his luckless crusades. He had with great success preached these endeavors every place, from the rural village churches of his ancestral Cotentin to the balcony of the Chartres Cathedral. He had traversed the face of Europe with his incredible circus of oddities from "the land of Rum" and had drawn young noblemen like flies to his famous lances. Babies received his name for simple honor, crowds gathered everywhere just to view him. He had stood in the mists of Normandy and stared across the Channel and been forbidden by King Henry to cross—a most high compliment to his potency in arms, if a slur on his intent.

He was for nine years wed to Constance, the French princess (a cousin to the one he had transported to his regent Tancred in Antioch), and they cherished a handsome fine red-haired son whom they called little Bo.

It was for no other reason than the desolateness of the sea-road itself that Bohemond had privacy today. For when he and Constance had traveled from their castle at Bari to attend the funeral of the Prince's half-brother, Duke Roger Borsa, it was a known event, and attended, as all his other movements, with publicity that was now and at long last unsought. Bohemond was only too happy for this unaccustomed peace, and for the fresh though familiar wildness of the scene, with the cliffy white rocks on the one hand, the sea-scape on the other. Looking far out, for he neared Amalfi now, he saw high-pooped caravels and bellied round-ships, which *might* be Mihera's like enough, and a sort of thrill assailed him, and he smiled.

Perhaps in Mihera he would recapture some of that old-time flavor that in these last days he had more than unconsciously looked for. So far nothing seemed the same. The people, the towns, even the blackguards were different, it seemed to him—those feudal monsters for which South Italy had been long so justly famous. Borsa had enjoyed a black enough fame, with murder of enemies and hanging of subjects the order of the day, and son William, it was said, bade fair to match him. Bohemond had watched his good, sweet, gentle Constance in that fabulous household all this present week—young William surrounded by Clutchy-Purse's roughs and his Lombard wife, the Lady Gaitlegrim. With some amusement he had watched poor Constance trying hard to think them civil and having a rough go. And yet, he thought now, not even Clutchy-Purse (God rest his puny soul!) had done black, thunderous evil like Raidulf Trincancote that Guiscard had used to tell of, or Gisolf of Salerno whom he himself had known. As for that (with a thought half of whimsy, half of truth), from King Henry of England on down to young William of Salerno, regarding him fearfully in his dead father's castle under Maia Torre, *Bohemond himself* was the one held villainous, it seemed, even by his own wife who, loving and sweet to him as she always was, had been doing daily penance for him, as she confessed one night when he had surprised her wearing a hair shirt.

A hair shirt indeed! True, it pricked one, sometimes, to remember that first Crusade, and to know what might have been done with the spirit of it whole, and it *did* bring twinges to be so worshipped by simple pious people everywhere. But he'd made too much talk to Constance; *that*, now, he knew. Of Antioch, of Tancred's vows of stewardship and his dreams of his own son to rule there some day. And on good days, when it seemed that Alexius *must* be passed, he had spun her his wilder schemes—of conquest, empire and undreamed-of wealth, beyond Byzantium. Blast that hair shirt, touching sweet, soft Constance . . .

There had been other things, though, that he did *not* tell her, nor ever would—things that had sent him only yesternight over to the Mere, across the Bridge, and up to Burg Ughol. Disappointment had met him. No cure for an aching memory, for a heart half-weighed by guilt. Where was she? No least hint of her in the gaping ruin of the hall; no sign in the mossy fen nor on the Bridge where he'd stood in the dank mists and made little fog-clouds with his own breath, alone. He had kicked at the bristly briar patch were Faustin's house had stood; he had kicked at it savagely, and left.

If the heart neither can nor dares redress old wrongs committed in the treacherous name of love, the conscience sometimes must, and to this end, finally, he sought Mihera. Zoë might still be east, might need them, might . . . The closest he had come to Byzantium in nine years of attempting it had been at one juncture to stand at Alexius's couch in his tent at Durazzo (Alexius not standing before *him* for many and ancient reasons), and hear a treaty that secured his descendants Antioch but which at the same time forbade his entry there, so that when, in the next year, there occurred a commercial treaty between Byzantine port-lords and Amalfi shippers, he had formed his design to face Mihera, tell him certain truths, and beg him to seek her. It was all, now, that he could do. But Mihera . . .

As Bohemond rounded the last spur and looked down on the white walls and turrets of the seaport town, he felt his courage falter as it had not faltered before kings, emperors, and desert lords, to think of that honest stare.

He was just approaching the town gate when an equerry accosted him from behind, bearing the Lombard crown-fess-and-fox of Maia Torre, and handed him a note. It was Constance!

Let us go down to Palermo for the Winter lists. Duke William tells me it is clement there. We would have it alone, in Sicily, without these crowds. I shall leave Bo with Lady Gaitlegrim. Meet me at that inn-road crossing they call Chestnut Point. Your nephew plans an escort there by horse. We decided on this directly when you left. Meet me at the point, dear, at Vesper-time tomorrow. If we miss, there's the Inn near. Romantic, our young Duke William!

Your loving

CONSTANCE.

Bohemond read it with mixed feelings, frowning at the part about Bo being left at Maia Torre. But immediately he felt silly. Had he not just been thinking how different this was now, how much more civil South Italy had become since the days of Tricancote. And Constance. He thought first of her coming as inopportune, and then, seeing it further, he speculated pleasantly about it. He was ill-natured now because of things pressing him. Yet, afterwards, would he not be a new man, resolved, confessed and perhaps forgiven? It might be an omen. Perhaps, afterwards, he and Constance—perhaps she would not bedevil him with her prayers and that hair shirt . . . Life could be folding to the best.

He tossed the varlet a coin and went on, the salt air fresh on his face, the note from Constance crackling in his leather jerkin.

It was still early, scarcely mid-way through the afternoon, but there was a crackling fire going in the small hall of the bay-side *palazzo* of Mihera of Amalfi. The sea-lord himself sat near it, playing backgammon with his private physician and long-time friend, Messer Jacoppo Poldi. Round and about him, at the back of his own and his guest's chair, at the door and tending the great central fire, was a company of servants, dressed in elegant silk tabard-and-hose, and rigidly attending. There were the finest tapestries on the walls, deep-piled eastern carpets underfoot, and on every tapestry as well as over the main doorway had been embossed the dolphin-head with a ship in its mouth, the emblem of the Amalfi fleet.

The two men at the game-board rarely spoke. The fire made all the noise in the room, with the exception of a huge, sharp-eared English mastiff who occasionally gave vent to lazy squeak-like yawns. He lay some distance back from the roaring fire, sprawled against a large harp-like instrument of the ancient Celtic fashion which was pushed back in shadows. The only activity besides those slow-paced strategies of the game was from one page or another, moving to serve Dr. Poldi with wine, meat or sweet things whenever he gestured for them. A good and useful life had enriched the doctor. His figure was naturally somewhat fuller, and in the dark Italian eyes was a look of true humor and ready sympathy especially to be met with in those fitly called to his profession. As to the game, he showed only fair interest.

Mihera, on the other hand, was all business, and his hand had not reached once for the goblet and tray, though both were waiting at his chair. He was still a well-sinewed man, leaner with the years, but possessing that knotty hardness which is the heritage of those with even a little of Saxon blood. Of his Norman sire he had retained nothing so evocative as the set, steely, almost threatening expression, which certain aspects of his life had done nothing to soften. The craggy brow, the thrust of shoulder . . . But what really had changed was his hair.

It was white, but not blond-white as his Viking-like thatch one time had been. It was white and coarse as flax is, and straight-cut, even shorter than before. It made him appear some older, but at the same time more striking, for his face, under that severe frame, was lean, tight-skinned and brown as tree-bark with a network of sea-lines besetting the eyes. And these, when he lifted them, appeared most startling, and they too were changed. They were veiled and hard, yielding nothing. There was a taut ridged muscle in his jaw, revealing to the medical all that was held within. It was this that Poldi remarked now and said, "Relax, Messire. Relax! There's all evening for the game, isn't there? And you'll best me anyhow, that I *know*, with that viperous luck of yours. But I try my best to foil it . . ." He enlisted more wisdom from his cup of wine and bent to the board.

A page whispered to the lackey at the door, and the first came forth, a glimmer of excitement in his carefully set face.

"Your Excellency, there's a visitor. The famous knight, the Seigneur Bohemond de Hauteville, and he wishes an audience with you."

Mihera flushed, looked at Poldi, and Poldi saw the tell-tale jaw-cords tighten like a bow.

"See him, of course," said Poldi, as if he had been asked, "but have a care, Messire. Don't let those humors of yours mount too high." He rose and advised something more.

"Keep an open mind to what the churl says."

"What?"

"About Lady Falloc, I mean. She has doubtless been with him, some-where behind this state marriage; we have both believed that. But do not set yourself against her. I advise you as a doctor, Captain. You pine for her presence in this drear hall more seriously than you seem to realize, If this is an appeal from her ladyship to come, than take her!"

"My God, Poldi! Do you think me fool as well as cuckold? You are not wise to nourish my memory on that subject now. I could gladly dispatch him in this room. As for her . . ." He spat on the rich rug.

Poldi shrugged, and left the room; and without disturbing the game table, Mihera sat and waited.

The entrance hall door-crown winked dully with the silver dolphin-and-ship emblazoned on its shield. On this Mihera set his eyes, hearing the bustling noise of his servants, the clink of steel, and a suppressed but unmistakable laugh. He only left off his deliberate scanning of the dolphin-and-ship when Bohemond stood beneath it.

He came, walking carelessly, with his long horseman's stride and one hand resting on the hilt of the heavy serpent-headed sword. He had left off his helm. His attitude was aware, careful, tentative, but there was also the bold shadow of a smile.

The mastiff rumbled and Mihera had involuntarily stood, and for an instant the two faced each other, young-old friends and enemies, with the thought of the third one in their ancient trio never more vividly with them.

"Remember," said Mihera half under his breath, "that when I left Antioch, I wished to kill you; I left that camp with murder in my soul as much as if I'd done it. I thought afterwards you had managed all that was possible of evil to me; but I was incredibly mistaken, and you piled up the score. She was coming home, when you . . ."

"Yes, Mihera, she was coming home; that's what I came about today." He was encountering in those steely eyes the same hatred and distrust he met elsewhere nowadays in those he knew best, or perhaps, who knew *him*. On this occasion he took it ill, he even began to resent it, before he thought. The just judgment—it was all there, in the straight stare, in the familiar lineaments of that bluff sailor's face that still to Bohemond looked odd above a merchant's gown. Bohemond began sincerely to appeal to him, sincerely wishing to banish that unbanishable distance. "Mihera . . . She may *still* be coming home . . . She may *still* be trying to come to you."

"Now that you've *done* with her?"

"No, Mihera. You know it's not that. She would not come near you then, if such had occurred, any more than she would return a helpless cripple—you have understood *that* much surely . . ." There was rebuke and anxiety in his tone, and a sudden new fear for Zoë's fate from the purport of his own chance words.

Indeed, Mihera had meantime regarded him with a new, quizzical look.

"What do you mean, exactly? She is actually not *with* you?"

"With *me?* Good God, no! Man, I'm . . . " he faltered, "I'm married." It seemed that everything in this interview discomfitingly smote him, and Mihera embellished his distress like a pit bull on the chase.

"Yes, I know. You are married. You have a child. You will excuse me, Bo, but you never seemed before to regard those things as considerable." He followed this shot with a silence in that already deathly silent hall that was far more eloquent than words.

"Listen," said Bohemond, at pains to sweep painful things aside. "She was on my ships from Antioch. She escaped with Panturge that very morning that we passed Alexius . . . But she was coming *home*, Mihera; there was nothing—" His voice trailed off, for once at a loss for words to win with. Mihera dominated the scene by his very presence. The fire crackled on in the strained atmosphere and then Mihera spoke.

"A certain captain was my guest here in '03, the one who brought the doors. He related an incident of that day; the skiff cut loose . . . the hunch-back . . . but I thought he erred about identity, since I had arranged with Venetians for her at the dock of Antioch. But the two things fit; I must believe that portion of it."

And, as if swiftly reshaping opinions he had nurtured all these bitter years, the mask-like hardness of his expression seemed to slip a little and he inquired in a tight voice, "Bo, where is she now?"

"By God's Arm, I don't know. That's why I'm here. When I heard of that shipping-grant between your captains and the Byzantines, I made up my mind to see you. I thought perhaps you— She might still be there, Mihera, in the city."

"At Constantinople?"

"It's a chance."

"So . . ." Mihera's whole attitude had undergone such a change in the past minutes that Bohemond mistook this softening for himself. But to Bohemond, Mihera said merely, "Is that all there is?"

"Of information? Yes . . ."

"Well. Good-bye, Sir."

Bohemond, shocked, incredulous of this curt dismissal, attempted bluster.

"By God, Englishman! Can I believe my ears? No tales . . . wine . . . catching up on things for old times' sake?" his gauntlet tentatively outstretched . . .

"No. No wine. No false forgetting. There are things that never are to be forgotten. And everything that can civilly be said by men between whom there is no trust has been said between us," said Mihera.

The fire crackled, the hound rumbled, the silence hung between them.

Bohemond shrugged. "If that's how you feel, Mihera, then that's it." He turned at the door, his steel-ringed breeches glinting in the light. "One thing still, Mihera, that I must know. You will look for her?"

The straight-cropped fair head nodded.

"Aye. I will seek her."

And he turned away from the bright figure beneath the silver shield.

Bohemond spent a restless night at an inn, and rode out of Amalfi early the next afternoon so as to gain to Chestnut Point in ample time. The rebuff from Mihera had struck home, had completed the sense of the passing of past good things and had done nothing to ease the deep ache of desolation that had lately troubled him. Yet why? he asked himself now. Zoë had someone looking after her, and he himself was riding away from the dead, discomfiting past, with Constance. He warned himself. Nursing nostalgia was a sign of age. He must watch it. For a young wife one must be young also—carefree, amusing.

And presently, with Amalfi far gone and the deepnesses of the Calabrian wilderness about him, he began to feel happy. The fir wood with its fragrant noiseless bed of needles, the half-descended sun slipping its soft shafts through—it was like a cathedral, of the sort he fancied, not stone, all-encompassing and narrowly windowed, but roofless, door-less, and allowing the virile motion he loved with his stout destrier beneath him. The blood coursed swift, to think of this romantic meeting with Constance. He would surprise her with his aging gallantry! The devil with the Winter Lists . . . There would be crowds again. He would take her off wandering; they would live as his father's crowd had—like gypsies, in certain spots he knew; wildly beautiful clefts in the Calabrian defiles, the Sila, the Basilicata . . . And then back to Bari, where he would live content for the rest of the peaceful years, like his Uncle Roger; and like him, too, die old, honored and surrounded by fair lands and a loving family.

For the first time in his life Bohemond wished to emulate his uncle, not his sire. The Great Count's had been a good life, at this end of it. He had enjoyed a fate which his father had missed by ill chance, since (so Bohemond had thought and advertised for his entire lifetime) Guiscard had been subtly done to death at Corfu by that Lombard trull. Well, it was sure, thought Bohemond, that he himself was more like Roger than his sire in this—that he was a lucky man both in love and marriage. To that marriage, to their son and his lands he would devote his time contentedly, endowing monasteries, tending farm-lands, benef-icent to the serfs he governed . . .

And yet, and yet . . . ! What a deal of things there *were* in this life, things as yet untasted, and what a good thing it was to *think* about them, to be hotly eager, as though to be a god gifted with insatiability at an everlasting feast! But *that* were one thought not to share with Constance, Constance with her beads and her penitential shirt . . .

Bohemond was laughing to himself as he reined in Volcan beneath the massive ancient chestnut tree. Presently, up the narrow defile, he saw them coming—three horsemen riding hard, one sure enough, side-saddle, in blowing kirtle . . . He waited until they had threaded the whole of those tortuous turnings and were almost abreast, and then he spurred out.

The squire-escorts were on his side, and as he approached he expected they would fall back and allow him to continue on with Constance. He noticed too late that Constance was veiled. Constance? Too late. The squire nearest veered from the saddle almost leisurely and sank the thin blade of the baselard expertly in the cleft between Bohemond's left pauldron and sleeve. They sped off, leaving him gasp-ing. Had it been young William's man? Had the veiled one been Lady Gaitlegrim or some castle wench disguised? He would never know. He brought to mind the direction of the Inn of the Horned Hood and urged Volcan slowly ahead.

They were roistering at the Horned Hood, dark men and thick-limbed women of the hills, dancing and shouting and dipping at the bowl. The musician Thibault plucked his lute so hard that his cultivated senses cringed at the din he made, but he did his best to compete with their revel. In their mood they minded nothing. They scarcely noticed the grey-faced horseman who swayed in, headed for the nearest table and collapsed upon it. And when his iron helm rolled onto the board, his shock of damp hair flung after it, someone shouted, "A drunken 'Cruse'!" But the ostler presently investigated.

"Ai, ai, this man is wounded. Get him upstairs there." But when they lifted him the blood spot on his jerkin alarmingly widened and the ostler frowned.

"No, no, merely here on the bench. A jacket for the lord's head!"

A woman on the edge of the crowd cried, "Hey, Thibault, sing us a gest! The 'Cruse' craves a soldier's lullaby."

But the inn-keep, dealing with iron fesses and tight clothes, growled, "No! It would not be decent. In this man's chest there is a mortal wound. A physician stops upstairs . . . Fetch him!"

For some time he lay, semiconscious and tossing, and the patrons of the Horned Hood quieted, watching the knight, massive in his sufferings, and presently, under the physician's hand, with herbs and hot ale, he appeared for a time to rally. He became lucid, seeing, and they smiled at him respectfully, having seen that he was an imposing one—intense, full of fortitude, princely, and they wondered, all of them. In his coma-like suffering he had seemed like a restive god, and this hour seemed something epochal, charming them to stillness, so that when the leech signed that death would come now, none of them wished to leave. The last change was swift. Suddenly he seemed to know—though to him, of course, the medical had indicated nothing, and he tossed from side to side, praying, speaking, uninhibited as a young child crying, or as a woman caught in child-birth, bereft of dignity, reticence, of everything but humanity. The end was abrupt, not gradual, so that they heard him, his great voice sure and audible in the brief, terrible trauma of his longed-for transfiguration. And before the heroic-proportioned body slumped, no longer quickened, against the bolster, before the great head fell, they listened to strange enigmatic snatches of a final orison . . .

"Far from truth! Hidden! My God, is there none to help me? None knowing my truth, my awful need? Pray! If there be one, pray that They may suffer me, with varlets and fools, through the gates of that shining . . ."

The musician, with sharp, sudden acumen, more sensitive than the rest, stepped closer, his lute slung at his shoulder-blade, and stood a long time, looking down at the deceased.

The Epilogue

MIHERA AND DR. POLDI both gave a start when at last the ivory portals of the Byzantine Imperial Ante-room were pushed ajar by the royal Varangians and the Princess Anna came into it. She *slid*, rather, thought Poldi; her feet were completely invisible under the rigid gown, making her look for all the world like a little jewelled queen-piece from one of their game-boards. Poldi watched as Mihera cut clumsily to the immediate question. No one could blame him; the process had been long enough, obtaining an audience like this.

"Your Excellency, can you tell me, please, the whereabouts of the Lady Zoë?"

"Lady Zoë? Zoë? Ah, yes," she said, perking her lips like a small bird's bill, as if the details of this requested interview had not been completely outlined to her, in official script. "Lady Zoë—the friend of Bohemond the Frank. It was long since, that herself and her varlet were dispatched from the orbit of the magnificent wrath."

"Dispatched?" Mihera repeated. "You mean she was done away with?"

"No; you interpret cosmic tongues clumsily, barbarian! My father is a just and merciful man, and she did not *wish* to be executed." She tapped a small closed fan on her pointed fingernail.

"*Did not wish to be*— What *then?*"

"The woman was punished according to her own self-judgment, and sent hence, I believe, to Italy."

"Italy!"

"Yes. You can *see* how the Basileus is merciful and just! It was too *good*, of course, for an accomplice of that wretch, Bohemond . . ." As she talked, her small head was motionless but the liquid eyes probed,

scanned, noted, examining each detail of the merchant and the medical
. . . hair cuts . . . costumes . . .

"If to Italy, then what *city?*" Mihera was growing impatient. "Where
was she to *go?* Indeed, in what manner was she punished, aye?" His
voice rose, he was annoyed with the vixen.

"As for her personal travels, how should *I* know? The rest we will
discuss presently. Tell me, Westerners, how died the knave, Bohemond?
Is his grave honored? What was his funeral like?"

Mihera's leather-clad chest began to swell and his face to redden. But
as yet his voice came quiet. He was holding himself. Poldi glanced
from one to the other.

"Let us not speak of that person. It is irrelevant," said Mihera.

"*I* am the judge of relevance!" Anna declared, drawing herself up.

"I don't care if you're the judge of Hell!" practically shouted Mihera.
"I don't intend to discuss him!"

The Varangians sprang forward; their axe-bill blades were presented
at Mihera's chest. Behind them Anna's nostrils flared visibly, and a small
icy glint now glowed in the lustrous eyes.

"You Franks," she said. "Always impossible."

And, seeming to pivot on her heavy gaud-hung hem, she turned
about and passed through the ivory portals.

"*Now* you've done it!" said Poldi. "When *will* you learn?"

"Come on," said Mihera. "Let's get out of here . . . Italy!"

All southern hostels, all hospitals and finally all pilgrim-shrines, that
next season, saw Count Mihera and his retinue. They followed a
tenuous thread—a lady and a hunch-back, perhaps making their way
by her ballad-singing. It was not as simple to cover the pilgrim-places
as it might once have been. Besides, these ancient historical attractions
like La Cava with its horrific grotto of monastic skulls, and St. Jacques
of Bari and the famous shrine of Michael on the wind-swept promontory
of Gargane, there were now Crusader-shrines, upwards of two score,
tombs of those knights who had met a hero's death against the Moor.
They were not all transported—a whole corpse was indeed not needed.
A hand, a head, a lock of hair, or even a tooth would do. These well-
visited sarcophagi dotted the byways of all South Italy.

Poldi knew Mihera could not help but think of Melfi and the
Venosa burial-crypts. There would be ample largess for a minstrel
singer there. Wealthy penitential voyagers would not likely pass up
the bones of old Tancred de Hauteville's famous and terrible brood.
But it took Mihera three months and much feckless journeying to
make up his mind. The implications were all too clear.

But finally with a camel caravan they traversed the Basilicata,
reached Melfi and rode out to the Abbey Holy Trinity, only to be

thwarted once more. It was not only that Zoë was not there. Neither were the remains of Bohemond. Guiscard himself lay slightly elevated, on the right side of his brothers, Drogo, Humphry and William Iron-Arm. And next to him, on his own right hand, a tomb that was empty, but which already had an inscription carved upon it.

Here lies Albarada, wife to Guiscard. Seek you Bohemond? He is not here. He is at Canosa.

The old dame herself still presided at Melfi Hall, they later learned!

Up to Canosa, then, they trudged. Not that Canossa of Hilde-brandian fame where the German Emperor had grovelled in the snow, but a small southern village, with little else commending it but pilgrim hostels.

They followed the flow of wimples and flat-hats, and located the tomb. Square, massive and severe, it hid its hero behind great bronze finely cast doors where Norman and Saracenic ornamental detail were artfully mingled. Mihera stood there for some time, observing the sand-gusts blow against it. Then he sought the usual little awninged pilgrim-booth (indigenous to all these places where scrips could be gotten for the Holy Land, if the inspiration struck).

"Yes. There is such a one who comes," the monk said. He handed the tall traveler one of his beautifully illuminated parchments which Mihera automatically read while the news passed over him, leaving him weak.

"Whosoever shows this scrip in genuine distress can in God's name claim from his fellow-farer sufficient portions of bread, water, and fire."

He returned the scrip. "I've no use for this," he said. "I wish but to wait here."

The caravan captain was relieved that his master had apparently now covered the trail. Gladly he transported him and Dr. Poldi to the monument from this day onward, and lolled in the lee-side of the wind-whipped goat-hides while they kept their vigil.

Finally, one evening, she was there. She wandered slowly on the edges of the pilgrim fires, tall and severe beside the hunched shadow of her wizen-faced page, singing.

Poldi approached her first; Mihera could not bring himself to move from the tomb-side column where they had waited—a prey to about-to-be-realized hopes and fears he had nurtured all these months.

The physician returned presently. "She seems to be in good health, Messire, and the accident that deprived her of sight, Messire, has never marred her beauty. The lids are closed. She smiles even, as she sings." He watched Mihera, watched as the shock of the long-dreaded news washed over him.

"Did you speak to her, Poldi?"

"Of course not. That is for you."

"What is't she sings?"

There was no sound for a time but the rush of the gusty wind as
Poldi hesitated. "A gest, as they all do . . ."

"Vaugh! I can tell from your face the half of it! I'll go for myself . . ."

Mihera went. In the flaring light of the fires she stood, singing, and
the resting pilgrims spared to the tall, richly dressed traveler only a brief
glance or two as he lingered, frowning and intently watching the blind
jongleuse.

> *My lords, would you know of Bohemond?* (*she sang*)
> *Hear then how first he came*
> *Whelped like a mastiff in the car of war,*
> *Winning his way through squirely Carousel*
> *And knightly trial.*
> *Hear of his voyages, his battles and his deeds*
> *Both fine and vile—*
> *Hear how his 'scutcheon darkened,*
> *How his sins were bared;*
> *Hear also how he tried to expiate,*
> *What deeds he dared.*
> *Hear too, my lords, how his good-friend minds him yet,*
> *With sighs, prayers, rememberings, till yon low yellow moon be set!*

Mihera came striding back to the caravan, his whole face darkened,
his light, deep-set eyes glowing like brand-coals in the troubled dusk.

"Start the beasts, Gerlin."

"But my lord!" said Gerlin, who with Poldi had been watching the
scene.

"Start the camels!"

Old Gerlin shrugged, and Poldi joined him on the head-seat.

"Better not cross him. Do as he says for the present."

"Aye, Doctor, I know what your Worship means. I mind the old
days here and Messer Falloc's father; I mind how in just such a choleric
spell he killed a horse once, with his bare fist's blow. I mind how—"

The gossip's voice droned on, blurred, and was summarily caught
up in the clamor of the fondak as it ground noisily onto the highroad.